CHORDUROYS
♥ AND TOO MANY BOYS ♥

EVERYTHING
ALL AT ONCE

CHORDUROYS
♥ AND TOO MANY BOYS 💔

BOOK ONE

EVERYTHING ALL AT ONCE

IVY CAYDEN

THE
HIDDEN
MERIDIAN

California

ISBN 978-1-949293-00-5 (Paperback Edition)
ISBN 978-1-949293-01-2 (eBook Edition)

Library of Congress Control Number: 2018948901

This is a work of fiction. Names, characters, businesses, places, events, and incidents are either the products of the author's imagination or used in a fictitious manner. Any resemblance to actual persons, living or dead, or actual events is purely coincidental and not intended by the author.

Spotify is a registered trademark of Spotify AB. Neither The Hidden Meridian, LLC or its CHORDUROYS AND TOO MANY BOYS™ books are sponsored by or otherwise affiliated with Spotify.

Editing by Andrew W. German
Author Photograph by C.W. Palmer
Cover & Interior Design by tslapointedesign.com

Published by The Hidden Meridian, LLC.
P.O. Box 876
Cambria, CA 93428

www.chorduroys.com

Table of Contents

Acknowledgments

The Team

Trish LaPointe: (Yes, you are at the top of this list.) Your professional design guidance enabled me to finally complete this first book and feel ready enough to release it. Thank you for the innumerable emails, calls, and versions. I treasure the bond we've forged.

Andrew German: Thank you for lending your seasoned eyes to this first installment.

Chase: Long ago, you looked at me with certain eyes and said, "Just write it." Thank you for that first life-changing nudge and for your unwavering support.

All About The Playlist

Do I have to listen while I read?

Listening to the playlist adds another dimension to the reading experience, but it is certainly not necessary. *Everything All At Once* exists as a story all by itself. (You never have to listen to the music if you don't want to.)

Where can I find the playlist?

The book's public playlist is on Spotify*.

You can find it by visiting www.chorduroys.com and clicking on the book's Spotify playlist link;

OR by searching inside Spotify for the playlist name: CHORDUROYS AND TOO MANY BOYS: Everything All At Once

How does this work?

The Spotify playlist is already organized by order of appearance in the book. As you read the story, you will come across songs in **BOLD**.

Here are some simple guidelines to follow while reading along:

1. PLAY the song as soon as your eyes reach it in the story. (Remember, you will only be playing the songs that appear in **BOLD**.) Continue to read the story while you listen.

2. If the song ends before you reach another song in the story, PAUSE the playlist. Read the story (without music) until you reach another song.

3. If you reach a new song in the story before the current song is finished, PLAY the new song. Continue to read the story while you listen.

4. If you reach a song at the end of a chapter, OR if you reach the end of the chapter before a song is finished, LISTEN (or continue to listen) to the song in full before moving on to the next chapter.

Two Special Cases:

Chapter 2: Three songs appear toward the end of the chapter. Be sure to listen to all three songs (at least once) before moving on to Chapter 3.

Chapter 14: The second song that appears in this chapter needs to be looped (played on repeat) until the story notes that one of the characters stops the music.

CHORDUROYS
♥ AND TOO MANY BOYS ♥

EVERYTHING ALL AT ONCE

For the dreamers (wearing headphones)

Under an ancient canopy of stars, the soft scent of dewy leaves mingled with the thick evening air. Kila's bare feet pressed into the damp earth. Her light eyes welcomed the darkness. Like the unseen rays of night, music poured through the protected redwood grove. **"The Way I Do" by Bishop Briggs** swept her mind into a weightless state. She felt as if she had unraveled gravity, the entire force of her essence focused on Angus's eyes. Like two rounds of chestnut-colored glass, they shone mere inches away, causing her breath to cease and her pulse to race like fire under her skin.

The cover of night blended as one with his black hoodie, and she struggled to determine where the cotton ended and his hair began. As if he had divined her thought, Angus tugged his hood back between his shoulders, revealing his dark locks and a shy smile. Kila searched his face like she searched his heart. The ache inside her whispered his name. His lips spoke of promise though they never moved.

I'm not waiting any longer. Kila silenced her hesitation, stretching up on her toes and spreading her fingers through his hair. As his hands gripped her waist, her eyes turned to prisms. His deep voice echoed in the capsule of her soul. Their noses touched and she knew what awaited her. As he closed his eyes, she knew he knew it, too.

When her lips parted, a flood of light shattered the dream just as swiftly as it had come on. She sat up from her resting position, eyes wide with anxiety, acknowledging Brixton's presence in the door with a single nod of her head. His peculiar half-smile eased her back into reality.

"I didn't mean to startle you, Kiki," Brixton whispered, "but your brother's been waiting for you."

"Yeah...that's right," Kila mumbled. Running her fingers through her chocolate hair, she realized the music she had heard in her dream had actually come from her speakers. Her head clouded with the gloom of confusion. *I can't even reach him in my dreams...WHY?* The tips of her fingers longed for his skin, and her lips tingled at the thought of touching his. *It still would have been my first kiss, if only in a dream.* Mustering a hint of a smile, she forced herself to her feet.

Brixton wondered what it was she had seen with her sleeping eyes. "Everyone's in the tree house and Ethan refused to eat his birthday cake without you," he pressed lightly.

"Is that so?" Kila asked, somewhat childishly, but mostly flattered by her brother's loyalty.

Brixton nodded.

"Alright…"—Kila searched for words—"…where have you been hiding out lately? It's been…a while."

"…I know." Brixton reached for the correct tone. "Your brother's grown accustomed to hanging out at my place. I guess you probably know we've been practicing there… for…a few months." He worked briskly to identify the song as she peered at him amidst her grooming. "It's Bishop Briggs, isn't it?" His lips smiled at her helplessly.

"Yeah," Kila breathed, her mind taking in the sight of him in her room.

"Your playlist?" he asked as simply as he could.

Kila half-smiled, catching his face in the mirror. "No… it's Tim's."

"Timmy's?" he asked for clarification.

"Yeah." Kila laughed lightly, noticing the seriousness in his face while she brushed her hair.

Brixton tilted his head. "I thought his Nektir account was private?"

"It is." Kila shrugged her shoulders. "We're connected, so we can listen to each other's lists. That's how I found Bishop Briggs—SUCH a fiiind…I love her."

"Do you and Timmy, like…"—Brixton watched her blue-gray eyes in the mirror—"hang out?"

"No," Kila rolled her eyes, "…we don't. Any more questions?"

"No," Brixton beamed and touched his right hand to his left bicep, "…at least not for now."

She bit her bottom lip, "I would have thought you would have asked me something else."

"…Oh…really?" Brixton struggled to mask his impending panic.

Kila talked herself through the emotions. She knew she'd be seeing him today but had convinced herself this wouldn't be awkward. *I was WRONG! It IS awkward. Sooooo awkward. It might even be worse than awkward. Like, if you took awkward's potential to devastate and paired it with the blind hope of a long shot. Play it COOL. Friends drift apart…sometimes. We just drifted, that's all…like different boats on the same ocean.*

Is it possible to drift back? Or, just BE back…the way that it was…I need to keep busy. I can't let him sense my scrambled thoughts. Pulling the wand from the square lip-gloss tube, she delivered a small dollop of sheer red to her index finger.

"Heart Is Full" by Miike Snow filled the empty space in the room.

Timmy likes Miike Snow, Brixton mumbled in his mind, wondering if Kila had already heard the group's music or if this was the first time she was hearing any of their songs. He couldn't help but ask in a roundabout way.

"Are you into this?" Brixton cursed his clumsy words.

Kila stretched her eyebrows together, "Song? Artist? Or both?"

He shrugged noncommittally to see how she'd respond.

"Of all their songs, this one's my favorite," she supplied minimal information.

"Mine too," he replied with honesty.

I believe him, Kila exhaled. *Makes sense that we'd share the same artist favorite. Guess it hasn't been that long, after all.* She busied herself with her grooming.

Brixton studied the way Kila's fingertip dabbed the strawberry glaze gently onto her plush, pliable lips, and finally acknowledged that the months he had spent away from his friend's house were ones in which Kila had changed physically. He shifted his weight from one foot to the other, then checked his phone. He found a text from Angus:

[Edging ever closer to eating this cake. Grab Ki and get back here…or sacrifice your slice.]

"Everything alright?" Kila asked in reference to the annoyed look on Brixton's face. "You need me to rush? I can rush, you know. Or, you can just head back now and tell them I'll be a few more minutes. You can start without me, I don't mind…."

"No, no. Take your time. I wanted to see you," he assured her, wondering if she would understand that he had missed her.

She liked Brixton's comment but didn't overthink it. Set on avoiding the dreaded "awkward," she disappeared with a smile into her bathroom.

When she moved out of sight Brixton tapped the reply on his phone:

[She just woke up! Must have taken a nap after track practice. Stuff your face if you're too much of a buffoon to wait for us. Touch my slice and it's WAR.]

Angus's reply assaulted the screen seconds after Brixton's text had left:

[Very well. I'm starving!]

Brixton, in defiance, opened the flap on his cargo shorts and slammed the phone down into it. He glanced at himself in the mirror. *Hair a mess. Figures.* He attempted to arrange it into some form of order.

"I'll take care of it," Kila offered from behind him, a circular jar of pomade in her hand.

Shyly, Brixton watched from the mirror as she rubbed the cream in her agile hands and worked a small amount into the ends of his golden hair, moving the sections carefully in opposite directions.

"Thanks," he spoke, growing ever aware they were alone together in her room. The back of his neck prickled from her recent touch.

"Don't tell Ethan I told you," she confided in him, "but he lets me fix his hair before school most days."

"I figured as much," he smirked, "but I'll keep quiet about it."

Kila smiled and nodded.

Brixton felt more at ease as the conversation evolved. Like a clean sheet lifted high, then draped onto the bed without a sound, his mind settled into a peaceful state.

"Your hair has really grown out—look at these curls!" she exclaimed with bright eyes, lifting one between her fingers. "Ethan's is fairly wild, but it's nothing like this."

While he fought with vigor to disperse the blush from pigmenting his cheeks, a thunderous sound rattled the glass pane. Kila shot like lightning over to the yellow curtains. To verify her suspicion, she opened the window.

Brixton retrieved the phone from his pocket to find another text from Angus:

[Time's up!]

So impatient! Brixton shook his head.

"Alright, sharpshooter!" Kila yelled towards the tree house, the long canary-colored curtains billowing beside her. "Once is NOT as impressive as twice. Let's have it, Ang."

Brixton dug the challenge, Kila's competitive streak having surfaced so easily.

"Twice with pleasure," Angus growled from the tree house balcony, stringing another rubber arrow into the bow and stretching his striking arm back.

The release was silent yet accurate, riding an arc right into Kila's window. Brixton studied her frame as she stepped toward the object in flight, catching it on the descent. In awe, she held it in her hands beaming.

"That was insane," she eyed Brixton, looking for acknowledgement of what she had just seen.

"Come on, Kiki," Brixton reminded. "You know that Ang's capable of practically anything when he's hungry."

"Well, if he's hungry we shouldn't make him wait," Kila quipped, shoving Brixton through her door and toward the stairs. Once her feet reached the first floor, she dashed down the hallway, sped through the kitchen, leapt off the deck, and sprinted toward the tree house.

Pleased that he had kept pace with her, Kila whispered down to Brixton as they climbed, "I swear this ladder gets smaller every time I come up here."

"Tell me about it. I've been warning E that our bodies have outgrown it. The beams are practically screaming for upgrades, but he refuses to make any renovations lest it lose any nostalgia for him and...," his words met their end as Kila leapt off the ladder toward a noticeably pleased Angus.

"UN.be.lieveable!" Kila high-fived him, moving inside the

small space which had served as the boys' private castle for almost a decade.

"Tell me you saw that, E," Kila gushed to her brother. "RIGHT through my window! Right through, and delicate enough of a trajectory to land right in my hands."

"Well, not right," Brixton amended. "It took some athletic coordination and general fearlessness on her part to catch it. Actually, I was more fascinated by the catch than the release."

Angus glared at him.

Ethan ruffled his sister's hair, chuckling at Brixton's inflated retelling. "It sounds like the whole endeavor should have been recorded and looped eternally in slo-mo."

"You doubted my aim," Angus promptly retrieved the arrow from Kila's hand.

"I figured it was unlikely you'd be able to target my window again…given the distance," she cupped a hand on his shoulder. Through his shirt, her fingers felt the warmth of his body and she didn't want to let go.

"Nothing is impossible, Ki," he reached his free hand to his shoulder to touch hers.

Brixton eyed Ethan to read his reaction to this unfolding. *Why is Angus touching her?*

"You're hungry, aren't you?" Kila posed the question to challenge Brixton's earlier remark.

"I wouldn't say hungry as much as I'd say starving!" Angus grinned, causing him at once to lose Kila's affection and then to suffer a flurry of laughter from her and from Brixton.

"Can't say that I missed that," Ethan wondered what had set his sister and Brixton off. He whacked Angus's shoulder in consolation.

"Me either," Angus shot a look at Brixton. "I thought their inside jokes ended with their friendship."

Kila bit her lip and looked to her brother for a life vest.

"No. The only friendship that's in danger of ending is ours," Brixton spoke his mind quickly. "Kiki and I have so many inside jokes, they will live on longer than we do."

Kila exhaled. *Still friends. Friends that drifted.* She smiled at Brixton, who offered a tilted nod in return.

"So...it's my birthday," Ethan angled for the spotlight. "Seems like that might have been forgotten for a few moments."

"Nope," Angus grinned widely. "Not forgotten. You are king for the day. Still. And as such, we will award you with sultry song, savory sweets, and an honorable gift. A gift fit only for a badass drummer such as yourself."

"NOW we're talking!" Ethan laughed, pulling his sister close.

"I better grab the cake before Angus drops from starvation," Brixton teased.

"Too late," Angus clutched his stomach and fell to the floor, dazed.

Kila erupted in laughter, allowing herself a long, uninterrupted glance at him lying down.

"And the ridiculous badge for the day has been claimed," Brixton shook his head, spotting Angus stick his tongue out at Kila as she helped him to his feet. He returned his irritated eyes to the cake, holding it up for Kila to see. "The box is… rather…ornate."

"Yeah, mom and dad picked up peanut butter gelato cupcakes from this place last week and they've been raving about it ever since," Kila gushed. "Apparently it's downtown a few blocks from Mayberry, and their head chef is nicknamed Noah because he's turned so many people onto veganism."

Angus grinned in part for the animals and in part for the cake.

Kila took the box from Brixton, placing it on the thick, knee-high oak table, and ran her fingers across the textured navy case. Embossed in gold on the lower left-hand corner, The Hidden Meridian logo featured a thin, vertical arrow intersecting the "i" in "Hidden" and the first "i" in "Meridian." She scanned the adjacent shelf for the candles, then noticed Brixton tossing them playfully in his hands.

"May I do the honors this time?" he asked.

"All this formality. Every time. Isn't anyone else hungry?" Angus whined, joking only partially, as he reached for his acoustic guitar.

Kila slid the round chocolate cake from the box onto the serving dish and watched as Brixton sank the candles into the sponge-like consistency with care. *It's nice to stand next to him again. I think he's...taller.*

"We forgot the matches...," Brixton looked through the cubby holes in the wall hoping to find an old pack.

"I didn't," Angus pulled them from his pocket. With a crimson grin, he tossed them over to Brixton. "Light 'em after this song. I've been practicing all week, but haven't played it for anyone yet."

"Got it," Brixton motioned for him to begin.

Kila dimmed the lights in the small space and took a seat on the floor opposite Angus, trying to keep herself from studying the frame of him and his guitar in this play of light shadows. Brixton settled in to her right while Ethan settled in to her left. As Angus strummed gracefully, Kila concentrated on his rhythmic catch and release of the strings. When she heard the thick sound of his voice, her eyes shut.

Ahhh. His voice, she basked in the melody. ***"Knuckles (Acoustic)" by Moose Blood.*** *I didn't know he liked this one. It's layered...but...why does he look pained? His face, his fingers, I can hear it in his voice. Is he singing about Reese? Are they over? Does he want it to be over? Has he finally seen it for what it is?* Kila opened her eyes in question when he suddenly stopped playing. She noticed Brixton's raised hand.

"It's a...tad somber for the occasion, no?" Brixton gulped, turning to the birthday boy for a second opinion.

"Actually, I don't mind it," Ethan smiled, "especially if he's singing about what I think he is. Finish it Ang, I want you to...," he lifted his head at Angus in encouragement. "It's a masterpiece of a song, and...it's fitting."

Kila bit her lip. *Why doesn't Ethan just say HER name? Everyone here knows who it is.*

"Thing is...I don't sound as good without Brix," Angus self-consciously plucked away again, too engaged in the chord work and his emotions to resume the lyrics or confirm Ethan's reference.

Brixton whispered, "I would have taken mine if you told me you were bringing yours."

"You should have it with you at all times," Angus spoke without his fingers losing focus. "You never know when the right situation will materialize."

"Valid point," Brixton agreed. "However, in this particular case, I'm glad I left it home. The weight of even one more guitar might cause the tree house to collapse."

A fountain of laughter escaped from Kila's lips.

Brixton's eyes flashed, grateful his comment had tickled her mind.

"Not another word," Ethan's voice threatened finality. "It's still solid."

Angus rocked back and forth in place while strumming, and

the boards below him shook for several moments.

This time, Kila heard Brixton's laugh before she heard her own, and she patted her brother's shoulder to soften the grimace on his face.

"It's been wobbling for a while now," Angus tried to appease Ethan with pleasant memories. "We built this thing when we were practically half the weight we are now. It was ideal for us then, but we've grown. Our love for it hasn't diminished. If anything, it's grown with us. It just needs a few tweaks, but… we don't have to talk about it anymore tonight."

Ethan nodded once without comment.

Angus tried to lift his spirits, "At least this round won't require any parental supervision."

"Yeah, maybe just Kiki's supervision," Brixton added for good measure, nudging her side.

Kila, caught up watching Angus's fingers, smiled in place of words.

"Alright," Ethan caved. "You guys MIGHT have a point. This summer…we'll make some repairs."

"Thank you," Brixton rubbed his hands together. "I feared one of us would end up in a cast before you came to your senses."

Ethan chuckled. "There will be no casts as a result of this tree house. We'll pick a few days for renovations, and, as a bonus, we'll equip our nest with some new features in the face of senior year."

Like flipping the bird to growing up?" Angus's subtle grin burned a new memory into Kila's heart.

I equally hate and love when he makes that face. When his lips press together then stretch to form red apple slices that work their way up the sides of his cheeks. Kila placed her palms on the wood below her, dragging her fingers slowly along the grooves in the floorboards to distract her mind. *His existence threatens my sanity. Falling for him was SUCH a bad idea...*

When the conversation ceased, Angus resumed the singing, investing all of himself and taking the song to its bittersweet completion.

"Nice," Ethan clapped a few times, feeling a nip of sadness himself. "I dread missing this. Sharing all of this. It'll never be the same," Ethan showed, for once, a rare bit of vulnerability. "In just over a year, we'll be scattered about the country."

Or possibly outside the country, Kila kept her nervous thoughts to herself. *Just a couple more months until I can get that application in.*

"Regardless of our locales, we'll always find a way to be together," Brixton assured him. "Friends for life, remember?" Standing, he lit one of the matches and gifted a glow to each of the seventeen candles.

"It has been fairly epic," Ethan spoke. "I wouldn't want to get into trouble with anyone else."

"Agreed," Brixton lifted his gaze off the small flames.

Angus, absolutely unable to wait for the cake any longer, began the chords of the birthday song.

Upon hearing a happier side of his voice envelop the room, Kila's eyes drifted from his fingers to his face. And in the soft darkness across from him, she peered straight into his brooding eyes as she entered in the song along with Brixton, singing to her brother.

When it was silent once more, Ethan closed his stormy blue eyes, releasing his wish as he leaned down to the candles. *May this year see the long-hoped-for rise of our band and bind us in such a way that college cannot tear us apart.*

After cutting the cake, Kila doled out pieces to her brother, Angus, and Brixton. By the time she moved her slice onto her plate, Angus motioned for seconds.

"Pause the stuff-your-face-fest and give him the gift," Brixton lifted his hands in the air. "It's his birthday, not yours. Don't eat all of his cake, either."

"Ease up," Angus warned, slipping more of the cake into his mouth with pride. "This is SERIOUSLY good, I can't help it. Seeing as though I'm the only entertainer tonight, I feel as though I'm entitled to two slices, or more, depending on how much E wants."

Beaming, Kila prepped the cake by slicing the remaining half. It served as a helpful means to break her eyes free from Angus's lips. *I NEED to finish that dream. There must be a way to pick up where I left off.*

When Brixton shook his head in annoyance, Angus shifted the guitar from his waist, transferred the cake crumbs from his fingers to his pants, and reached for his oversized backpack.

Ethan rubbed his hands together in anticipation.

Kila bit her tongue, then moved it to the inside of one of her cheeks to distract herself from Angus's frame. *Maya should have been here. WHEN is she going to tell him?* She watched her brother's face, feeling the nip of anxiety.

"Aha! Buried, but I found it," Angus tossed a black square envelope to Ethan with some backspin. "If you like it, it's from the three of us. If you hate it, it's from Brix."

Kila rolled her eyes and nudged Brixton. "I see he's still quick to throw you off the roof," she whispered.

"Tell me about it," Brixton caught her smile, "I don't think that'll ever change."

Ethan broke the silver seal of the envelope to reveal a gift certificate for Casper's Music Underground. "This is beyond generous, you guys," he beamed. "I don't even know what to say, other than 'thank you,' but that doesn't seem to reflect how grateful I am...."

"We all know you need an upgrade," Brixton smiled. "This should be the remainder you need for the new set."

"And to be honest, it's not a selfless gift. Think about how sweet our whole setup's going to look with the midnight-hued drums. Happy Birthday to the hottest drummer EVER," Angus fake flirted with him, fanning his face in jest.

Kila hoped he'd be fanning himself over the thought of her one day. *Yeah right*, she accidentally laughed aloud, as Brixton issued an inquisitive look at her.

By the time the four descended the ladder an hour later, the cake was no more and Ethan could not have been more pleased. He thanked his friends several times over for the sizeable gift certificate, then asked them which upcoming album they believed to be the most anticipated of the summer.

Kila remained quiet, but listened to their answers. Lightheaded from a near Angus overdose, she found herself equal parts enticed and enraged. *My heart is out for my demise. Surely there is no other explanation.*

Brixton, on the other hand, scrambled to arrange circumstances that would enable him to see more of her. "Guys…my mom's hinted more than once we should think about rotating our band practice locations. Why don't we spend some hang time here this weekend?"

"SOME?" Angus laughed, almost giddily, high-fiving Ethan and leaping through the air.

Ethan's half-smile all but screamed he was hiding something. "SOME will be an understatement, Brix," he hinted.

Brixton looked from Ethan to Angus, wondering who would budge first. When neither spoke, he added, "I would like to comment that this is rather lonely, the two of you snide with your secret and myself left only to guess."

"Perhaps if you hadn't been so lame staying home every night for the past two weeks, you would have had time to conspire with us," Angus rubbed his hands together.

Brixton erupted, "Lame?! How convenient. You've forgotten, YET again, that we're not all child prodigies. Some of us have to take the time to study for exams in order to pull As. We can't simply walk into the room, grasp our pencils, and ace every standardized we touch, like Angus Lyr."

"Hey! I studied, too," Ethan jumped into the line of fire. "I just don't have an issue with the letter B."

Angus grinned wider.

Brixton's frustration peaked. "Okay," he held his palms up, "I'll admit it. I may have gone a bit overboard this semester prepping for exams. I WAY over-prepared, but it wasn't about the letter as much as it was about securing a certain GPA for a certain school. And I thought you two would understand that."

"WAIT!" Ethan practically jumped in place. "You said you were applying for early acceptance to Cypress U with me in the fall?" Ethan touched his hand to his hair in thought.

"I am, but I want placement in the new advanced pre-med program," Brixton crossed his fingers behind his back. *God, that was close. Deflect. Deflect.* "ANYWAY. One of you fill me in. Now. Before I lose it."

Angus pointed to Ethan.

"My parents are leaving early tomorrow morning," Ethan paused just long enough to see Brixton's right eyebrow raise, "and not returning until late Sunday evening."

"Welcome to the wild," Angus quipped. "Pack your bag tonight, so you don't miss out on ANYTHING tomorrow afternoon. E's REAL birthday festivities kick-off tomorrow, promptly after last period."

"He's right," Ethan slapped Brixton's shoulder. "Pack and prepare."

Brixton couldn't recall Ethan ever looking this mischievous. It was a strange but fitting look for him. He wondered if Kila would be around at all, or if she would be spending the entire weekend at Maya's since her parents would be away.

"Alright boys. Let's have it," Angus executed the ten-year-old handshake seamlessly with his two best friends.

The trio then walked across the lawn toward the house, plotting tomorrow night's adventures. When Angus left, Brixton steadied his mind to say goodnight to Kila. He looked around anxiously but didn't see her anywhere.

"Already snuck away," Ethan explained. "She's been a bit skittish lately."

Instinctively, Brixton looked up the stairs in the direction of her room. The hallway was dark, and, from that angle, he couldn't even make out the lines of her doorway. *If she's distant, it's my own fault.* He had hoped he might score a hug from her. It had been months since he'd had one.

"How was it?" Brixton felt certain Ethan would understand his ambiguity.

"Pretty good, I think," Ethan nodded, "considering Angus's tank of a reference to the death of the friendship."

Brixton double-blinked, "What THE HELL was that, anyway? Just because Reese makes him miserable, doesn't mean he has to make ME miserable, too."

"You know it always comes back to that," Ethan exhaled loudly. "It will always come back to you. We have to get him over her. It'll be better for everyone—you, me, and Kila."

"Kila?" Brixton nervously fished for information. "Has Reese spoken with Kiki lately?"

"Not that I know of," Ethan confided in him. "I just don't like the situation. I feel like there's a lot Angus hasn't told us. Tonight's song choice revealed more than he may have wanted to. And the heartless looks Reese gives Kila in school are hard to ignore. Kila claims she's taking it in stride, that she has more important things to focus on than Reese's bitterness, but still…I worry about her. I worry about her a lot lately."

Brixton's eyes glazed over and did that weird thing he does sometimes: look off into the distance in reflection. "Yeah. Kiki's really, well she's…I guess she's," Brixton found it impossible to finish his thoughts aloud.

"Different?" Ethan filled in the blank. "Guys keep asking me about her, and girls who didn't know she existed a few months ago are talking about her. I hear it in class and I see it in the hallway. I know, in some ways, she's oblivious to it, and her focus lies elsewhere, but I can't figure out what she's after and how to talk to her about it. I'm kind of worried. I think everything accelerated with her tutoring Annabelle."

Questions poured from Brixton's mouth like water from a spout. "Kiki's tutoring Anna? Since when? Why didn't you tell me? How come you never mentioned it until now?"

"My sister didn't want anyone to know. I guess Anna was embarrassed about it. Her teacher told her if she didn't get a tutor she'd fail her math class. When Kila was recommended, she agreed to keep Anna's secret. And I kept Kila's secret… well, up until now," Ethan laughed. "I think the arrangement has actually been beneficial for both of them. I mean, Anna's grade skyrocketed, of course. That part didn't surprise me. Kila's almost as obsessed with math as Angus is. But, Anna's not like she appears at school. She's not pretentious by any means. Actually, she's fairly down-to-earth, and not at all like the superficial hollow-head everyone makes her out to be."

"I CANNOT believe you kept this from me," Brixton shook his head. "You know I never would have said anything to anyone."

"I know," Ethan whispered, "but I didn't know if you and Ki would start talking again, and I didn't know how that would play out if I told you. Anyway, you know now. So stop griping."

"Annabelle Delancy. At your house. Hanging with Kiki and My. Studying together. Weird," Brixton, with some difficulty, envisioned the trio in his mind.

"It's not just a school thing, though. The three of them have grown inseparable. They're always here, not only engaging in an unending mixture of schoolwork, but also airing nearly incomprehensible fashion dialogue. When I leave the house I usually slip out the back to avoid the critique that would SURELY end me if I walked through the line of fire."

"Hang on," Brixton held a hand up. "I think you might, in reality, favor this situation. It's clear why I haven't been coming over the past couple months. You have three desirables primping over you after school. Hell," he smirked, "I'd have kept that a secret myself."

Ethan tilted his head, "It's not as glamorous as it sounds. You'll see this weekend."

"Are any of the girls dating anyone?" Brixton fixed his eyes on Ethan's. "With all of these secrets floating around, I figure I might as well ask in case you already know and you're simply not telling."

"Nope," Ethan replied, thinking of something that wasn't readily apparent to his friend. "But, I imagine it's inevitable. That's why I'm worried about Ki. What if she decides to date a weasel?"

Brixton shrugged. "Said weasel will be subject to the ultimate punishment."

Ethan nodded for him to elaborate.

"Chaucer-style. We immortalize his defeat in the lyrics of one of our songs and sing it in the courtyard. Case closed," Brixton rubbed his hands together. "Angus would be more than down for it. You know how well he sings when he's ticked."

"I wish it were as easy as that," Ethan mused, shaking his head.

"She's not going to fall for someone who's only interested in…she's intelligent. And you'll probably see it coming before she does. Who knows?" Brixton hinted, "Maybe she'll pick someone you already like and trust?"

"I doubt it," Ethan semi-smiled. "I don't trust anyone around her. It's worse because she skipped a grade. She's not even sixteen."

"She will be in a few weeks," Brixton shuddered at his own words.

"Good, but scary point," Ethan noted. "Anna's been somewhat of a good influence, but I'm afraid to admit Ki and My have grown wild in her presence."

"Oh. Wow. Hmmm," Brixton digested his friend's last statement and scrambled to supply an appropriate response. "Don't worry, Kiki was headed in this direction anyway. It's not as if she was going to stay a child her whole life. She was bound to come out of her shell. She's always been beautiful, she just hid it well. It is necessary and just as healthy for her to grow up as is her obsession with schoolwork." Brixton paused to see if Ethan was still following. He seemed to be, so he proceeded. "I've noticed the change myself. It started out with her no longer wearing sneakers to class every day. She has flats and platforms and everything in between. Then she started letting her hair down; it seems bouncier, and most days she's wearing lip gloss."

"I know. It takes forever for her to get ready now," Ethan huffed. "Before, we could leave the house within five minutes to run errands or eat together."

"Yeah, she was always faster than Angus," Brixton recalled, "but on the flip side, now she smells like ginger sometimes...," he stopped himself from further embarrassment.

Ethan shot an amused glance at Brixton, "I was about to ask if you could help me keep an eye on her...but it seems as though you already are."

"We'll take care of it," Brixton assured him, "we always have."

Ethan walked Brixton to his car. Afterwards, he headed inside to thank his mom once more for his birthday cake. She pretended to be forlorn that there was nothing left of it. In the shower, he imagined he was playing his new drums; and, amidst the airplay, he knocked all of the bottles off the tub ledge.

* * * * *

A few doors down, Kila, with phone in hand, paced barefoot in circular loops about her room. **"Dreams" by The Cranberries** delivered a sweet-scented bouquet of sound; and, though she spoke sincerely with Maya about something very serious, Kila couldn't help but see Angus in every corridor of her mind. *I just…need to be older. I need to be wiser. That's all. I'll age. I'll educate myself. I'll find a way to make him recognize me as something more than Ethan's sister.*

"Maya, you NEED to tell him! You'll regret it if you don't. You're my best friend. I'm serious. We've been talking about this for weeks now. Come on with it," Kila glanced at Nektir, her music app of choice.

"I just…can't seem to get the words right. When I see him, I want to tell him. I do!" Maya insisted, "I've TRIED. I just don't want to risk him hating me for it. And I can't bear to leave it that way, in uncomfortable regret."

Kila continued, "The ONLY regret you face is waiting THIS long to talk to him."

"Maybe I've waited this long for a reason," Maya's heart beat faster, "maybe he's not supposed to know…."

"My—him NOT finding out is NOT AN OPTION. No wonder he hasn't found out already! That's a miracle in itself, the way news finds its way around Cypress. Do you REALLY want him to find out from someone else? Seriously?" Kila reasoned with her.

"Okay. I'll tell him the first part, which almost everyone knows. But I'm NOT telling him the second part. I know we talked about it, but I just can't tell him. Some things are better left unsaid, Ki. What if the second part IS one of those things? It could be!" Maya yelped, feeling nauseous at the thought.

"Nonsense," Kila kept her voice soft yet firm. "Tomorrow.

Promise me you will tell him both parts tomorrow. Promise! PROMISE BOTH PARTS!"

Maya acquiesced, "I promise, both parts...but, only because I trust you. And IF you are WRONG about this, I might never speak with you again. I SWEAR it!"

"It's a deal, then," Kila pursed her lips. "Get your rest. Your worries officially end tomorrow."

"More like begin tomorrow," Maya huffed under her breath.

"Enough of this," Kila's strides quickened as she continued to traipse about her room. "You want my help? You need my help?"

"YES!" Maya looked up at her ceiling, "I can't do this without you." She collapsed in a heap of desperation onto her bed. "I'm begging you! Don't make me beg...please...oh, it's useless now. I'm begging, and you know it."

"Alright," Kila laughed a little, loving that her friend needed her in such a way. "**Joss Stone's 'Baby Baby Baby,'** at least twice, before bed."

"Ki," Maya huffed, then giggled. "You KNOW what happens when I listen to that song."

"You love that song. It makes you happy and hyper," Kila was pleased with her own advice, "and I think, I hope with all my heart, it just MIGHT push you over the edge. Commit to the song and commit to the telling. Both parts. Come on. I want to hear it."

"Okayyyyyy…both parts," Maya whispered already feeling sleepy. "I'll put the song on repeat while I get ready for bed… know that I'm trusting you."

"Good," Kila breathed easier. "It'll help you think it through. Correction, I know that it will."

"I hope so," Maya hunted for the song on her phone, so she could play it as soon as they ended the call. "Night Ki—love you."

"Love you, too," Kila softened for just a second. "After school you will tell him. Both parts."

Seventeen minutes after saying goodnight to Kila, Maya lay buried under her covers, peacefully listening to Joss Stone's breathtaking voice. Each time the song looped, she plunged deeper into rest. When the misgivings of her mind unhinged completely, she walked past Brixton and Kila's intimate conversation to land a better view of Ethan playing his new navy drums. The moment Ethan saw her, he smiled and motioned her to move closer.

While Maya welcomed her sleep to find it better than reality, Kila, still awake, lay atop her duvet listening to her playlist in an act of rebellion against time. *I don't care what the clock says,* she declared in her mind, as she remained in the same clothes from her brother's tree house party. Her palms rested on her emerald-colored corduroys, and her fingers—the only part of her that moved—tapped the tiny grooves in the fabric. The state Kila found herself in was the state Ethan had fondly coined as a "music coma"—the condition Kila opted for more times than not. And the song—which sent her on a new journey through the past day, the past year, and nearly every event that had led her to her present predicament—was none other than **"Coming Over" by Dillon Francis, Kygo, and James Hersey**.

As the memories took their turn one by one, Kila's fingers continued to move along the grooves of her front pockets, the plushness of the fabric comforting her through the more difficult recollections. While no one knew yet, she often daydreamed about having her own clothing line, a small boutique for both sexes offering nothing more than corduroys, button-downs, T-shirts, and sweaters. She longed to give corduroys the proper praise they were due but never seemed to receive.

Corduroys, Kila felt, were the ultimate garment; they possessed the ability to gift their wearer with an untouchable magnetism. Available in an eclectic range of colors, deep or washed-out hues, and every cut imaginable, they were the treasures of her closet. Jeans were an everyday staple, but corduroys offered something more: a softer, chicer fit, with built-in vertical stripes that hug the lower body's landscape better than other fabrics. And the fondness for that particular fabric, which had been worn for decades by struggling musicians and rock stars alike, existed as yet another outcropping of Kila's absolute love of music.

She viewed music and corduroys as so intertwined that, in 7th-grade, her English teacher deducted points on a creative writing piece on account of her spelling corduroys with an "h." It practically pained Kila to learn that the first half of one of her favorite words wasn't a reference to musical chords.

After venting to Brixton, her then best friend, she vowed to continue spelling it her way on everything unrelated to schoolwork. The new spelling caught on quickly within her inner circle, and the addition of the "h" had, by this time, more or less been anchored to the word forever by her friends.

On the surface, the love of corduroys seemed like a harmless, innocent tendency, but Kila knew it had the potential to land her heart in some serious trouble. It already had. She recalled the first time she saw Angus in a pair, nearly two years ago. She breathed in the memory, reliving it in her mind, as the music swirled about her.

Ethan had an epiphany and decided to rearrange his room. Angus rode his bike over to help. I watched from the hallway. To justify my guard, I held two glasses of fresh-squeezed lemonade in my hands. The movement of Ethan's bed and desk was hard enough for me to handle. I had always laughed at my mother's friends who spoke of magnetism, thinking it foolish. Yet here I was at thirteen struggling to decipher why I couldn't keep my eyes off Angus. The mammoth bookcase did me in. I'm still recovering from it. Perhaps it was the way he carefully pulled out all the books, stacking them with my brother in order on the floor. He asked Ethan if he could borrow two of them, and all I could think about was wanting to borrow him...

By the time his hands touched the empty bookcase, I could hear my heart pounding. My hands clenched the chilled glasses of lemonade as Angus's chalky, marled sweater rose up with his arms exposing the bottom of his abdominals. The sight of the toffee-colored chord's waistline kissing his bronzed stomach all but made me float. I drowned in the ridges and grooves of my favorite fabric wrapped around the smooth skin of my only crush.

With heated cheeks, I leaned against the door trim when he spotted me and thanked me for the drink. That grin, coupled with those chorduroys, caught me in a net, one I have yet to get out of...though I've tried. God, I've tried. I should have known RIGHT then it would never work. I couldn't even respond, Kila laughed aloud, surfacing from her music coma. *After I gave Ethan his lemonade, I tiptoed back to my room, collapsed onto my bed, and daydreamed the rest of the day away. I can't do that again, though. Here I am two years later, minus my best friend, and I'm in no better place.*

A long huff escaped from Kila's mouth, and though the thought of Angus still held real estate in her mind, she pushed him to the background and reached for her laptop. Sprawling onto her stomach, with her feet in the air, she wiggled her toes and moved her fingers along the touchpad. As she reflected on her recent conversation with Maya, she scrolled through her music feed on Nektir. Where a multitude of usernames had once inundated her music feed, now only one remained: "1HighKite," the handle of Timothy Cardiff.

The nature of this happenstance existed in what almost felt like an alternate reality. When Kila opted to unfollow Brixton's Nektir feed, due to their fallout, she also made a firm decision to unfollow everyone else's. Brixton's feed, at times, had felt more nourishing to her than meals, and she already knew that subtracting him without subtracting the others would produce more or less the same result as subtracting everyone. So she axed them all. Her stubborn mind forced her on a months-long solo expedition, granting her the complete listening freedom she wasn't sure she wanted. Listening to anything at anytime without anyone knowing seemed dull. Her dad, Dil, encouraged her to embrace it. Laughing in a caring way, he explained to his daughter that this used to be the norm.

But, Kila couldn't embrace it because she didn't like the former norm. It seemed dusty...and incomplete. She didn't just want the sounds in her ears. She wanted to taste the lyrics in her mouth, wanted to type her feelings on the screen, and wanted someone to share those exchanges with. About two weeks ago, the state of Kila's music affairs changed drastically when 1HighKite sent an invitation to connect on Nektir. Knowing that his account was private, the invitation echoed of intimacy. With immediacy, she accepted the request and followed him back, feeling a bit mysterious for it. *Did he notice I'm not connected to anyone?*

She first sifted through his playlists and then continued to listen to his music on and off for the past couple of weeks. The two shared interest in some of the same alternative and indie artists, but Timothy had a whole host of other artists in his queues, including some Kila had never even heard of. She listened to those songs with the nervous intensity of two strangers who had agreed to meet for the first time.

* * * * *

Here she was once more, at ten o'clock on a Thursday night, watching 1HighKite's feed again. *He's a night owl like me,* she smiled at the thought of knowing a little bit about him without ever having conversed with him in class. Scrolling through the list, her eyes landed on the new song he'd begun,

"Stand on the Horizon–Todd Terje Extended Mix" by Franz Ferdinand.

Oh *&^%! I clicked on it. She bit her bottom lip as the same song he was listening to began to play in her room. She looked up at the ceiling, shifted onto her side, and prayed he wouldn't see she was listening. She knew she could simply switch to one of her own songs, and he might never notice, but the melody of his song had already mesmerized her.

Doubtful he'll notice, she took in the lyrics, feeling strangely connected to the boy she knew only from a distance. The boy who rarely spoke in school, but somehow morphed into Salt for Swordsmen's frontman on the weekends. *Does he know I've been to a few of his shows? Can he identify who's in the crowd from the stage at a night show or he is too focused on singing to care?*

There WAS that outdoor show they did in the fall, during the day...I toyed with the idea of talking to him after the performance when he passed through the pumpkin patch...but by that time I was already with Brix and E, and Maya more or less laughed at me for simply quasi-hinting I wanted to talk to him. Despite his rousing performance and epic crowd-surfing, he looked lonely amidst the hundreds of pumpkins, his onyx vegan leather jacket and equally dark, ripped jeans...all those zippers and chains, and that melancholy mouth, all sewn shut when he's not on a stage.

The chatter of her mind scattered like the shriveled pieces of a popped balloon when she saw the fluorescent orange dialogue box appear with a message from 1HighKite:

< 1HighKite: You've never done that before... >

Kila's widened eyes stared at the screen. *HE'S MESSAGING ME! What's my play? Ignore? Reply? Delayed reply? I should be able to talk to him...right? Without it being weird? I mean, we're in the same grade, since I skipped one. He's sixteen. I'm fifteen. He's the same age as my brother's friends. He's in my Calc class. And, I WANT to talk to him. Hell, I'm too curious NOT to.*

After a deep breath, she typed with caution:

< K.Lorens: It was unintentional. >

What are the odds he'll reply? Maybe HE'S playing the delay game...ugh, I should have exercised more patience! Committing to an air of indifference, Kila opened up a new window on her screen to check her email, but when the fluorescent orange notification flashed in the lower left-hand corner of her screen, she switched back to Nektir faster than she ever had to see his reply:

< 1HighKite: It's okay. I confess to listening to your feed in tandem, too. I just set mine to private when I do, so you can't see. >

Kila squinted her eyes. She couldn't place how she felt, but typed a reply just the same. With that, the conversation developed organically:

< K.Lorens: Whether it's true or not, it made me feel better... >

< 1HighKite: It is true. (I listened to the entire Bleachers

Strange Desire album with you last night.) ⟩

⟨ K.Lorens: OMG, you did NOT… ⟩

⟨ 1HighKite: Yeah, I so DID…"Wake Me" is my favorite on that album, too. I was into the fact you hit it five times. ⟩

⟨ K.Lorens: I've listened to that song longer than that before. I thought E was going to kill me by the pool one day last summer, I couldn't stop playing it. ⟩

⟨ 1HighKite: Yeah. Sometimes you need to invoke the repeat. It's there for a reason. Song must be worthy, though. If it is, there's no shame in it. ⟩

⟨ K.Lorens: This Franz track is most definitely worthy. Tell me more… ⟩

⟨ 1HighKite: Me? There's nothing to tell about me. ⟩

⟨ K.Lorens: There's everything to tell. I know less about you than anyone else at Cypress. You talk to no one but Miccah and Vik, and they barely talk to anyone else, either. ⟩

⟨ 1HighKite: Don't let Miccah and Vik fool you. They're just as vain as everyone else, but they happen to be my bandmates. ⟩

⟨ K.Lorens: I know, but…I can't imagine them worrying about anything… ⟩

⟨ 1HighKite: They do. Vik's texted me twelve times since we started this thread…he's sweating this date he has tomorrow night… ⟩

‹ K.Lorens: REALLY??? With who? Are you allowed to tell? ›

‹ 1HighKite: Yeah, don't say anything. Her name's Gretchen, but she goes by Greco?!?! (Neither of which I'll be addressing her by, of course.) She's a high-strung metalhead from Watsonville. He met her at a festival a few months back. They text religiously on the daily, and he finally asked her to meet him out. I'm a little surprised she agreed to it. ›

‹ K.Lorens: Whoa...so Vik's got some game... ›

‹ 1HighKite: ...still open for question. They're both effing nuts if you ask me. Worse part is, I have to go...not looking forward to it, as you can probably tell. That whole "no way it won't be a disaster" double date scenario. I would bail if it were anyone else. I swear it. ›

‹ K.Lorens: Why? You might like the girl. ›

‹ 1HighKite: Doubtful. I need substance. ›

‹ K.Lorens: How do you know she's lacking it? ›

‹ 1HighKite: I've seen her pages—it's all gumdrops and absurdity. There's none there. ›

‹ K.Lorens: Maybe she's hiding it, just like you. MAYBE she's the girl of your dreams. ›

‹ 1HighKite: I'm a fan of the positivity...but... ›

‹ K.Lorens: ...??? ›

‹ 1HighKite: …I don't want to upset you. ›

‹ K.Lorens: How could you? ›

‹ 1HighKite: IDK…by being myself. ›

‹ K.Lorens: You shouldn't be anything else. ›

‹ 1HighKite: …I was just thinking that dreams and reality don't converge as often as people might like them to. ›

‹ K.Lorens: Yeah, that's apparent. ›

‹ 1HighKite: Really? I can't imagine anything's out of your reach. ›

‹ K.Lorens: Wow. Wish that were true…I mostly feel foolish. ›

‹ 1HighKite: Same here, strangely. I've never messaged anyone on here before. What do people talk about? ›

‹ K.Lorens: IDK…I don't care what they talk about. Just keep typing—where do you have to go for the date? ›

‹ 1HighKite: Probably some overpriced place that doesn't offer vegan options. ›

‹ K.Lorens: Nasty…tell Vik you'll meet up after dinner… or, there's always the garden salad. Everywhere has one of those, but you know you have to order it without dressing if you really want it vegan, and then ask for oil and balsamic on the side to be safe. ›

‹ 1HighKite: I know, you're right. Better safe than sick to my stomach. The whole thought of it annoys me. I hate relinquishing my time for such trivial things. ›

‹ K.Lorens: ...I kind of can't picture you on a date... ›

‹ 1HighKite: Why not? Am I that awful? ›

‹ K.Lorens: What? NO! Not at all. ›

‹ 1HighKite: Tell me then. ›

‹ K.Lorens: You just, well, you, have this presence about you. ›

‹ 1HighKite: Like a bad presence? ›

‹ K.Lorens: No. ›

‹ 1HighKite: You like doing that, don't you? ›

‹ K.Lorens: ? ›

‹ 1HighKite: Telling only a portion of something. Why won't you tell me what you're actually thinking? ›

‹ K.Lorens: bc I'm nervous. ›

‹ 1HighKite: Of me? ›

‹ K.Lorens: Yeah. ›

‹ 1HighKite: Why? I'm the one who should be nervous. I

don't know how to talk to people like this. Our social circles only overlap inside Casper's or at shows. >

< **K.Lorens:** Screw our social circles. They do nothing but alienate people. >

< **1HighKite:** I like talking to you online. It's…enlightening. >

< **K.Lorens:** Likewise. I didn't expect you to message. >

< **1HighKite:** I've been hunting for a reason to. >

< **K.Lorens:** Really? I wanted to talk to you, too… >

< **1HighKite:** You don't have to say that. I'm not as delicate as your brother's friends, you know. >

< **K.Lorens:** I figured as much, considering you could build a time machine solely out of the metal you're wearing on any given day. >

< **1HighKite:** Congratulations, I cracked a smile. >

< **K.Lorens:** It's about time. I didn't know if that ever happened. >

< **1HighKite:** It does. (On occasion.) >

< **K.Lorens:** Noted (with a smile). >

< **1HighKite:** UGH. I bet I won't be smiling tomorrow. It's fated to be the worst, and I already know it, which makes it even worse, if that's possible. >

‹ **K.Lorens**: You really are as dark as you seem, aren't you? ›

‹ **1HighKite**: Maybe, but I'm still a work in progress. ›

‹ **K.Lorens**: Aren't we all? ›

‹ **1HighKite**: Possibly. So…what is Kila Lorens doing up so late? ›

‹ **K.Lorens**: She's messaging Timothy Cardiff. ›

‹ **1HighKite**: You didn't call me Timmy… ›

‹ **K.Lorens**: Would you rather I did? ›

‹ **1HighKite**: No, I hate being called Timmy. ›

‹ **K.Lorens**: COME ON. You don't like being known as "gothic Timmy"? It's only the most obnoxious, stereotypical name someone could have given you. To be honest, I can't believe the name held for so long. ›

‹ **1HighKite**: I KNOW! Thank you. Miccah and Vik both swear I should embrace it. (I question them more often than not, by the way.) Miccah claims he would bow before anyone who called him "gothic Miccah." ›

‹ **K.Lorens**: Hysterical. ›

‹ **1HighKite**: I need a new nickname. ›

‹ **K.Lorens**: Clearly. How about you let me pick it? ›

‹ 1HighKite: What are your qualifications for this? ›

‹ K.Lorens: None needed. I pick a name. If you don't like it, you don't use it. I'm pretty sure I could pick the right one, though. ›

‹ 1HighKite: Right now? Or after we message some more? ›

‹ K.Lorens: I didn't realize there would be more messaging. ›

‹ 1HighKite: There doesn't have to be if you don't want there to be. ›

‹ K.Lorens: Relax. I was teasing. I like talking to you. ›

‹ 1HighKite: Nickname me, then. Right now. ›

‹ K.Lorens: Okay, but on one condition. ›

‹ 1HighKite: I'm listening. ›

‹ K.Lorens: You can no longer "once-a-name" me EVER again. ›

‹ 1HighKite: You do realize that NO ONE, including my sister and bandmates, has that exemption. ›

‹ K.Lorens: Exactly why I requested it. If I'm going to brand you with a new name, I need something equal in exchange. And I see that as an even exchange. ›

‹ 1HighKite: People will notice you have preferential treatment. ›

‹ K.Lorens: Will that embarrass you? ›

‹ 1HighKite: I was concerned for your sake, not for mine…
although I do like naming people on the spot and confusing
the newbies, like Gretchen. (I've been brushing up on my
"g" names.) ›

‹ K.Lorens: Don't scare poor Gretchen. Call her NICE "g"
names, and not anything awful. Who knows? She could turn
out to be perfect for Vik. ›

‹ 1HighKite: Not holding my breath on that one.
Unrealistic expectations have a tendency to choke the life
out of relationships. (Not based on experience, but on
observation.) Enough of that. Back to our new names…what
were you saying? ›

‹ K.Lorens: What if you named me, but it was a perma-name
in place of a once-a-name, but no one else could have a
perma-name? That would work as well, as long as I liked
the name. ›

‹ 1HighKite: Yes! I already have one in mind. Is that weird?
I could never use it on you, because it didn't fit the "once-a-
name" naming convention. ›

‹ K.Lorens: Wait. You already have a perma-name for me in
mind? How?!!! ›

‹ 1HighKite: Don't pry. Let's do it this way. If I like your
nickname, I'll tell you the perma-name. If we both approve,
we move forward with the new names. Then we only refer
to each other on here with those names moving forward. ›

‹ **K.Lorens:** Deal. But don't say you like the name if you really don't, and I won't either. The last thing you need is another name you hate. ›

‹ **1HighKite:** Agreed. But first, tell me something about you that no one knows. I'll never tell anyone, just between us. ›

‹ **K.Lorens:** Like a friend thing? ›

‹ **1HighKite:** Yeah. I mean, unless you want to be enemies and tell me. I'm down for that, too, as long as we can still talk on here. Whatever you're feeling... ›

‹ **K.Lorens:** Okay, "enemy," I'll tell you something if you tell me something. Only one thing. It'll be a first step towards trust. ›

‹ **1HighKite:** On the count of three, we both type it. ›

‹ **K.Lorens:** 1 ›

‹ **1HighKite:** 2 ›

‹ **K.Lorens:** 3 ›

‹ **1HighKite:** I'm a potter. I've been making pottery since I was twelve. Started with mugs, but I'm dabbling into sculpture—it calms me down. If you tell anyone, I will never forgive you. Well, maybe not NEVER, but close to. ›

‹ **K.Lorens:** There's a wooden box under my bed, full of canvasses I've painted. Mostly of things and of people I love—oil paintings. No one knows except for E and my parents. ›

‹ 1HighKite: Not what I expected. That's rad. ›

‹ K.Lorens: Doesn't surprise me. You're inherently artistic. ›

‹ 1HighKite: We're not as different online as we are in reality. ›

‹ K.Lorens: Different doesn't always mean separate. ›

‹ 1HighKite: I think I'm learning that (right now). ›

‹ K.Lorens: I knew you had a s o f t e r side. By the way, do your pajamas have zippers? I've been dying to ask this whole time, but I wanted to wait until we had at least some semblance of rapport… ›

‹ 1HighKite: That might be the most bizarre thing anyone has ever asked me in my life. ›

‹ K.Lorens: Are you mad I asked? If so, I take it back. ›

‹ 1HighKite: No! Don't take it back, I'm laughing too hard. ›

‹ K.Lorens: Is it because your pajamas have zippers? ›

‹ 1HighKite: Yes, my pajamas are solely comprised of zippers! They're a mechanical masterpiece and overwhelmingly uncomfortable, thanks to their lack of any fabric. Actually…(I don't wear pjs) ›

‹ K.Lorens: Oh… ›

‹ 1HighKite: Don't worry, I'm not the type to insert a tasteless comment or embarrassing pic here. (I'm still fully dressed from the day & I might even sleep in my clothes tonight 'cause I'm feeling lazy & I'm pretty absorbed in our convo.) ›

‹ K.Lorens: Ollie. ›

‹ 1HighKite: ??? the name? ›

‹ K.Lorens: If you want it to be. ›

‹ 1HighKite: Unrestricted yes, but I'm feeling disinclined to tell you yours now. I mean, you just flipped yours out there without an introduction, and now that I've instantly taken to it, I'm experiencing a high level of concern you might be repelled by yours. ›

‹ K.Lorens: It's hard to believe you're this self-conscious. I HAVE seen you onstage, you know. ›

‹ 1HighKite: Are you going to tell anyone how I really am? ›

‹ K.Lorens: Not a chance, Ollie. This thread belongs to us. ›

‹ 1HighKite: Aurora. ›

‹ 1HighKite: Do you like it? ›

‹ 1HighKite: ??? You aren't responding. If you hate it, I can pick another. Don't bail on me. ›

‹ K.Lorens: I'm here. Not bailing. I…don't feel worthy of it. ›

‹ 1HighKite: ??? Is that your way of saying you don't like it? I can't read you…help me. Please? ›

‹ K.Lorens: When I read it I thought of someone else. Someone stronger. Someone who wasn't subject to the restless crushing without return, which has become my life as of late. ›

‹ 1HighKite: You confound me. Who is this ignorant fool? This person who hasn't returned your affection. Does he even exist? Is he like a college guy or something? ›

‹ K.Lorens: A college guy? Ha! NO—that'd be a little creepy considering the age diff. Just…never mind. But, thank you for being sweet about it. ›

‹ 1HighKite: Does he know that you like him? ›

‹ K.Lorens: IDK? Maybe, maybe not…anyway, he's into someone else, so it doesn't matter. ›

‹ 1HighKite: Are you heartbroken? ›

‹ K.Lorens: OLLIE! Come on! You're making it worse. ›

‹ 1HighKite: Sorry…not my intent. I'd rather you were happy. Let's pick another name for you, then. ›

‹ K.Lorens: No! I've changed my mind. I'll take Aurora. I couldn't imagine anything better. ›

‹ 1HighKite: Good. Neither can I. ›

‹ **K.Lorens:** Is it really you? ›

‹ **1HighKite:** ??? Who else would I be? I mean, look at my playlists—not proof enough? ›

‹ **K.Lorens:** Yeah, I just…you seem pretty unapproachable in school. ›

‹ **1HighKite:** There's a reason for that. I'm not good at all of the…false charm, which seems to be required for high school approachability. I also hate making plans, unless the plans are music related. Does that make it impossible for us to be friends? ›

‹ **K.Lorens:** No. It makes it more possible. Do I come across as stuck up? ›

‹ **1HighKite:** …Only a little? ›

‹ **1HighKite:** …I'm joking! ›

‹ **K.Lorens:** Good, because I was just about to tell you that I like your new haircut, and I nearly decided against it. ›

‹ **1HighKite:** Oh, I thought it looked horrible—my sister got a little too carried away with it. ›

‹ **K.Lorens:** Naomi!! How is she? The cut is perfect—it was too long without any direction before. Now, it has angles and a life of its own AND it's the perfect length for a boy bun. ›

‹ **1HighKite:** Naomi is Naomi—can't make up her mind between theater and hair, so naturally she's in school for both. Theater at UCSC and hair at Aveda. Girls are too into hair. PS: I'll NEVER wear a boy bun. ›

‹ K.Lorens: Please tell her I said hi. She is seriously the coolest. Maybe I'll have her chop my hair off this summer! PS: Never say never. ›

‹ 1HighKite: The day I wear a boy bun is the day I have entirely given up on life in general. So...if you see me in one, you might want to notify Naomi and anyone else who's crazy enough to care that my time on this whacky rock is nearing its end. ›

‹ K.Lorens: UGH! You're such a drama king. Maybe you should study theater, too. ›

‹ 1HighKite: No time. I'm too into music. (Don't chop your hair—it's nice the way it is.) Are you bored? ›

‹ K.Lorens: Bored more than ever, lately. ...This is helping, though. ›

‹ 1HighKite: Me? Truthfully or comically? ›

‹ K.Lorens: Truthfully. Why do you keep questioning me? ›

‹ 1HighKite: IDK...because it's you. ›

‹ K.Lorens: I don't know what that means. ›

‹ 1HighKite: I know, it's okay. You're just...suspiciously easy to talk to. I didn't expect it—I expected something a little more superficial. ›

‹ **K.Lorens:** I KNEW it! You thought I was snobbish, didn't you? ›

‹ **1HighKite:** NO! Definitely not. It was simpler for me to think you were someone else. ›

‹ **K.Lorens:** … ›

‹ **1HighKite:** Don't go. I shouldn't have typed that. It's just weird to see you with Anna now. ›

‹ **K.Lorens:** Anna? (She's not the person she once was. Most people don't know that. She's not like Reese anymore… to be honest, I don't think she ever was.) ›

‹ **1HighKite:** She was either just like Reese OR very willing to go along with whatever Reese wanted. I'd rather not talk about it. Is that alright? I hope it is…I don't care if you hang out with her. It shouldn't change whether or not we message on Nektir, should it? ›

‹ **K.Lorens:** No. I'm good with you being honest though, Ollie. I like reading what you have to say. I won't repeat any of it. Not one word. Actually…I wish I could come to Bitters Saturday night… ›

‹ **1HighKite:** Yeah, I was about to ask you a little while ago when we first started the thread, but then I remembered you obviously have to be somewhere else. How are you holding up, by the way? I saw Maya fighting back tears in Calc the other day, and it tore me apart a little. I guess, because that girl is never sad about anything. She's your best friend, right? ›

‹ K.Lorens: Yeah. It's been pretty rough, but I've been trying to make the best of it. We're basically going all out for the party. ›

‹ 1HighKite: So I've heard…from the nonstop chatter in the hallways. ›

‹ K.Lorens: Do you want to come after your gig? Or do Miccah and Vik have other plans for you? ›

‹ 1HighKite: Is this an official invitation, or merely an honorable mention? ›

‹ K.Lorens: IDK, are we friends at Cypress High or friends on Nektir only? ›

‹ 1HighKite: IDK, do you think people could handle us being friends? ›

‹ K.Lorens: Do you think I care what those people think about? ›

‹ 1HighKite: I tend to think you care what your brother, Brixton, Angus, and Anna think about. I doubt any in that sequence would approve of our friendship—Maya, I'm on the fence about. She could go either way, I suppose, based on what I know. ›

‹ K.Lorens: Ollie, come to the party if you want to. I'm not going to beg you to come. ›

‹ 1HighKite: Alright. I'll think about it. I'm not a party person, though. (I'm best onstage or in my bedroom.) ›

‹ **K.Lorens:** (Ooo. I'll keep that in mind…) ›

‹ **1HighKite:** Are you flirting with me? ›

‹ **K.Lorens:** I kind of REALLY wish I could come to Bitters. ›

‹ **1HighKite:** (You didn't answer my question.) ›

‹ **K.Lorens:** (Intentional.) Did you pick the set list yet? ›

‹ **1HighKite:** it's in process…I want to add something unexpected in this time, but every time I've suggested it, Miccah and Vik shut it down like it will ruin SforS forever. I guess I just get tired of the hard songs every show—all the screaming—it sometimes takes me two or three days to recover my voice. I mean, although I love him, I'm not Dave Grohl, and there are only, like, a handful of legends who can continually stress their vocals like that without it rendering them useless the next day. My Sundays are the laziest, you have no idea. ›

‹ **K.Lorens:** I can't fathom you singing something softer… what track were you thinking? Can I hear it? Please? ›

‹ **1HighKite:** OMG, not now. I can't just send you a file on the spot. ›

‹ **K.Lorens:** I'm sorry. I didn't mean to get so excited… ›

‹ **1HighKite:** Don't apologize for that. Please. I just don't know what to sing. It's paralyzing how many options there are. ›

‹ **K.Lorens**: May I make a suggestion? ›

‹ **1HighKite**: Yes, please. Not only do I need a song, but I need to convince Miccah and Vik to play while I sing it. ›

‹ **K.Lorens**: ? Miccah and Vik are the easy part. In this instance, you have two things going for you. #1, you can tell them you refuse to perform at all unless they agree to play your chosen song at the end of the set. #2, (and this is an assumption, so tell me if I'm right in making it) I'll bet Gretchen will be there, and it could be the perfect platform for you to work in a softer song. A softer song, a little romance, and lots of kissing—you know how it goes... ›

‹ **1HighKite**: Your assumption is spot on—Vik's crush has already committed to Bitters even if tomorrow night's date is a bust. By the way, IS THAT the way it goes? (I have no idea. I've only kissed one girl, it was years ago, and it didn't end so well.) ›

‹ **K.Lorens**: ...Even you have me beat, Ollie. I haven't been lucky enough to make it that far. ›

‹ **1HighKite**: Wait, wait, WAIT, Aurora... ›

‹ **1HighKite**: Hang on... ›

‹ **1HighKite**: I nearly fell off my bed! (NOT joking, my laptop almost snapped in half at the hinge.) ›

‹ **K.Lorens**: ??? ›

‹ **K.Lorens**: Is your laptop ok? ›

< 1HighKite: Ha. Yeah. It's fine. YOU have never been kissed? Is that right or did I somehow misinterpret? >

< K.Lorens: Forget it. I shouldn't have told you…let's talk about the song. It'll make me feel better. >

< 1HighKite: So…Brixton NEVER kissed you? >

< K.Lorens: No. >

< 1HighKite: Is he OUT OF HIS MIND? >

< K.Lorens: …IDK. We were never dating. Did you think we were? >

< 1HighKite: Um…you were together every day for…let's see, YEARS. It's not too wild of an assumption for me to make. Did you specifically tell him NOT to kiss you? >

< K.Lorens: No. I didn't. That would have been weird of me to say. >

< K.Lorens: And no one has ever tried, as in EVER, okay? >

< K.Lorens: I really, really, really don't want to talk about it anymore. >

< 1HighKite: Don't worry. My mind is too boggled to press any further. I think you need to get out of your circle more often. Have some adventures of your own. >

< K.Lorens: You're probably right about that… >

‹ **1HighKite**: You feel bad, don't you? It's not your fault… I swear it. You just…it hasn't been the right situation, yet. You have something to look forward to instead of look back upon. I wish I could erase mine, if it makes you feel any better. Mine wasn't what I thought it would be. It felt cheap and empty soon afterwards, and I hated myself for it. It kind of messed me up, to be perfectly transparent about it. ›

‹ **K.Lorens**: Do you want to talk about it? ›

‹ **1HighKite**: Not now…maybe someday, though. ›

‹ **K.Lorens**: Ok. Promise me you won't just stop talking to me without telling me why…I know this might seem crazy, but I just need to know…like right now before we talk any further. ›

‹ **1HighKite**: I promise. No matter what the hell ever happens here in Felton or anywhere else in California or anywhere else on Earth either of us might be, that I will NEVER stop talking to you without an explanation, ever. ›

‹ **K.Lorens**: Thank you. I'm sorry about your first kiss. It sounds like she didn't deserve it. ›

‹ **1HighKite**: Yeah, well…it more or less married me to my music, so for that part I'm grateful. ›

‹ **1HighKite**: I have an idea: Why don't you pick the song for me? ›

‹ **K.Lorens**: OMG. (Seriously?) ›

< 1HighKite: OMG. (Yes) (haha) >

< K.Lorens: OK...I can never pick just one, though, so I'll pick three and you can pick one...is that alright? >

< 1HighKite: Sure. Hit me, and I'll listen to them now. Or, we could listen to them together, if I put them in the shared queue? What do you think? >

< K.Lorens: Oh! Definitely shared queue...let me think... >

< K.Lorens: ...Thinking...thinking...thinking... >

< 1HighKite: Waiting (patiently) >

< K.Lorens: **"Sweater Weather" by The Neighbourhood, "Cardiac Arrest" by Bad Suns**, and **"I'm Into You" by Chet Faker**. All will sound dangerous dressed in your vocals, all have the softer but edgy side you mentioned, AND...besides that...I think the crowd, particularly, the girls in the crowd, will LOSE their minds if you sing something along those lines. >

< 1HighKite: I'm in. I'll pick one. BUT, if I'm forever teased about this, know that I have you to thank for it. >

< K.Lorens: You won't have to thank me for the teasing, because there will be no teasing. >

< K.Lorens: This is something I know about—one of my specialties. I wish I could trade specialties. Mine don't seem to serve me in the ways I wish they would. >

‹ **1HighKite**: Maybe we can share specialties...I must have some that aren't serving me, too. ›

‹ **K.Lorens**: Shhhhh! Close your eyes. The Neighbourhood just started. You need to imagine it, the storylines in the lyrics, and singing each of the songs...to see if one of the three will work for Saturday night. ›

‹ **1HighKite**: OK. (Please keep in mind I don't know the rules until you inform me of them.) ›

And with that last message, Kila Lorens and Timothy Cardiff, with closed eyes, listened to the three songs in the shared queue and fell asleep at almost the exact moment towards the end of "I'm Into You." The queue, which had auto-set itself to repeat, continued to loop for nearly six hours until each of their alarms beckoned them awake for school. Timothy stopped the queue from playing only when it was time for him to leave for class. He could see that Kila hadn't signed off, but that she had switched to the mobile app. He did the same, and hoped he'd see another message from her soon.

Fridays at Cypress High were always something to look forward to. One could nearly hear the glorious bells of weekend's call as students angled to get written into the plans of those they fancied. And an almost palpable angst for summer tugged at their teenage minds on the morning of this particular Friday, exactly one week before the last day of school.

At her locker before first period, Kila invested three-quarters of her focus in the conversation with Maya and Anna. The remaining quarter she split in half, between scrolling through last night's Nektir thread and watching the hallway for Timothy to pass by with Miccah and Vik. *Am I inflating the importance of last night's conversation? It probably means less to him than it meant to me. Have I already attached myself in some way… on a friend level…on possibly another…and should I regret that?* Kila had no sooner blinked when she saw Anna poke Maya. Then she received a sharp jab in her own side.

"I think Salt for Swordsmen is coming over here," Anna hissed. "Do either of you have any idea WHY?"

Maya's brows danced in confusion. "No," she whispered.

Both girls eyed Kila, who remained unreadable even as the three boys approached.

"Mabel, Andrea," Timothy rushed through his greetings to Maya and Anna.

"Hi guys," Maya spoke, wondering why he hadn't addressed Kila.

He's not giving me a once-a-name! Exactly.as.promised, Kila positioned her gaze halfway between Vik and Miccah. Her eyes landed on the tightly rolled persimmon-embroidered lime bandana, which loosely held back Miccah's messy honey brown hair. The edges of her lips curled upwards.

"While I don't like that the majority of our grade is torn on where they should be Saturday night, I do understand why," Miccah nodded to Maya.

"Thank you," Maya smiled warmly. "I WILL watch the entire show online afterwards, so it better be good."

"If it's horrible," Miccah lifted his chin, "I cordially invite you post a 'no mercy' review in the comments."

"Invitation accepted," Maya grinned, turning to Kila. "You'll watch the SforS show with me, right?"

"Course," Kila kept her words to a minimum and her eyes from reaching Timothy's.

"So, why'd you guys stop here?" Anna asked, to Maya's confusion and Kila's irritation.

"Besides cashing in on the rare opportunity to annoy you," Timothy pursed his lips, "I have something to give to...her." He ceased talking to Anna and stepped toward Kila with a folded piece of paper, "You...dropped your worksheet in Calc class yesterday."

"Thanks," Kila swallowed the nerves in her throat and instructed her arm to reach for the equation-stamped paper.

"See," Vik squinted at Anna through his black 'n' blue eyeliner, "there are at times reasons for guys dressed like us"—he motioned to Timothy and Miccah's dark attire—"to speak with girls like you. Wait, to be perfectly clear I'm not grouping the three of you into the same category, because, well...only you know why."

Kila looked at Anna in question.

"Easy, V," Miccah touched Vik's shoulder and smiled at Anna. "I'll apologize on his behalf. He's extra sharp today—long anticipated date tonight. Timothy, too. I guess this is also somewhat of a public service announcement that both are officially off limits."

"Oh yeah?" Anna smiled for the first time. "And what about you?"

"Insanely available," Miccah grinned nervously, "but I guess that's always been the case."

"Hey, I know someone who has a mega-crush on you," Maya held a hand over her mouth. "I TOTALLY shouldn't have said that, though."

Kila and Timothy shared the briefest glance, then just as quickly looked away from one another.

Barely able to breathe, Miccah rubbed his hands together. "Is she coming to Bitters tomorrow night?"

"No," Maya pursed her lips in thought, "she'll be with us, BUT, I do know that she has never missed an SforS show. And she's one of a kind and one of the coolest girls I know."

"You're not going to tell me who, are you?" Miccah realized as the first bell rang.

"No," Maya shook her head, "I'd be in all sorts of trouble if I did. But I might be able to convince HER to tell you, though. Or at least talk to you a little more, so you could figure it out on your own."

"I would exist exclusively in your debt," Miccah vowed with both his words and his eyes.

"Miccah," Vik scolded him openly, "we've talked about not being a pushover. Do we need to have that conversation again?"

Kila suddenly found it possible to speak more than one word

at a time. "No, Vik, you don't need to have that conversation AGAIN, because you never NEEDED to have it in the first place. Control yourself, not your friends. Miccah's curiosity is not misplaced. In fact, I vow to assist Maya in convincing this girl to talk to him. Admittedly"—she linked her arm in Maya's—"I don't know who it is yet, but I already have my guesses."

"You guys are the best," Miccah beamed at Kila. "Can you come to our next practice? I can pay you in cold-brew coffee and force Tim to sing the songs you like."

Before Kila could speak through her smile, Vik huffed, "Five minutes with these three, and you turn to mush. It's downright embarrassing."

"GET over yourself," Kila rolled her eyes in an exaggerated fashion. "If you think this little five-minute interaction represents an unabridged accounting of who we are"—she motioned to Maya and Anna—"your perspective is mush. And it's downright embarrassing."

Vik snarled without reply.

Timothy's unapologetic laughter and the warning bell sounded in unison.

In an instant, locker doors slammed shut and students scurried to class. The group of six dismantled slower than it should have, Anna the last to leave Kila's side. Once alone, Kila opened Timothy's Calc worksheet to see his two-word note: "Message Me." She opened the Nektir app on her phone the moment Ms. Backster rolled out the AV cart and resumed the biopic on Oscar Wilde.

‹ **K.Lorens:** I'd be lying if I said that wasn't weird. (Good Morning, Ollie.) ›

‹ **1HighKite:** I told them as disinterested as I could that I had to hand you something, and the two of them followed me without warning. (We Nektir-slept together, Aurora.) ›

‹ **K.Lorens:** (I know.) Now we are prisoners in class once more. Where are you? ›

‹ **1HighKite:** Snoozing hall, playing ping-pong with Miccah, who pretty much idolizes you now. ›

‹ **K.Lorens:** I thought only seniors were allowed to take study hall first period? How'd you two swing that? ›

‹ **1HighKite:** Mr. Kolter's absent. ›

‹ **K.Lorens:** Yes! That means I'll have study hall for 5th. Go easy on Miccah. ›

‹ **1HighKite:** I need him to go easy on me! He's an animal at p-pong. ›

‹ **K.Lorens:** You'd have a better chance at winning if you stop messaging. ›

‹ **1HighKite:** No way, I'd rather lose. Besides, we're waiting for the table again…could be a while as the seniors are having a legitimate fight over who's up next…they're so anti-chill sometimes…hope they work that out before college starts. ›

< **K.Lorens:** I know…could be a rude awakening for a few of them. Hey, on the topic of rude, what's with the animosity between Vik and Anna? >

< **1HighKite:** There's a history between them, which began in middle school. Might be best to leave that alone for now…What's happening where you are? >

< **K.Lorens:** I'm staring at a giant image of Oscar Wilde's tomb. Beside me, Nolan Anderson's sleep-sitting with his face on the table (about a centimeter away from drowning in his own drool). So, yeah, it's pretty mind-bending over here. >

< **1HighKite:** Ha! I don't know if I can watch you and Vik mince words again without it being obvious I'm on your side. >

< **K.Lorens:** All it took was a 10 hr Nektir thread to win that honor? >

< **1HighKite:** I'm not answering that question, but you've been right about everything else so far. >

< **K.Lorens:** Oh yeah? >

< **1HighKite:** Yeah. The double tonight—the girl I mentioned, the one I'm matched up with. Her name's Jocelyn. She's been texting me all morning… >

< **K.Lorens:** …So your dreams have been answered? >

< **1HighKite:** Not sure about that…guess I'll see what she's really like tonight. Truth: I'm nervous. >

‹ **K.Lorens**: I imagine that's natural...you totally like her now. I can tell... ›

‹ **1HighKite**: We'll see if you're really right on this one tonight. Where will you be later? ›

‹ **K.Lorens**: Mostly at my house, maybe a little shopping. Anna and Maya are crashing with me. I need to make sure Maya does something before tomorrow night. Send me some swagger if you can lend some. ›

‹ **1HighKite**: ? You have more swagger than I do. ›

‹ **K.Lorens**: False. ›

‹ **1HighKite**: Fine. I'll lend you what little I have until my date. Then, I need it all back and maybe some of yours, too. ›

‹ **K.Lorens**: Deal, Ollie. ›

‹ **1HighKite**: Will it be weird if I fill you in afterwards? ›

‹ **K.Lorens**: Hell, no! I want every detail, less the kissing. Omit the kissing for me. My only request. ›

‹ **1HighKite**: You've really never been kissed? ›

‹ **K.Lorens**: ...We covered this last night...review the thread. ›

‹ **1HighKite**: Hang on...I have a better idea... ›

‹ **K.Lorens**: ??? ›

‹ 1HighKite: A U R O R A ›

‹ 1HighKite: Look at the back of the room, by the door… ›

‹ K.Lorens: OLLIE! ›

‹ K.Lorens: What.the.hell? ›

‹ 1HighKite: Come out here. ›

‹ K.Lorens: No! OMG. ›

‹ 1HighKite: Come out and kiss me. ›

‹ K.Lorens: I am NOT kissing you. ›

‹ 1HighKite: Why not? You look totally bored, and no one else has tried. I'm trying, so let's do this. ›

‹ K.Lorens: Your slither dance is exceptionally adorable, but…1) I don't want a fake kiss and 2) Jocelyn tonight. ›

‹ 1HighKite: #2: Fair enough. #1: it wouldn't be fake. (I knew you wouldn't come out, but @ least now you know someone tried.) ›

‹ K.Lorens: Totally doesn't count as "a try," but I do love messaging you. Better go for now—Ms. Backster's flashing the demon eyes at me. ›

‹ 1HighKite: …Guess I'll have to settle for p-pong w/ Miccah. Just don't forget →Deal's always on the table: a kiss whenever you want it (with or without slither dance, your choice). ›

< **K.Lorens**: You're nuts (but thank you). >

Timothy Cardiff never returned to study hall. Instead, he snuck out of school, hopped into his car, and headed to Wild Roots Market for his morning snack. Halfway through his Muesli Munch and cold-brew coffee, he realized he had carved an underground tunnel to Kila Lorens's world. He wondered why she had let him, and if this were more likely to be a short-lived or a long-lasting entanglement. And he couldn't make amends for this happening on the same day he had a date with Jocelyn.

* * * * *

Periods two through four proved equally as dull as the first to Kila, but in fifth she took comfort in the cold metal seat she chose in the auditorium. Placing her backpack on the floor, she reached to retrieve her phone and Audeze headphones. *Ollie. He's hilarious...and hours away from being Jocelyn's. Would he have kissed me if I met him in the hallway, or was he bluffing to make me feel better? Yes? No? Ugh. Reese. Jocelyn. (Insert any random girl name that's not mine.) Will I ever get to date someone I like? Someone I love?*

Music and daydreams, Kila reminded herself, slipping her headphones into place. With a swipe and a few taps on her screen, she selected **"Love Right Now" by Eon MC Etc.** and closed her unsettled eyes. *At least Eon gets it. Lyrics always tell all. He's such an ace. Too bad he's at least a decade older and doesn't know I exist. I wonder what his teenage life was like. I bet he wouldn't have let himself be played by someone like Reese. No way...*

Angus. I could write that name a thousand times over in my notebook and never tire of the shape. Never tire of the sound. I always see him when I close my eyes. These lyrics. That face. His smile. Reminds me of when he first started driving. When he came to the library after school with me last year. The only time I rode in the Jeep without his mom and without Ethan. Alone. He and I.

It was a Tuesday. In late October. Everyone at school that day had been obsessing over their costumes for the Halloween dance. For once, I didn't care about it. Why? He had decided in our Math class he would be joining me at the library. There was some reference material he needed there, which he didn't have access to online. I thanked everything that was good in the world for the existence of that reference material, several times between his mention of it and the end of classes that day.

It was nearly 2 p.m. when I met up with him in the parking lot. He took his sunglasses off when he spotted me. The weather was crisp and he was wearing a pair of blue-gray chords, a long-sleeved granite-and-white ribbed T-shirt, and an almost black puffer vest. I couldn't keep my eyes off him. He kept making me laugh. The way he purposely exaggerated the singing in the car and repeatedly asked if I was warm enough. I kept hoping maybe he'd want to go somewhere other than the library to do our homework, even though that's where we both needed to go. I wanted him to drive somewhere else. Anywhere else. And homework was the last thing on my mind.

I purposely chose the table in the farthest back corner of the reference room. The section is more like a cubby than anything else. He sat next to me, instead of across, which kept my heart racing. I was taking notes for my project but I may as well have been copying words written in an ancient language. I had no idea what I was writing in my notebook, I just knew I wanted to stay there forever. Next to him. In the corner. Behind the towering bookshelves. Close enough to smell his woodsy cologne and hear his steady breaths. Close enough to watch him read and see his sharp mind at work.

For hours he studied quietly, and I attempted to do the same. The time passed mercilessly despite my wish for it to stop. The light, which had once poured through the windows, faded until it was dark. It grew cold in the large space, cold enough that I nearly shivered, even with my double layers of flannel button-downs. I popped both my collars to warm my neck, buttoned both shirts to the top, and unrolled my cuffs until they reached my knuckles. I did everything I could to project an appearance of comfort. I worried if he noticed I was cold he would suggest that we leave. And if he did, I knew it would be odd to insist that we stay.

Despite my efforts, he noticed and offered his vest. I let him slip it through my arms and over my shoulders. Neither of us spoke, but every few minutes afterwards he looked up from his work and smiled at me. Each time, like lightning to my chest. My nervous note-taking turned into sketches of him, depictions of his face and of his hands. My fingers refused to occupy themselves with anything else. The drawings seemed to take shape of their own accord, leaving my mind free to think of other things.

The feeling of his vest reminded me of a sleeping bag. We had shared one when we were much younger, on a camping trip down to Big Sur with our families. He was seven and I was six, and he was angry that Ethan had chosen to share a sleeping bag with Brixton instead of him. He pouted for a hearty fifteen minutes, until he realized Ethan and Brixton had already fallen asleep. Of the eight inside, he and I were the only two still awake in the "kids" tent. For a long while we whispered about very unimportant things. We giggled and we sang. We even snuck out of the tent to peek at the stars. I remember feeling small, but liked feeling that way with him. Young in years but somewhat already adult in our thinking. When we shimmied back into the gigantic sleeping bag, he kissed my cheek goodnight. I wiggled because I was happy, and he snuggled up to me. He smelled like his dad's cologne. The same woodsy cologne he wore in the library.

While Angus continued to work, I wondered what that scene would have been like in present day, without our parents or friends, just him and me and that same oversized sleeping bag. I imagined we gazed at the stars through the redwoods, just as before. And talked about anything and everything. He smelled better than the fire, the two of us pressed together, the strands of our dark hair meeting up for a nightcap on the pillow.

In the stillness of the library, that fantasy hadn't felt so farfetched. I blinked and found his chair closer than before. A new reference book lay in front of his notepad, and I realized then he must have left and returned. His knee brushed against mine under the table, and I was working up the courage to ask if we could hang out again. He spoke first and asked if I'd like to take a drive to the beach before he took me home. Naturally, I agreed...but, that never happened. Brixton and Ethan turned up at the library. Minutes later I returned his vest. I hugged him goodbye, but I'll never forget how forced it felt on his end.

Kila exhaled, feeling the pulse of her elevated heart rate. Its beats seemed to match the rhythm of the song. Drained from the layered recollection, she leaned her head past the edge of the metal chair and arched her back into a deep stretch. *Is it possible to reverse a crush?*

The answer never made itself known. Two warm fingers touched Kila's forehead, stealing her attention. She rotated her torso to catch them and recognized the hand they were attached to. *Angus's. How long has he been behind me?!?* Kila washed the smile from her face before turning around to face him. He raised his eyebrows as she rolled her eyes, neither of them removing their headphones.

With the aid of his watch, Angus let three minutes pass before hopping over the row to sit next to her. Two teachers scolded him for the maneuver, but he wasn't asked to return to his seat. Kila elbowed him and he elbowed her back. No words were exchanged. He busied himself writing feverishly in what looked like a new journal until his phone vibrated in angry succession. His eyes tense, his fingers replied to the multiple messages he had received.

Knowing the signs all too well, Kila turned toward the back of the room and spotted her. *Of course! I knew it. Can't let him have a moment of peace. At least not with another girl. She doesn't want to sit next to him. Yet, she doesn't want him to sit next to me, either. How CLASSIC in her world. What a waste. I was closer to Angus when I was six. Seriously. Screw this,* Kila shook her head. Without hesitation, she gathered her bag, tapped Angus on the shoulder, and made her way to the main aisle. She exited the auditorium from the upper level, opting for the door just to the left of Reese's seat.

The two girls exchanged frigid glances.

Kila spent the last twenty minutes of fifth period wandering the hallways and listening to music. When the next bell rang, she didn't meet up with Anna and Maya as she normally would. She was too annoyed and knew they'd see it on her face. Instead, she slipped into last period early, smiling at Timothy when he took his seat at the other end of the room.

He pointed to his phone, and Kila opened their Nektir thread to find his latest message:

‹ **1HighKite:** I've been informed that I'll be relinquishing my phone to Vik right after class. Guess these girls have a no-phone rule…just wanted to let you know in case you messaged and I didn't reply right away. I'll fill you in later. Promise. ›

They're smart, Kila inhaled the reality of the situation. She replied quickly and a short exchange began:

‹ **K.Lorens:** I understand. It'd be pretty rude to text someone else when you were on a date. I hope it goes well! ›

‹ **1HighKite:** Truth: I'm not sure what I'm hoping for anymore. I seem to keep changing my mind. ›

‹ **K.Lorens:** Just let it happen, Ollie. (Fall & don't fight it.) ›

Timothy sent five more messages, but Kila didn't see them. She had placed her phone facedown on her desk, feeling more somber than before. That expression remained in place as Angus slipped into the seat in front of her. To make her laugh, he slammed his bag down on top of hers and pushed his chair backwards until it met her desk.

She huffed loud enough for him to hear.

He raised his eyebrows and whispered over his shoulder, "You're less than fifty minutes away from a parentless weekend."

"...So...?" Kila humored him.

"...So you should be wearing a smile...," Angus insisted.

Kila's face lightened as she thought more about it.

He sensed it, and took the opportunity to say something more meaningful. "Why'd you bolt from the auditorium?"

"I was getting antsy and wanted to take a walk," she spoke to the back of his neck.

"Not like you," he turned around briefly to look at her face.

She waited for him to face forward before replying, "Maybe you don't know me as well as you think you do."

His slight laugh melted her heart, and she squeezed his shoulder to quiet him.

"What I do know is that Timmy keeps looking over here," Angus covered his mouth when he leaned back to talk this time. "How about you tell me what that's all about?"

"How about no," she tucked his shirt tag, which had been sticking out, back into place.

"Thank you," he tilted his head back. "Took double gym in lieu of lunch today—wait! Is that why you left? Do I smell?"

"Yes," Kila spoke instantly, "like a huge, muddy frog in a fly-infested swamp."

As punishment for his disruptive laughter, Angus was assigned several advanced calculus problems at the blackboard. All the while grinning, Kila watched him finish them in less time than it would have taken anyone else in the room, including Dr. Goldman. Angus returned to his chair like a king who scored an easy victory, his subtle aloofness sending Kila's mind on another journey through her past.

On the same floor but in another wing of the building, Brixton received a tap on the shoulder from Josie. She passed him a folded square with Ethan's name scribbled across the top. *No name of sender? No problem. I'll find out for myself.* With a pair of curious eyes, he examined the row of faces sitting on Josie's other side. Josie, irked he hadn't delivered the note the instant he received it, tapped her fingers next to his.

Brixton brushed her hand away, continuing the search. When his eyes fell upon Anna, he found her gaze glued to the note. The moment she felt his glance, she squeezed the pen between her fingers and forced her focus to the whiteboard. *Possibly. Potentially. Yes, I'm thinking definitely...Anna.* He held his eyes tight to her face while she shifted in her seat, her sun-kissed hair falling over her shoulder, her right leg crossing over her left. The once-innocent folded page in his hand immediately assumed a greater weight. *What does she need to tell Ethan that can't wait ten minutes? And why today?*

She's never sent him notes before...

Kiki and I used to swap notes all the time. Her musings and anecdotes, often conjured up in stressful times, never failed to amuse me. Her rants and her hopes. Passed in class. Passed in the hall. All the creased pieces. Silly sketches. I have them all. Still. In a box in my room.

*I need a hug. From her. Embarrassingly bad...and it's my fault, the lack. All the times I saw her listening to **"Bros" by Wolf Alice** in my music feed, night after night for the first couple weeks...then nothing. All her listening sessions set to "private" so I couldn't see...disconnect. Complete darkness. Musical murder. And I deserved it.*

Brixton's mind, so musically inclined, played the song without request. His emotion climbed while his body cursed the decision that robbed itself of her company, of her laughs, and of her hugs. *It's been long enough. The risk tied to seeing her is trivial compared to what I've missed. Consequence be damned. Nothing is worse than lost time. Time I can't rescue. Months without her. Months of uselessness. Months of practice without execution. I won't let another day pass like this. I can be a better best friend. I can be more...I can be whatever she wants...whenever she wants...*

Brixton's hand touched his neck. He remembered the way Kila touched his hair last night. *Her demeanor towards me. That warmth. When we were alone. Could it have been my invention?*

The unnatural sound of Josie's double fake cough roused Brixton from his private thoughts. He issued an instant look of indifference, which came as no surprise to Josie. Then he made sure Professor McGavern was looking elsewhere before he slid the note next to Ethan's left hand.

Ethan, feeling the paper meet his fingers, stretched back in his seat, pleased to be thought of enough to receive a message this close to class end. Slyly, he placed the note inside his book and unfolded it slowly. Adjusting his dark chocolate locks so they no longer obstructed the view from his bluish-gray eyes, he began reading. When he detected Brixton's spying eyes, he used the cover of his book as a blockade.

Scrunched and strained, Brixton's face leaned closer to catch Ethan writing a reply. Though he couldn't make out the words, Brixton watched him fill up the remainder of the page, flip it over, then cover more than half of the backside. *My god, is he penning a short story?* Brixton eyed the clock. *Two minutes left!*

By the time Ethan returned the note to Brixton to pass back through Josie, the final Friday bell rang. Brixton opened his mouth to bombard Ethan with questions, but Annabelle's immediate presence quieted him. While he had known her since elementary school, he had never spoken with her.

"My note," Anna said shyly.

Brixton tilted his head and slid it towards her hand.

"Thanks," she moved a section of her hair in front of her shoulder and looked to Ethan.

He smiled, zipping up his bag smugly.

"Welllll?" she asked.

"I replied," Ethan stated simply. He walked toward the door and she and Brixton followed.

In a matter of seconds, a swelling sea of students consumed Ethan's frame. Anna thrust herself into the crowd, nearest Brixton, hoping to reach Ethan. After taking a few strategic strides, and narrowly avoiding a staged collision with Nolan (a sometimes ill-mannered and always pompous senior) Anna had a hand on Ethan's shirt.

"Wasn't fast enough," Nolan grumbled to his long-time wingman, Elliot.

"We have one week left of senior year," Elliot's unusually deep voice carried farther than he realized, "and you're STILL too chicken to talk to her. How am I supposed to play ball with KL this summer if you can't even get me onto the field?"

Brixton, three body rows ahead, snapped his head around to glare at Elliot's scheming eyes.

"Dude. We have all summer," Nolan rolled his exposed, rugby-playing shoulders back, "Quit complaining. All you have to do is buy some running shoes and run the trails at Henry Cowell—early summer mornings. Wake up before seven, go a few days in a row, and you're bound to bump into her alone. You'll have a better chance working your lines there than at the beach with her brother and the rest of his goody glam friends swarming around her."

Brixton, no longer content with a simple glare, upgraded his expression with a pair of squinty scorching eyes.

Elliot, noticing the gesture, unfolded his middle finger and waved it prominently in the air.

Nolan had no idea why Elliot's finger was flying at full mast, but soon caught sight of Brixton's unmistakable scowl.

What a rooster! Kiki would never date Elliot. Never. Not in a centillion years. And his lines have zero chance of working on her. ZERO! The epitome of clueless, Brixton shook the frustration from his mind, just as he heard Anna speak to Ethan.

"Aaaaannnnnnd?" Anna's voice hit a higher pitch. "Are you really going to make me unfold the letter to find out?"

"Yup," Ethan smirked. "Well, technically you don't have to read it and you could just wait until later."

"Ethan Lorens—I swear!" Anna pouted her lips.

Brixton yearned to learn the truth of the situation. *Whatever it is, it's something worth hearing. Something entirely unexpected. Something that will change things.*

Kila emerged from the crowd with Maya, who appeared to be fretting. "Is my brother being mean to you?" Kila asked Anna loudly enough for Ethan to hear.

"Not entirely," Anna whispered, quickly inserting herself between her two best friends. With one hand she stroked Maya's arm to calm her; with the other she held onto Kila's shoulder.

I wish I was touching Kiki's shoulder. We used to be inseparable. Brixton's mind leapt from its cage when Kila's eyes met his. "Hey," the singular syllable word fell like an anvil from his lips.

"Hi," Kila replied, laughing when Maya reached around Anna to squeeze her side.

"Last night…you went upstairs before I could say goodnight," Brixton's private thoughts flooded into public speech despite his former fear of approaching her.

"I know. I had to call Maya," Kila wanted to feel less self-conscious around him, but the blaring unanswered question in her mind stood in the way. When Maya squeezed her side again, her honest feelings trickled out with another round of laughter. "I'll take a goodnight tonight. Is last night's still available or has it expired?"

"My goodnight offers have no expiration," Brixton's green eyes flashed.

All Kila could do was smile. *Are we drifting back together? Has it finally started or is he working another agenda?*

Ethan grinned at Maya, wondering why she seemed to be looking in every direction but his.

"Okayyy then," Anna attempted to draw the somewhat-disjointed meeting to a close, "I suppose we may or may not see you later, Mr. Ethan."

Ethan nodded, still withholding the information he knew she so clearly sought.

"Wait! What's happening before later?" Angus leapt into the group, confused to see Anna unfolding and reading a note in between Kila and Maya.

"Doesn't pertain to you," Ethan motioned to Angus. "You're coming with us."

Maya glanced at Ethan only long enough for him to wonder if she had.

"Why? Maybe they need me to go with them," Angus looked from Kila to Maya, hoping one of them might speak up.

Kila bit her top lip, locking her thoughts inside her mouth.

"They might, but, truth is, we need you more," Ethan speedily added, "We're headed to Casper's." He watched Anna's expression change as she flipped the note over to the backside.

When Anna finished reading, she met his eyes.

Ethan nodded in a slight, barely visible way.

Brixton acknowledged Angus's presence but was mostly focused on Ethan's strange behavior. He eyed Kila, trying to decipher the situation by her body language. About a half year ago, when they were hanging out all the time, he wouldn't have had to wonder. She would have resorted to coded signals, or speed-texted him. *I want all access to her world again. The secrecy. The intimacy. The high.* All but one faded into obscurity as **"Lightning Strike" by A Silent Film** pounded in Brixton's mind. His fingers tapped his pants in time with the beat no one else could hear.

I never held her like I wanted to. All those times we fell asleep in the same room. Not once next to each other, not once under the same blanket. I'd keep talking, just like she liked, until her eyes no longer opened. And I'd lie there, full of feelings for her, until I fell asleep myself. Knowing she'd be there when I woke up. Knowing it was Saturday or Sunday morning and we'd go to Lazy Tortoise for brunch. That we'd find a million and one ways to enjoy the weekends together. It was never awkward. It always felt right. Like a poem without a forced form or a story without a certain ending, our friendship burned through the days and nights like a sun that never set. To be with her again like that, to tell her how I felt and how I feel...

Brixton's eyes cascaded over Kila's face and hair like a cloaked waterfall. He vowed to impress his interest upon her. A fluid interest, which could morph from a drip to a deluge at a moment's notice. The conversation continued, despite his detachment from it.

"Guess I'm going with them," Angus relented, purposely bumping into Kila on the way to Ethan.

Right before Angus was out of reach, Kila smacked his shoulder and he looked back at her grinning, teeth and all. In that moment, Kila wanted nothing more than to feel him bump into her again. She couldn't believe how his frame had filled out this past year, and she wondered when she would get to see him by her pool again. *What if I'm that girl that's always in love with the boy she cannot have?*

"He makes my heart race," Maya finally spoke as she watched the boys drift farther and farther down the hallway. "I like everything about him. What if he doesn't come back to the house until super late?"

"He'll be home before dark. Trust me," Kila pursed her lips, "they won't pass up a parentless house, a clean pool, and a stocked fridge."

"Nicely put," Anna applauded her. "Come on!" She pulled Kila and Maya outside the school toward the parking lot. "From Ethan's note, I estimate they'll be at your place in about an hour."

"That soon?" Maya gasped.

"You're NOT getting out of it this time," Kila warned. "A promise is a promise and you are telling him tonight. Both parts."

The trio slipped into Kila's navy Saab. Maya took the passenger seat and Anna sat in the back behind Maya. When they drove past the boys and Ethan's mouth formed a bright smile, Maya cringed and slumped down beneath the window.

"My. You're doing this," Kila aimed to prepare her. "I think you're having such a hard time envisioning the talk because you're worried about what to say. And I think the secret key to all of this is actually asking instead of telling."

"What questions?" Maya looked at her, blankly.

"One question, consisting of three words," Kila piqued her interest. "Also happens to be one of his favorites." With a cheeky grin, she increased the volume on her car's console. **"R U Mine?" by Arctic Monkeys** thrust through every speaker, a seductive chaos of drums layered between the sultriest of verse. Kila held a single finger up in victory.

"Ki-la!" Maya yelped, unable to fight the urge to bob her head.

"Ooo!" Anna moved about rambunctiously in the backseat. "When did you set that? This morning?!"

"Maybe this morning. Maybe just a moment ago," Kila dramatically lip-synched to Maya instead of supplying Anna with a definitive answer.

Maya grinned.

Anna, backseat dancing, stretched an arm toward the center console to low-five Kila. "How? Always on point. You know it. I know it. Maya knows it. I bet Bates would like to know it," she poked Kila's shoulder playfully.

Kila fantasized for just a moment, laughing the notion off. *Even if I could...I'd probably still take Angus...not that Angus is an actual option, either.*

"Come on. He's our age. Well, mine, not too far off from yours," Anna continued. "If you keep up with these skills in a few years' time you could be dating him," she pressed her lips together, liking the thought of it, "and then he could hang YOUR poster on HIS wall." Anna batted her eyelashes.

"I could see it!" Maya jumped in.

"You guys," Kila beamed, "I'm sure he's not lacking options right now. His latest mix is pretty much cemented at the top of the Indie chart."

"Reese told me he kissed your hand at last summer's concert," Anna tapped Kila's shoulder for emphasis.

"He was excited when he found out Brix and I snuck in. Besides, Bates was barely known then. He was probably trying to do whatever he could to build a fan base...," Kila felt her defense was adequate.

Anna couldn't let go. "Reese said he didn't kiss anyone else's, and that you were one of the only girls he talked to... despite the fact that she forced Angus to introduce her to him. Apparently, Bates wanted nothing to do with her."

"Yeah, well," Kila grinned, "Bates is...intelligent."

Maya pointed accusingly at Kila, enjoying the momentary distraction, which also happened to be juicy.

"I advised Reese against it," Anna recalled aloud, "but she bashed him on all her social media accounts, and anywhere else her defacing comments weren't blocked."

"Oh yeah? I'm sure Bates REALLY felt the heat from that," Kila laughed, shaking her head. "Did she think her trolling would actually affect his career? It's not as if she's in the music business or holds any sway in...well ANYTHING in the world outside of Cypress High," she laughed. "What the hell is she thinking?"

"She's not," Anna tried to temper her partiality. "Well, she is. It's just all caught up in someone she'll probably never have...so, it's turned her a bit...cuckoo."

"What if that's about to be my fate?" Maya huffed in between head bobs. She focused intently once more on the song, recalling that Kila had mentioned it was one of Ethan's favorites.

Kila touched Maya's hand, bringing the conversation back to its origin, "You don't have to approach him as soon as he arrives. Just sometime before midnight, ANYTIME before midnight."

Anna distracted Maya by dancing behind her seat, hugging her intermittently.

"As much as you're outwardly fighting this, I know you secretly want to take the plunge," Kila pulled her bottom lip into her mouth thinking of Angus.

Maya buried her face in her hands, blushing.

"Don't give me that!" Kila laughed. "It's going to be better than you think. Don't you think I know my own brother? I would never lead you astray."

"I suppose you're right," Maya moved her hands away from her face.

Anna giggled lovingly at the sight of Maya's blushed cheeks.

"But it doesn't make me any less nervous," Maya admitted. "I'm still freaking out!"

At Maya's request, Kila played "R U Mine?" on repeat all the way to her house. Once parked, Kila unhooked her phone from the console, increasing the volume as Anna twirled Maya across the front lawn. Halfway up the stairs, Kila's bedroom speakers picked up the signal from her phone. The addictive song blaring, the three went wild, Anna and Kila acting as silly as they could to bolster Maya's courage.

Shortly after the three settled down on Kila's bed, Maya reached for one of the colorful photo albums stacked in the cubby of the reclaimed-wood side table. Anna, who had contemplated squeezing in a pinch of shuteye, sat up in delight to catch a glimpse of the images. Maya served as curator, while Kila and Anna gasped and giggled their way through the many middle-school photos. Minutes were spent discussing each image of Ethan, Brixton, and Angus.

When they came across some group photos of Ethan's 8th-grade baseball team, Kila spotted Timothy standing tall in the back row, one of his earbuds barely visible in the shot. *His inky hair was so short back then. You can barely see it coming out of his hat. I wonder what song he was listening to? I probably should have waved to him after Calc class. Our last exchange was odd. I didn't know what to say, and then Angus…everything else falls out of focus when he's around.*

Kila touched her phone. Convinced that Maya and Anna were too absorbed in the conversation to notice her momentary absence, she opened the Nektir thread to find the additional messages Timothy had sent in last period:

< 1HighKite: Falling for a girl like Jocelyn could ruin me. >

< 1HighKite: She doesn't seem to be the fall-for-and-forget-about type. >

< 1HighKite: (If you had just come out into the hallway

earlier, I would have had a proper excuse to bow out of the double and dodge this bullet…) >

< 1HighKite: Anyway, looks like you're caught up. I'll check in with you later. Let me know if you find out who likes Miccah. >

< 1HighKite: Fingers crossed we both get kissed tonight, Aurora. >

More likely you'll be kissed tonight than me, Ollie. Angus is forever out of reach, and my hands never seem to want to reach for anyone else…at least there's music. Music and friendship. It'll be good to have Brix at the house again. I still miss him. Maya HAS to tell E tonight. She promised, and she has to follow through.

* * * * *

Leaving the school parking lot, Ethan followed Brixon's white station wagon to the Kading house. There, Brixton greeted his mom, left the keys with her, and reunited with Ethan in the old Range Rover. Mrs. Kading stepped outside to see them off, reminding the boys to be safe as she often did. On the road, the California Central Coast summer breeze took advantage of the open windows and whipped through the strands of the boys' longish hair without either of them speaking. **"Electric" by Atlas Genius** filled the car with invisible sparks.

Close to Angus's house, Ethan noticed the time on his dash and remembered his parents were in Houston. *Far away from Felton. Far enough to be in another time zone.* An uncharacteristic smile spread across Ethan's face from cheek to cheek, and Brixton, who had pretended to be preoccupied with the music en route to Angus's, could contain himself no more.

"E, if you don't clue me in on what's REALLY going on, I'm going to lose it," Brixton confessed from the passenger seat, "and, you know how rare that is for me."

"I know. I'm sorry…just wait 'till Ang is in the car, so we can all talk about it," Ethan inhaled the unforgettable scent of the redwoods. "By the way, what was the deal with Elliot and Nolan in the hallway after last class?"

"They're scheming to get Kiki and Anna," Brixton huffed.

Ethan grinned, amused by the idea, "Which one wants Ki?"

"Elliot," Brixton spoke the name through clenched teeth.

Ethan's full-bodied laughter enveloped the interior of the SUV.

Brixton released some harmless chuckles himself.

When they pulled into the rocky driveway, Angus pointed to his watch. He leapt into the roomy backseat before the wheels had rolled to a stop.

"Reckless rebel," Brixton shook his head, semi-seriously. "Don't you know we prefer to keep you in one piece?"

"You do? But, I thought more pieces were better for sharing. Hang on. You DON'T want to share me?!" Angus reached his hands around the back of the passenger seat to embrace him,

"Brixton Kading, YOU ARE the sweetest!"

"Get OFF me!" Brixton flexed free from his grip.

Angus turned his attention to Ethan. "Did you make out with Anna? Tell the truth," he settled comfortably into the backseat, pleased with his bluntness.

"NO!" Ethan adjusted his grip on the steering wheel. "What gave you that idea?"

"Well, for starters, both of you had some overly intense private interaction in the hallway that was not as hidden as she had hoped it was. Beyond that, she was looking at you like you had something she wanted," Angus spoke swiftly. "I know that look pretty well, since…I'm usually the one who's giving it."

"Yeah, well, besides all that," Brixton added with a grin, "they were passing novels back and forth to one another in Geo class."

"Wow, you guys have drawn some pretty wild conclusions." Ethan shook his head, "The truth of the matter is Anna wanted to know if both of you were staying over the house tonight."

"Weird…," Brixton gazed out the window. *I prefer to give Kiki her goodnight in private. Last night slipped through my fingers.*

"Why is it weird? I like this plan. Why aren't we there now?" Angus asked. "I bet they're in the pool already. You know what that means." He raised then lowered his eyebrows three times.

"I doubt they're in the pool," Ethan spoke coolly. "I know it sounds ridiculous, but Anna's actually super-shy when it comes to the whole beach/pool thing. Ki says she won't even wear a bathing suit if guys are around."

"Seems like for someone not hiding anything, you certainly know some very intimate details about Miss Annabelle Delancy," Angus pointed out.

"Seriously," Brixton agreed with him.

"We're just friends. I swear. You'll see," Ethan rolled his eyes. "Besides, even if I like her, which I honestly don't, I wouldn't have a chance with her because she's pining for one of you. If she was pining for me it wouldn't matter if both of you were sleeping over. She wouldn't have asked." He watched as Brixton and Angus looked at one another and then looked back at him.

"It's Brixton," Angus stated matter-of-factly. "It's obvious. She'd never go for me because of my history with Reese, even more so now that she's not friends with her. Plus, I heard she's changed a lot. Going for Brixton makes sense. Beyond that, I'm sure Kila would validate his likeability."

Brixton gulped. "That makes no sense at all! Anna doesn't know anything about me," he pressed his back deeper into the seat, wondering what Angus meant about Kila thinking he was likeable. "You honestly think Kiki WANTS me to date Anna?"

"I don't know. I have no idea," Ethan realized, as he pulled into Casper's Music Underground. "That's the thing. It was really important to Anna that all three of us were around tonight. I have no idea what the girls are up to, but I do know I'm not ready to walk into it right now." He removed his sunglasses and tousled the hair out of his eyes. "I mean, maybe we need to instate some ground rules here."

"Such as?" Angus asked.

"My parents are gone," Ethan lifted his hands up, "three boys, three girls...what if this turns into a disaster?"

"...What if this turns into the best weekend we've ever had?" Brixton's thoughts, again, found their way to Kila.

"I hope Brix's right!" Angus replied. "I don't think there's much to worry about...just much to hope for."

Brixton grinned.

"Maybe...I guess I'm on the fence with this one," Ethan spoke aloud but thought the opposite internally. He knew his sister, and he sensed the girls were hiding something. "Come on. I want to order these drums. I barely slept last night thinking about them."

"Alright," Angus shouldered them. "Let's get the drums dialed in and head back to your place for a dip. We'll conspire while we swim and then see what happens with the girls," he concluded, jumping ahead so he was the first through the store's revolving door.

Brixton slipped into the next section. Once inside, the two took in the iconic classic rock vibrations of **"Wheel in the Sky" by Journey**.

"MY BOYS! Just.in.time!" Casper held an aged hand up, pointing to Angus. "You're never going to BELIEVE what I received word of today. Where's Ethan?" his hazel eyes looked beyond Brixton toward the entrance.

"Stuck in the door. Again," Angus shrugged. "Pull him out Brix," he shook his head.

"You pull him out," Casper's raspy but friendly words were final. "I have to talk to Brix real quick. When you get back with Ethan, I'll tell you all the news."

"Fine by me," Angus spun around and made his way back toward the entrance, wondering why Casper needed to speak with Brixton in private.

"You know, I need to get that door repaired again. I don't think it's always Ethan's fault," Casper eyed Brixton, his teeth far too snowy for his age not to have been whitened a few times. "Got your email. Now, what in the blazes of rock anthems were you doing up at 2 a.m. on a school night?" he stared at Brixton with the likes of a scolding parent.

"Thinking. What were you doing?" Brixton flung the question back at him.

"I was…placing orders for the store," Casper's thin, shifty smile more or less negated his answer. "Anyway, this morning I reached out to all my contacts, first the ones that owed me something, then anyone I could think of. No one—I mean no one!—can get these sold-out Bates tickets. I even tried asking for singles, thinking if I found one some place I might be able to source another separately and come up with the two that way. Brix. I've got nothing. I'm sorry," he hated relaying disappointing news. "I wish I could tell you otherwise."

Brixton slapped the counter. "Thanks for trying, Cas'. If you can't get 'em, it pret-ty much means no one else can. I've exhausted my final option," Brixton mumbled out the last few words, "I'll proceed in another way."

Casper recognized the look on Brixton's face. Though he'd never before spotted it on Brixton, he'd seen it countless other times, frosted on the faces of other hungry young men in his music store. "Who's the lucky girl, anyway? Rumor, and by rumor I mean your mother," Casper snickered, "thinks you've never dated. I didn't let her know she was right," he teased him. "That means you should tell me who it is. Who's convinced you to swim with the sharks?"

Brixton panicked and made the quiet sign.

Casper noticed, then promptly ignored it. "They're all sharks, just remember that. No matter how good they look. Sharks. All of them!" Casper chuckled for just a moment before his hazel eyes took on a seriousness Brixton hadn't seen. "If you want to LAND a shark, you have to BE a shark. None of this 'nice guy all the time' business. That only works when the sharks are old and battle-worn. Be nice, but don't get strung along. I've seen a lot of bait, and I don't like to see sharks pretend to be bait. Take my word for it, so you can avoid some scars. BE A SHARK, Kading!" he slapped the counter where one of Brixton's hands rested.

Brixton jolted, finally nodding at Casper with an endearing half-smile.

Angus made his way to the front desk. He pressed his hands into the counter and bent his elbows in a semi-push-up, "So. What's all this about sharks?"

"Nothing of importance," Casper assured him.

A flustered Ethan took his place next to Angus and Brixton at the counter.

"Ahhhhh! We now we have all three! I've been on edge ALL DAY waiting for you guys," Casper took a deep breath to settle himself. "I couldn't dare put this in an email and risk it," he scanned the vicinity of the front desk to be sure no one else would hear. Then he proceeded, his deep voice just a little louder than a whisper, "From a reliable source: Emerald Rock is launching another Emerald Open." Casper joyously tapped his hands in swift succession on the cash register.

"I thought they weren't doing it anymore?" Angus pushed himself upright. His mind prepared to race.

"They weren't. Yet, they are," Casper rubbed his weathered hands together. "You guys could win it. You have it. I know you do."

"Have what?" Ethan asked, his blue-gray eyes wide with wonder.

"The moxie to win the next Emerald Open. My buddy Al Finnereck is EmRock's new editor in chief. Messaged me with the news this morning. They aren't just searching for new talent. They're hunting it, like giant, hungry cats. Al's been in the industry for over thirty years. He's overdue for retirement but won't take his break until he unleashes the newest big band. The world is begging for new rock. We can't survive merely on pop anthems and whiney ballads. You guys have to submit to this. I'm convinced it's your calling."

"Our calling? How?" Brixton squinted. "We can't even agree on a band name! We have nothing together, no originals, just covers. All we have is the want, and, at best, somewhat of an ability to play."

Ethan's mouth filled with the bitter taste of confusion. *How many leagues out of our league is the Emerald Open?*

"You may think that way, but I see something else," Casper reasoned. "Don't forget I was sound-check for The Cuffed Renegades all those years. Many, many years. I watched them and all their opening acts. No other band has come close to their talent or fame."

"How could they?" Angus grinned. "Who the hell else can play instruments while handcuffed?"

"Sweet britches undone, I'm NOT talking about THAT!" Casper stood up, "The cuffs were badass; they always will be. But, I'm talking about the chemistry, the look, the passion. You guys have it. I've seen it."

"...And you're making these judgments based on our recent performance at the school picnic?" Ethan rubbed his hand through his hair. "We can't submit and look like a joke. They always take the unprepared or untalented and rip them to shreds online. I won't have us shredded. I won't have us ridiculed. It means too much. We can't. EmRock is the most recognized leader in rock music news and the EmOpen is the ultimate contest for up-and-coming serious bands. I wish we were there, I really do. But...," he shook his head, looking at Brixton.

"The picnic wasn't your best performance," Casper had no plans of surrender, "I was there. Angus wasn't into it. He had something else on his mind. The kids didn't notice. You may not have noticed. But I noticed. You let Salt For Swordsmen outshine you. Now, I'm not going to say anything negative about those boys. They're great musicians, great customers, and they put on a fiery show with some real heart, but you guys could be BETTER. You have so much untapped potential. You need to TAP IT!"

Brixton and Angus held back their laughter.

Casper directed the next message to Ethan. "You have to manage your group. It's yours. You started this. You're the one that dreams about it, every night I imagine, and you're the only one that can bring them forward."

Suddenly empowered, Ethan nodded. *I did notice Angus was distracted. I should have said something to him at the picnic. I saw it. That dull look of loss in his eyes. Was it Reese? Damn her and her games!*

Without needing a reply, Casper continued. "Who cares if you don't have originals this second? I get the Cypress Branch. I see the three of you always listed in the Honors section, every quarter, and Mr. Lyr, here, nominated for the Keats award three years in a row. It's unheard of. You're freaking intelligent. The lot of you," Casper pointed at Angus, "and you're a goddamn WRITER! Write some music, practice it, and play it like your future depends on it. Do you know how many people would love to have the chance that you already have but are too frightened to recognize?"

In his fever, Casper breathed heavily, eyeing each of them as if his gaze could convince them one by one. As the silence laid hold of them, he continued, in a lighter tone, "Sorry that I'm fired up. I mean, I'm not sorry I got fired up. I'm sorry I cussed. And I'm sorry you're not seeing it. Guys, the EmOpen is for on-the-ground bands. Like yours and SforS. Not up-and-coming bands already playing circuits. Bands in the very beginning of the process. Barely hatched. The past few contests were a disgrace to what the contest was originally intended to represent. At your age, those are, unfortunately, the only ones you probably remember. Al's making sure they get back to what it was meant to be: pure. Right now they're itching to find a band in its infancy that has the potential to make rock history. They want to document the journey. Massive media, massive coverage. And this EmOpen differs from all others previous."

"How so?" Ethan looked to Angus and Brixton. They seemed as wishy-washy as he was about this idea.

"The votes are exclusive to EmReaders, not allotted solely to industry execs. No cash prize and no runners up. EmOpen will produce a single winner. And the winner this time, since they have a lot of ground to cover for their mishaps two years ago, will tour all-expenses-paid for two months in the states AND earn a spotlight blog about their growth on EmRock online for two YEARS. That's an organized tour, plus two years of publishing your words, feelings, experiences on EmRock's homepage. Two years of unadulterated feedback from fans. Unprecedented. It's more than any riser could hope for."

"Whoa. That. Is. Tight," Brixton, lifting his shoulders, eyed Ethan. "What were the mishaps two years ago?"

"FeatherClaw took the prize money and squandered it on lowbrow pleasures," Angus jumped in, rubbing his hands together. "They never released an album or even an EP, but then again they weren't very talented to begin with. Street word was they won based on their ties to EmRock's upper management."

"Yup," Casper confirmed. "Major setback. That's why they let a blank year pass to restructure the contest. They couldn't risk another flop. It bruised their ego and put their entire namesake in question. Their forum became so brutal they ended up purposefully crashing their own website and listing it 'under maintenance' for a day while they regrouped. But, before that, there were upsides: EmOpen's best and brightest win to date was We Dream of Scuba—they took the title in 2000."

"Wait. WeDOS was an EmOpen win?" Angus grinned. "Pure platinum. I have ALL their albums! Well, most of us do, I imagine. I had no idea…," his mind churned, trying to sift out the emotion from his thoughts on the matter.

"I might be the owner of a small music store in a small town, but in my younger years I was embedded in the rock scene. Embedded. You reach a certain age, and you need to rest. Partying for a few decades takes a toll on you. It takes a toll on anyone," he laughed, knowing the boys wouldn't understand this until later. "Trust me. I know talent when I see it. Your energy, your balance, your connection to each other...wayyy beyond the superficial. Al's not making the official announcement for at least another week. He couldn't release the details of submissions to me, but he did hint at a tight deadline. In the past, they specified a six-week submit period from moment of announce to final close. I bet the window will be narrower this time. They can't chance non-interest. And they want to get started as soon as possible. They're aiming for big buzz and serious commitment."

"Thanks for telling us, Cas'. We'll think about it, and let you know as soon as we have an answer," Ethan surprised Angus and Brixton with both his reply and the fact that he spoke on behalf of the band.

"YES!" Casper rattled on the cash register some more, "That's all I was looking for today. Just to plant that seed, the gooooolllden seed." He moved a clump of his well-seasoned, curly salt-and-pepper hair away from face. "Now, I gather the real reason you came in here was to order those drums you've been drooling over. I saw that hefty credit that was purchased for your birthday...," his ultra-white teeth made an appearance again.

After Casper extended Ethan his best price on the new drums and the ordering process was complete, the boys checked out the new-equipment wall. Brixton, pulling a vintage maple acoustic Fender from its lime velvet stand, began playing **"Water Stop" by Dispatch**. Following suit, Angus picked up a nearby guitar and plucked away. Casper stopped the store's classic rock from playing, motioned for Ethan to step up to the set like the one he had ordered, and hurled a pair of drumsticks his way. Ethan caught them on the fly, and Angus's voice belted out the lyrics in perfect time and pitch.

Praying the boys would give in to his wish and cast their lot in the EmOpen, Casper snatched his professional camera from under the register and began recording their performance. He steadied his aged hands, aiming to hold the device still. After all, he reasoned, the band will need ample footage for their entry package. The music store patrons, practically sunbathing in the energy shift, set their own thoughts aside to experience the gift of live music. Emerging from the aisles and alcoves, they followed the sounds of the instruments and vocals until they spotted the memorable trio of high school boys.

Not worried about Reese today, Ethan grinned watching Angus spin around with his guitar, dancing and singing. Brixton leapt in place, the tip of his tongue barely visible at the corner of his mouth. *And THIS…THIS is why we play,* Ethan reminded himself, striking the drums and loving the honest, unshakeable high the music delivered.

In seconds, a small crowd formed around them comprised mostly of zealous older men and amorous women. Angus winked at one of the ladies, who gasped aloud and laughed nervously before disappearing down one of the aisles flushed with excitement. Brixton laughed when, moments later, the same woman peeked over one of the displays with her phone. Angus posed for the picture despite the fact that he pretended not to notice her.

At Brixton's direction, the middle of "Water Stop" blended into **"Hey, Hey" by Dispatch**. The boys, knowing it would be their last today, gave it their all, earning Casper an influx of visitors from neighboring stores who packed themselves in behind the initial onlookers. Brixton, feeling the pull in his heart, mouthed the words but held his voice back. His fingers moved agilely about the strings without thought, his mental focus too invested in Kila to concern himself with the crowd.

When the applause died down, Casper thanked the band profusely for playing in-store and letting him record. In exchange for the flood of customers they attracted, he opened his coveted "plectrum treasure chest" and let Brixton and Angus each dip one hand in to grab a variety of new picks. "Remember what we talked about last time. I want you both to experiment with material, shape, and texture."

Angus and Brixton cupped their hands together, unwilling to let even one of their many new picks slip from their fingers and fall back into the chest.

"Kind of feel like it's my birthday now, too," Brixton wore an unusually large smile.

"Seriously," Angus slipped his picks into the small satin bag Casper held out for him, then helped Brixton get his into a similar bag. "I don't believe it! You pulled a Timber Tones out!" He gripped it, turning it about.

"Hey! No trades yet. We'll check 'em out next practice and make swaps IF they're fair," Brixton set the tone, issuing a firm look at Angus, who was less than anxious to return the pick to the appropriate bag.

"Keep him in line, Brix," Casper chuckled. "And Ethan, since you have no need for picks, I'll order some extra sticks and things for you at no charge, to help move that little decision of yours along."

"Thanks, Cas'," Ethan shook his hand, grateful for the storeowner's unwavering encouragement. *He's always been there for us. Always.*

"Hold on! Wait! Wait!" Casper tended to his music station. "After a performance like that, you can't just walk out to nothing."

Angus raised an eyebrow.

"You need an exit song. You can't go out without one. It's a thing. Or, it was. And, I plan to resurrect it," Casper leaned back in his trusty swivel stool.

Brixton smiled.

"Wait for it!" Casper pressed his favorite button on his retro remote.

Ethan backhand-fived Casper as soon as he identified the song. **"Travelin' Band" by Creedence Clearwater Revival**.

"Nice," Angus approved of his choice. "If only WE sounded like this…."

"You'll sound like yourselves. And THAT is what the world needs," Casper gushed, rattling on his cash register as only he could. At his signal, the boys slipped out the door with light hearts and heavy minds.

"Let's keep all that between us, think about it individually, and talk about it as a group later," Ethan instructed in the car. "Too much to take in all at once. And I don't want the girls hearing about it—that includes Kila," Ethan quickly glanced at Brixton, "at least until we have it sorted out ourselves."

"Best idea," Angus's mind reeled, questioning whether or not he possessed the gumption needed to draft a platinum song. The idea burned a new desire into his mind. A desire greater than his want for the girl who had poisoned his mind for months.

Brixton busied himself with brainstorming new band names, though the thought of Kila cut through his focus more than once. *The right band name...the right goodnight...the right band name...Kiki...*

At Ethan's house, they raced up the stairs, climbing three steps at a time. Music blared from Kila's room, and, since the door was shut, the boys figured the girls were holed up gossiping inside. Brixton pressed the palm of his hand into the door as they walked past, wishing he was on the other side of it, alone with Kila.

Inside Ethan's room, the three changed at Mach speed into their swim trunks. Then, they trampled back down the stairs shoulder-checking each other along the way. Ethan swung open the French doors to unleash Angus and Brixton, who rocketed toward the pool. As the giant splash from their double cannonball drenched him, he heard a chorus of high-pitched, playful giggles.

Ahhhh, Ethan straightened his stance. *They weren't in Kila's room.* He brushed the water from the splash off his arms, patting his face to catch the drops from his hair. The reality of the parentless weekend shined like a beacon in front of him, as he looked at Brixton and Angus wrestling merrily in the pool and then to his sister and Maya reclined regally on the chaise lounges.

Glued to the boys in play, Kila's light eyes offered not an ounce of attention to her brother. In response to the quiet, her fingers reached for her phone. *Deck speakers make all the difference. The only thing better than being outside is listening to music WHILE outside. Music always helps. And Maya needs all the help she can get right now…she's cutting this WAY TOO CLOSE…*

One of Kila's hands made the Nektir selection while her other slapped the cushion on Maya's chair. **"Closer" by Tegan and**

Sara tiptoed from the deck speakers and painted new scenes above the pool. The nerves accompanying the thoughts conjured by the song stole Maya's voice away. In a pair of amber-hued surf shorts and a broken-in white T-shirt, Ethan stood less than a few feet away from Maya's lounger. Fearful he might walk away, she turned and lifted a hand to him.

"At least someone says hello," he smiled warmly at her.

"I'm glad you're back," Maya spoke, immediately wishing she hadn't uttered those words. Just an innocent phrase, she feared it might have been out of line.

"Is it because you're hungry?" he attempted to guess the reason.

"Yes, she more than me." Maya, thankful he had jumped to his own conclusion, pointed to Kila.

"I figured. She's always hungry. Like Angus," Ethan laughed. He blushed when his eyes drifted to Maya's skin and he realized he was staring at her bare, bronzed torso. Quickly, he looked to his friends in the pool.

At this point, Kila's attention split in half between Angus's face and Maya's task. Her eyes stole several successive glances at her brother. The first time he looked excited. The second time he looked at Maya's mint-green bikini. The third time he looked nervous. *Too painful to watch,* Kila exhaled and took solace in Angus's smile. *I wish he was always at the house. I wish we could just hang together, without any of the others.*

"...Were you okay back in the hallway after last period?"

Ethan's eyes followed the curve of Maya's right shoulder.

Kila cringed.

"Yeah," Maya's voice wavered. "Why? Did I look weird?" She tried to appear normal. Anxiously, she moved her long dark hair aside and retied the mint-green bikini top bow behind her neck.

"No," Ethan laughed strangely, watching her hands at work, "you never look weird." His eyes dropped like marbles to the stonework under his feet.

Maya sat on top of her hands, not having any idea why.

"You know, maybe it was me. You just seemed elsewhere, that was all...," Ethan looked at her face again, first at her smooth cheeks, and then at her attentive eyes, "...I probably shouldn't have said anything."

"No...you're right. I mean, I was elsewhere. I was...," Maya worried her heart might rupture. Each beat felt like it moved the whole of her upper body.

Ethan waited for her to finish.

Maya forgot she needed to finish and waited for Ethan to say something.

"...So, where was elsewhere?" His funny smile, which accompanied his characteristic half-laugh, brought a fog of calm over her.

She settled into some semblance of normalcy. "Oh," she laughed, "I guess I was wishing I was here already. I've been looking forward to this pool time."

"I've been looking forward to finishing our Jenga game," Ethan touched his hand to his abdomen, searching her face.

Sparks ignited behind her coffee eyes. "You didn't take last weekend's tower down?" Her heart beat with such enthusiasm.

"No. How could I?" He grinned, "It was our best tower yet."

"But Peaches?" she wondered how his dog hadn't knocked it over.

"I locked her out of the library all week," he explained, "tower was still intact as of this morning. I have…been keeping an eye on it."

Maya laughed at his blue-gray eyes, her fears leaving her with every exhale. "I guess we better finish the game, then."

"Yeah," Ethan ducked to avoid another incoming splash from the pool, "let me know when you want to."

She couldn't bring herself to say "now" despite the fact that every part of her body seemed to want to besides her mouth. "I will," she spoke the words slowly before changing the subject, "so, did you get the new drums?"

"Yeah," his honest expression revealed his honest excitement.

"Are you setting them up tonight?" Maya gushed. "I can't wait to hear what they sound like!"

"I WISH!" Ethan exhaled, explaining, "They're on order. Shouldn't be too long, but I'll need a little time with them once they arrive before I'll let you hear. I have to get used to them," he placed a hand on the back of his neck, picking up on the fact that Maya's almost intimate smile had faded. "You growing scared I might win at Jenga?"

"No," she smiled again, covering her hands over her mouth to hide her peek-a-boo nerves. "I'm not!"

"You should be," he warned her warm eyes. "I do intend to win this time."

"We'll see," Maya gazed back at him. She wished she could take him down as easily as the last misplaced piece in their Jenga tower, wooden blocks stacked in a mess on the desk like she wished their bodies could be.

Noticing her closed eyes, Ethan inhaled what he mistakenly believed to be the end of the conversation. He looked around, then asked, "Where's Anna?"

"...She's inside," Maya took a deep breath, adjusted her position on the chair, and questioned the feelings in her heart.

Kila's single huff was loud yet unintentional. *Just when it's getting somewhere...COME.ON.E.* She wished she could take her brother aside and somehow make him realize what was at stake.

Beads of water flung from the pool, salvaging the situation.

"Kiki," Brixton bobbed up and down next to Angus, "which one of us can jump higher?" He liked that her eyes had already been on him.

"In the water?" Kila asked. "You can't measure that in the shallow end, it's too easy! You have to jump up from the deep end," she giggled, watching Angus spin about in circles, the same way he used to when he was only about ten or eleven.

"Deep end is better!" Angus roared, pushing Brixton to the left.

"Must everything be a competition?" Ethan lifted his shoulders.

"Ease up. It's not our fault you're so afraid to lose that you won't join in," Angus teased, as he and Brixton prepared themselves for the "dunk and jump."

"I think it's noble you don't opt into their games," Maya whispered to Ethan. "You'd win them all anyways."

Ethan liked the way that sounded, but didn't let it go to his head. "I don't know, My. They're ruthless at times."

"You can sit, if you want," Maya moved her legs to the side, hoping he would. "This is bound to take a while."

"Thanks," he sat at the edge of her chair.

"No thanks necessary," she wanted to move closer but couldn't bring herself to. "It's your chair."

"You always take mine. Why is that?" he laughed at the sight of Brixton and Angus looking so serious.

Maya squirmed beside him, watching Angus and Brixton's heads disappear under the water. "Because it's yours," she dared the words from her mouth.

"Fair enough. But, since you always take it, and I've never mentioned it, you owe me something in return," he chuckled as Brixton and Angus shot straight up, a sheet of water headed in their direction.

Maya gasped, ducking behind Ethan to shield herself.

"Oh, so I'm your umbrella now, too?" he turned toward her.

She shrugged with a wide smile.

"I still need something in place of my chair. Of the eight out here, it's obviously the best. You know it. You recognized it. Otherwise, you would have sat in one of the others. You haven't even bothered to try them out, have you? And we've had them for years...," he expertly held a straight face.

"Nope, no reason to," she looked to Brixton and Angus, who were fighting loudly, but tuned out their words. "There IS actually something I've wanted to give you," she pulled the glossy golden brown sunglasses from the top of his head and put them on, covering her eyes. She figured it'd be easier to say the words if he couldn't see in.

"No, no, no!" Ethan shook his head. "Chair, okay. Umbrella, on occasion. Sunglasses, no way," with his coy smile, he pulled them off her face.

She pouted and he grinned some more.

"Ethan! Stop whatever you're doing!" Angus ordered. "Ki is a biased judge—it's obvious. She keeps saying that Brixton is jumping higher than me when I can, at times, see over his head."

Kila flashed her poker face at Maya, and they shared a sneaky understanding.

"Are you messing with him again?" Maya whispered. "You know he can only take so much." She covered a hand over her mouth to keep from laughing, but it was to no avail.

The pout on Angus's face was priceless, Brixton all the while knowing he hadn't won every single jump.

"Okay, okay," Kila came clean. "Both of you were pretty even. Honestly. It was hard to see most of the time. Sometimes Brix was higher. Other times you were."

Beads of water fell from Angus's dark hair, rolled down his face and neck, and gathered to form a mini pool inside his collarbone.

Kila watched the rivulets flow on his skin. *I wish I was one of those drops. Those lucky, lucky drops.*

"In cahoots. I KNEW it!" Angus thrashed about some more in protest, flashing his crimson smile and dunking Brixton under water. "He CANNOT be trusted with her."

"Are my funny dolphins hungry yet?" Ethan asked, hearing Maya's playful laughter beside him.

"STARVING!" Angus exclaimed, noting Brixton's snarled face. "Bro, who cares what he calls us, as long as he feeds us," Angus tossed him around some more.

Brixton stuck his tongue out at Kila before he was dunked again against his will.

"I told you Angus was hungry. Just like Ki," Ethan turned to Maya. "What do you think? Do veggie burgers sound good?"

Maya nodded, sensing another opportunity slip from her.

"And kale, puh-lease!" Kila begged, linking her arm through Maya's to cheer her.

"Oh. Someone remembered she had a brother, just when it was time to eat. How convenient," Ethan ruffled Kila's hair when she stood to move her lounger closer to Maya's. "I got you, don't worry. Just keep an eye on my dolphins," he patted his sister's arm and half-smiled at Maya. Then, he made his way into the house.

"Need to make room for the food," Brixton launched himself over Angus's shoulders, rushed toward the thick grass, and sank into a set of masterfully controlled clap push-ups.

"Hey! Not without me," Angus pulled himself up and out of the pool.

Kila's full eyebrows rose when she caught the definition in Angus's engaged arms. She continued to study his form as he pumped out the plyo next to Brixton. The concentration in his dark eyes and the rise and fall of his body sent a wave of heat through her cheeks. Feeling her lips spread apart, she breathed through her mouth, hoping he would never discover he held such a grip on her heart.

"You getting in some extra sets without me?" Angus asked by means of whisper. Unable to keep pace with Brixton, he felt self-conscious for falling behind in front of the girls.

"Perhaps," Brixton let him wonder, "but, I think the real issue at hand is you used all your energy on those jumps you thought you were losing."

"Ready yourself," Angus huffed, downgrading to non-plyo push-ups. "Retribution will be swift and unavoidable."

"Just the way I like it," Brixton smirked, his airborne claps still as loud as they were at the start of the set.

Maya mentioned Brixton's high energy several times.

Kila's eyes grew curious, but they never fell upon Brixton's skin. *I hope we're still drifting back. Maybe this weekend will help it along...he did mention a goodnight...and...I miss him, without understanding why. Just as much as the first few confusing days without him. All that time, consumed by the void of his absence.* The simple admittance brought back to mind memories of Brixton's free-spirited laugh, his thought-provoking conversations, and his second-to-none playlists. *No one builds them like Brix. No one. Not even Bates...and Bates makes a living building them. I can't look at his playlists until we've reconciled. I made that promise to myself when he quietly bowed out of my life without reason...the empty nest of our friendship is his doing.* Needing to speak through the speakers, she scrolled through her songs. Her finger touched **"Motions" by Kostka** and her eyes closed, sinking into the bleeding past.

"Which are you thinking of?" Maya whispered, "Come on, Ki. I can't tell." Her brown eyes leapt from Brixton to Angus in question.

"Which do you think?" Kila opened her light eyes only long enough to offer an ambiguous answer. She was afraid to tell herself these days, and telling someone else, even her best girlfriend, seemed all the more daunting.

At the first few seconds of the song, Brixton looked to Kila. What he saw broke his focus, her athletic legs curled towards her chest, her bare eyelids sealed tight in reflection. His push-ups ended that instant, due not to increasing fatigue but to increasing emotion. *This is it.* Brixton stood up. *This is the first song of her choosing I'm hearing since she cut me off from her Nektir feed. "Closer" was for Maya. It was obvious. That wasn't what was on her own mind. This is…this perfect hard-hitting track is about what she's thinking right now. My first fuzzy look at the blueprints of her new house. The one she planned without me. Is there a place for me? If there is, I'll stay. As long as she wants. I'll help her build. I'll sleep in the kitchen. I'll sleep in the garden if I have to. Draw me in, Kiki. Paint me into the plan. There's so much music to share, so many things left unsaid, and so many ways I want to show you.*

Though Maya had long ago suspected Brixton's feelings for Kila, she had never spoken of them. A guess is just a guess, Maya told herself, and she didn't want this particular guess to influence Kila and Brixton's relationship or, rather, best friendship as they had always referred to it. When the best friendship came to a screeching halt, Maya sensed there was something more to it than happenstance, and for good reason. The past didn't add up to the decision, and the present never seemed to reflect what was really there. And the hungry look on Brixton's face, which was somehow related to the song Kila had chosen, gave Maya the feeling she may have been right all along.

"Ki," Maya spoke as quietly as she could.

Kila opened her eyes at Maya's secretive tone to find Brixton looking at her. He stood shirtless in the grass, but all she saw was his face. His eyes held a weight she was unacquainted with, his expression naked and his smile barely traceable. A tilt of the head was all she could muster, nervous that he might be judging her appearance in some way. *I can't read him anymore.* She grabbed the towel behind her head, unrolled it, and covered herself from her neck to her toes.

Maya inhaled air in such a way it sounded more like hiccup. "Ki," she whispered again.

"It's eighty-something degrees, Ki," Angus pushed himself off his hands. "You can't possibly be cold." He eyed Brixton wondering what he might have missed.

"I am," Kila insisted, twice as self-conscious as she had been before. She sat up without a smile, her towel covering her bathing suit, and pivoted so her back faced the boys and her front faced Maya.

"Retribution time!" Angus tackled Brixton in the grass, the two of them laughing heartily.

When the boys ended their shenanigans, they discussed the band. Brixton, fearing he might be locked out forever, looked at Kila only when Angus tapped on his phone. Maya noticed Brixton's glances more times than not, and Brixton hoped Maya's smile meant he could count on her as an unspoken ally.

To relieve her uneasiness, Kila channeled her focus back to Maya. At first she teased her for not having spoken with Ethan moments ago when she easily could have. Then, she gently reminded her of the finite timetable. New suggestions and kind words were offered. Maya regrouped mentally, preparing herself to move ahead at the next opportunity.

Choosing once again not to bring up her guess about Brixton, Maya instead hinted to Kila that Brixton may have been taken by the sight of her in her pastel-and-white-striped bikini. Kila's instant fit of giggles caused Maya to shake her head. Though Maya couldn't help laughing herself, she wished she could explain how things appeared from her vantage point. That Brixton seemed especially interested.

After Kila settled down, Maya drove home the notion that it was quite possible Brixton wanted to reactivate their friendship and that Kila should determine if she wanted the same. Kila's contemplative eyes stirred the questions behind Maya's hopes. The next time Brixton gazed at Kila, Maya smiled up at the sun, grateful to know such a secret.

* * * * *

In the house, Ethan gathered the ingredients from the pantry. Having made dinner for his friends a number of times, he already had an idea of how much of what to make without having too little or too much left over. As he made his way into the kitchen, he bumped into Anna. She was in the midst of devouring one of his blueberry-peach popsicles.

"This is the greatest!" Anna slurped away, "Kila told me you've been making them for her for nearly a decade now—so sweet of you...."

Ethan grabbed a paper towel square for her from the dispenser, "Thanks. I think my mom thought we'd outgrow them, but I guess we haven't yet. You are TOTALLY getting it all over yourself, though," he laughed at the pink and blue watercolor-like outlines around her mouth and the matching splatters on the front of her shirt.

"Don't worry about the stains. It's worth it, and I'm sure they'll wash out," she bit her tongue. "I packed my bag to the limit this weekend. Your sister couldn't make up her mind on what we were going to wear tomorrow night. I could stay for about a week with all my options."

"Well, let me know if you decide to," he grinned. "I'll make sure we have plenty of popsicles."

A soggy Angus appeared in the doorway right as Anna smiled at Ethan. Patting his wet hair, he was careful to let his drips fall only on the small rug behind the French doors. Seeing Annabelle and Ethan paired and alone, Angus wondered if Ethan had been completely honest during the car ride to Casper's. He raised an eyebrow at Ethan, who immediately glared back at him. Before words could be exchanged, Kila whirled into the house.

"You found the pops!" she greeted Anna.

"Yeah. I'll never be able to bring myself to have another out-of-the-box frozen pop again," Anna admitted, adjusting the paper towel around the bottom of the flattened stick as she continued to munch away at the iced juice and fruit. "I love that you can see the fruit, and then you can select your slurps based upon which flavor you want to taste that moment."

"He makes the juice in the juicer—it's not store-bought," Kila boasted about her brother's particulars.

Ethan half-smiled, "I think you're overdoing it. They're pretty easy to make."

"Uh. No. I don't think you realize how much we love them," Angus moved to make room for Kila. Then, he decided to have some fun and pressed up against her side.

"Ugh! Ang. AGAIN?" she pulled her shirt away from her midsection, to keep the wetness off her skin.

"I can't help myself," Angus grinned in such a way that his nose scrunched a little.

Kila instantly forgave him.

"He does that every time," Brixton appeared behind Kila. "You should know by now how childish he is, Kiki," he whacked Angus's shoulder.

Annabelle blushed and looked down at her sandals, far too nervous to continue slurping the pop with a shirtless Brixton present. Some of the liquid dripped onto her fingers and she wiped it with the paper towel.

Brixton swallowed hard, turning to Angus for a silent second opinion. *Anna doesn't really like me, does she? This is scaring me. This could complicate things. How am I supposed to get close to Kiki if Anna is trying to get close to me?*

Angus, offering not a trace of emotion, looked at Ethan, then at Brixton, then at Anna.

Kila reached for Anna's hand and whirled around quickly to pull her outside. In the flurry of the escape, Kila forgot Brixton was behind her, and she collided with his body when she pivoted.

"Ugh. Brix!" Kila huffed under her breath, "You're like a wall now." She slid to the left and pulled Anna to safety outside.

Brixton's unhideable smile caused Ethan to laugh.

"Somebody just received a rare compliment," Ethan reached for a mixing bowl.

"Is it just me, or is anyone else dizzy?" Angus took the towel Brixton handed him, "It's like a girl merry-go-round in here. I can't tell if I'm in love with it or if I've grown ill."

"I'm with you," Brixton exhaled, wrapping his own towel around his waist to absorb some of the water from his shorts. "I feel like someone's digging my grave. I thought this sort of thing was supposed to be fun? Whatever I say or do seems to be the wrong thing."

"Yeah, well, you definitely said the wrong thing to Ki back there," Angus looked at Brixton with a pair of dark, serious eyes.

"I didn't say anything," Brixton grew worried. "No words were exchanged on either side. What are you even talking about?"

"All I know is that everything was fine. She and Maya were lying next to each other, talking, in their bright bikinis. Not a terrible view if we're being truthful," Angus paused to look at Ethan, who laughed. "Next thing I know, you're done with your push-ups and Ki is covered in a towel from the neck down. Not more than fifteen minutes later, she changed back into her normal clothes in the poolhouse."

"Ang, I just looked at her," Brixton mumbled, looking at Ethan, "I swear it."

"Yeah, well, don't look at her like that again," Angus crossed his arms, pleased with himself. "She obviously doesn't like it."

"You two are a crack-up. My sister probably thinks one of you is cute and she grew self-conscious," Ethan spoke lightly as he chopped vegetables and filled the bowl. "And who could blame her? With the two of you topless, muscular clowns showing off in the grass, one is bound to grow a bit flushed. I bet Maya did, too," he smirked.

"Nope. Maya has failed to realize Brixton and I exist. She's nice to us, but it's very clear her interests lie elsewhere,"

Angus looked to Brixton.

They both looked at Ethan accusingly.

"She won't even flirt with us," Angus pressed his lips together.

"No way. It's not me," Ethan laughed. "Be realistic."

"We are," Brixton nudged.

"It's getting to the point that everyone but your sister is into you! Of the three of us, who would have guessed YOU would turn out to be the girl magnet?" Angus slumped onto the barstool at the counter.

"You are far too striking for that sort of defeatist talk," Ethan placed a hand on Angus's shoulder, "and I'm far from a girl magnet. The only reason they talk to me is because I'm approachable, I'm Ki's brother, and I don't make them nervous. Anyways, they might just be using me to get to Brixton."

"Oh yes, the boy in the poem with the golden nutmeg-colored hair and glistening jewel-like eyes," Angus quipped, "I will never forget that. EVER!" He amused himself into such a fit a laughter he could barely speak.

"I will get you Lyr," Brixton threatened, edging towards him, "I never wanted to be the center of Reese's poem. I wish it had been centered on you, so you could stop bringing it up every two weeks."

"You say that, but I'm not sure I believe you," Angus continued, the once-light-hearted conversation suddenly feeling heavier.

"There were some advantages that came from it. Even Mrs. Epstein was partial to you after the reading."

"I was twelve! Your so-called advantages are imaginary. I worked for my grades just as hard as you did back then. Maybe harder. You are ridiculous, Ang," Brixton shook his head, looking at Ethan in disbelief.

"The only one who's ridiculous is you. Once you admit that you liked her poem, and the attention that came along with it, I'll drop it," Angus rubbed his hands together.

"I'll never admit it, because there's nothing to admit! It's caused nothing but problems. Clearly. It's still causing problems, years later," Brixton's playful mood ended. "You think I like problems? I don't. You might be attracted to her, but I'm not. I don't care what she looks like. If she were naked in my bedroom I still wouldn't touch her. She's empty, and spends all of her time screwing people over to get what she wants. Her beauty will fade with age, trust me. And if she continues to undervalue intellect, she'll have nothing left."

"You know NOTHING about her," Angus glared at Brixton, slamming a hand down on the counter.

"I know A LOT more than you think I do," Brixton's eyes were set, so fixed on Angus he stopped blinking.

"Enough!" Ethan boomed, "It was a poem written in 7th-grade by a little girl with a crush on her writing partner. Can we forget about it now?"

"He can't, obviously," Brixton muttered, "Reese is a nightmare, and the sooner he realizes that, the happier his life will be."

Angus scowled at him and looked out the sliding glass door. He caught a glimpse of Kila fixing Maya's hair, admiring the tenderness she had for her friend. "I won't bring it up again," Angus muttered, his eyes reluctant to return to the kitchen. They much preferred studying Kila's movements.

"That's all I'm asking," Brixton came clean. "I'm looking out for you, not looking to fight."

"I know," Angus clapped Brixton's shoulder. "It's all messed up...still."

"You'll figure it out," Brixton slapped him back to seal the apology.

Ethan, happy that the tension had cleared at least temporarily, resumed the peeling and chopping. He poured the wet ingredients into the dry, then mixed and kneaded the batter. Brixton and Angus hovered close to the counter where he was working, in case they might offer assistance or, more likely, serve as vultures, consuming any edible scraps that might fall outside the bowl.

Annabelle and Kila sauntered inside, acknowledging the boys in the kitchen via nods only. Quiet and relaxed, they nested in the living room, flipping through nature and travel magazines, commenting here and there in a trance-like state.

Brixton wanted to visit Kila in the living room, but with Anna present the arrangement seemed too tricky. *Patience. Some test of my patience. I blew it out there. So painfully that Angus noticed. I must time this out. Wait for the ideal. Alone, without the girls, without Ethan or Angus.*

When the mixture was ready, Ethan tasted the batter. Then he enlisted Brixton and Angus to form the burgers and strolled outside to fire up the grill. **"I Dare You" by The xx** seeped into the balmy early evening air, and Ethan took in the lyrics, feeling high.

"Oh good!" Maya's excited words startled him, "I'm super hungry now."

He laughed to find her still sunning in his deck chair.

"Scared you, didn't I?" Maya grinned.

"Maybe," Ethan bit the inside of his upper lip, "but only because I'm focused on feeding all of you."

Easier to talk to than any of Kila's other friends, Maya dressed more like a tomboy and less like a princess. She and Ethan often spent time talking when Kila was lost in her studies or when Maya was sleeping over and Kila had fallen asleep early. Now that they were older, Ethan found himself feeling a little uncomfortable around her when they were alone. It had never been that way before.

"It'll only be a few minutes. I just need to start the grill," he waved the tongs in front of her. "You can have the first one, bunless, as an appetizer if you want. I won't tell the others," he raised his eyebrows in secrecy.

"Oooo," Maya grinned, "yes, please."

"Consider it done," he said smartly, looking at her stomach again before turning to walk away.

"Wait," Maya sat up, looking a little more serious.

Ethan turned back to her, "You want two for a warm-up? I can make that happen...."

"No," she whispered. "One is plenty. Otherwise I won't be able to eat anymore with everyone else and then they'll know our secret," she laughed.

"One it is," he nodded once, noticing her tense eyes. "You're out here alone. Is something on your mind?"

"Yeah...I'm actually nervous about something," she shifted her position.

"What?" he moved closer to her chair, in case anyone attempted to listen in from inside.

"It's Reese," Maya hated saying her name.

"Reese?" Ethan couldn't help but notice the polarity of that name as he repeated it. *Her. Always her.*

"In case you didn't notice, Anna likes Brixton. REALLY likes him. Reese knows, and she's insanely jealous of Anna. I'm not supposed to say any of this to you, but I thought it'd be better if you knew. Please don't tell Ki or Anna I said anything. They'd be miffed if they found out. I...wanted to tell you," she glanced at Ethan, "I'm worried."

Ethan wasn't anxious to cast his thoughts, but forced himself to only since Maya had confided in him. "Well, we both know that Reese isn't happy until everyone else is unhappy. We've seen the likes of this before. Actually…I was just dealing with it in the kitchen."

"Not the poem again?" Maya held her hands up, her eyes shifting to the side, annoyed.

"Yup," Ethan pursed his lips. "Are you sure Anna likes Brix? Is this something she told you, or is this something you inferred?"

"I'm pretty sure of it," Maya answered indirectly. She pulled the hair elastic free from her head, letting her thick hair tumble down to the side.

Ethan looked the other way.

"But," Maya said softly, "I am not so certain he's the ONLY one she likes, so if there is any interest there….well, you know what I am saying, I think." She looked at Ethan's face, but he was hard to read.

"I don't get it," he opened and closed the tongs in his hands mechanically. "Why does everyone want me to like Anna?" he whispered under his breath.

"Huh? I don't want you to like her! I mean, Ethan, you know what I mean…," Maya whispered back. She clutched the edges of her chair, white-knuckled and wondering if she should use this as a springboard to talk to him. But, the words were lost to her and so was her breath.

"Good. At least you haven't lost your mind like the rest of them," Ethan tapped the top of her head playfully with the handle of the tongs. "Consider that you have another recruit on 'Reese watch' now. I'll let you know if I hear of any new developments, and you do the same for me. Will that relieve your mind at all?"

"Yeah," her feelings slowly found their way toward him, "you always make me feel better."

"Glad I could help," his grip on the tongs tightened.

Maya smiled.

"Care to hang with me at the grill?" Ethan warmed up to her varying emotions. "I think it'll be easier to get you that first burger."

"Of course," she found her footing, standing to adjust the towel on her lower half, "but I need to get out of this suit first." She grabbed her sweatshirt from the side table and held it in her arms. As she walked past Ethan, she whacked him in the butt with her sweatshirt.

Ethan fumbled with the tongs and nearly dropped them.

Maya smiled with full cheeks as she slipped through the open sliding glass door.

"On second thought," Ethan cleared his throat, "I think it's best if Brix helps out. I'll have him get you the first burger just the same, and he's used to the grill drill, anyway." He stopped himself from rambling and resorted to shouting, "BRIX—GET OUT HERE!"

Without having to be called twice, Brixton shuffled out to the grill. Ethan wanted to tell him that Maya had just smacked his backside with her sweatshirt, when she somehow appeared again with the burgers, buns, and fixings. No longer in her mint-green bathing suit, she wore relaxed light-wash bell-bottomed jeans, a fitted oatmeal tank, and a particularly curious smile.

As she placed, arranged, and rearranged the items on the table next to the grill, Ethan attempted to convey his message to Brixton via hand gestures. Brixton, confused, thought Ethan had asked to be left alone with Maya; he began walking towards the house. Ethan hurried after him but only managed to take a few steps.

Maya intercepted Ethan's body with hers. She wrapped her arms around his sides, and leaned her head on his shoulder. Channeling all of her feelings into her arms, she squeezed him, wishing he could learn her thoughts from this one giant hug.

Ethan clenched and looked at the sliding glass door.

Brixton stood outside with Anna, both watching intently.

"Uh? You guys playing truth or dare or something?" Ethan let his hands touch Maya's back. He felt her lean in. With the exception of his hands, his whole body remained tense.

"Um. I…just…you know how…that…I…it's," Maya's thoughts twisted together. Her hands fell from his upper back to his lower back, and she loosened her hold on him.

Ethan took a step to the side, freeing himself from her embrace. "You girls and your crazy games. Just let me cook and we can play after. I'm sure Ang and Brix will want to join in on the fun, too, if they're not already in on it," Ethan huffed, playfully opening and closing the tongs near Maya's face. "But no one else's getting in on our Jenga game. That's something we need to finish on our own."

When Maya didn't smile, he looked back at the house. Anna seemed upset and she motioned Brixton inside with her. Kila, who had been standing behind Brixton and Anna the whole time, could now be seen through the glass.

Maya's blank expression walked past Ethan along with the rest of her body.

He sped up to her, hooking his finger through one of her bell-bottoms' belt loops. "Maya," he spoke her name.

He had planned to ask her what was really going on, but, when she spun into him, he froze in place. Her body arched too close to his for him to think straight. His grip tightened on her belt loop, the smell of cinnamon bark and sweet orange drifting from her hair to his nose. His eyes took flight from her bouncy hair to her dark eyes to her raspberry-colored lips, which sparkled in the sunlight. In an instant he felt dizzy, like when he rode the Rock 'n' Roll Express too many times in a row at last summer's fair with Brixton. *Say something and stop staring. She's going to think you're a creep, otherwise. Jenga. No, I've mentioned that twice. Something else…*

Maya looked up at him, frustrated with herself.

"It'd be nice to know what game we're playing," he spoke softly. "Just tell me, so I can play my part. I won't let on that I know," he tried to remain calm.

He expected her to speak or move, but she was still there, close to him. And he could still smell the orange and cinnamon. It wove a pattern through his nerves. He fought to imagine it wasn't detectable in the air.

"Ethan, my belt loop…," Maya whispered, hopelessness filling her mind.

"Oh, sorry," he released his grip on her pants, somehow regaining his poise. "T minus fifteen minutes until the burgers are done. Please instruct Ki to set the table—that's the least she can do if I'm cooking for everyone."

When Maya entered the house, Brixton sped outside, flashing a sly grin. "I'd say I detected some chemistry, but that would be an understatement," he eyed Ethan.

"No chemistry, Brix—I have no idea what that was all about. I'm beginning to think all the girls at Cypress have spring fever."

"Conditions are favorable for us, then," Brixton offered quietly, a half-smile spreading across the right side of his face.

The two friends laughed a little.

"Hey, if nothing else," Brixton continued, "we can always play some music tonight and debate whether or not to cast our lot in the EmOpen."

"The EmOpen sounds sweet," Ethan admitted, "but the probability of massive failure is greater than any other outcome."

"E," Brixton straightened his posture, "it's nothing new. Failure always lurks closest to what you want to attain. It's not like any of us is in this one alone. There's three of us, and we each bring a unique skillset. Failure's never dealt with us as a team. At least, not on this significance level. In fact, us failing to enter the EmOpen is also us failing to give failure a fair match. I mean, when you think about it, we have to enter, for failure's sake."

Ethan smiled, crossing his arms. "You made a few good points. I'll give you that. But, don't forget, even if you can convince me, we still have to convince Angus."

"Oh, please. Angus is easier than you," Brixton replied matter-of-factly. "All we have to do is pitch it as a low-loss gamble and he'll ante up."

"I'm not sure why anything makes Angus nervous," Ethan shook his head. "With the single exception of Reese, Angus has always gotten everything he's ever wanted."

"I know," Brixton shook his head, "that's partially why he can't move on. Reese is a constant reminder of his only failed attempt at anything. Reversing that outcome has become a sick obsession of his. It's like his personal quest for invincibility."

"...No one is invincible," Ethan's eyebrows stretched together.

"I know," Brixton laughed. "If the low-loss angle doesn't do the trick, we'll threaten him with Timmy."

Ethan's eyes widened. "Do you think he'd believe us?"

"If we were convincing enough," Brixton shrugged.

"Alright," Ethan nodded, "I'm in."

"Good," Brixton took a deep breath, "it's settled."

When the first burger was grilled to perfection, Ethan slipped it onto one of the small plates. He surrendered the tongs to Brixton and ventured inside with the burger, stealthily looking for Maya. Unfortunately, she was standing in the living room with Kila and Anna, and he couldn't avoid the wave of embarrassment he felt as he passed the plate to Maya in front of them. Shortly after the burger changed hands, Kila and Anna rushed into the dining room. Alone with Maya yet again, Ethan recognized the pattern.

"I figured you forgot," Maya clasped the rim of the plate,

worrying about what he might say next, and then what she should say after that.

"I didn't," Ethan noticed his chest expand. *Oh NO! I took in too much air. I have to let it out slowly,* he fretted, never having had this experience before. *Does this look ridiculous?* He worked to time-release it. *If I don't, I'll risk sounding like I'm huffing and puffing for no reason.*

"Hey!" Angus scowled, "You didn't tell me they were done."

No sooner had Angus finished his complaint than Kila and Anna grabbed hold of his arms, pulling him without a fight into the dining room. Angus, smiling excessively as he veered out of sight, didn't seem too bothered by the ordeal.

"WHAT is going on?" Ethan laughed, as the final bit of excess air escaped from his nostrils. "You have to tell me. It's not fair, anymore. Really, My," he pulled his hair into his face, then swept it back in place.

Maya switched her stance, juggling her weight from her left foot to her right foot, unable to find a comfortable position. Giving up, she pulled a chunk of the burger apart from the rest and shoved it in her mouth.

Ethan studied her expressions.

She hid them well with all the chewing.

"Let's have it," he crossed his arms. "I'm in on it. It makes sense now. You're the distraction. You're pretty good at it, too," he grinned at her, thinking how perfectly she played her role. "What new joke are the boys up to now, huh? Booby-trapping my car? Spray-painting my Chucks? What is it? And why are you in on it this time? I thought we were tight back there with the secret swapping, and all? Or was that all part of it, too?"

For the first time, Maya wondered if he might be flirting with her. Still, she wasn't prepared to break the news, not even one part of the two parts she had promised Kila. "We ARE tight. That's...the problem. I'll tell you later on, seriously. It's not a dead-end promise."

"I don't know if I trust you now," he studied her face. "Why should I?"

"Because I still owe you something for your chair," Maya crossed her fingers, "remember?"

He looked at her, skeptically.

When she offered him a piece of the burger and he took it without comment, she knew she had landed herself a little more time.

"SO, 'I'll be right back' REALLY means 'take over the grill because I'm gonna hang with My while you cook all the rest'?" Brixton snidely made his presence known behind them.

"Something like that," Ethan smirked when he caught Maya's smile.

Brixton held up the piping-hot plate of burgers, then delivered them to the dining room table. Ethan, acknowledging he forgot to cook the kale, rushed into the kitchen to prepare it. Kila, in an attempt to impress her friends, set the table with the best dishware.

Mom would have laughed about the dishes. Ethan contemplated the nature of Brixton and Angus's apparent scheme. With each push of the silicon spatula through the lacinato kale, he guessed: *Uploading embarrassing photos to my account? Duct-taping my toilet? Toothpaste in my socks? Hot sauce in my sheets?*

When the garlicky kale reached the table, six hungry teenagers dug into to the meal. It was anything but dull. They discussed who had the biggest burger, and then debated over which vegan cheese and toppings best complemented the veggie patty itself. Ethan swore by the Pepper Jack and classic ketchup 'n' mustard combo. Maya opted to keep hers simple, with American, a little Vegenaise, lots of lettuce and sprouts, and sliced tomato. Kila's plate mirrored Maya's, only without the sliced tomato and with triple the lettuce. Angus took the other route, cramming everything from coconut bacon to pickles under the hood of his rosemary ciabatta bun. Kila glanced at him while he ate it, trying not to stare too much at the stripe of barbeque sauce resting on the edge of his upper lip. Brixton's mountain of kale stood taller than the veggie burger he put together, but he took them both down with equal enjoyment. Anna, who wasn't yet a fan of kale, decided to add a few forkfuls into her half-eaten burger. She mentally scratched cooked kale off of her "foods to avoid" list, and Ethan smirked when she opted for a second helping.

It wasn't long before all the serving plates were empty. In less than twenty minutes the whole group sat stuffed and contented, floral cloth napkins folded on the table, quietly enjoying each other's company.

To Kila's amazement, the boys had been on their very best behavior. Not one belch was heard. And no bathroom humor was had. *Things are certainly different*, she glanced at her brother, hoping Maya would tell him soon, and then at Brixton, who smiled at her.

"Ethan," Annabelle spoke, "thank you for making such nice, homemade food for us."

"You're welcome," Ethan returned a grateful smile. "Credit is also due to Brixton, as tonight's grill master."

"Hey," Angus looked down at his plate, "you never mention when I'm grill master."

Ethan laughed, "That's because when you're grill master, no one else is around but Brix and me."

"Still," Angus insisted, building up his plea, "you can announce it to Brix next time. If I'm grill master, even if it's just the three of us, he needs to know. He should know. It's important."

Chuckles infected the table for a few moments while Angus pretended to turn away in frustration. Once the group had grown quiet again, Angus offered to help Kila clean the table and return the kitchen to order. Brixton masked his annoyance, but Kila was taken by Angus's willingness to help. Frightened she might drop one of the heirloom dishes, Kila reminded herself to fix her attention on the cleaning and not on Angus. She counted her breaths and counted the plates as she picked them up one by one.

"Brix, why don't you bring your guitar down here?" Angus's suggestion brought light to everyone in the room.

"Yeah…I thought you wanted some of that. Since you didn't have any last night," Brixton winked. "E, how about breaking out the bongos? Then we can put on a balanced show for these girls."

"He's really going to sing while he's doing dishes?" Anna laughed while looking at Angus.

"Yeah. He sings wherever," Ethan smirked. "Brix, remember our history final last year?"

"How could I forget?" Brixton placed both of his hands on the table. "He sang that song he made up about Johannes Gutenberg while we were taking the standardized. Dr. Kentworth was torn between reprimanding him and rocking out to it. It was legendary."

"I was there! I remember," Maya laughed. "And I had a better view of Dr. Kentworth's internal struggle than the three of you did. My desk was practically attached to his. There was no space in that room, and I always hated it with the exception of that moment. It made the whole semester of him being able to see everything I was doing worth it."

Angus's crimson grin stole another piece of Kila. She fell into her thoughts. *There'll be nothing left of me if I keep looking at him. It's a curse,* Kila exhaled. *How is he able to do this to me? It has to stop.*

"Too bad you weren't there, Ki," Angus touched Kila's shoulder. "I would have had some honest feedback."

WHY does he keep touching her? Brixton clenched his teeth before leaving the room with Ethan to grab the guitar and bongos.

"So...they're really going to play in the kitchen?" Anna's eyes widened.

Kila nodded as everyone made their way out of the dining room. Anna and Maya took a seat at the counter while Kila and Angus moved the dirty dishes to the sink.

"Oh my gosh. Brixton is SO good at guitar it gives me shivers. Shivers! I've never seen him play up close," Anna gasped when she remembered Angus was in the room.

"Well, then. You're in for a treat tonight. Playing up close is his specialty," Angus couldn't let the moment pass him by. He played it expertly, without a trace of humor in his expression.

Kila, biting her lips together, squeezed Angus's arm.

Maya rubbed Anna's back.

"I won't say anything. You don't have to fret," Angus looked at Kila's face when he spoke the words even though they weren't directed at her. "These things can't help themselves sometimes."

"I know," Kila accidentally touched Angus's hand when she reached for the dish in the soapy water.

"So what do you want to hear?" Angus's question swept Kila off her feet.

"Oh. Me? I figured we'd let Brix pick the first," Kila adjusted her hair. Then she worried it might have looked better before she touched it with her wet fingers.

Maya whispered in Anna's ear how attractive she thought Ethan was when he played the bongos. "It's because he plays them standing up, and he moves his hips a bit."

Anna's giggles caused her and Maya to incur a series of soapy splashes from Angus.

The two girls shrieked while Kila attacked Angus from behind, gripping his biceps and pulling him back towards the sink.

"You want some of these suds, don't you?" Angus's verbal threat to Kila was quelled by the peculiar sensation of wetness atop his hair.

"I have crowned you the dish king," Kila held a hand over her mouth. "A sudsy crown for a sudsy king."

"You're lucky you're so cute," Angus moved close to her.

"Don't let him do it, Ki!" Maya laughed.

Kila eyed Angus, challenging his intent at revenge by remaining in place.

He swept his fingers under the curve of her chin and grinned. "I would never soap your hair, Ki...I'll get you back some other way."

That's the very moment Kila melted, and Brixton and Ethan

returned with their instruments.

Anna couldn't keep her eyes off Brixton now that he was wearing his guitar. She didn't even attempt to look away, because every moment of this sight was worth any embarrassment that might arise from it.

Maya tapped at Anna's leg to insert a break in her obvious stare.

Adjusting his bongo stand, Ethan announced in a serious tone, "Brixton has decided that Kila should select the first song."

Kila, busying herself with the dishes, smiled with her head tilted down. *Drifting back. DEFINITELY drifting back.*

"So we have a riddle," Angus aired demurely, "if Brix wants Ki to pick the first song, and Ki wants Brix to pick the first song, who ACTUALLY gets to pick the song?"

Naturally, everyone turned to Ethan.

"Let me see," Ethan rubbed his hands atop the bongos in thought. "Brixton picks the first song. My sister picks the second."

"The chief has spoken," Angus smiled, handing Kila another stack for the dishwasher. "You're up, Brix."

"Okay. I'll, um, I'll just start," Brixton closed his eyes.

All the quiet nights returned to him. Nights when he was alone in his room. Nights when he practiced guitar. Nights when he clocked second workouts. Nights when he wondered what music she was listening to. Nights he should have been chatting with her. She loved staying up late, and he grew to love the late as well. Late was time they more or less had alone. Time when parents were sleeping. Time when Ethan was sleeping. Time that was theirs, on the phone or in person. Time for music, time for laughter, time for sharing, time for emotional intimacy. Time for falling asleep on the phone together. And then waking up and remembering it.

Brixton opened his eyes to find his fingers already playing something. Ethan nodded at the song choice, knowing it from Kila, but never having practiced it with the band. Angus shrugged his shoulders and shook his head; he didn't know all the lyrics.

"Let's wing it, Brix," Ethan could tell Brixton didn't want to make another selection. His hands struck the bongos at a soft rhythmic pace.

"Yes! Yes, you guys," Angus laughed, wrapping an arm around Kila's shoulder. He whispered into Kila's ear something only she heard, "Anna and Maya are about to lose it."

Kila wanted to look at Angus, but instead found her eyes on Brixton and her brother.

"I'll join in the chorus, so I don't feel useless. I know that part, at least," Angus stayed next to Kila, though both his arms now rested at his sides.

If Angus is only singing chorus, who is singing verses? Kila wondered.

"Alright," Brixton closed his eyes, "in three." He forced himself to disappear into **"I Can Make You Feel Young Again" by Copeland**. It was the only way to beat the shyness.

Kila's heart raced for so many reasons. For the unexpected proximity of Angus's body, for the repressed memories the song conjured, for the crisscross emotions darting through the air. Her eyes bounced from Anna to Maya, their faces full of wonder. And that's when she realized the soft, angelic sound she heard was her brother and Brixton's voices layered together. *They're singing! I didn't know EITHER of them could sing. It's beautiful.* Kila had aimed to look at Ethan, but it was Brixton's face her eyes found. His closed eyes in focus, his open mouth in song, his bare fingers dancing about the guitar strings.

Angus offered his vocals during the chorus. His voice, more practiced and powerful, drowned out the sound of Ethan and Brixton's harmony. Although most times Kila pined for Angus's deep voice, she found herself here sifting through the joint vocals to locate Brixton's quieter, graceful sound. *There it is.* It emerged when the chorus ended, sweeping the months without his friendship away. She felt like he had never left her. That the two of them could pick up right where they had left off, the time in between fading like thick haze in the midday sun.

We could hit up Henry Cowell for a hike before dark, check in at the gallery to get his summer schedule, wander the beach until it either gets too cold or we get too hungry, and round off the outing with an enormous Italian herb pizza. Starlight convo at my house or his...but...I wouldn't even know where to start. Maybe if we just looked up at the stars long enough, it would all start to make sense?

*One day everything was normal. And then the next...
emptiness...as if the friendship were something that had
happened, but had happened to two OTHER people, and not
to us. Ethan knew no more than I did. Angus was polite—it's
possible he knew why and it's possible he didn't. My wanted
to talk to Brix on my behalf, but I wouldn't let her. Something
clearly pushed him away, and if he couldn't tell me what that
something was himself—with all that we shared in the past—I
didn't want him telling anyone else. It seemed better that way.*

*I hated the semi-smile he started giving me in school. If we were
no longer friends, why waste energy on pretense? I never told
any of his secrets, and I assume he's never told any of mine—
even now. Growing apart from some people is part of growing
up—so "they" say—but I never thought Brix would sever the
connection. I never thought he'd leave the space we created.
The place where we could talk about anyone or anything and
figure things out. With music.*

Guess I was wrong.

And now what?

*He pops up into my life last night, like he never bowed out, and
I'm supposed to dial it back to where we were before the rift,
just because he wants to, it's easy to, and he sounds like this?*

*I need something. An explanation. A reason that isn't
conveniently crafted to sound like it's the real one. I need the
real one. He owes me that.*

Even though this is helping...

Pinned by her past, time passed without her noticing, and suddenly Kila heard nothing. Confused by the quiet, she touched Angus's hand, which was caressing her arm for some unknown reason. The lump in her throat throbbed uneasily. Three times she tried to swallow it unsuccessfully.

"Come on, Ki," Angus's crimson grin ushered her sadness away, "it couldn't have been so bad that you're speechless."

"No," Kila turned away from his dark eyes, "there was nothing bad about that."

Brixton, mid-conversation with Ethan, stopped speaking when he noticed Kila looking at him.

"Your voice," she felt her chest rise and fall. "I thought I heard it that time we were in the midst of yard work at your house. When we were blasting **'All The Lights' by The Cinema**, and I called you out on it. I knew I caught you singing—it was gorgeous, and you were all 'I wasn't, I'm just really good at the lip synching.' I KNEW it!" Kila blushed when she felt the weight of everyone in the room looking at her.

Brixton didn't mind that everyone could hear. "I couldn't tell you," he shifted his guitar to the side. "I mean, I wanted to, in a way, but I didn't want you to think that I could REALLY sing, because I can't. Every once in a while, you get into a song. You fall into it, completely; and, if it's not too out of your normal vocal range, you can sing it modestly well. It doesn't happen often, and, therefore, it's unpredictable. One afternoon last fall when Angus had bronchitis, E and I found out that the two of us could, KIND OF sing. And by kind of, I mean wing it enough so that we could still practice until

Angus's voice returned."

"But you never kept anything from me...until," Kila couldn't tell if she had blushed again or if the first blush had decided to linger.

"I know," Brixton prepared to remove his guitar strap. *I'm going in. It's time. I don't care if the whole school is present in this kitchen right now. It's happening.*

"Hold up!" Angus severed the moment. "Don't take it off. I'm going to get mine," he ran out of the room before anyone could comment.

Brixton's fingertips pressed tightly into the strings of his guitar as he looked back at Kila.

Maya noticed.

Ethan, unaware of the underground conversation, spoke with Brixton about the surprise of the Copeland song. He more than hinted at the want to elicit Casper's feedback by staging a similar performance next visit. Brixton replied to Ethan with words alone; his eyes lingered on Kila's face.

WHAT is happening to me tonight? I'm ALL OVER the map! Flickers of 9th-grade sex-ed class twisted like a disco-ball in Kila's mind. Biting her lip and feeling grateful Ms. Jun wasn't around to notice her body's practically textbook change in posture, she turned around to face the remaining stack of dirty dishes and cookware. It enabled her to regroup and think about what she had just heard, what she had just learned. *Was it the song? Why do I feel like this? I need to pause. I need to think before I speak. I'm blending time and feelings from the past into the present where they have no place.*

Anna appeared by Kila's side, taking over for Angus. Plates and utensils were rinsed and loaded into the dishwasher. Pots were scrubbed with hot water and placed upside down on the drying rack. Maya moved closer at Anna's prompt.

"All three singing," Anna whispered. "WHAT was that?"

"I might be dead. Am I still alive?" Maya anxiously looked at Ethan, then hushed the volume of her voice. "Ki, pinch me. Pinch me right now. I need to know."

Kila's lips stretched into a smile. "You will not receive a single pinch until you tell him."

Maya pouted.

"Angus kept touching you," Anna whispered to Kila. "I was watching Brixton and then I saw you space out, and Angus was, like, more or less massaging your arms with his hands."

"Wait," Kila's eyebrows twisted in surprise. "I thought he just touched me for a second so I'd open my eyes."

"No," Maya shook her head. "He serenaded you at each chorus."

Kila gasped, then looked straight ahead at the tiles above the sink. "We need to get out of here," her definitive words startled them. "The three of us are out of focus. We had a plan, and that plan has failed. Massively. The timing of everything is off. Things aren't playing out the way they need to. It's all… twisted. The most important goal is to get Maya to talk to E. That's never going to happen if the boys are playing music all night, and Ethan's trapped behind a pair of bongos."

"I love the music, and I hate to leave it, but you're right," Anna agreed.

Maya nodded somewhat reluctantly. "You call the last song and we'll tell them we have to go to…."

"To the mall," Anna filled in the blank. "That's where we'll regroup, talk about what just happened, and gush over how smolderingly hot the three of them are. After we've calmed down, we'll come back and give this another go."

"Yes! Well," Kila shook her head laughing, "I'm not into Ethan like that, obviously, but yes to everything else. We'll return in a few hours when it's dark and time for…other things."

Maya and Anna nodded, more so with their smiles than with their heads.

Kila felt in control again after the plan laid down roots in her mind. *I fumbled. The one time he touches me sweetly I'm too wrapped up in the past to notice. WHY? Why! And when my parents are away, sweet surrender. Will I be ridiculously awkward my whole life?* She all but leapt at Angus when he walked through the kitchen door with his guitar.

He grinned in the midst of the attention.

Brixton eye-checked Ethan.

"The second song choice is mine, right?" Kila's eyes assaulted Angus's face with a concentration of feeling he'd never received from a female.

An undeniable energy burned inside her words, but Angus felt uncertain of its nature. "If you're that excited you can call the second AND the third," he watched for a change in her expression.

"I just need the second," Kila explained. "My and Anna and I have to run out to the mall right after."

"Oh? The mall? Fun," Angus soon after realized his reply had come across as lackluster.

"You're not meeting up with anyone there, are you?" Ethan posed the question before Brixton had a chance to.

"No!" Kila laughed. "We want to meet up with you guys when we come back...."

"Good," Brixton jumped in, "that works out, because we have some band things we need to discuss on our own, but we'll be free to chill later if you're up for it."

Angus shot a quizzical glance at Brixton, who ignored it.

Ethan pretended to scratch his nose so no one saw him laugh.

"Alright," Kila looked at Anna and Maya, and then at Brixton. "I need some of The Strokes," she eyed Angus, "and I need '12:51' to be exact."

Ethan nodded to Brixton, then motioned for Angus to move into place.

Brixton's pick grazed his guitar strings but quickly pulled away. "Can I just say that this is one of the greatest songs in the history of Friday night hangout songs?"

"You can," Angus beamed, "but I think almost everyone in the kitchen already knows it is."

"Do you know the song?" Ethan asked Anna when she had looked away.

"No, but Kila's only had a couple months with me, remember. I'm still learning all this stuff," she smiled bashfully at Brixton.

An odd and clumsy mix of bongo sounds filled the air. Everyone laughed when they noticed Maya hiding behind Ethan's shoulder, her small, caramel hands looking especially guilty.

Ethan smirked, then pulled Maya backwards when she tried to scurry away. "Come here. You want to play with me?"

Maya nodded with the joy of a child.

"Alright," Ethan's voice held more warmth in its tone than seriousness. "Put your hands on top of mine, and then we can swap yours for the bottom if you get the hang of it."

"Okay," Maya's fingers wiggled in anticipation, "where should I stand?"

Ethan motioned her to stand in front of him and behind the bongos.

Kila nudged Anna, internally praising her brother for this moment. *That's it, E. This might happen now, after all. Late as hell, but still in the works. Ah, my brother. As cool and smooth as marble in the most unforeseen moments.*

"Everybody ready now?" Angus's sly grin had Kila smiling. "Wait! Hang on," he took advantage of the timing. "Ki, do you want to come over here and get between me and the guitar, and we can play together, you know, both strapped in, your fingers on the top, mine on the bottom until you get the hang of it?"

"I will kill you," Ethan looked at Angus straight-faced.

Anna pinched Kila's side.

"Enjoy the lead singer's antics while you can, girls," Brixton rolled his eyes. "When you return tonight there might be a little less of him. Or, he might not be here at all."

"Hit it," Kila spoke through her laughter, daring to imagine what it might feel like to fill the space between Angus and his guitar. *Too intense. Way too intense. Time to watch Maya.*

"12:51" by The Strokes came alive in the Lorens kitchen. With two acoustic guitars, a pair of bongos, and one impeccable voice, Anna fell in love with the song without ever having heard the highly contagious original version. Kila, in control of her eyes but not so much in control of her heart, looked from Angus to Brixton to Angus. *I love how he smiles when* *he sings the songs he likes. He can't help it sometimes. That voice. The way he makes it roll from his mouth in waves of rich words. The way it comes across as effortless to him, as if he were simply walking down the hall or driving to school.*

Kila stroked Anna's blonde hair to give her eyes a break from Angus. She watched the way Anna looked from one boy to the next, always lingering on Brixton's face. *I'm not sure who's more excited right now, Anna or Maya?* Kila wondered, loving the crazy smile on Maya's face. Her tiny hands on top of Ethan's large hands were something Kila had to take a picture of. *I hate doing this, but she'll thank me for it later.* Kila reached for her phone. She captured how close Ethan stood behind Maya, how breathless the two seemed, and how in awe of Ethan's talent Maya appeared. Then, for good measure, she took a few pictures of Angus and Brixton, following up with a couple more shots of Angus alone.

"I want this every weekend," Anna whispered in Kila's ear. "You have changed my life, K Lorens. This is way beyond the B+. Way beyond."

"And you have changed mine, eternally for the better," Kila pulled Anna in for a hug. "We just need to make Maya come clean. Tonight. It HAS to be tonight."

"It'll happen," Anna spoke, louder than intended.

"What will?" Angus asked, removing his guitar.

"More fun when we return," Kila smiled strangely, sticking out her pointy tongue to distract him.

"You better not flirt with me with your brother around," Angus tilted his head. "You heard what Brixton said."

"Yeah," Brixton walked towards Kila, free from his guitar. "Brixton said you shouldn't flirt with Angus at all because he's in another relationship."

"That's right," Kila rolled her eyes, leaving Brixton to his own thoughts.

"I can't believe this is the best concert I've been to...and it was in your kitchen," Anna rescued Kila from the dead-end conversation. "You guys are going to be rock stars," she looked at Ethan.

"Oh yeah? How's that?" Ethan smirked, watching Maya have her hand at the bongos without him.

"I don't know that part," Anna smiled, "but I believe it, even without the details."

"Come on," Kila patted Maya's hand.

"Thank you," Maya touched Ethan's shoulder, moving in for a hug although she hadn't planned to.

This time Ethan opened his arms easily and relaxed into it. "Can you tell me now?" he asked during the embrace.

Maya squeezed him with her eyes closed.

Anna turned to Kila.

Kila crossed her fingers.

"No," Maya gazed into his blue-gray eyes after the hug. "I'll tell you later. I promise. It'll be better that way," she noticed Brixton and Angus's smiles and worried that Anna or Kila might not have kept her secrets safe.

"Neither of us breathed a word of it to the boys," Kila assured Maya as they passed through the hallway alone.

Outside, Anna fanned herself with both of her hands. "Thank you, night air! My heart rate was so wild back there I felt like I was working out!"

Kila and Maya burst into laughter as Anna fanned the fabric under her armpits.

"I'm re-applying my deodorant as soon as we're in the car," Anna thrust a hand into her purse, rustling the contents around to find it.

Maya wrapped her arms around Anna's torso.

Kila walked behind them all the way to her car, wondering if Timothy was enjoying the double date and also if he was enjoying Jocelyn's company. *I bet Ollie's farther along than I am already. I have to turn this around.*

After the highly successful two-song kitchen concert, the boys watched the girls group together in a whispery fever and leave for the mall. For a strained twenty minutes Ethan, Brixton, and Angus kept at the music; but, without the flirtatious energy bubbling in the air, the scene seemed a bit stale. Left to themselves in an otherwise empty house, the bandmates of No More S'mores sprawled out lazily on the couches in the living room, quietly thinking and staring at one another. To prompt new conversation, Ethan played **"Skull and Bones" by The 10x, Ben Schuller** from his phone.

"Seeing as how Kiki took a bunch of pictures, I thought we played it pretty well in there," Brixton broke the ice.

"Obviously not well enough," Angus snapped, "we didn't score an invite to the mall."

"You hate the mall," Ethan tried to soothe him.

"Yeah, but I mean, it wouldn't have been so bad…with the girls…," Angus trailed off.

"You know," Brixton looked to Ethan, "after the bongo bonding you had with My, I'm surprised she didn't ask you to go to the mall with them. I bet if you had hinted you wanted to go, she would have jumped at the chance to have you there, and then Ang and I could have tagged along."

Angus's face flashed in momentary annoyance, "How could E have hinted we were free to go after you mentioned we had other things to do? You used the words 'on our own,' Brix. We lost our invitation LONG before the bongo connection."

"No, we ran the risk of looking ultra-lame. At that point they didn't want us to go. I had to say something," Brixton lamented mildly in his mind. "How was I supposed to know that Maya and Ethan were going to have a moment? The look on her face when Kiki told her she had to leave…did you catch that, Ang?"

"Caught it. She didn't want to leave him. Definitely heavy. Admittedly jealous," Angus smirked. "You know, I wouldn't mind feeling admired like that."

"I'm onto you two, by the way," Ethan warned with an upturned lip.

"Onto what?" Angus looked to Brixton in question.

"All the cover-ups. Leaving me alone with Maya to hide your tracks. You're not as smooth as you guys once were, you know," Ethan shook his head. He wanted them to know that he knew. "She couldn't keep a straight face around me. Dead giveaway. I could have pulled it out of her if I tried a bit harder, but I'd rather hear it from the two of you. You know the rules. I'm calling it, so you have to come clean."

"Hold up," Angus found this comical. "You think we're pranking you?"

Ethan eyed Brixton.

"Yeah, E, we're not in on anything," Brixton explained. "You have my word."

Ethan looked at Angus.

"In all seriousness," Brixton rubbed his hands together, "I think she likes you. She hugged you before she left for no reason. You usually only score a hug from her when she leaves for the day. She's coming back, and she's staying over, so there was really no need for a hug before the mall."

"Kila and Anna DID hint at her liking you," Angus confessed. "While they didn't come out and say the words, they did pull me out of the room when you were about to share the first burger. I didn't tell you about the hint because I figured you'd freak out and overthink it."

"I have to admit," Brixton tilted his head, "that whole 'first burger' thing struck me as romantic."

"I'm going to figure it out," Ethan vowed, straight-faced. "Then I'm going to get you guys back, in such a way that you won't attempt to mess with me again. You took it too far this time.

You involved one of the girls."

"...And he continues to live in denial," Brixton spoke under his breath. "She likes you. Do something about it."

Angus lifted a foot in the air in agreement.

"E, if I was getting those signs from...the person I liked, I'd be all over it," Brixton's fingers closed over his palms thinking about how he would feel if Kila embraced him the way Maya had embraced Ethan.

Angus looked at his phone in frustration, then tossed it onto the coffee table. "By the way, why'd you have to say that to Ki, about my being in a relationship?"

"It just came out," Brixton wondered what level of a lie that was. "We were teasing each other and I took it a little farther than I should have. But, I didn't say anything she didn't already know...."

"Yeah...I hate this," Angus rolled his shoulders back into the cushion. "I need more from Reese. What we have isn't enough...I guess it never has been."

"Because Reese isn't the answer," Brixton stretched his legs out. "I know you don't want to believe me, but I wish you would. Has she agreed to meet you out this weekend or at ANY point in the future?"

"No," Angus huffed, "I stopped pressing it."

"Good. End it," Brixton closed his eyes thinking of Kila.

Angus laughed, "I know. I want to. I'm trying, but...she's such a brat." He picked his phone up from the coffee table with the guilty look of a child about to chase trouble.

"If I was dating someone, even in secret, I'd want to see them. It's like you're having a long-distance relationship with someone you go to school with. It's...kind of odd. It'd be different if this girl wasn't a snake, but you already know she is!" Brixton spoke his final thoughts on the matter, "For the record, I'd be in favor of anyone other than her." *Anyone other than her and Kiki, that is.*

Unsure if the continued Reese conversation was yet another staged distraction, Ethan pulled his phone from his pocket and texted Maya:

[Asking an honest question in hopes of receiving an honest answer: Are Brix and Ang pranking me?]

Ethan nestled into the couch. *As soon as I have confirmation, I'm launching a counterattack. I'll be silent. I'll let the boys think their plan is still in play. Then I'll strike. I'll get Maya to help, and, with her acting as a double agent, victory will be mine. I'll ride the wave of glory in quiet composure, and Maya will take note of my sportsmanship.*

"The girls will be back at some point," Brixton sat upright. "I'd rather we do something else than risk staying here, falling asleep, and fulfilling our ultra-lame prophesy."

"Wanna play some more?" Ethan asked, hurling a pillow at Angus to halt his obsessi-texting.

"Nah. Not in the mood," Angus replied flatly, setting his phone down once more. "I could, however, go for some dessert. Any birthday cake left?"

"How could there be?" Ethan laughed. "You ate the last piece. It doesn't just replenish itself."

"It'd be awesome if it did," Angus grew hungrier at the thought. "I bet there's more at the restaurant. It's right off Mayberry. Why don't we go check it out?"

"On foot?" Brixton pulled up the map on his phone. When circumstances allowed, he preferred to walk. "It's The Hidden Meridian, right?"

"Yeah," Ethan confirmed, "love that name."

"Fitting, I think, for the level of sumptuousness of that cake," Angus added, glad his hunger would soon be sated. "I wonder what other decadent delights that Noah character makes."

"I'm anxious to see the inside of this place," Brixton jumped in place a few times, warming up for the experience. "Professor Dalton did say he dug the maps, remember?"

"Yeah. That guy's obsessed with maps, though," Ethan laughed.

The three grabbed their sweatshirts from upstairs and headed off on foot to Brixton's satisfaction. The weather was perfect for the walk. The type of weather where the air is neither noticeably warm nor noticeably cool, and your muscles are so relaxed it seems like your legs are more like gliding forward than mechanically stepping along.

In between the two boys, Ethan set the pace. Though he would never admit it, he often found himself at the nucleus of the friendship. Brixton and Angus frequently looked to him for guidance; and, more times than not, it was Ethan who coaxed the group to cross over into new terrain. While "girls" had always been on their minds, it was only recently that Ethan began wondering how their relationships with the opposite sex might shape the rest of their lives. He thought of Maya, first in one way, then in another, and he itched to see her answer, which hadn't yet come.

"I don't see it," Brixton again referenced the map on his phone as they veered off Mayberry towards Maple. "7980. It's supposed to be over there, across the street."

"Maybe it actually IS hidden," Angus faked a gasp.

"Let's walk over and see," Ethan calmly directed the group as he often did. "It has to be there."

As the boys waited on the corner for the traffic light to change, they were whistled at by a cluster of twenty-something-year-old females in an excessively shiny, banana-yellow convertible. **"Free" by Broods** blared from its many speakers until the girl in the passenger seat softened the volume in hopes of kindling a conversation.

"Ladies," Angus greeted their enchanted smiles, "a little tip: playing hard to get is never a bad idea...."

The girls hardened in their seats. The driver, in particular, prayed for the light to change. Her bedazzled, claw-like fingernails pressed into the peacock-feather-themed steering wheel and her glittered face stared straight ahead in concentration. At the first sight of green, the metal toe-bed of her right stiletto dug into the gas pedal, the sports car racing away from their monstrous flirtatious flop. The boys, left in various states of emotion, discussed the incident.

"I always forget how much I love that song," Ethan pulled his phone from his pocket and added "Free" to one of his current playlists.

"That's all you're going to say?" Angus shook his head at Ethan. "Wrong in so many ways, and not the 'good' kind of wrong."

"Obviously, but the song choice was on point," Ethan added, "you can't deny them that. Broods is top notch. Wayyy up there."

"They are," Brixton agreed with Ethan and then scolded Angus. "You keep quiet next time. What if they get into an accident because of your little tip?"

"Maybe they'll behave themselves next time in order to get what they want," Angus's words rolled off his lips. "If they had pulled up without saying anything and kept to themselves, we probably would have given them a quick glance."

"Speak for yourself," Brixton cast his vote. "I didn't see anything worth a second look. Their lips were smothered in overconfidence and entitlement. No interest. No thank you."

Ethan smirked, "We couldn't even land an invite to the mall from my sister and her friends. Hunting college girls is a bit outside our existing strengths."

"Correction," Angus noted, "THEY hunted us. Whistling, no less. Who whistles anymore? Maybe they're older than we thought...that'd explain the whistling."

Brixton laughed. "Yeah, being whistled at doesn't exactly put me 'in the mood.'"

"I didn't know you could GET 'in the mood,'" Angus laughed. "I was beginning to think you were asexual."

"I'm not attracted to Reese," Brixton gritted his teeth. "That does not make me asexual."

"Breaking news: Reese is no longer up for discussion tonight." Ethan resorted to drastic measures, "Whosoever brings up her name again loses the privilege of staying at my house this weekend."

The temporary sound of silence let Ethan know they took his ultimatum seriously. Crossing the street, they continued to track the supposed location of The Hidden Meridian. Pacing back and forth, Angus noticed peculiar purple arrows painted on the sidewalk. He motioned to his friends and they followed the trail of arrows, which led them under the thick canopy of a sprawling tree, around a bend lined with exotic succulents, and finally down a terra-cotta cobblestone pathway. Brixton ran his hand along the wall to his right. Plastered in old world maps, his fingers touched the outlines of islands, countries, and continents.

"See," Angus grinned, "if I hadn't polished off last night's cake, we never would have had this adventure."

Brixton jumped towards him, "Does this mean you're officially over us not getting an invite to the mall?"

"Yes," Angus responded without hesitation. "AND, we can brag to the girls we came here first. Thus, it will always be 'our' spot and never 'theirs.'"

"I like the sound of that," Ethan reached out his hand to open a large walnut door, etched with hieroglyph-like symbols.

Brixton's eyes widened when he stepped inside and his ears were greeted with **"The Island" by Parade of Lights**. "The décor, the smell, and even the music is a ten. Maybe higher," he whispered to his friends as they stood in the short line.

Angus lifted his shoulders up and down in semi-dance, leaning close to Brixton. "Yeah, I've been crushing on this song since the first time I heard it. I bet you could sing this one well—it has that whimsical tone you like."

Ethan shook his head. "Sometimes I fear one of you will kill the other. Other times I fear quite the opposite. Not that that would be a problem. I just think it wouldn't be fair if you didn't tell me…."

Brixton patted Ethan's shoulder, attempting to speak through his laughter, "Our interests lie elsewhere. Trust me."

"Come on," Angus puckered his lips. "Now that he knows…."

Brixton laughed harder.

"Enough, you two...there's plenty of time for that later," Ethan attempted a straight face without success. "I love you both. Equally...I think."

Angus sized Brixton up.

After the couple ahead of them had been seated, a tall, muscular gentleman in a dragonfly costume motioned them forward. The boys took note of the vegan arm patches sewn onto the front of his shirt and along his sleeves. Ethan pointed out his favorite to the dragonfly's appreciation, while Brixton and Angus admired his neatly trimmed strawberry-blonde beard and tidy hair bun.

"Gentlemen. Welcome," he theatrically handed them menus and began orating the long list of specials for the day.

Angus, driven by his growing craving for dessert, peered around his wings to scope out those already seated at the small establishment. When he confirmed there was no one they knew, he scanned the open areas to determine which table might suit his trio best. At the first pause of the dragonfly's impeccable speech, Angus jumped in with his request.

"We'd like to sit at the counter and order dessert," Angus spoke in his politest tone hoping they wouldn't be forced to listen to the rest of the dinner specials.

"Dessert?!? My good gents dessert is the very reason we are in business!" boasted the dragonfly with a pearly smile. "Noah has just arrived, and I've been told he's in a most experimental mood!"

All three boys smiled, their stomachs clearing space in anticipation. Ethan followed Angus to the counter, while Brixton lagged behind, eyeing each of the manuscripts and vintage art pieces hanging on the walls. *Kiki would LOVE this. Maybe once our friendship locks into place again, I can take her here...the two of us.*

"Come on!" Angus motioned for Brixton to claim the stool next to him. "Aren't you hungry?"

"Yes," Brixton laughed, "but I will never, at any point, be as hungry as you. There's a bit of ridiculousness to it."

Ethan was too busy drooling over the dessert menu to participate in the regularly scheduled friction-fest starring his two best friends. He continued ordering the selections in his mind and hooked one of his shoes under the footrest below the counter. *WHERE is Maya's reply? The sooner I see it, the sooner I can plan...*

Brixton placed his hands on the marble countertop, pretending to peruse the menu but really thinking of Kila and the promise of the goodnight. When the lights in the restaurant dimmed to almost darkness, he eyed Angus and Ethan.

Before any of them could speak, a series of eight, equally spaced strokes to a gong gave flight to identical notes, which reverberated in the trio's ears. Three seconds of complete darkness invited the whooshing sound of torrential rain. As the lights returned in a softer state, a new level of calm washed over their minds. Behind the counter, they could see what they had first mistaken for a normal wall was a giant stone slab, slick and shimmering, with the final drops of water cascading down its front.

"Wow," Angus's dark eyes took in the sight, "it didn't sound like a recording, but I didn't think it was right here." He admired the unassuming stone wall in front of them.

Brixton and Ethan nodded, their thoughts suddenly stolen by the sultry pulse of swanky house music. **"Hot Hands" by Darius** touched their ears, and the romantic cravings of all the patrons in The Hidden Meridian seemed to cloud the air in an invisible mist. A few of the guests moved closer to one another, holding hands and issuing private looks. Several others, who weren't coupled off, clapped in excitement and shouted for Noah. The increasingly adult atmosphere caused the boys to straighten their posture in their stools. Without realizing it, they all neatened their hair at once.

When the first of them had turned sixteen last year, Angus insisted they honor the pact they made at thirteen to grow longer hair for their junior and senior years of high school. The pact, which began as a joke, aimed to improve their creative image and attract girls. It all started after Ethan insisted Brixton and Angus watch a series of documentaries with him on their favorite bands. All three were required to take notes, so that at the end of the docu-session they could correlate their findings and identify similarities that might help their own band mature and flourish. In comparing the many pages of notes, Ethan reached the hysterical conclusion that the only similarity between the three sets of scribbles was the words "longish hair." Now, on the surface, the idea that a hairstyle could bring about such change was a rather silly notion. However, honoring the pact, as ridiculous as it seemed, had caused a chain reaction in their favor, forever to Angus's self-satisfaction.

While none of the boys opted for a drastic new do, they all agreed to grow beyond the dreaded awkward stage, where it looks like you need a haircut but it's not quite long enough to style. Angus suffered the brunt of this brutal stage. While Ethan's chocolate hair was finer and could be combed down, and Brixton's golden hair was curly and seemed to look natural at every state, Angus's thick, almost black hair assumed the shape of round globe about his head. For a while, Angus's older brother, Hunter, called him a clown; but, after a few patient months, Hunter grew envious, opting to adopt the style himself. Despite how justifiable it would have been, Angus never evened the score on the name-calling.

At its current length, Ethan's hair was no longer than an inch below his earlobes. He kept his silky hair almost in line with the shape of his head, the longest sections sweeping across his face from the top of his scalp. In the summer, his chocolate hair color took on a reddish undertone. Kila insisted his color wouldn't change as much if he used her hair sunscreen, but he found this recommendation laughable and chalked the color shift up to a seasonal happening.

Brixton's hair always appeared to look different. Sometimes it appeared curly, sometimes it appeared wavy, but always it appeared longer than Ethan's, by anywhere from a half inch to an inch and a half, depending on both the tightness of his curls and his mother's suggestions to have it trimmed. After seeking distance from Kila, Brixton grew self-conscious of his growing hair, lacking both her valued opinion and her arsenal of products with which to style it. Last night, Kila's touching his hair for the first time in many months felt something like a homecoming. In the summer, Brixton's hair lightened several shades in the sun, and at any given time during the year his hair naturally possessed four or five shades of blonde and brown, ranging from bleached to nutmeg.

A singular, striking color, Angus's dark hair was mostly straight, save for the ends which tended to flip upwards, especially while and after wearing one of his characteristic beanies. Angus, unlike Ethan and Brixton, tended to experiment with his longer hair. Most recently, he had it cut into a few layers, the shortest just long enough to tuck behind his ears, and the longest a little less than halfway down the sides of his neck. This newest cut was Reese's least favorite to date, as she claimed it made him look too playful. Although Angus had no idea, Kila liked this cut above all the others. She felt it meshed more with his personality. In times of hardcore crushing, Kila swore to herself she would darken her hair to his shade one day. At least, she figured, if she couldn't have him, she'd have the color she'd fallen so hard for.

The boys, who had long ago finished adjusting their hair, sat with superb posture in the super-tall stools reviewing the menu without knowing how watched they were. Close to every female in the establishment had taken note of them, three almost-fully-grown boys approaching the cusp of their defining years. Ethan began to wonder when might be a good time to resume discussions on the EmOpen, when a lively, well-dressed older gentleman with a French accent asked them if they'd like to order a drink.

Brixton, who had been silent for quite some time, spoke up, "We'd all like a round of the elderberry kombucha."

"Splendid choice," the server nodded in approval, "an in-house specialty."

"Were the gongs for Noah?" Ethan asked.

"Yes! They ring when he arrives, and they ring for him and him alone," the server spoke proudly, leaning in as if he were about to share a secret. "Newbies, aren't you?" he asked.

"Sort of," Ethan replied with noticeable wonder. "We had one of Noah's cakes last night, but this is our first dine-in experience."

"Then we must make it unforgettable! In addition to what you see on the menu, and what you've heard from Fredrique, there's a small selection of what I daresay will be Noah's latest blue-ribbon creation."

Angus's eyes widened when the server raised his eyebrows.

"Oooo…what is it?" Brixton asked in anticipation.

"A secret mixture of cake, fudge, and orange. What has so far been named"—the server looked around suspiciously before he whispered—"coco'range."

"We want that!" Ethan answered for the group. "All of us."

Angus and Brixton nodded in quiet agreement.

"You've made the right choice by a landslide," the server pursed his lips. "Besides my chef, my partner, and myself, you youthful gentlemen will be the first to try it. It is…delightfully addictive," he shook his head with pride, taking the menus from the boys. With one fluid movement, he stuffed them back into place on the wrought-iron shelf behind the counter.

Ethan tapped his hands on the table, thinking of his new drums. "Our server must be the owner. We really should have asked his name…."

"I know," Brixton smiled. "We'll get it before we leave."

"Yeah…so I've been thinking, and to follow up with our discussion from a few hours ago," Angus played with his place setting, "we should enter the EmOpen next year, not this year."

Signaling to Brixton he'd begin the plea, Ethan addressed Angus. "We don't even know if they'll be having one next year! Plus, even if they do, the bands will have a whole year's time or more to position themselves for it compared with this year's, which will be a surprise to the majority of the bands. You heard Cas'—there's going to be a short time between announcement, entry, and close. Besides that, this time next year we'll be on the verge of parting ways for college. It'll be too hectic. And who knows where our minds will be at, then. This year's Open is our only REAL chance."

"Then we don't enter," Angus folded his napkin again.

"Why not? There's hardly any risk! No one will even recognize our band name when we enter, because it will be different than it is now," Ethan, by default of this argument, came to grips with the understanding that his own decision had just been made.

"Wait! You don't want to enter the competition with our current name, 'No More S'mores'?" Angus shook his head in silence. "As a side-note, it was cute for a couple weeks in

8th-grade, but that name has been holding us back for years. If you want to get serious about the band, I say we table the entry into the EmOpen and start by renaming ourselves."

"A new name is a given," Brixton jumped in. "That's already been discussed. It's a small detail."

"Picking a band name we all agree on is not a small detail," Angus argued, "and until you both admit that, this serious band discussion is anything but serious."

"Okay," Ethan acknowledged, "band naming is not an elementary task. However, whether we enter the EmOpen or not, we still need to rename ourselves, so the renaming is not in question. We all agree that 'No More S'mores' will soon be no more. We HAVEN'T all agreed not to enter the EmOpen."

"We haven't?" Angus looked at them both.

Brixton pulled the conversation out of overdrive, settling on an easier gear. "We've been playing together in our parents' garages for years. We've played at school, done a few very small gigs, but we've never fully challenged ourselves or really put ourselves out there."

"Wasn't that the point?" Angus asked. "We were sick of playing sports season after season, year after year, and we wanted to broaden our horizons. Playing has and always will be fun, not forced. The whole reason we picked up instruments was because we longed for an escape from structure."

Ethan cranked the gears in his mind to determine a few ways to take the conversation from here. Before he could set himself on a new path, he heard **"Hearts Like Ours" by The Naked And Famous** grace the room, and Brixton continued to hammer away at Angus's defenses.

"Don't you feel like there's something more to accomplish before we graduate? We've spent nearly all of our years together, we know each other like we know ourselves, and we share a love of music unparalleled by most. If we love the music so much, why not try to PLAY for a living? THAT would be the ultimate escape from structure. I'm not saying we're destined for fame or even inferring that we deserve it, but if we don't give this a shot we might always wonder." Brixton looked directly into Angus's eyes. "I don't want to be those old guys playing poker on the porch, talking about how we bowed out when we should have bet big. I want to be those old guys playing poker on the porch, talking about how we bet big when we could have easily bowed out...I want to be those old guys playing poker on the porch in vintage T-shirts with our new band name on it, who, after two or three scotches or gin and tonics or iced tomato juices or whatever the hell it is that old guys drink, aren't afraid to pick up their instruments and rock out, because those old guys still have it in them, and they always will have it in them as long as they're alive."

Angus unfolded his napkin, deliberating on Brixton's full-bodied statements.

Sensing he had hold of Angus, Brixton continued, "You're not just going to stop playing when you get to college, and neither am I or E. And, any band we might join in the future will NEVER have the history and chemistry we've already cultivated. Cas' is right, we have a RARE chemistry. You can't deny it. We anticipate one another. We support one another. We grow together."

Ethan studied Angus's face throughout Brixton's entire delivery. When Brixton was finished with his plea, he eyed Ethan to bring it home, and Ethan obliged.

"You're a huge part of this, obviously. And this is something that Brix and I really want. No one will know we're entering, unless we tell them. The fact that we haven't settled on a new name yet is actually a godsend. Unless our entry is accepted, no one will have any idea it's us. We can keep it a secret from everyone except Cas' if you want." Ethan's hands gripped the end of the counter, "I know it's crazy, but maybe we need crazy right now. I'm tired of going with the flow. I say we step out of line. Together."

Angus, silent and unreadable, looked at them blankly.

Brixton issued the threat, "If you won't get on board with this, we'll be forced to ask Timmy. He's the only other guy at Cypress that plays flawless lead guitar, has a deep singing voice, and fits the 'dark and handsome' descrip. New rumor has it he's been feuding with Vik and Miccah...but if we pull Timmy in, we can kiss the slightly wholesome edge we had goodbye."

"Oh. NO. There is no way in hell gothic Timmy is taking MY place on stage! The thought alone irritates me more than anything," Angus cracked his minutes of silence.

"So you're in?" Ethan pressed his hands into the counter, sensing the end of the battle.

"Yeah," Angus smiled at last, giving in to them, "but we need a second singer for when my voice taps out. That person also has to play bass. Don't forget we have no bass. And without bass, we don't stand a chance in the EmOpen."

"Alright," Brixton agreed, "it's not going to be the easiest of tasks, but we'll comb Felton and the surrounding areas for someone who doesn't kill our chemistry and that we all agree on."

"And," Angus set another bar, "I need the two of you to work on your backup vocals. Especially Brixton. No offense, E, but I think he could lead a few songs. I think he SHOULD lead a few songs, once he's more confident and...," Angus worried about vocalizing the last part, "he's able to open his eyes comfortably."

Brixton shifted in his seat.

"I didn't know he closed his eyes," Ethan looked at Brixton. "Since when?"

"Just when I sing...or when I'm playing and...certain...people are around," Brixton's nervous smile somehow flew under Ethan's radar.

"It's not our worst problem," Ethan assured Angus, "we'll work on it as a team. He'll practice and we'll watch him. When he's improved some, we'll set up a couple test shows in my backyard. Ki can invite some of her friends, just a couple for the first, maybe a dozen for the second, and then we'll increase the numbers as necessary."

Angus nodded.

"We can even assign my sister the role of Brix's eye-check," Ethan shrugged his shoulders. "I think she'd be game."

Brixton's gulp was quiet enough that neither Ethan nor Angus heard it.

"Alright," Angus grinned. "I'm into the idea of the backyard shows…it's dual purpose. Practice for Brix and practice for the group." Feeling Ethan's weighted glance, Angus tipped his head up slightly, "We all need improvements though, not just Brix. As a band, we must learn to self-evaluate AND solicit criticism from others."

"I'm in agreement on that," Brixton's mind had cleared itself of concern. "This has to be about more than practicing instruments, more than mastering songs. We have to identify and work on other things, too, like our band's image, what we stand for, what we're willing to do, and what we're not willing to do. If we don't have the answers to those questions now, someone else WILL fill in the answers for us later… and I don't want that. I've never wanted that. Our bond has to be strong enough so that no one else can get in, unless we INVITE them in. I don't want to bleed myself into this group, only to end up as another example of a failed band. I don't want to see our tireless efforts culminate in the finality of a hyperlink that leads to a story detailing where we went wrong. Some angry blogger or journalist, who never made it in the music business, snidely putting out our dirty laundry for the worldwide web to sniff, so he or she can go to bed with a little more self-worth knowing someone else took an irreversible nosedive, too."

"...So, I'm taking it you still read all those mags and sites?" Ethan smirked.

"Whenever I can," Brixton held a hand up, "and I get notifications via email and phone, too."

Angus laughed.

"Look," Brixton smiled, "we're either serious about this or we're not. If we're serious, we need to assume new roles. I've always been up on the industry—it's an obsession of mine I'll never shake. But it should be important for US, not just for me. We need to know who's out there doing what. We need to remember what worked in the past and why, and what hasn't worked in the past and why. We need to identify new trends, so we can either be a part of the movements or steer clear of them. We need to identify our competition. Not to trash them, but to make sure we're different, and we should try to befriend some other bands. We're musicians, and we should surround ourselves with musicians and with anyone else who inspires us."

"He's got a point," Angus's dark eyes softened along with his voice. "We have to think beyond practice. In my opinion—and final decision to you, E—Brix should officially hold the role of 'industry intel.' He's been doing it for years, and it's time we gave him credit for it. That, and song order. I think almost the whole world's in agreement that no one can stack 'em back to back like him. He assumes those roles and we leave those to him."

"Entirely in favor," Ethan's words echoed his enthusiasm. "For your role, Mr. Lyr, Brix and I are finally going to put you to the test like we've always wanted to," Ethan looked at Brixton, then back at Angus. "WRITE us some originals. BE the lyricist. We want you to. Cas' wants you to. And I think deep inside, you want to, too."

Angus grinned and Ethan and Brixton exchanged looks with one another.

"We want to hear the words," Ethan crossed his arms. "We want you to tell us."

"I'll write some originals IF, and only if, you agree to act as manager," Angus leaned back in his stool. "You've taken the role too lightly. You lay the heat when it's easy, but the second Brix or I get friction-y with one another, you take a step back. You need to make the final decisions. We need direction, and on occasion Brix and I need to be put in our place," he laughed. "Brixton more times than me," he whacked Brixton. "Besides those reasons and many more, Brix would never approve of me as manager, and I would never approve of him as manager; and, since Brix and I already have our new roles, and, since you were the link that connected the three of us to begin with, the management role can only fall to you."

Ethan inhaled, feeling the significance of his decision. "I'll do it. I'll manage us. I'll really do it this time. For real."

"AL-RIGHT!" Brixton let out a celebratory yell.

"All in," Angus turned to Ethan. "All in, THIS YEAR."

"The legendary EmOpen," Brixton issued his classic far-off gaze. "History in the making. Right here, right now."

In a fervor, Ethan tapped his hands on the counter. "I wouldn't have it any other way, you guys. I wouldn't enter with anyone else. I wouldn't push myself with anyone else. Failure be damned. We're comin' for you! I've wanted this SO bad I didn't even realize it." In triumph, he held his hand up, prompting Brixton and Angus to seal the deal with their secret handshake.

At the trio's course-altering decision to enter this year's EmOpen, The Hidden Meridian assumed a brighter ambiance. A sense of calm settled upon Ethan's shoulders. It whispered words of comfort, as if he and his friends were merely actors in a play, and the scenes were unfolding exactly as they should. **"Never Going Back Again–2004 Remastered Edition" by Fleetwood Mac** stirred the room in heartfelt fashion, and the boys discussed how the track was of the rarest class. The kind that allowed it to rise through the barriers of time, to be listened to and loved by multiple generations.

The animated waiter, who they already suspected to be the restaurant owner, returned even more exuberantly than before, and slid the drinks down the length of the counter. Each glass nearly touched the hands of its recipient. "And without further ado, my three new lads, I bring you the greatest pastry chef currently living. The Hidden Meridian's very own Noah!" He extended both hands up in the air, proudly introducing the youthful boy standing next to him.

"Jacques, just call me Jacques," the boy spoke warmly, in a French accent, similar to the waiter's. "Whether Noah or his ark existed is still up for debate, so we don't know if 'Noah' actually saved any animals or not."

The server quickly piped in, "Let's say he didn't exist, which is worst case because he did. SOMEONE has to make that name mean something. It might as well be YOU, since you're so passionate about saving animals."

Jacques smiled politely and released a small huff, "I think the crux of this whole matter is that you poured Gary a little too much of the good wine before he wrote that review."

"Gary LOVES that wine! It's a fine, fine, organic wine and I'd be doing the rest of the patrons a disservice if we didn't have it on hand year-round," the server retorted, unfazed by Jacques's comments. "You're Noah to me and to everyone else at The Hidden M...and I WILL NOT have it any other way," the server clasped his hands tightly in front of his waist. "I know you have a hard time with the loftiness of the introduction, but the accolades are those given to you by critics, not by me. I have people coming in here every day telling me they've changed their way of life because of you and your gentle ways. I have people writing to me on our social sites asking if we can ship your cakes halfway around the world. You're the star of this place, not me...if I don't see it as a burden and it's my place, you shouldn't either. You should enjoy the attention. It's for your artistry, after all. The guests love you...they LOVE your creations," he rubbed his hands together, "and I do, too."

"Calm down, Uncle Horace," Jacques replied with a detectable tenderness in his voice. "I am most happy working as your baker, even if I have to respond to the silly name of Noah."

"The name's an ideal fit. It really is. Not silly at all. You'll see," Horace boasted to the boys, contented once again. He slid the desserts, three coco'ranges, down the length of the counter in the same fashion as he had the drinks. Beckoned by Fredrique, Horace sped away to tend to another matter.

Jacques lingered to see their reactions.

Brixton, in a well-mannered fashion, placed his cloth napkin on his lap and took a tiny bite. A smile on his face, he tilted his head back and closed his eyes in gracious approval.

The pastry's sweet orange scent reminded Ethan of Maya's hair. His cheeks flushed at the thought, such an innocent connection, yet such a terrible time to blush. He could all but feel Jacques's confused expression. Without another moment's pause, he used his spoon to deliver a medicinal dose of the cake to his mouth. "SO, so good!" Ethan praised the chef, the delicate blend of flavors pulling his thoughts back from Maya's bronzed stomach.

Angus, never one to follow suit, took the entire mini-cake creation into his left hand and shoveled it between his lips.

"That's the way to do it," Jacques clapped his hands with a small chuckle.

"Let me introduce the animal." Ethan smirked, pointing, "This is Angus. He's Brixton, and I'm Ethan. We're delighted to have tasted first-hand the art of Noah."

"The honor was all mine, gentlemen," Jacques answered. "Hey, you wouldn't be THE Ethan I baked the cake for yesterday morning, would you?"

"That's me," Ethan smiled. "And that's how we ended up here today. The animal ate most of it and was craving more."

"I admit it," Angus held a hand up. "But you're to blame," he forced it back on Jacques. "Making a cake like that. I couldn't stop, and it wasn't even my birthday."

"We knew you'd be exceptional, but we didn't expect you to be so young," Brixton's emerald eyes took on a friendly nature to match his smile. "How did you learn to bake so well, and how old are you anyway?"

"I'm sixteen and three-quarters. Baking's not that hard if you love it like I do. It's mostly just a lot of trial and error. You guys are tasting the good stuff, but there's a lot of experiments that don't make it out of the kitchen, and for good reason," Jacques replied modestly.

Angus admired Jacques's accent. "You look more like eighteen or nineteen than you do sixteen and three-quarters," he couldn't help but speak his thoughts to him.

"The kitchen ages you," Jacques joked. "Must be all the heat...."

"...And he possesses a sense of humor, too," Brixton lifted his spoon to Jacques as if toasting to him in some way.

Angus nodded and pondered which question to ask Jacques next.

Ethan's mind froze his thoughts when he heard the start of **"Make It Easy, Under the Sea" by We Are Scientists**, and saw his phone light up with Maya's long-awaited text reply:

[Honest answer: no pranks (that I know of). Sorry if I made you uncomfortable earlier. I was trying to tell you I like you (much more than I'm supposed to). Guess that kills our friendship, but I had to come clean today. I promised Ki.]

Let loose, Maya's words bounced around like rubber marbles amidst the ice cubes in Ethan's brain. *More? Uncomfortable? Kills? ...her face...the bongos...my chair...the hug...her stomach...how?* He struggled to remember what he felt like prior to reading her text, so he could resume those thoughts and that conversation and his friends wouldn't notice his internal circus. *I need to read it again, alone. Maybe I should excuse myself to the restroom...*

The building pressure behind Ethan's forehead prompted him to rub his temples.

Angus, who had been speaking with Jacques and Brixton, quickly noticed the change in Ethan's demeanor. He pulled the phone from Ethan's hand while Ethan was still staring at the message. "Whoa. This is thickening nicely. Especially the 'much more' part," Angus passed the phone to Brixton with a double eyebrow raise.

"Ah! Told you!" Brixton placed a hand on Ethan's shoulder. "She likes you. Time to decide."

"Relationship issues?" Jacques lifted his shoulders in question.

"Pre-relationship issues," countered Angus. "Although I wouldn't count this one as an issue at all. More like a profoundly fortunate occurrence."

"I see," Jacques eyed Ethan's blank stare. "I have the misfortune of attending Parker. The only girls I see come here for my dessert, and nothing more."

"Ha!" Brixton chimed in, "they LITERALLY want your sugar."

"Can't blame 'em though—your desserts are mighty temptational," Angus wondered why the accent hadn't helped Jacques on the girl front.

When Jacques pointed at Ethan, the others took note of his confused state.

"So you guys really aren't pranking me?" Ethan asked sheepishly. "Swear to me in a way that I know, before I embarrass myself."

Angus nodded, picking up on where Ethan's mind might be. With one hand in the air, Angus pledged: "We swear to you, on the decision we just made a moment before Noah delivered his drug-like addictive dessert, that Brix and I are NOT pranking you. And, I personally swear that I think she likes you, and has for a while, and that you should text her back as soon as possible, before she comes to her senses and decides to crush on Brix or me, or on both of us at the same time." He grinned when Jacques laughed.

"Yes," Brixton secretly enjoyed Ethan's concern, "the reply. You have to reply. How do you want it to come across?"

Ethan blushed without words. Then he shook his head, laughing. The phrases from the text rushed about in his head like children running amok with glow sticks in the dark.

"Well," Jacques joined in, "is it possible for me to see the text? Do you trust me?"

With a single nod, Brixton handed the phone to him.

Ethan's cheeks flushed with conflicting emotions, "Maybe we should just make the rounds with my phone and have everyone in the restaurant chime in with advice. I'm sure Maya would want everyone to see it. It's not personal, after all...."

"Don't be a toad," Brixton scolded. "If he can make flour, chocolate, and oranges taste like that I think we should hear his advice."

"I second that," Angus agreed. "Let Jacques give us his opinion."

"Okay, okay," Ethan rearranged his hair nervously, "I'm sorry, Jacques. I'm freaked out about this, if you couldn't tell. Let's have it. I won't erupt again."

"Don't worry," Jacques's accent soothed the group, "I'll probably get a bit crazy if a girl says she likes me, too. I guess, since I don't know anything about her, other than your two friends seeming to think she's desirable, I'm left with just one important question—what do YOU think about her?"

"Huh?" Ethan's head spun in circles, first clockwise, then counterclockwise. "About Maya? What do I think?" He felt the words leave his mouth but barely heard them.

"Yeah, about Maya," Jacques hoped to relieve him, not frighten him. "Do you want her to remain a friend, or do you want to make her feverish?"

Three pairs of eyes centered on Ethan.

Welcoming the attention, yet feeling a little overwhelmed, Ethan admitted, "I just don't really know how I feel. This just…doesn't seem real. She's so much better than me…she's out of my league…like, wayyy so much, and maybe she's confused, and she's going to change her mind. Then, when that happens, what happens to me?"

"Nonsense. Forget the circumstances. Forget your fears. Those aren't important," Jacques boiled it down. "Let's dissect the text," he picked up Ethan's phone from the counter. "Maya confessed she has feelings for you. She attempted to tell you about those feelings but couldn't. Why? Because you're already friends, which she mentions here. Her feelings aren't new, but how long has she had them? We don't know for certain, but what we do know is that she's had them long enough for whoever Ki is to not only know, but also for Ki to make Maya promise to tell you. The words 'much' and 'more' were used in her reference to the liking. Those are heavy words. Do you or do you not like this girl?"

Brixton and Angus shared a pleased glance with one another.

Jacques slid Ethan's phone back across the counter toward his hands just as **"Edge of Seventeen" by Stevie Nicks** began to mesmerize everyone in The Hidden Meridian.

Ethan, feeling resolve, was about to answer Jacques when a long-legged, bright-haired, spider-like woman in knee-high cowboy boots and a short skirt dashed toward the counter with a sense of urgency, asking which of the boys was Noah. Angus was about to point to Jacques, when he dreadfully realized Jacques was pointing at him. Brixton flinched and Ethan covered his mouth. First, the woman's freshly painted face lit up with honest joy. Then that joy congealed into a goblin-like gel. It rushed into her eyes, boiling into a creepy, lustful stare.

Angus gasped as she approached him. He expected her to stop at a safe distance, but she quickly invaded his personal space, running her fake fingernails through his hair and motioning to her female accomplice to snap a picture with her phone.

"Make sure ya get a good one, Tina," she ordered her friend. "Take a couple if ya need to."

The others watched silently beside Angus, in disbelief at this woman's highly questionable behavior, which had not yet ceased. Swiveling Angus's stool toward her, she climbed onto his lap and popped her most canned pose. He held his hands up and out, so he wasn't touching her, and attempted to grin, which was difficult given his obvious frustration. When Tina gave the "thumbs up," the woman slid herself slowly down Angus's thighs, angling her head back sensually and kissing him on the cheek.

"I'm Dawn," she exclaimed, locking her hand onto his, "and I'd be lying miserably if I told you I wasn't praying for your eighteenth birthday. You've given me such hope for men... the taste of your food...the taste of your...chocolate. But, you're still a boy. A boy...," she rubbed her hands on the back of his neck. "A quiet boy. I haven't heard that accent. You haven't said a word. Oh, but you will one day. One day you'll be running this place. You'll be forced to talk. If I have it my way, this building will be remade into an ark and your name will be the most sought after, the greatest name in confections. And I'll have your picture, you'll have my affection. And I might be a food critic from Manhattan who has had a bit too much of your uncle's champagne, but I know in just over a year and a quarter you'll turn eighteen. And then I'll be back. And this will all be a bit different...you and I...and this deep, dark hair."

Angus shivered at the thought.

"Shhhh," she held a finger to his lips, "you don't have to say a word. Not now. Not necessary. They'll have to add another star for you. Five isn't nearly enough. You are six. Six stars."

Though Angus's eyes had doubled in size, he mustered a smile, hoping she might leave faster. He waved to her as she slowly walked away, swishing her hips in an exaggerated manner. Right before she reached the exit, she turned back to wink at him.

Jacques held his hand up until she was out the door and out of sight. Then he nodded to Angus.

"She should be ashamed of herself! MY GOD!" Angus's disgust

exploded from his lips. "That was…should we call the cops? Was any of that even legal?"

"Her thoughts weren't, that's for sure," Brixton cringed. "She was thinking beyond her words. I could see it clearly, especially before the cheek kiss, if you know what I'm getting at…."

"The first girl to sit in my lap was probably closer to my mom's age than she was to my age," Angus puckered his face in sheer annoyance. "I might throw up…and burn my clothes. She touched my mouth!"

"Swish with the kombucha," Ethan tried to stop laughing. "Get some on your lips. It'll cleanse you."

"See what I have to deal with?" Jacques quipped. "Most are not like that. If I had known, I wouldn't have pointed to you. I was trying to avoid a photo, that's all. I'm sorry she mauled you. I won't let anything like that happen again," Jacques held a hand up in promise. "Free dessert all week? Can we still be friends?"

"Yeah," Angus grinned, "but if I happen to see Dawn or Tina again, I'm making a beeline out of here. I don't care if it costs you a bad review."

"Understood and accepted without question," Jacques beamed. "This time, though, I have to give you credit. You were quite impressively up to the task! I would have screamed for my uncle the second she touched me. And she absolutely could not get enough of your hair between her fingers! I wouldn't be surprised if she pulled a strand out on the sly and plans to put it in that rhinestone locket she wore about her neck."

They all cracked up, including Angus, who rearranged his hair back into place in good sport.

Without further interruption, Brixton brought the conversation back around to Maya's text and the appropriate reply. "Ethan, you can't leave her dangling out there. Her feelings are exposed. Even if you're torn about it, write something nice back. Anything. Just respond before she changes her mind!"

"No! No! Don't do that!" Angus roared, grabbing the phone from Ethan's fumbling hands. "Okay, I don't know a ton about girls, but I do know they pick apart everything you say and do, especially what you write, since they can read it over and over again. That's happened to me before. So, think about it before you send something back—she could be staring at that damn message the rest of the night, trying to extract some ancient secret like a kid with a decoder ring."

"Right...right," Ethan mumbled softly, searching for the right answer.

"I've never been texted by a girl, but when it happens I plan to make the most of it," Jacques thought aloud. "I'll ask her what her favorite song is, and I'll tell her I'd like to sing it to her while feeding her some luscious raspberry cheesecake."

"Whoa Jacques!" Brixton exclaimed, "I'm liking the passion, which totally came out of nowhere, but I have a problem with you using the term 'luscious' to describe the cake and not the girl."

Brixton's comment prompted Ethan to crack a smile and return to his senses. "I think I just experienced my first faux freakout…this isn't a problem." Snapping his phone back from Angus, he tapped at the screen, pausing to look up at Brixton and Angus. "I'm not sharing my reply, so feel free to talk amongst yourselves."

Brixton eyed Angus, then engaged Jacques again to include him in the group. "Maya is Ethan's sister's friend. They're the same age and have known each other for a while. Ang and I kind of saw this coming," he grinned, fist bumping Angus.

"Don't gloat," Ethan spoke without looking up from his phone. "You don't know what I'm writing, remember?" He proceeded to tap at the screen like a madman, writing and deleting, writing and deleting.

"Regardless of what you do or don't write, we should probably get back there," Brixton's mind flooded with thoughts of Kila and how he'd respond to her if she ever confessed the words Maya had. *I'd tell her she can like me as much as she wants, as long as I'm allowed to feel the same way about her. I'd ask her if we could be alone as soon as possible. I'd play the secret playlist, the one I made for her that I'm constantly tweaking that's hidden from view. I'd take both her hands in mine. We'd drown in music. We'd drown in each other…*

"Is this is your ploy to rush back to your sweet Annabelle?" Angus teased.

"No," Brixton snapped back from his pointless daydream. "I've never even spoken with Anna until today."

"Doesn't mean you don't like her," Angus challenged, confidently.

Brixton rolled his eyes, thinking of Kila again. *The drowning... in music...in her...*

Ethan crossed his fingers under the counter, closed his eyes, and triggered his reply:

[I wasn't uncomfortable. I thought you were playing with me, that Brix and Ang put you up to something. Since our friendship is dead, and you still owe me something for my chair, take me as your boyfriend. Warning: proceed at your own risk. (My lips are sealed.)]

"Eyes-closed text reply!" Brixton stood up, pointing. "He is DIALED in! I don't care what you say, E. You basically read us the reply with that tell-all tactic."

"From ice to boil," Angus joined in the group tease. "It's on tonight. This is imminent. I wish I could watch," Angus raised his eyebrows in upgraded three-round fashion.

"You're gross," Brixton laughed. "Get rid of Reese and get ahold of yourself."

"In process," Angus looked at his own phone, swiping away and grinning.

"Sounds like you guys juggle a lot of drama," Jacques laughed. "I kind of like it."

"Come over tonight! They'll be plenty of it. And to be frank, we could use some help," Ethan put his phone in his pocket. "My parents are away, and we're all just going to crash there."

"Really? Sounds like fun—but I'm not off until ten," Jacques looked at his watch. "Will you guys still be hanging out?"

"Are you even serious with that last question? Did you hear him say his parents are gone? It's a Friday night. There are girls over. We'll be up late, Jacques—come over!" Angus ordered.

"Alright—I'm in. Where is it?" Jacques asked.

Brixton texted the address to Jacques.

When Ethan tried to pay their bill, Jacques wouldn't let him. "Late birthday present, partial courtesy of Dawn and Tina. I'll see you later," he waved, escaping into the kitchen, donning his chef's hat, and wearing a new smile.

"He has no idea what he's in for," Ethan smirked as they began the trek back to his house.

The air was much cooler on the return walk, and the boys were thankful they had taken their sweatshirts along with them. There was hardly any traffic on the street, just the low hum of streetlights and the occasional biker whizzing by.

Brixton, missing the music from the restaurant, called up his "Wishful Wandering" playlist on his phone, opting for a shuffled order. When **"Shot At The Night" by The Killers** played first, he felt it fateful, his thoughts ever circling around Kila. *Is it really considered drowning if it's willful and you enjoy it? If it isn't, I couldn't drown in her. I'd have to call it something else...immersion? I want to see her music again, hear her laughter, and be the person she always comes to for anything and everything. I want her to understand WHY and* *not hate me for it. I want it to mean more...and I want her to know I'd never look elsewhere, if she were to look to me...*

Angus took note of Brixton's contemplative face and wondered whether he was thinking of Kila or Anna. He tried to figure it out. "Ki liked your singing even more than Anna did. Kind of a shocker, no?"

Burying his smile, Brixton avoided the trap with a question of his own, "How could you possibly know what either of them were thinking? Kiki rarely confides in you, and you barely know Anna."

"Easy you two," Ethan warned. "I don't want to hear the dreaded R-name, so if that's where this nugget of tension is headed, you both better remember what we discussed earlier."

"I wasn't headed there at all," Angus explained to Ethan. "I was actually headed in the opposite direction. I want to know where his thoughts are at. See, Brix and I always knew Maya wasn't available, but now I'm wondering about the availability of Ki and Anna."

"My thoughts are inside my mind. I've kept them there for a reason," Brixton smirked. "As far as Anna and Kiki, I see no limits," he felt his mouth tighten with his last two words. "But I would advise against starting something new before you have ended your present, um, circumstance."

"Understood," Angus grinned. "I had no plans. I was just curious about yours."

Brixton squinted, doubting the truth in Angus's words. *Not*

Kiki. Not Kiki. Please don't pick Kiki.

"In case anyone wants to know MY thoughts, I'd like my sister to remain single." Ethan worried when neither Brixton nor Angus issued a reply.

"Uncle Pete will be happy about our band plans," Angus changed the subject to Brixton's relief.

"I figured as much," Ethan replied. "That guy can rock out! Remember when your mom used to have him play at your birthday parties when we were little? That was the MOST intense version of 'Row, Row, Row Your Boat' I've ever heard!"

"You should totally have him teach us that version. I mean, who doesn't know and love that golden oldie? Brilliantly re-done," Brixton gushed. "It has enough potential to be a sick cover in our lineup. And no one would ever expect it. We could blend into it and people would sing along. You know they would."

Ethan watched as that wide-eyed look swept over Brixton's face, accompanied by his destiny-driven smile. Angus's white teeth shone in the moonlight between his crimson lips. At this union of thought, Ethan realized his music dreams were no longer just his own. They were the band's dreams, too. After only one euphoric moment, he remembered that Maya hadn't responded to his last message. He fussed silently.

"You two sure know how to lay it on thick." Angus grinned, "Since when have you two been angling to get me in on the EmOpen? Was Cas' in on it?"

"Cas' was NOT in on it. We didn't hear about it until you did. After that, there may or may not have been some angling between E and me," Brixton skated away from further explanation. "Speaking of laying it on thick, let's get E thick for Maya," he pointed to a street sign, conveying they were only a block away from the house.

"Get me thick?" Ethan broke free from his worry, "Let's just make sure we're still a rock band, and not a boy band. The industry's already maxed out in that department, and I have no desire to wax my brows, my legs, and any other part of me that makes me feel masculine."

Angus snickered, "Band Rule #1: No manscaping. I want to see bushy brows, furry legs, and a forest around your—"

Ethan covered Angus's mouth to cut him off, the three of them laughing so hard their stomachs hurt.

"Don't say it," Ethan warned, removing his hand. "Ugh!" he wiped his fingers on his jeans. "Your mouth was wet."

"Believe it or not, the mouth is home to our good friend saliva," Angus pulled his hood up to keep the breeze from blowing his hair in his face. "On to the thickness. Brix, help me out."

Before Ethan could protest, Angus and Brixton fixed his clothes and adjusted his hair.

"Is this really necessary?" Ethan fought with words, despite his knowing the complaints wouldn't free him. "I'm just going back to the house to talk or something. Besides, she hasn't even replied to my reply."

"Reply, schmeply, it's the 'or something' that we're prepping you for, E...," Angus reminded him. "Did she or did she not throw her arms around you a few hours ago?"

"You told him?" Ethan eyed Brixton.

"I had to! He had to know the situation," Brixton defended his decision to release the juicy news. "You haven't talked about it since...what were you thinking when it happened?"

"I don't know...," Ethan evaded the question. "I thought you guys were pranking me! I guess I wasn't expecting it."

Angus pressed, "Wasn't expecting it like a hair in your food, or wasn't expecting it like a winning lotto ticket?"

"Those are two very opposite sides of the spectrum, Ang," Ethan huffed.

"Yeah," Angus nodded proudly. "That was kind of the point."

"It was the lotto ticket," Brixton answered for Ethan, "wasn't it?" he asked rhetorically. "It was, because E would have said the hair right away otherwise." He was pleased with himself. "That and the eyes-closed text reply make it a certainty. Now, we just need to find a non-sketchy way to get the two of them in the dark."

·"Done!" Angus remembered, "I actually brought a movie. I forgot to tell you guys."

"Is it romantic?" Ethan asked.

Brixton looked at Angus.

"Of course NOT!" Angus grinned widely. "It's *Camp Fright*."

"*Camp Fright!*" Ethan frowned, "All the reviewers claimed they had nightmares for weeks! I swear your last movie, *Bedroom Beasts,* scared my sister to her core. She's still afraid to sleep in the dark. She has a night-light now."

"Yeah, that one was pretty bad," Brixton played mediator. "Even I was a little scared. Maybe we can wait to watch it until the girls go to bed."

"After they go to bed?" Ethan raised his shoulders. "I don't even know if Maya sleeps! I stay up pretty late, and most times she outlasts me. Last weekend I stayed up until 4 a.m. When I finally sauntered off to bed, she was still reading in the living room."

"A scary movie will make things easier for you," Angus encouraged the idea. "Trust me. She'll be scared. She'll get closer. I think it'll work."

Brixton thought about Angus's words. *I must sit next to Kiki.*

"Brix, back me up," Angus felt confident he'd win this vote.

"Fully backed, Angus," Brixton cast his unlikely approval. "We go the scary movie route."

"Because he likes her," Angus couldn't tease Ethan enough. There wasn't usually anything to tease him about, and Angus took full advantage of the situation. "Not only does he like her today, but he's liked her for a while. I can recall more than a few times when you didn't stay out late with us 'cause you wanted to be home at a certain time, when Maya just hap-pened to be sleeping over."

"Yeah," Brixton joined in the harmless taunt, "and we all know Claire never gave you a curfew!"

Angus high-fived Brixton.

Ethan laughed but wouldn't affirm their guesses. They were now in his driveway. As they strode through the backyard, they heard a rustle in the trees. Something leapt out from the bushes, and the three boys jumped backwards in unison.

"Peaches!" Ethan greeted her furry face, "We forgot to let you back in...."

In purest joy, the large charcoal-colored Great Dane ran circles around the boys. She pushed her grass-speckled head into Ethan's hand, then offered her full attention to Brixton. Leaning on her hind legs, she patiently waited for his affection. Brixton pet her from her ears to her snout. She wagged her tail in devotion, looking at Ethan with her great glassy eyes as though she were thanking him for bringing Brixton back to the house.

"Looks like you're in for it tonight, too," Angus whispered to Brixton. "Maybe she coordinated with Maya."

Flashing a few canines, Peaches turned her snout toward Angus and let out a low, threatening growl.

"Watch it," Ethan warned. "She's just as sensitive as the rest of us."

The boys exchanged last-minute nods and whispers before walking into a quiet kitchen and equally quiet living room. Annabelle and Kila, stretched out on the area rug, lay on their stomachs amidst a heap of science and fashion magazines. Maya, dressed in a Kelly-green sweatshirt, sat curled up on the smaller of the two couches with a book and a blanket, her fingers combing her hair slowly as she read. Angus and Brixton studied the girls on the floor, while Ethan's body thought about moving closer to the couch. His eyes traced the soft caramel contours of Maya's face, then lingered on the shape of her shiny, plump lips.

Brixton watched the bottoms of Kila's bare feet, which seemed to slowly escape from the edge of her bright blue corduroys. "You're in a trance, Kiki," Brixton couldn't help but address her by that name. He loved the sound of it; he knew she liked it, too, and his eyes caught hold of hers just as her smile took form.

Maya, at the sound of Brixton's voice, mechanically slid her bookmark into place. Sensing Ethan's presence, her mind morphed from bored to ballistic and targeted his light eyes. The sound of everyone else fell away. She never heard Kila's reply. She never saw Angus steal the magazine from Kila's grip, nor the gusto with which Brixton returned it to her. Without taking her eyes off Ethan, Maya closed her book and stood up, not knowing why.

Ethan swallowed a mixture of nerves and anticipation. *It's not a prank. This is really happening.* His nose could almost smell the sweet orange of Maya's hair. He noticed every blink of his eyes, taken more and more by her each time his lids opened and he confirmed her line of sight. Anna spoke to him. Angus and Brixton laughed with Kila, but it was all static. Nothing more. All static, except Maya. Nothing, except Maya. Maya and more Maya, in his eyes and in his thoughts.

When she left the room he followed, leaving the others behind without a single word or gesture.

"Oh my gosh…this is…oh my gosh," Kila breathed the words out, rustling through the multitude of magazines on the floor. "Where is it? Anna, help me," she whispered through nervous laughter, "my phone. Hurry! I need it. WE need it!"

Anna tossed magazines to and fro. Brixton joined in the hunt, willing to do whatever it took to earn some of Kila's gratitude. The three continued to flip issues about, pushing them to one side and creating an open space. After what seemed like too long, Kila stood and looked from the coffee table to the larger L-shaped couch.

She huffed.

"If I find it, can I grab it?" Angus asked, his crimson smile surfacing.

"I don't see why not," Anna laughed, sensing the invisible drops of flirtatious precipitation falling throughout the room.

"DON'T even think about it," Brixton snapped his body upright. "Kiki, it's in your back pocket," he glared at Angus.

"What?" Angus mouthed to Brixton through his recently retracted grin.

"You know what," Brixton mouthed back without a trace of forgiveness.

"Oh…," Kila, miserably attempting to hide her smile, pulled the phone from the back pocket of her corduroys. "Brix, I need you," she whispered, motioning him closer. "Come here. We don't have much time."

If only in another context! The tip of Brixton's tongue felt as if it had been glued to the back of his bottom teeth. *The things I could tell this girl. I'll explode if she ever touches me. Explode. Dead. Dead before I could even enjoy it.* His feet tingled in his shoes as he walked towards her.

"Pick a good one!" Anna begged Brixton. She turned toward Angus to fill him in. "Ki had a feeling Maya might run off to the library, so we're going to play music in there to set the right tone for My and E…and hopefully they'll…."

"…kiss," Angus's dark eyes flashed with a hint of romance Anna hadn't expected.

"You haven't, have you?" Anna whispered to him softly.

Angus shook his head "no."

"I won't tell," she promised, although he hadn't asked her to.

"Have you?" he felt it only fair to whisper back.

"Yes," Anna whispered, hoping her laugh wasn't loud enough for Brixton and Kila to hear.

"Who?" Angus didn't know if she would tell, but he was curious.

"Long time ago. 8th-grade. Timmy…," Anna's fingers touched her smile. "Strange, right? Nice kisser, though…."

"More than once?" Angus liked hearing her secrets enough to keep up with the whispering. "Did he smother your lips with gothic caress?"

"No to the first…yes to the second," Anna recalled giggling, this time loud enough to catch Brixton's attention.

That's ONE flirty laugh. Maybe Anna and Angus will pair up, and I won't have to worry about him chasing Kiki. Caught up in his thoughts, Brixton touched one of his hands to Kila's upper arm.

"What do you think?" Kila's concern assaulted him. "We have to hurry!"

Brixton felt Kila's smooth skin under his hand, and his eyebrows rose when he came to the realization she hadn't shrugged him off. He took a step closer and looked at her phone, the words he needed somehow rushing from his lips. "No, no, it can't be THAT song. It has to have that vibe…that vibe that makes you so unbalanced on the inside, you have to reach outside yourself for that person, and only that person. To the point you can't wait anymore for it. To the point you almost start shaking."

"Yes," Kila bit her bottom lip, "I think I know where you're going. I think I know what you mean. I mean…what we need." She inhaled as she scrolled through another one of her playlists. "THIS. This should do it. You know how Maya can't resist the throwbacks. It's one of her faves, which should help. What do you think?" she held her thumb under the song, crossing two of the fingers on her right hand.

"Yeeeeaaahhhh, Kiki. I LOVE it. Play that," Brixton's mind felt like it had been shrunk into the size of a tiny pellet, which had been thrust into the tank of a hungry goldfish. *I've seen her account again, even though I don't have access to it. I just saw her music…and she could not have picked a better song. So RIGHT. Everything about her is right. Classic early '90s. God…* His hand slid down her arm to her elbow, his heart leaping at the sight of her hopeful eyes.

"Alright. It's about to play," Kila tapped the song. "It's on!" She grinned as **"You Want This" by Janet Jackson** danced its way from the library, down the hallway, and into their ears. "You think this will work?"

"Yeah," Brixton high-fived Kila. "I'd make out to this easily. All night long."

When Anna gasped at Brixton's words, Angus nudged her and whispered, "Guaranteed my boy is a better kisser than Timmy. Guaranteed."

Anna shushed him.

A bit hopeful and a pinch jealous of Maya and Ethan's current predicament, Angus, Anna, Brixton, and Kila conversed in the midst of their own budding frictions. At first they agreed to wait in the living room until Ethan and Maya returned. Then they amended the plan to wait only until the end of the song before letting Angus loose for reconnaissance.

* * * * *

In a bit of a trance, Ethan found himself in the library. Maya paced around the bookshelves and he shadowed her, about three paces behind, staring at the green hood of her sweatshirt. His hands numbed at the thought of touching her and it meaning something more than friendship. His mind ordered words and phrases in his head, replies on deck should she speak first. The even pacing helped him focus. He counted laps. He counted steps. Seventy strides later, he felt calm, his numbness faded, and his speech expressed itself naturally.

"Talk to me," he sensed her hesitation.

"How serious were you in your last text?" she kept walking.

"How serious were you in yours?" Ethan laughed a little, noticing the music for the first time. *My sister…or Brixton…or both. They are more dangerous together.*

Maya's heart fluttered. She slowed down on her fifth lap, near the desk that held their unfinished Jenga game. She remembered how Ethan looked while playing last Sunday. How she wanted to touch his hands every time he wrapped them around his mug to sip his coffee, how she wanted to kiss his forehead every time he studied the tower to pick his next piece, how she wished she could have found a way to record his laugh on her phone without him knowing.

"Want to play?" Ethan stopped a respectable distance beside her.

"No, not now…," Maya felt the pressure build inside her body. She looked at his hair.

"Want to play…something else?" he touched a hand to the back of his head.

She nodded without a verbal reply, her hands nervously clasping the top of the chair behind her.

"May I move closer?" he pulled his top lip into his mouth, waiting for her next signal.

Maya nodded a second time, watching his shoulders rise and fall with his heavy breaths.

He took a step towards her. They were close enough to embrace, but he fought the urge to reach for her. His hands remained pinned to his sides, and he looked at her eyes with a yearning new to him. "Your turn."

She loved his simple game, jumping right into her play. "May I touch your hair?" she looked at his lips, praying he'd say "yes."

He nodded, closing his eyes once he felt the calming sensation of her fingers in his hair.

The strands, far softer than she had imagined, tickled the spaces between her fingers. Starting at the top of his head, she combed all the hair down into his face. Then she rustled the sections all out of place, her heart pounding with the beat of the song when she saw that his eyes were still closed.

"Your turn," she heard her own exhale as her fingers pulled away from his face.

Ethan wanted her hands on him again. He didn't know his hair could feel such a way, and he likened Maya's touch to the wonder of starlight. "May I...," he watched her lips, the way they opened and closed as he reached for her caramel-colored cheeks.

She nodded, running her hands up his neck and right back into his chocolatey hair. Every moment his lips neared hers felt like an eternity. He leaned in so gradually it pained him, his world reinvented the instant his lips pressed against hers.

"Mmmm," Ethan knew he shouldn't be talking, but the sounds tumbled out. "Ooh," he grinned, thrilled by the taste of her jelly lips. *Raspberries...* He traced the outline of her sides to keep his noises at bay, but they found a way out from his mind through his lips. "Mmm...Mayyy-AHhh."

She giggled at his funny, breathy noises but kept her lips moving. "You're so much better than you think you are," she spoke against his mouth, reminding herself she was kissing Ethan Lorens every time her lips crashed against his. "I am miserably attracted to you and your geekiness...you knew, didn't you? You must have...."

"No," he gripped her lower back, pulling her into him. "I always liked the sight of you in my deckchair, in my house, and...everywhere else I ever saw you," he pressed his lips into hers, letting them linger long enough to feel a few of her exhales. His nose grazed hers before their smiles collided. "I want more," he kissed her mouth in rapid succession. "Come on. Stop laughing at me."

She pulled away from his lips and pressed her face into his shoulder.

"What happened?" he felt her cling to him. "Did I say too much? Am I really bad at it?" He rubbed her back in panic.

"No," Maya whispered. "You're incredible…it's Angus."

"What about him?" Ethan hardened.

"He's in the doorway," she whispered, letting out a nervous giggle.

"Oh," he kissed her dark hair in relief then rotated towards the door.

Maya's face remained hidden against his shirt.

"Remind me why we're friends again," Ethan eyed Angus. "I seem to be having some difficulty with that right now."

"Many reasons, not just one," Angus stood tall, crossing his arms. "However, the most relevant right now: without my encouragement, that might not have happened."

"So, you find yourself entitled to watch anything I do that you feel, in some way, responsible for?" Ethan shook his head, rubbing Maya's back some more, "I have a problem with that, and I think you would, too, had this been the other way around."

"Apologies," Angus amended. "I came in to invite you both to watch the movie, but found myself instead caught up watching yours."

"Alright. We'll be in soon." Ethan shook his head, "I'd like the next scene not to involve you."

"I'm leaving...but, you both look good together. Really good together," Angus grinned. "I mean it. You should...get back to it."

"Thanks Angus," Maya composed herself enough to turn toward the doorway, smiling.

Angus gripped the edge of the door, moving it back and forth with his hands as he stood in place.

"Ang...," Ethan hinted.

"I'm gone," Angus moved from sight.

"Keep it that way till we come in there," Ethan shouted at the empty doorway.

Maya, not upset to be left alone with Ethan, moved her hair to one shoulder and applied a fresh coat of raspberry gloss.

Ethan worried the interruption may have reverted his relationship with Maya back to the way it was before their kiss. "Are you gearing up for the movie?" he touched his hands together awkwardly.

"No," she leaned into him, "I'm gearing up for our next scene."

She laughed at his pleased glance. Then, she laughed against his mouth, feeling his hands on her face and loving every moment of it.

"I'd be perfectly happy if this was the only movie I ever saw," he rotated his kissing from her lips to the spot above her lips.

"That tickles," she wiggled her face.

He took the opportunity to kiss her cheeks and her chin. "Why haven't we done this before?"

"I don't know…but, we should try our best to make up for all the lost time," she playfully blew air into his open mouth.

"I'm down," his lips stretched towards hers. "You taste so good. You are so good. So brainy. So beautiful. So kind. You…never laughed at how terrible my drumming was when I first started," he rubbed his nose against hers, touching his lips to hers at every opportunity.

"…It was never bad," she pressed her fingers into the back of his neck. "You always moved me."

"Yeah well…," Ethan debated whether or not to tell her what he was thinking while he ran his finger down the slope of her nose. "…You were always my muse," he pulled his upper lip into his mouth when her warm eyes looked into his. Worried his comment might have been too thick too soon, he gulped.

Taken by his sweet confession, Maya's heart swelled. She

kissed him like she had always wanted to, with the sole intention of making him feel loved. His shoulders in her hands, she kissed his mouth, washing her innocent adoration over his soul.

"Thank you," he opened his eyes.

She almost laughed but held it in, instead using the time to get a better look at his eyes.

Ethan shook his head, "I guess that wasn't the suavest thing I could have said."

"I don't want you to be suave," she touched his cheeks. "I want you to be you," she softly bumped her nose into his. "And thank you, too."

He touched her hair with both hands, feeling its fullness. "I guess we should go back, even though I really, really don't want to."

"I know," she rolled her face into his, kissing his left cheek over and over and thinking of things she knew she probably shouldn't. "You better not act like this never happened after the real movie is over."

His hands touched hers for the first time and his gray-blue eyes were as serious as his voice when he said, "I will never act like this never happened."

They left the library hand in hand.

"Good…'cause I have other ideas for us, and something else

that I have to tell you," she looked at the wall in the hallway before gazing in his eyes again.

"I also have some ideas," his half-smile made her swoon.

"Do any of them lead to taking advantage of your parents' absence?" Maya's eyes pulsed at the thought.

"Yes…actually, all of them do," his once inescapable shyness slipped into playful desire.

"Ummmm," Maya stopped walking. "Hold on."

Ethan remained silent and attentive.

"It's just…that…if you're going to tempt me like that, can I at least have another before the movie?" she closed her eyes before she finished. "I mean, it could be hours before we get to again…and…."

"My…you can have as many as you want," he came in quick. Somehow, each kiss felt better than the last, and this time her hands in his hair drove him wild.

The kissing continued for longer than either had planned.

He pulled his lips from Maya's only when he saw Anna making her way through the hallway.

"Sor-ry guys," Anna blushed hard, looking at her toes as she sped past them.

"Can we sit together?" Maya whispered in Ethan's ear as they neared the living room.

"Yeah," his hand moved to her lower back. "I'm not watching it, otherwise."

Maya felt Ethan's thumb press into the bottom of her spine. The rest of his fingers wrapped around her side, and she already longed for the end of a movie that hadn't yet begun.

Kila appeared in the doorway, reaching for her friend. From the guilty look on his sister's face, Ethan correctly gathered Angus hadn't kept his findings to himself.

"First kiss," Kila whispered into Maya's ear. "Both parts?" she asked hopefully, pulling Maya away from her brother.

Ethan couldn't hear the exchange, but he saw Maya shake her head "no" and hold up her index finger.

"I didn't expect to see you so soon," Brixton addressed Ethan's entry. "We were beginning to wonder where you two had run off to, but Angus let us know you were lip-locked in the library so we figured we'd let you have your fun."

"How tactful of you," Ethan eyed him.

"Hey," Brixton winked with his reply. "I'm always here for you, E."

They shared a light laugh.

When Anna returned, Angus scanned the living room, "OKAY! Now that everyone's here again," he raised his eyebrows a few times, obnoxiously pointing to Ethan and then to Maya, "WHO is daring enough to watch *Camp Fright* with me?" He cast the bait with the vigor of a star actor.

"I hoped that might be what you were hiding," Anna bit the line, bouncing in her seat. "Count.me.in!"

Kila peered at Angus. "Just how frightful is it?" she asked, knowing full well he would dilute the truth and hint that the recent reviewers couldn't handle a dash of scary sauce.

"It's not going to be that bad," Angus strung seven ambiguous words together and chased them with a grin.

Kila reconsidered. *Hell, even if it is "that" bad, if I can score a seat next to Angus, it will be WELL worth any number of sleepless nights.*

"Why don't we just watch it later?" Brixton assumed the protective role since Ethan was preoccupied. "We have all weekend. We could even watch it in the morning, so it's less, well, frightening."

"No, it's alright," Kila realized if they delayed the movie, it would also delay her chances of sitting next to Angus. "I can handle it, Brix," Kila assured him. "Load it up. If I start to panic, I'll leave at the crazy parts."

"That's my girl," Angus grinned at Kila as he rushed past her to dim the lights.

Brixton turned to Kila to gauge her reaction to the possessive comment, but she was staring at the L-shaped couch, adjusting her long T-shirt over her corduroys. Annabelle, bubbling with excitement, organized the magazines, which still lay in a mess on the floor. She stacked them by category, then moved the short towers to the smaller of the two coffee tables.

There was that brief moment of awkwardness in the dark when the boys didn't know who should sit where. They looked back and forth at one another, without talking or pointing, in an attempt to assign places. Angus, making the first move, athletically leapt over the back of the couch, wedging himself smack between Kila and Annabelle. The girls looked at each other with amused glances behind his dark hair, Kila inwardly much more pleased than she had let on. The right side of her body, where the edges of her silhouette skimmed his, felt electric. She closed her eyes, escaping back to her dream from yesterday afternoon. If she had just fallen asleep a mere fifteen minutes earlier, she might have seen how it ended.

"Wow, that maneuver was entirely unexpected. And you usually try to escape the spotlight," Brixton teased Angus, who grinned indulgently at his remark. Shifting one of the cushions, Brixton fell into the spot on the other side of Kila next to the armrest, purposefully leaving no available space on the L-shaped couch.

Maya was pleased by this play, and she tugged Ethan towards the loveseat. He showed zero resistance. Reaching his hands toward the back of the couch, he stretched his arms wide, casting an ivory quilted blanket to catch Maya inside. She snuggled into his shoulder without needing any additional prompts, and he wrapped both of his arms around her. Warmth enveloped his senses, and his mind was quickly consumed by thoughts of what might happen later.

Annabelle sat strangely silent, peering every so often around Angus and Kila to steal a longing look at Brixton. *If only there were a way to make Angus and Brixton trade places*, she thought to herself. *Why does he have to look like that ALL THE TIME? He should be required to take breaks, and cycle in some bad days amongst the good.*

During the previews, Kila gradually shifted her weight towards Angus to see if he would get the hint. He pushed back half-heartedly, but he was too busy texting someone to be sincere about it. Kila stole a look at his phone to confirm the textee was Reese. *Ugh! She doesn't even like him*, Kila complained to herself. *Why, oh why, did I have to fall for someone who's in love with a vicious airhead? WHY!* She demanded, as if someone, other than herself, could respond to her internal bickering. *I blew it when he touched my arms earlier in the kitchen and I didn't respond in kind...*

On Kila's other side, Brixton remained petrified in place. Unable to make a move, his eyes watched Kila and not the screen. Every time her body shifted next to him, he thought about how he had missed her. *This was my chance. Now that she's right here, she seems farther away than before.* His fingers bent when he saw her look at Angus again.

While the opening credits were lackluster, the first few minutes were riveting. Every so often, Kila shook between Angus and Brixton. The third time she shook, Angus set his phone down and placed a hand on her knee. Kila, far too frightened by the sight of the serial killer onscreen, hadn't noticed Angus's hand. Brixton, however, had. He also caught Angus look at her in ways that made his veins sizzle. Three more minutes into the movie with Kila still unaware of Angus's hand, they all heard an unusual noise.

"Oh my god!" Kila latched onto Brixton's forearm.

When Brixton's other hand touched her arm, her knees sprung into his abdomen. Angus's hand fell away without mention or acknowledgement. Shaking in waves, Kila gripped Brixton's shoulders, hiding her face in his neck. The song **"Young Legends" by Sleigh Bells** began to play just as the camera panned from one tent of sleeping campers to the next.

WHY was I ever rallying AGAINST the scary movie? Brixton savored Kila's attention. As she pushed further into him, he wrapped both arms snugly around her shoulders. "Kiki—it's alright!" He laughed with his nose in her fresh-scented hair, rocking her back and forth, "It's just some silly actors with a ton of professional makeup and special effects." *Is she really on top of me?!*

"I'm sorry," Kila's hot breath on his neck caused him to shudder. "Am I squishing you?"

"No. It's okay. I have you. Don't worry," he rocked her back and forth again, treasuring the feeling.

With a clenched jaw, Angus eyed Brixton's unusually toothy grin. Annabelle kicked Angus in the shin to thaw the tension in the room. At the sound of his laugh, Kila lifted her head from Brixton's shoulder to take in Angus's unforgettable lips. He winked at her, and she hid her face behind Brixton's, experiencing a mix of jealousy and relief when Angus looked down at his phone.

"Your singing...the Copeland song," Kila shook in Brixton's arms. "I don't believe what you said."

"About what?" he spoke into her hair only loud enough for her to hear.

"That it was, like, a fluke...," the harsh, gripping sounds onscreen kept her shaking in his arms. "You sang The Cinema just the same...so per-fect I could barely distinguish it from the r-rrreal vo-ho-cals."

"Nah, I think you were just happy that day...you loved jumping in the leaves," he held her a little tighter, wishing his lips could pass through the silky chocolate curtain of her hair and show her how he really felt. *I need to tell her. She's not going to stay in my lap all night. I mean, I'd like her to, but this is merely a result of the movie plot. Not how she feels about me. Did she notice Angus's hand and not care, or did she not notice his hand because she was scared? Ugh...this is excruciating...*

"I was happy...we used to have fun, or, maybe it was just me," she pressed her fingertips into his back, leaning her head on his shoulder. "I...don't know what happened to us...but I still don't believe you about the singing...," Kila gasped when she heard another one of the serial killer's victims scream. The high-pitched desperation in the actress's voice sent chills up her spine.

"Would it be alright if we talked tonight?" Brixton pressed his face into her hair and felt her ear on the other side. "You did promise me a goodnight to make up for last night...," his words were so soft he couldn't hear them.

"I remember…," she blinked against the soft fibers of his shirt. "We can talk…if…you don't disappear," she closed her eyes tight, fearing for the killer's next victim.

"I'm not going anywhere…Kiki…," Brixton swallowed the growing lump in his throat and held her closer. *I hurt her… how could I have done that? What nonsense I gave in to. I'll come clean after the movie. I'll put it all out there, and she can know. She can judge me or forgive me. We can resume our friendship or part ways, our hearts never to cross paths again. But at least she'll know. I owe her that…*

As the time passed, Angus's jealousy grew. While keeping up with Reese's unending texts, he wondered why Kila had landed in Brixton's lap, and what poetry Brixton might have whispered in her ears to keep her there. Every so often, Angus looked to Anna and smiled, recalling the look on her face when she spoke of Timmy's secret kiss. Like a solar flare in his heart, he ached for his own first kiss. He remembered the euphoric look on his older brother's face when he'd confided he had had his first. Hunter claimed it was impossible to describe the feeling, later touting kissing to be better than anything else, even all the things that came afterwards in the relationship.

That was seven years ago, but it didn't seem like it. Angus thought of that conversation daily, at first wishing Reese's lips would be his first, and now wishing only for the feeling. The girl he imagined on the other side of his lips hadn't taken shape yet. He wondered who she would be. He wondered if he already knew her, or if maybe he would meet her this summer. Without the certainty of her face, he longed for her just the same, just the same as he longed for his first kiss.

When the unidentified noise grew louder, Angus jumped at the opportunity to pause the movie. To his suspicion, the sound wasn't coming from the speakers. It was coming from outside. Ethan prepared to stand up, when Brixton motioned for him to remain seated. With Kila beside him, Brixton walked slowly over to the narrow window by the door to investigate the sound. The others watched from the couch, pretending they weren't as startled as Kila.

"Noah's here!" Brixton announced, unlocking the door.

Kila looked at Brixton curiously. *I couldn't have heard that right.*

"Well, hello again," Jacques entered, navy boxes in hand.

Kila stared at Jacques in awe, half wondering if he was real. She looked back at Annabelle, to relay something with her eyes that Ethan did not understand.

"What'd you bring? Oh baby! TELL me its more coco'range!" Brixton pleaded.

"Nope!" Jacques shook his head. "All out, and I figured you wouldn't want the same thing twice. I opted for a fresh batch of tiramisu instead."

"Man, you are spoiling us," Brixton took the boxes from his hands, "but, I have to admit, we don't mind being spoiled."

"I couldn't come empty handed. You'll soon learn that about me," Jacques studied the girl attached to Brixton's arm.

"Is that really vegan tiramisu?" Kila asked in a shy but hopeful tone.

"It is—I work at The Hidden M," Jacques replied, unsure if this was the response she was seeking.

"Oh, right...so you're...the...Noah...and it's...oh...," Kila mumbled, making the connection that the up-and-coming vegan chef and the handsome boy standing before her were one and the same. Without another word, and to everyone's surprise, Kila left Brixton's side and sprinted up the stairs to her bedroom.

Ethan introduced Jacques to Maya and Anna, and explained that the girl who disappeared was his sister. The whole party was thankful for the dessert, but no one wanted to indulge in the treat until Kila had returned. Other than Jacques, the group knew how much Kila loved tiramisu. Realizing something was awry, Annabelle grabbed Maya and the two scurried up the stairs to fetch Kila, under the guise of procuring more blankets for the movie.

As soon as the girls left, Brixton cleared his throat, "So... how's things on the cuddly couch?"

"We're not cuddling, Brix—we're just sharing a blanket," Ethan lifted his head with a half-smile.

"Really? From the doorway, it looked like the two of you were quite cuddly, but, I mean, I'm just the baker," Jacques teased.

"They were also QUITE cuddly in the library, where they kissed, MULTIPLE times, a little while ago," Angus crossed his arms.

Brixton snapped, "Too bad they couldn't enjoy the intimacy without your prolonged hovering."

"Sounds like you rather successfully solved your girl problem," Jacques smiled at Ethan, "but in the process may have landed yourself a peeping tom."

"Would you guys stop?" Angus grew uncommonly bashful. "I stumbled into a soap opera starring people I know. It wasn't my aim to linger. I was sent for reconnaissance by these guys, and just got caught up in the romance of it all. Don't make me out to be a perv. I'm not a perv!"

"We're only teasing you, Ang," Ethan laughed. "We know you're not a perv."

"Speak for yourself. I still have my doubts," Brixton's comment was met instantly by a flip-flop to his chest. "Good aim," he laughed it off. "For that, I take it back. I declare this room to be perv-free."

Angus caught Brixton's return throw of the flop and slid it on his foot, feeling vindicated.

After a moment of silence Jacques addressed Ethan, "Did I upset your sister? I was thinking about bringing a German chocolate cake, but for some reason, I made a split decision to make the tiramisu. Did I strike a bad chord?"

"No! She's actually OBSESSED with tiramisu. She's just...in a...weird mood, I think," Ethan thought on his feet.

"What's her name?" Jacques asked.

Brixton looked at Angus to find Angus looking at him.

"Kila," Ethan smiled, "but she usually goes by Ki or Kiki."

"Ah!" Jacques made the connection. "The Ki from the text. I got it. Wait. How do I address her, Ki or Kiki? Which is best?"

"Brixton's the only one who calls her Kiki, so I'd stick to Kila or Ki," Angus suggested, to Brixton's satisfaction.

"Thanks for the head's up. Wouldn't want to say the wrong thing," Jacques rubbed his hands together, feeling the weight of Angus and Brixton's stares. "How long have you guys been together?" he looked at Brixton.

"They're not together," Ethan laughed, "my sister glued herself to him because she was scared."

Great, E. Great. Brixton worked to maintain his composure. *Last night you're supposedly worried about her. On the walk, you mentioned wanting her to remain single. Now, you give someone you just met a couple hours ago the green light. Why not give him a spare house key while you're at it? Her bedroom is upstairs and to the right. Take your shoes off and make yourself comfortable...*

"Yeah, we're making our way through *Camp Fright*," Angus explained, internally questioning Brixton's twisted brow, "and Ki and Brix are pret-ty much best friends again. It's annoying sometimes; but, we deal with it."

"I see," Jacques read hints of fluctuating emotions on Brixton's face but grasped nothing conclusive.

Ethan detected a touch of angst in the air and he aimed to nip it in the bud. "So, basically, there's nothing to worry about, Noah. All friends here."

"All except for Ethan and Maya," Angus grinned, "they're friends who kiss."

Jacques chuckled at the sight of Ethan's proud expression.

Brixton, recognizing that this tension wouldn't bring Kila any closer to him, retrieved the deck of cards from his back pocket. "Alright fellas. Poker time."

"Now THIS I support," Jacques smiled, reaching for the cards as they were handed to him.

Like clockwork, the boys began their game, playing with Jacques for the first time. Though none of them spoke the words, it was acknowledged that he had been accepted into their private, inner circle. Ethan, Brixton, and Angus had never before felt a lack in their friendship; yet, Jacques already seemed to fill some void, which had, up until now, existed without notice. The fullness of their hearts reflected in the fullness of their smiles as the discards and draws created winning and losing hands.

After about thirty-five minutes the girls came tiptoeing down the stairs empty-handed, their giggles giving them away before their footsteps. Ethan noticed that Kila had changed yet again. This time she wore a deep V-neck, long-sleeved heather-gray T-shirt that gently hugged her frame. What he hadn't noticed was that she had also switched her pants, opting for vintage green distressed corduroy bell-bottoms. Her hair was quite different, too: voluminous, wavy, and without a doubt the product of Anna's expertise.

What. The. Hell. Is going on? Ethan's mind flinched at the sight of Angus's eyes wandering along places they normally wouldn't have on his sister's body.

Brixton whacked Angus's upper arm in an effort to snap him out of his eye expedition.

"Sorry about that," Kila announced, in a soft tone, touching the tips of her fingers to her corduroys. "I forgot I had to take care of something," she looked at Annabelle and Maya for support.

The two girls smiled at her. Then they smiled at the boys.

Kila's eyes fell upon Jacques's navy-and-yellow skater shoes. *He's not real. He can't be,* she looked at her palms before looking at her brother.

Ethan lifted his head and his shoulders to communicate his encouragement.

Kila side-eyed Maya, the tiniest smile stamping its mark upon her lips.

"Wow, you guys sure brought back A LOT of blankets," Angus addressed all the girls, yet looked only at Kila.

"How about that tiramisu?" Annabelle aimed to deflect his comment.

"Oh man, you wanted some?" Angus wiped the corner of his mouth, "You should have said something." His dark eyes swam the perimeter of Kila's frame without remorse.

Brixton whacked him again.

On any other occasion Kila would have gladly met Angus's flirtation, but the recent sight of him texting Reese lingered behind her working thoughts like a screensaver waiting to take over. Second place was never something she wanted to be a part of, if she could help it, so she set her attention elsewhere. Somewhere new. Away from the boy who still wanted Reese and away from the other boy who broke off their former best friendship without an explanation.

Jacques had initially intended to play along with Angus, but that plan changed the instant Kila's clear blue eyes waited kindly for his reply. "Every piece remains…in the kitchen," he caved, feeling his heart swell as she smiled at his face for the first time.

Ethan liked the way Jacques had handled himself. He nodded to him in approval. Maya and Anna tugged Kila toward the kitchen, and the boys followed. Angus, questioning the uneven dynamic of four boys and three girls, toyed with the notion of asking Kila to invite Josie over. Upon thinking it through, though, he decided to leave the ratio as it was, fearing Kila might suppose he liked Josie if he asked for her specifically.

Brixton took the liberty of opening the boxes. The sweet smell alone seemed filling, and it took his mind off Angus's all but verbal admission of interest. *We need to get back to Camp Fright. I want to feel her next to me, to let her know it could have been us kissing in the library. It could have been us months ago, years ago, and it could still be us tonight…* his palm touched the cool stone countertop. His nose took in another breath of courage.

Ethan offered a serving knife to Jacques, who carefully sliced the dessert and indulged his own urge to pass the first plate to Kila. She accepted it gratefully, leaning on her toes to relay her excitement. Jacques hoped his version of the Italian dessert would top the others she had tried in the past. It's always a gamble to offer someone a new version of their favorite, and the weight of her review pressed heavy on him now. He studied her face, to break himself away from the worry.

An image of youth, Kila was stunning, with long dark hair in soft waves, light eyes, and full lips. She was athletic in appearance, full of form. While Maya and Anna were just as attractive in their own ways, Jacques found himself partial to Kila, so much so that he began a full visual audit.

When he felt Brixton's eyes on him, Jacques redirected his own eyes to the counter, awaiting Kila's verdict. Pausing only to giggle, Anna and Maya whispered furiously to one another, leaving Ethan, Brixton, and Angus to guess their dialogue.

After a few quiet bites, Kila set her fork down on her napkin. In quick succession she stepped close to Jacques, touched her hands to his shoulders, pressed up on her toes, and touched her lips to his cheek. She retreated from his personal space just as speedily as she had entered it. Then, she sang his praise. "Un-be-lievable. I didn't know it could taste like that… each layer had something to offer. Together, they created something almost indefinable, something almost divine," she beamed, looking to Anna and Maya once her cheeks began to blush.

Jacques, completely caught off guard by her advance, didn't know if he had imagined her kissing him, but his left cheekbone tingled and that was proof enough. "I worried you might not like it," he felt the space between his nose and lips grow warm and wondered why. He spoke to her as though no one else was present, "I'm glad I made it the traditional way tonight."

Kila's eyes glistened, "The traditional way…what other ways can you make tiramisu?"

"Oh, lots," Jacques laughed a little nervously before composing his thoughts and voice again. "Sometimes, I drench the whole thing in a dark chocolate glaze to give it another dimension. I also added a raspberry reduction to it once…that was interesting," Jacques liked that he'd made Kila so energetic. "Oh, and I like to make a frozen version when it gets a bit hotter…that's my uncle's favorite. And I make a raw version for my best friend's mom. She really likes that; but, then again, not everyone is into the whole raw thing."

"I want to try it ev-er-ry way," Kila jumped up and down in front of him. "Promise that I can!" she squeezed his forearm. "Promise. Please? Come on, you have to!"

Jacques grinned, too overwhelmed to speak, and patted her hand with his.

"I'm counting that as a yes," she squeezed his forearm once more, then reached for her plate, "and it's a yes that you can't take back. I'm holding you to it."

"Good," Jacques watched her take another bite, "I want you to hold me to it."

Now allies by default, Brixton and Angus rolled their eyes at one another. Ethan chuckled at what he imagined to be a little light-hearted competition. He was accustomed to seeing his sister dodge advances from the opposite sex. Seeing her play offense tonight was entirely new. He looked to Kila, who appeared more contented than she had been in months. She smiled while she ate, but Ethan guessed the tiramisu wasn't the real culprit for the glow on her face.

The whole group gushed over Jacques's tiramisu. Even Angus paid his compliments, noting he'd tried three different offerings in less than twenty-four hours and still found himself only wanting more. Proof, Angus insisted, that Jacques's desserts were, in fact, addictive. Anna confessed she believed Ethan's veggie burgers and Jacques's tiramisu were the perfect pairing for a Friday night, while Brixton argued they were the second best pairing and that Maya and Ethan were the first. When Kila and Angus clapped, Maya kissed Ethan on the lips, and he blushed, pulling her closer.

With one unopened box of tiramisu remaining, the seven shuffled back to the living room, ready to resume the frightful plot of the movie and the nervous excitement of the darkness. Ethan and Maya returned to the smaller couch, nesting under their blanket as if it were an every weekend occurrence. Brixton, knowing that Jacques needed a spot on the L-shaped couch, turned to Angus for counsel. Angus relayed with his hands that he'd move to the floor.

Per Angus's willing rotation, Brixton took Angus's former seat in between Kila and Annabelle, begrudgingly leaving his former seat on the other side of Kila open. Delighted the space had been made available to him, Jacques settled down close to the armrest. At the feeling of Brixton's leg brushing hers, Anna bit her tongue, remembering what he looked like singing in the kitchen with his eyes closed.

A pinch queasy, Brixton brought to mind the way Kila thanked Jacques for the dessert. *A cheek kiss??? Does she like the tiramisu more than him, or does she like HIM more than the tiramisu? Ugh...I don't even know...I hope something VERY gory happens onscreen VERY soon. Why is Anna's leg so close?* He shifted his body closer to Kila to allow himself a little freedom from Anna's leg, only to see Kila then shift her torso closer to Jacques. *I bet she likes him MORE than the tiramisu! She MUST...Does she like him more than Angus? That might be worth figuring out before I focus on anything else...*

As he dimmed the lights, Angus smiled. He knew there'd be no shortage of things to discuss after the movie, and during the boring parts he'd text Reese. This weekend was already working its way into one of his favorites, and it was only Friday night. With growing optimism, he reclined on the floor, propped against the couch nearest Annabelle. Still feeling flirty, he reached over Brixton's legs to grab one of Kila's bare ankles.

Kila shook Angus's hand off without a second thought, and when Brixton turned to the right to release his smile, Anna mistakenly thought his smile was intended for her. Full of hope, Anna edged her leg closer to his, and Brixton, recognizing his next shift could cause another chain reaction putting Kila even closer to Jacques, decided to remain where he was. Anna was pleased. Her leg tingled again.

Since Ethan had openly shown his affection, Maya was less reserved. It was the release of pressure from wondering if that person you long for also longs for you. Under the blanket, she pressed her hand into his chest, resting her chin above his thick collarbone and inhaling the cologne on his neck. It was never a secret to Kila how Maya felt about Ethan; she had known for years. When Ethan was out of the house,

Maya would, on occasion, sneak into his room and smell the rectangular bottle of Dusk by Herban Cowboy atop his dresser. Maya had grown to love the inviting scent, but smelling the glass would no longer suffice now that she had smelled the cologne on his bare skin.

Taking joy in the strange sensation of being sniffed, Ethan pulled Maya closer, running his fingers through her hair from the roots to the ends. She nuzzled her face into his skin, holding his body much tighter than before. *I have waited for this*, he realized. *I have waited for her.* Reclining deeper into the cushion of the couch, he stroked her arms and rested a hand on her thigh. *How still she is*, he looked at her face, planning to gaze into her eyes, but saw only lids where her dark eyes once were. Two curtains of lashes had lowered shut to block out everything except the feeling of being in his arms.

He marveled at her serenity, yet wondered if something was amiss. She was the night owl of the group, but the first asleep this evening. *Hopefully she only needs a quick nap,* Ethan grinned at the thought of kissing her again. Unable to wait until later, he quietly kissed the top of her head and wished for her affection. *Every day. Every chance. I will kiss her. And I'll figure out why she lets me, so I don't mess this up. My summer will consist of Maya and the band and little else,* Ethan declared in his mind.

On the other side of the room, Jacques, Brixton, and Anna continued to struggle with their own ambitions and internal dialogues. Angus, amidst them on the floor, texted every so often, generally unfazed by the movie. Kila, in contrast, felt her heart throbbing in her ears and wondered how everyone else in the room could be this nonchalant about the horror unfolding onscreen. Though she repeated to herself over and over again it was only a movie, she soon feared for her life.

Jacques tapped on her hand to offer the blanket next to him, and she jumped about three inches vertically. Her eyes, full of fright, flashed to verify he hadn't morphed into the murderer. Following the lines of his face with her eyes, she exhaled loudly and reached for the burgundy blanket. Calmly, Jacques fed the smooth edge into her hands, wishing he could move himself there instead. Kila, driven by fear, yanked the blanket towards herself. She tucked it all around her body, praying it might provide her with some comfort. To Jacques's disappointment, not a corner remained for him to grasp. He rested his palms on his pants and faced forward, tasting the bittersweet flavor of a touch-and-go affair.

Brixton was pleased by this play. Kila's fingers had grazed his ribs when she was securing the blanket, the sensation throttling him back to his inner dialogue. *Maybe the tiramisu MORE than him. He wanted to share the blanket, but she wasn't having it. And she hasn't even LOOKED at Angus after that failed ankle grab attempt. This movie needs to draw to a close so I can talk to her...alone. I'm not afraid. I'm ready.* Brixton came out of his head when he noticed the brilliance of Kila's face smiling at him.

Maybe it's not as complex as I thought, he grinned back at the face he favored above all the others. He prepared to lift his arm to touch her face when he realized Anna was holding onto that arm. *Why me?* He hated that he had no choice but to go along with it. Well, he had another option, but the projected outcome was too bleak for comfort. Shaking Anna's arm free from his would have been likened to dating suicide. *If I hurt Anna, the unspoken girl code might prevent Kiki and me from EVER having a relationship.* Brixton fell back into watching the movie, acutely aware of Anna's skin on his, and unsure about everything he had once been sure about.

Jacques remained discouraged by the blanket mishaps, but up to the challenge now that Anna had laid claim to Brixton and Brixton hadn't issued protest. After all, formulating an award-winning recipe rarely happens overnight. It could take days, weeks, even months of calibration. Likewise, Jacques guessed having a real chance with Kila might also take some time, and he was more than willing to allocate some of his to what he believed to be a valuable long-term investment.

As if the movie jockeyed for the teenagers' attention, the sounds on the screen, without warning, increased in volume and intensity. When the seven were fully alert, the sounds were swallowed up by a surge of silence. Only muffled grumbles and growls speckled the air at this point, the familiar sounds of Peaches wrestling ferociously with her bone in the hallway.

The moment the serial killer crept into the tent of the unsuspecting campers, Kila yelped and covered her face with the blanket. *It's all fake. It's all fake. It's all fake. Just actors and makeup and special FX,* she repeated over and over to herself. *Fake limbs. Fake blood. Fake screams. Fake limbs. Fake blood. Fake screams.* When she felt a tap on her shoulder, she moved the blanket to the side of her face, revealing only an ear and an eye.

"Any chance you might share your blanket shield with me, since I shared my classic tiramisu and promised to share all other versions in the future?" Jacques whispered. "It's possible I might be more frightened than you are."

His French accent and well-spoken words drew Kila's mind away from the movie, and she anxiously untucked the blanket on his side, letting him come under with her. Covered in blanket from head to toe, they were unable to see each other but spared from the graphic scenes.

"Thanks Kila, this is much better," Jacques spoke the words merely because her silence made him anxious.

Too afraid to talk, she tried to touch his arm, but he was adjusting his shirt and their hands touched. Her fingers clung to his as shrill screams pierced the air. A slight rotation of his palm allowed his fingers to slip between hers.

We're holding hands. I haven't held a boy's hand before, Kila realized. She had been so hell-bent on trying to rush into her first kiss that she had underrated the magic of interlocking fingers. And these weren't just any fingers. These were the fingers that were capable of crafting the most enchanting tiramisu on the planet. *I wonder what else he can make...*

"Do you have a girlfriend?" Kila shut her eyes just after she asked.

"No," he whispered. "How about you—will you be in trouble for this?" he slid his fingers deeper between hers.

"No," she laughed, leaning her body toward him.

He tilted the side of his head so it rested next to hers.

Am I dreaming? Did I fall asleep while Anna was curling my hair? No longer irritating her senses, the movie fell away from her mind. With his hair against hers she envisioned his freckled face. She squeezed his hand. He squeezed hers back. There were several rounds of this before Jacques placed his other hand on top of hers, and Kila felt her five fingers caressed by his ten. *Is this? No one's ever...* her mind took flight, her heart danced pirouettes, and her hips shifted on the couch cushion. *WHAT is happening to me right now?*

Before Kila could reach her own conclusion, she felt a rush of air on her head. The blanket, which had before shielded their bodies and conversation, had been pulled from their heads and dropped onto their laps. Kila glared at the silhouette in front of her, her eyes struggling to adjust to the light from the movie.

"Just making sure no one suffocates," Angus tapped Kila's head mid-grin. "Don't forget what we learned in class. It can come on quicker than you think."

Brixton, for once, was thankful for Angus's rowdy nature. He had been stewing beside the questionable blanket fort for what seemed like an eternity. In gratitude, Brixton nudged Angus with his foot, and Angus tapped Brixton's shoe in nonverbal reply.

Although Kila and Jacques's upper bodies were now visible, their hands remained hidden under the blanket. She squeezed his hand. He squeezed hers back. When she hooked her ankle around his, he smiled so wide he covered his mouth with his free hand.

On the screen, Deacon, one of the more athletic campers, began piecing together the grisly clues. Emboldened, he dressed himself in only his darkest clothes, hid whatever could double as weapons inside his backpack, and set out to rescue both the girl he secretly loved and what few friends of his remained. **"Machinehead" by Bush** raced into the air as he sprang from his tent. With knees bent and his core close to the ground, he edged around the tents and looked to the clearing where Tori, the girl of his dreams, had set up camp.

Kila, now engrossed in the movie as a result of its current music accompaniment, bobbed her head to the song, one that more often than not made it into her playlists.

Jacques liked her response to the song and, also liking the song himself, decided to squeeze her hand to the beat.

Kila grew excited and pressed herself closer to him.

Right about that same time, the serial killer took note of the gutsy camper. The masked man, who had previously planned to enter a tent full of angelic toddlers, gladly amended his plans when he set his eyes on the supposed hero to be. Diving beneath a picnic table, he flexed his gloved hands, all too eager to hunt a moving target. A hair-raising, spine-tingling stalking scene commenced, and Kila's fingers shuddered inside Jacques's hand.

Jacques stroked her fingers with his and turned to face her. "We don't have to watch the rest, if you don't want to."

His thick French accent made a puree of her mind, and she couldn't deny the opportunity to learn more about him away from the group. "Yeah, I, I think I might enjoy the night better if I stop watching…."

"Me too," those two words Jacques whispered so faintly in her ear nearly left Kila in a state of mental paralysis.

She blinked tightly, hoping it might reboot her brain. It worked, her thoughts in mid-race as if they hadn't stopped. *Can I take him up to my room or will Ethan come up right away in concern? NO, NO, not my room. Wait. The "where" doesn't really matter, does it? It's the "alone" I care about. Seeing him without anyone else there to see us. And the sooner Jacques and I leave the living room, the more "alone" we will have.*

Without planning to, and still in thought, Kila had slipped her fingers free from Jacques's and found her hand around his knee. He looked at her in fierce surprise, his eyes questioning her intent. She wondered how many of her hormones were lit up as a result of the song versus the proximity of the French chef beside her. She found her answer when she felt his hand circle her knee, and her hips shifted on the couch cushion once more. *It's HIM and my knee is tingling. TINGLING. Is this what happens? Things tingle? Like when your foot falls asleep, only it's not the bad tingling but the good kind? Like when Brixton kissed me on the forehead after I won the hula-hoop competition at field day last year? NO. That doesn't count. We weren't…in a situation…like this…this is different. This is much more tingly. This is…*

"So…," Jacques spoke quietly again to her, "by the not watching, do you intend that we close our eyes or go somewhere else?" One of his fingers tapped on her knee, and he felt her inhale. "I'm fine with either...equally," he pressed his hand atop hers.

"Go," Kila slipped her fingers back between his, "I'm actually pretty thirsty. Let's get a drink in the kitchen and hang out down the hall in the library. Sound alright?" She prayed he'd agree. His fingers weren't too short or too long. His palm was thick but not too thick; and, more importantly, it was completely dry and not clammy at all. *Oh, how I have feared clammy hands!* She mused to herself, wondering just how long she could keep her fingers wrapped in his. *Should I open my palm to give him the easy out? Am I being clingy? Everyone throws that phrase around, but no one will actually define it. I need the definition so I can make an accurate determination,* Kila fretted.

Jacques's reply put a stop to her overthinking, "Sounds perfect as long as I can make some hot tea."

Pulsatingly loud, the movie thundered on. Spurts of blood sprayed across the screen, dripping in long rouge lines. Kila wasn't sure which body the blood had sprung from, but she felt especially grateful for that when the sound of new screams filled the air. Her eyes closed in fear.

"Come on," Jacques tugged on her hand, "let's leave before it gets worse."

Kila liked the connection more and more. Since he didn't release his grip, she didn't release hers either. And as they stood free of the blanket, their linked hands were visible to the others.

In a flurry of excitement, Annabelle nudged Brixton to point it out, but his huff left her wondering what was on his mind. She let go of his arm to receive no reaction from him. With Ethan wrapped around Maya, Angus texting on the floor, and Kila leaving the room with Jacques, Anna was feeling less and less like a "how to get boys" guru. She slouched back into the sofa cushion, facing the movie but paying much more attention to her internal quarrel.

"I thought the movie might be too scary for you. I'm sorry," Ethan studied his sister as she and Jacques made their way towards him.

"It's okay. Noah's scared, too," she blushed when her brother saw she was holding Jacques's hand. "We're just headed to the library...," Kila stopped trying to explain herself when she caught the sight of Maya asleep in his arms. "She has more to tell you, so make sure she does," Kila ordered without further detail.

"Why didn't you tell me sooner?" he mouthed to her.

"It was Maya's secret, not mine," Kila ruffled his hair with her free hand.

She took a couple steps past the loveseat but jolted backward when Jacques hadn't followed. Looking over her shoulder, she could see Ethan talking to him. *WHAT is he saying? Please, please, please let it not be a silly older brother threat, or worse, something embarrassing! Be cool about this, E. Just tonight. Just with Noah,* she hoped her internal begging might be of some use on this rare occasion.

The stop was brief, which was good, at least she thought, and Jacques was following behind her again, his fingers still locked in hers. In the kitchen, Kila dimmed the lamp to fit her mood, and realized it would be silly at this point not to release her grip, light though it was. She wanted to tell him how nice it had been, but couldn't find the way. Everything she thought of saying sounded creepy, so she decided to run her thumb down the center of his palm before letting it go.

"I must confess I sort of hoped you'd get scared so we could run away together," Jacques leaned against the counter. "Scary movies are far from my thing."

"Same. The last one I saw messed me up pretty bad. Anyway, what is your thing?" she asked, anxious to score as much Q&A as she could before the others were finished with the movie.

"Well, for starters, I'm liking tonight. I met your brother only a few hours ago with Angus and Brixton, and here I am with you now in a—I have to say this, don't laugh—a rather marvelous kitchen. Who's the cook in your family that gets all this space?" he pointed to the expansive marble countertops running the length of the room.

"Honestly, it's mostly Ethan. Both my parents enjoy cooking, but they're always working so much, the only time they really make use of this room's potential is on Sundays."

"Ethan didn't tell me he cooks; but, then again, I did just meet him. What is his specialty?" he asked.

"He makes these super-delicious veggie burgers—they have this really...sophisticated taste. What's funny is that he came up with the recipe when he was about twelve. He'd had some dream about it, and miraculously, it worked. We never get tired of eating them. He made them for everyone tonight."

"Your brother seems cool."

"Yeah, well, his current coolness hinges upon what he said to you a moment ago. I'm scared to ask," she looked at him.

"You just did," he closed his eyes when he laughed. "He basically told me you were delicate and to be careful with you."

"Delicate?" Kila rolled her eyes to the ceiling. "What am I? A vase?"

Jacques grinned. "I do like vases, but a vase you are not. Rest assured of that," he made it a point to look in her eyes.

Kila tried not to blink.

"He was just playing big brother, that's all," Jacques defended Ethan. "I respect him for it. I'd have said the same thing, too, if my sister was holding hands with someone she just met."

"So you have a sister?" Kila's eyes lit up.

"No…but theoretically," he laughed, leaning close to her in confidence. "What your brother doesn't know is that I've never held a girl's hand before, so it wasn't as if I was tapping into my repertoire of tricks."

"I haven't held a boy's hand before, either," Kila admitted since the conversation allowed.

"Really?" He believed her yet couldn't grasp how it could be true. "Are you sure?"

"Yes," she smiled, "but...I'm kind of glad about that now."

"Me too," he looked in her eyes again, pleased with her last reply. "Seconds for both of us, then?"

She nodded, anticipating the sensation of his touch.

He moved his hand into hers quickly, this time running his thumb down the line of her palm.

Tingles shot up her forearm. *Yup. It's him.*

"I have to tell you something else," Jacques looked at her intently. "My name's not Noah. It's a silly thing from the restaurant."

"You know, I somehow knew that from my mom, but I forgot to ask your real name," Kila grew excited, imagining the possibilities in her mind. *Something French, maybe, but what is it?* "Will you tell me?" she couldn't help but touch his hand again.

"It's Jacques. Jacques Noir," his fingers slipped inside hers as if that's where they now belonged.

"Oh," Kila managed to say the two letters as his name resonated inside her mind. *Jacques Noir.*

"I mean, if you like Noah better, we can stick with that," Jacques added, hoping he hadn't disturbed the growing chemistry between them. "Whatever you prefer," his thumb touched her wrist.

"I really like Jacques," Kila assured him, liking the way that phrase sounded in her mind.

When he smiled just a little, she closed her eyes and tried to continue breathing.

"Are you still shaken from the movie?" he asked.

"Yeah," she fibbed, too nervous to tell him the truth about his affect on her. "So...you wanted tea?" she changed the subject. "What kind?"

"Don't laugh, but I have it with me. I'm pretty particular about... almost everything," he blushed, pulling a small wrapped envelope out of his cargo pocket with an upturned lip.

"I didn't laugh. I'm intrigued," Kila grabbed the two tea sachets, looking for the label or any indication of what kind it was. These were, without a doubt, the fanciest tea bags she had seen. They felt like satin, with what looked like whole dried flowers inside. The top of the bag was tied with a cord that ran in elaborate knots right to the end. A saffron glass bead took the place of what would normally be a square paper label.

"No label. It's my tea. Well, I don't grow the leaves, but I have the loose leaf shipped to the restaurant, and then I make a special green blend, adding a few extra bits here and there from our kitchen. And the bead...I just always thought tea deserved a better topping than the normal paper thing."

"You...I...I don't even know what to say to you," she pushed on his shoulder with her hand.

His upper body didn't roll back when she pushed it. It wasn't like any boy's body she had seen to date. It was unquestioningly firm—something she wasn't expecting. *Tea cannot happen without boiling water*, she prompted herself, filling the kettle and grabbing two ceramic mugs from the cabinet.

As the water heated, she asked Jacques why she had never seen him at Cypress, and he relayed that he attended Parker, the all-boys private high school.

"Parker, huh? I heard that Professor Olquist is the greatest Lit Phil teacher in the US—have you had him yet?"

As her intellectual side surfaced, Jacques welcomed it with open arms. "Yes, I have him now," he watched the light dance behind her eyes. "I think I'll appreciate his tough love a little more when I'm certain I've passed his class."

"Oh," Kila giggled, "I'm sure you'll pass, but if you ever want to share any of your papers with me, I would be honored. I wish there was a way for him to teach a class at Cypress, too. My Lit Phil teacher is more worried about being current than actually challenging us. It's kind of a downer because he's chosen some really epic writers for us to examine this semester, but when it comes to the critique, he only scratches the surface."

Jacques couldn't believe she was as geeky as she was attractive. Each glance and each word made him sense he had previously yearned for this night without knowing. He looked over at her distressed vintage green cords, which were bunchy near her ankles. The tops of her feet were lightly bronzed and her toenails were the whitest of all the pastel blues.

"I painted them after school today," she spoke a little shyly, "I was trying a new Lauren B. Beauty polish."

"I love the shade," Jacques replied, "it reminds me of the baby-blue frosting I sometimes make for my cream cheese cupcakes. And…just so you know, I'm in favor of trying new things."

Kila blushed right as the kettle whistled.

With precise movements, Jacques poured the liquid into the almond-colored mugs and began the timer on his phone to ensure the exact steep time for the tea.

"I've never timed my tea before," she smiled, then tried to keep herself from smiling. *I can't smile every time he says something. He'll think I'm weird.*

"Sometimes the smallest things make the biggest differences. This just happens to be one of them," he spoke confidently when it was in reference to the culinary.

"I could listen to you talk all night," Kila gushed.

"You'll get used to the accent," he grinned. "Then, I'll be boring like the rest of them."

"We'll see," Kila decided to show a half-smile since he had offered a full one.

When his phone vibrated, Jacques removed the tea bags from the mugs and Kila led him through the hallway and into the library. Though she hadn't remembered, her phone still remained synched to the speakers, and they opened the door to the sound of soft alluring music. **"Easy Yoke" by FAVELA** had just begun to play, and her eyes caught the recognition on Jacques's face.

"You know it?" Kila's heart pirouetted faster than before.

To serve as his answer, he mouthed the words in exact time.

Her heart leapt in such a way that her whole body shifted. Hot tea escaped from the mug, burning her index and middle fingers. She moved the cup to her other hand and dried her fingers on her corduroys, feeling embarrassed.

"It's alright. It happens to me...nearly every day," Jacques placed his mug on the coffee table and reached for hers. "I think I hold the record in tea burns." He set her cup next to his.

The grip of the song's message and the low-level light from the stained glass lamps scattered about the room made Kila wish he would reach for her. *What would it feel like to be in his arms?* Her eyes followed his body as he moved along the bookcase. *I'll always see this when I hear this song. How is he single?*

"Astounding," Jacques mumbled, looking up at shelf after shelf of early edition classics.

"Brix and I used to spend hours in here all the time"—Kila stopped her thoughts, realizing her words required some clarification—"reading," she added, feeling the echoes of the loss of Brixton's best friendship.

"I can see why," Jacques replied without concern. He pulled a well-preserved, turn-of-the-twentieth-century edition of *Aesop's Fables* off the shelf and carefully opened the spine to look inside.

Kila fidgeted in astonishment. Her eyes gaped and her stomach tightened. It was her favorite collection, her favorite book of all time. The fearless and uncompromising spirit of Aesop's life, not only his fables, which had been passed down orally for several centuries before finding themselves in print, had always captivated her. To live a life of purposeful truth, peace, and higher wisdom was to be immortalized as one of the greats.

Of the hundreds, possibly thousands of books in here, Jacques chose this one. Why? Her breathing slowed. *Why Aesop? Why tonight?* Her heart took over for her mind. She examined him in full for the first time. It was like he had walked off the cover of an outdoors magazine. His rough olive cargo pants coupled perfectly with his soft cream-colored, long-sleeved shirt, the arms rolled halfway up his freckle-dusted forearms. *Those freckles. They're everywhere. I didn't even know I liked freckles so much...*

"It may seem silly, but these are my favorite," Jacques looked at her, surprised to notice she was studying him. "They were my favorite as a child, and yet, they are my favorite still."

"No, it's not silly at all—I...quite enjoy them," Kila felt her limbs turn to crème brûlée as she looked into his espresso-colored eyes and then to his squared mahogany sideburns. *The barely there reddish tint to his deep brown hair...* She leaned on the daybed behind the bookshelf for support. Her legs grew weak, and Jacques surmised she must be tired from whatever it was she had done earlier in the day.

"You should try the tea. I'm anxious to know what you think." He grabbed her mug for her, placing it in her hands.

She liked his old-fashioned manners.

The smell from the cup was quite a contrast to any tea she had smelled before. Sipping its velvety texture, she was greeted by a complexity of taste. Notes of the green leaves and what seemed like flowers danced upon her tongue.

"Wow. I don't normally drink green tea. I prefer Earl Grey. But this, this mixture you made, might be my new addiction— is there some type of flower in it?" she sipped again, then touched her tongue to the roof of her mouth.

"Jasmine. I think that's what you are referring to. That's what helps to lend the texture."

"Yeah, I taste the texture," Kila feared she might like him too much. "Can I take you everywhere with me?"

He nodded his head warmly, hiding his smile inside his mug.

If it were possible, Jacques would have framed the moment. The tea was exquisite, but not as exquisite as the conversation.

Between glances and sips, they took turns reading to one another and discussing each fable in detail. After just a dozen pages, they jointly confessed Reynard the fox to be their favorite, and insisted, despite his cunning disposition for trouble, he could do no wrong.

To uphold their unfounded position, Jacques and Kila felt it necessary to verbally revise the fables moving forward, painting Reynard in only the highest of moral lights, even in those fables he hadn't previously held a role. This improvisation incited a host of grand dramatizations, colorful additions, and flirtatious laughter. Lots of flirtatious laughter.

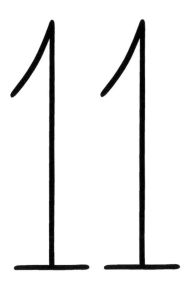

Back in the living room, Annabelle's leg no longer tingled. When Jacques and Kila left, Brixton scooted closer to the armrest, leaving a whole cushion's length between them. Though Anna pictured Brixton's face, she kept herself from looking at him. His body language all but voiced he wasn't interested, and she wasn't about to push it. *I'm shifting into neutral,* Anna reflected. *Time to chill and wait it out.*

Questioning the feasibility of a real relationship with Brixton led Anna to think of her parents' state of unrest. The bickering between her mother and her father had grown intolerable. Every night the squabbling took hold of the house. Anna never questioned whether it would happen, just when it would happen. And it never seemed like there was any real reason for it, either; at least not one that Anna recognized.

She remembered a time when she looked forward to coming home after school. Her father, who was a master-carpenter, always made meal prep into more of a humorous challenge than an arduous chore. Anna loved helping him in the kitchen, and she took pride in seeing his dinner success rate surpass 70 percent. Those shared moments—even the ones where she jumped up and down with a towel to wave the smoke away from the alarm—were ones Anna truly cherished.

Things hadn't been that way for months, though. Now, as soon as her mom came home from the office, the tension set in. It was impossible to make it through dinner without one of them storming off. And Anna found it most disconcerting that the tension rose regardless of the meal's success. Always caught in the crossfire, Anna struggled to console the one left at the table. She feared the continued repetition of this new routine could disband their marriage, and she began feeling resentful herself.

Yet tonight, for the first time in a long time, Anna felt thankful. Things with Brixton weren't ideal by any measure, but she enjoyed the time away from her parents. Time without bickering. Time without having to take sides. Time when she could actually think of herself. Spending the night at Kila's house with her now closest friends seemed more normal and natural than being at home. And she hoped, within the confines of all her other thoughts, that her parents might have a bit of a rekindling while she was away from the house.

When did discomfort become this acceptable to me? Annabelle grew suddenly self-aware as if waking from a dream. Her toes throbbed inside her pointy fabric heels, her jeans squeezed the life from her thighs, and her bra's underwire pressed mercilessly into her upper ribs. *I just can't feel like this anymore. Comfort must reign over fashion…at least at night, anyway.*

"Excuse me," Anna climbed over Brixton's legs, "I'm off to change, but I'll be back in a few minutes. Will you count the new deaths for me?"

"Of course," Brixton smiled for the first time since Kila left the room. "You think the count will come into play at the end?"

"Yeah…it might," Anna looked back to return his smile before she walked away.

Brixton leaned down to speak with Angus, "It's a good thing Kiki left before the heads started rolling. I can't believe Deacon was forced to kill two of his own friends. This is maddening! How can Anna be counting deaths? I can barely watch it myself."

"Bro," Angus whispered, "she's counting because she's starting to figure it out. The fatality toll has come into play a number of times already. I didn't want to tell her and give it away. The killer is obsessed with numbers. Don't tell me I'm the only one to notice. You usually pick up on these things before I do. I mean, I saw it, and I've been texting the whole time…," he elevated himself from the floor to the spot on the couch next to Brixton.

"No," Brixton shrugged, "I didn't notice. My radar's all off tonight."

"WHAT are you taaalking about? Your radar's at an all-time high. First, you have Ki in your lap for, like, fifteen minutes. Then, Anna's ALL over you. And now she's going to change," Angus raised his eyebrows.

"Get ahold of yourself," Brixton eyed him. "Her changing is not in any way correlated with me."

"Brix. She likes you. Don't be like Ethan and let the months pass by without mention," Angus crossed his arms. "You should test the waters. She wants you to."

Brixton eyed him suspiciously.

Angus continued, "You know, I can sleep in Ki's room tonight if you want me to."

"ANG," Brixton all but growled at him, "WHY would I WANT you to sleep in Kiki's room?"

"Brix, I wouldn't be with her," Angus grinned.

Brixton's shoulders rose.

Angus shared his train of thought, "Ten-to-one she sleeps in the library with Noah. Since it's pretty obvious Anna wants to stay with you, you two should take the guest room. I'll stay in Ki's room and find out if her new sheets are really worth all the hype she's given them."

Brixton's face threatened to twist in such a fashion that he didn't know what to say next. "I'm NOT staying with Anna," he barely managed to come across as carefree. "And, even if Anna sleeps down here of her own accord, and, even if Kiki does stay with Noah, you should leave Kiki's room free in case Maya doesn't want to spend the night in Ethan's room. I think it's only fair for Maya to make that decision for herself and not be put in a situation where the decision has been made for her."

"Good point about Maya...I hadn't thought of that," Angus pulled his eyebrows together recalculating the possibilities of who might sleep where.

"We're staying in the guest room," Brixton knew he'd won his case with the Maya angle. He looked at the screen and added two more bodies to Anna's kill count.

"Guest room it is," Angus softened, "but, sleeping arrangements aside, you can't tell me you don't find Anna to be sweet."

"It's not that she's not sweet," Brixton thought of her. "She is, absolutely."

"Then what is it?" Angus asked. "I'd love to be in your position, with someone like Anna who thought of me like that. I've always been on the other end, like with Reese."

"Is that all you want?" Brixton shook his head, "To be adored?"

Angus offered a slight nod.

Brixton smirked, "You already are. Adoration aplenty."

Angus lifted his shoulders, creasing his brows deeper than before.

"Open your eyes," Brixton whispered. "Cypress is teeming with girls who adore you."

"Name one," Angus challenged him, "one you could see me with."

"Josie McCellum. Martha Albernin. Delaney Williams. Vanessa Jeffreys. Aida Blackwell. That's five, and I could keep counting for a while longer, but I don't want to risk bolstering your ego too much. It could negatively affect the band, and, in general, make you more of a shallow punk."

"MORE of a shallow punk?" Angus eyed Brixton.

"Yes," Brixton remained firm throughout his explanation, "that was my way of balancing out the delivery. I see that it has worked."

Angus biffed him with a small cushion to the face.

"Watch it, Lyr," Brixton held his hand up.

"Okay, I'll take that into account. In return, for me, at least appreciate some of Anna's attention," Angus pressed. "You might regret it if you don't."

"I might regret it if I do. My feelings lie elsewhere," Brixton's fingers pressed into the fabric of the armrest. "You asking me to do that is like me asking you to go out with Josie or Delaney." *She was in my arms only an hour ago...for the sake of fear, not for the sake of love, but still. Still in my arms. Another lost chance.*

"Enough, then. I won't press it, but I hope you figure it out in time," Angus looked at the screen. "By the way, did you catch Ki in that gray shirt? I thought I was losing my miiiiind," he pushed his phone away from his body as if he ran the risk of Reese hearing him. "With her intellect, she shouldn't be allowed to look like that."

Brixton's face tensed. "Kiki's entitled to dress the way she wants, when she wants, regardless of her IQ. And, while we're on this topic, you need to control yourself around her. Ethan saw you drool, just like I did. When I whacked you, you should have cooled yourself down," Brixton clenched his teeth. "I had to whack you twice! What was that all about?"

"I couldn't help it. I never saw her look like that," Angus defended himself, "and Ethan would have had the same reaction if she wasn't his sister."

"No! He wouldn't have. Do you even know our best friend? He hasn't looked at anyone like that but Maya in a long time. It's referred to as self-control, something you might want to take a look into."

"Roughness tonight," Angus pouted, "but, you know, it really doesn't matter, anyhow."

"How so?" Brixton wasn't sure he was ready to let it go. Angus hadn't even hinted at remorse, reinforcing Brixton's initial reasons for concern. *If Angus makes a mental leap from Reese to Kiki, this whole ship's going down.*

Angus leaned forward to look Brixton in the eyes. "...Because Noah is probably making out with her right now. If he's not, he's either too nervous to make a move OR too modest to know she wants him."

"You think Kiki wants Noah, like WANTS him, wants him?" Brixton felt sick to his stomach. "Like physically wants...to be physical?" He shook the vivid visuals from his mind and looked instead at Angus.

"Yes," Angus grinned matter-of-factly.

"How can you be so sure?" Brixton wondered just how apparent his own feelings were, given his outburst. He waited for the answer just the same.

"Um," Angus thought back to Jacques's arrival. "Let me see. She changed as soon as he arrived. He brought her favorite dessert. She kissed him on the cheek. They hid under a blanket. They held hands in front of us. They left us to be alone," Angus clamped his jaw in a scarcely noticeable way. "I don't like saying this, but Noah might have the best timing. In history. Kind of a bummer for us," he leaned into Brixton.

"Get off me," Brixton shoved his shoulder away, laughing. *There's NO WAY they're making out! They can't be. She's never kissed anyone before...is she kissing him now?* His stomach churned.

When a barefooted Annabelle returned a few minutes later in a pair of yoga pants, sports bra, and an oversized, off-the-shoulder thermal, Brixton blinked and welcomed her with a half-smile. Angus moved to the opposite end of the couch, and she hesitatingly took her former seat. Pretending to text, Angus held his phone but kept an eye on Brixton.

"Four since you left," Brixton, more conscious of Anna's feelings, faced her when he spoke.

"Four!" she gasped. "I was hoping I'd only miss one or two. Were they notable kills?"

"Nah. Fairly dull and unimaginative," Brixton smirked. "Deacon passed out from the shock of it all. Tori's still safe, but the killer's on a roll now. You came back at the right time...."

Anna touched her hands to her knees, fighting the urge to reply with a forward comment.

"You look comfy," Brixton spoke again, wondering why she'd turned quiet. He issued what he deemed to be a friendly smile.

"Thanks. I feel better," she wiggled in place to keep her face looking calm. Then, she folded her legs into a new position.

Brixton found Anna's relaxed look refreshing. Her hair was loosely pulled back into a ponytail, buoyant and full of bounce. With all her hair out of the way, he could see the ovular shape of her face. His eyes touched the center of her apricot cheeks, then traced a line to her glistening floral earrings.

Easily the best dressed at Cypress High, Anna could pull off things fashion magazines normally advised against. Perhaps it was her carefree confidence or the fact that she somehow already knew that one's status in high school was not the end-all-be-all to a person's worth in life. When she and Reese were still best friends, they would often make high-stakes bets with one another for fun, never involving money but always involving fashion. On one such occasion Anna lost a bet, and for her punishment she was to wear metallic silver pants to class. Not only did she wear them without a fight, but she also wore them with a smile, nicknaming the style "baked potato" when questioned about it. Needless to say, Reese wasn't pleased with all the compliments Anna had received in place of what should have been humiliation, and that day marked the beginning of a falling-out that would end a several-year connection.

Brixton gathered that, like Reese, many of the other girls at Cypress envied Anna. While her female admirers once swarmed around her like bees, they weren't the nicest of friends, or really even friends at all. He was grateful Anna found an unlikely connection in Kila, the antithesis of calculating. And seeing Anna in such a relaxed state made Brixton suddenly aware that Angus might be right. Part of him hoped she'd stick around for a while so he could sort his feelings out.

"Brix, do you want it or not?" Annabelle leaned over him.

"Huh?" He panicked, noticing her hazel eyes, perhaps for the first time.

"Angus wants more tiramisu. Are you going to have another piece? If so, I'll get you one," she smiled at his contemplative face. "I asked three times."

"Oh, sorry," he looked at his hands. "No thanks—I'm good." Brixton waited for Anna to leave the room before scolding Angus, "Why can't you get your own dessert? She's not your slave!"

Angus discerned, by the sharpness in Brixton's voice, he might have changed his stance on Anna. He addressed Brixton's biting comment piece by piece, explaining both his circumstance and his intentions. "She wanted to split the tiramisu with me since she only wanted half. Plus, she wanted to get some water, so she offered to get the tiramisu while she was out there. Tone down the self-righteousness, tonight. Please. And don't even so much as hint at sexism. You know how I feel about that. I wait on my mom nonstop at home, since my dad passed away. You know I'd never act like that, believe in that, or condone that. Besides, Anna's into YOU, she's not into me. I already know what that feels like, remember? I'd never go there again…willingly."

"Sorry—I, I'm feeling messed up," Brixton softened at Angus's subtle reference to Reese. "I think this movie's getting to me. I need a break. Can you count the kills for Anna?"

"Yeah. I already promised her I would…," Angus laughed. "Go pace a bit. It'll do you some good."

Brixton stretched his legs and snuck around the couch. Ethan, in a daze, kept one eye on the movie and the other eye on Maya. Both of his arms held her. Seeing them together seemed so right that Brixton yearned even more so to make a similar connection himself. *Kiki…*

Though he angled the walk to Angus as though it were ambiguous, his real motive was to check up on Kila. Treading lightly down the hall to minimize the creaks from the wooden planks, Brixton fretted over what state he might find them in. Earlier in the evening, he had learned that Jacques had been inexperienced with girls; then again, it had only taken Jacques an hour on the first day he met Kila to hold her hand, something no one else had been able to do up until now. *I never really went for it, though*, Brixton chided himself.

From the half-open doorway, the music caught his heart before her face could. **"A Rush Of Blood" by Coasts** sent his mind soaring through a stream of memories, quick glances back in time when it was he and not Jacques in the library with her.

As the years molded their friendship, Kila and Brixton had read through the classics. They debated each story's worthiness, sometimes so staunchly that one or both would need to stand and pace to hash it out. They categorized authors. They learned of their lives. They discussed their troubles, not just their triumphs, and tried, without reservation, to take something positive from each of them.

The fire in her eyes always egged me on. I took the opposing stance even when I agreed with her. Her analytical ability might be my biggest turn-on. I wanted her to uphold her position. I wanted to know how she thought and what principles she held higher than others. Sometimes she'd shut me down. Sometimes I'd shut her down. But, no matter how tightly she crossed her arms or scrunched her nose, I loved her all the more.

When we tired of books we turned to cards, and when we tired of cards we turned to talking. And music. EVERYTHING centered on music. The one, unfailing, undeniable connection between our two hearts. We'd agreed there's a song for everything, for each occasion, for each feeling, and, though she didn't know it, I wanted all the occasions and all the feelings to be with her. The convenient emotions as well as the inconvenient ones.

I'd stay up all night the night before I knew I would see her to construct the following night's playlist. A hope that I could speak to her in songs the message my mouth lacked the courage to voice. E and Ang thought the playlists were for the band, and I let them think that to protect the truth. They were always for her, and they were always about her. That those same playlists inspired the band was merely a secondary return.

The sound of Jacques's voice tangled up in Kila's laughter

tore a rip in Brixton's heart. No longer able to escape into his precious memories, Brixton was forced to see the burning present. In the short time since Jacques and Kila left the living room, things between them had somehow accelerated. Jacques gazed at Kila as though she alone held the answer to some longstanding question he'd been wrestling with. And while this was to be expected, it was Kila's body language toward Jacques that surprised Brixton. *She keeps touching him. On his shoulder. On his arm. Before they laugh. While they laugh. After they laugh. He only touches her after or while she touches him. Her hand. Her elbow. Her foot. He knows he can't come on too strong. He senses it. He's smart. Is he smarter than Angus?*

We used to be alone ALL the time, just like this. Maybe I spent too much time debating and not enough time connecting. I didn't know she wanted affection...I could have used some of that myself. I guess I'm not so great at reading her anymore... or maybe I never was.

Reluctantly, and with a heavy heart, Brixton returned to the living room, collapsing into the couch cushion with an immense huff. He felt his dreams slip from his mind, and, the image of Kila he once held so high lost a single percentage grade of its brightness. He wondered if he should attempt to minimize his feelings, at least temporarily. And he hated that thought.

As if she read his concern, Peaches sprung into his lap, slamming her boxy, boney head into his jaw.

"I miss the days when you were a puppy and couldn't crush me like this," he laughed into the Great Dane's ear, patting her shiny coat.

She wagged her tail, unfazed, and settled her head on his shoulder.

At least someone's into me, Brixton shrugged, leaning his head onto hers.

She stretched her giant pink tongue to touch his skin and snarfed when he looked away laughing.

Annabelle, sitting with Angus at the other end of the sofa, smiled at the endearing way Brixton cuddled with Peaches. The single piece of tiramisu she and Angus had shared was close to crumbs. When Angus's phone vibrated on the coffee table, Anna took one look at the screen and glared at him.

"What?" Angus asked, as if nothing had happened.

"I just don't know why you even talk to her still," Anna used the opportune timing of Angus's blank face to swipe the last morsel of tiramisu from the plate.

"Hey!" he struck his fork into hers.

The sound of clanking metal caused Peaches to issue a warning growl.

Brixton enjoyed the snappy back and forth that unfolded before him. *They don't exactly look terrible together, her light features contrasted against his dark features.*

Anna shifted her weight and readjusted her legs on the couch. She ran a hand through her ponytail and began again, this time facing Angus. "Okay, I get it. I of all people do. Reese is gorgeous, she's charming, and she makes you feel a certain way about yourself. She makes you feel the way you want to feel, which, in your case, I'm guessing is: wanted," Anna side-eyed him.

Angus smiled, "And what's wrong with that?" He dabbed his finger on the plate, consuming the last bit of the cream.

"Well, the fact that she's convinced you of something that may or may not be true. And you believe her, all of it, despite what she did to you last year," Anna kept herself from looking at Brixton. She knew it would only upset Angus further and he already looked upset to begin with. "You don't get it, do you? You're brilliant, but you can't see it because you're in the MIDDLE of it. She's winning this one, and I HATE to see her win, especially when it affects people I care about."

Angus found himself caught between enlightenment and aggravation.

I can't believe she's ACTUALLY getting somewhere with him! Brixton's spine moved into proper alignment against the couch cushion and his head lifted from its previous downward tilt.

Peaches, sensing a shift, too, lifted her ears and her tail.

Anna continued, "Look, I know you message Reese around the clock, but you have to hear me out. She will do ANYTHING to make you crave her approval. And, I know you may not feel that way, but you don't need her approval. You don't need her. No one should need someone else's approval to be happy. She doesn't want a RELATIONSHIP with anyone. She wants to RULE them." Anna repositioned herself again, growing more compassionate, "I don't want to upset you. I want you to look past the illusion she's created. See, when you realize you no longer need her to feel that way, that's when you'll find out who she really is. I, unfortunately, had to learn that the hard way."

"I'm sorry about what happened between you two," Angus spoke sincerely. "To be honest, I don't really know much about it. She's never brought it up."

"I know. She has good reason not to. It wouldn't serve her in any way, so, it's useless to her," Anna reiterated her stance. "It's alright, and, actually I prefer it this way. I wouldn't trade Ki or My back under any conditions."

"I don't think they'd trade you, either," Angus thought of them fondly. "From the looks of it, the three of you have grown inseparable, much like Brix, E, and me."

"We have. Like sisters...look, you may or may not know this, but you do have a bunch of options. I know of quite a few, and I bet there's even more," Anna nudged him, "so why waste anymore time with Reese?"

"I love how I keep hearing about all my options tonight," Angus grinned. "How do I know you and Brix aren't embellishing? I wouldn't put it past either of you, seeing as how you both want me to move on so badly."

"We're not embellishing," Anna played with the ends of her ponytail. "If Ki were in here, she'd agree with Brix and me, too. She knows more about your options than I do."

Angus looked perplexed.

Brixton at last joined in, erupting with words so fervently that Peaches shook under his hand. "I named NAMES and he STILL didn't believe me!"

"You named names?!" Anna exclaimed. "Unethical! You can't name names! What were you thinking?"

Her voice sounded so high-pitched that Angus laughed helplessly.

"I had to prove it to him somehow," Brixton defended himself. "How else other than supplying names?"

"You broke the code," Anna shook her head, flirtatiously. "You can't be trusted now."

"I may have broken code, but I would break it again, if necessary, to shake him free from Reese," Brixton patted the Great Dane's head as she flopped her enormous body across his lap. "Goodness, Peaches," he whispered into a laugh, trying to settle her down by patting her lower back.

"Well," Anna loved the sight of Brixton and the dog together, "the good news is there will be plenty of opportunity for Angus tomorrow." Anna wiped her mouth with her napkin and applied some powder-pink conditioning lip balm to hide her smile.

"I KNEW it!" Angus screamed. "Movie ends at a kill count of thirty-three—and Anna was right. Deacon's still passed out. Tori is still in hiding with her best friend in the woods.

And the killer walks, free from the authorities, after killing them and stealing their armored car, racing toward the glory of a sequel, which hasn't yet been made, but which we will see nonetheless, the very MOMENT it's available. I'm talking in the theaters, for those of us that dare to face the fright again."

Anna burst into laughter, holding up a finger to celebrate the victory of her sequel prediction.

Angus hurled a pillow at Brixton's head to punish him for his eye roll.

Peaches barked when the velvety cushion bounced off Brixton's hair and onto her snout.

"Shhhh!" Ethan hissed, breaking his lengthy silence. "I'll END you guys if you wake her up! Don't you DARE turn the lights on, either."

Angus motioned Brixton and Anna into the hallway, where the three continued their conversation safe from further threats.

Annabelle spoke first, "You have to admit it's cute to see Ethan like this. I mean, who would have suspected he was 'grade A' relationship material? I always thought he was adorable, even handsome at times, but, this, this I was not prepared for."

"He is pretty handsome," Brixton joked, "when he's not busy being adorable."

"Whaaat?" Angus pretended to be forlorn. "Is he more adorable than I am?"

"Yeah," Anna laughed. "By far. Sorry, but I feel the need to be honest."

"It's alright," Angus explained. "Everyone knows the real adorable order is Brixton, Ethan, myself. You think I would have come to grips with that by now."

"Clearly," Anna gushed. "But that's just MY adorable order. Each girl has her own," she batted her eyelashes, only half joking. "Okay, I think I ought to go up to bed. I have to help my dad out with some things in the morning."

"Alright," Angus shook his head, "if you must, you must."

"One more thing," Brixton felt, for the first time, drawn to her. "What were you mentioning about tomorrow's presenting plenty of opportunities for Angus?"

Anna looked at them perplexed. "The party tomorrow night?" she smirked, then tightened, realizing she shouldn't have mentioned it yet.

"WHAT PARTY?" Angus and Brixton asked in unison.

"I—uh, I'm really tired guys, and I shouldn't have mentioned it. Kila will need to explain in the morning. I'm afraid I might be in trouble for this," she hopped from one foot to the other, biting her lip and hoping Kila would forgive her for this accidental spill.

"Wait—will you be at the party?" Brixton asked, a little self-conscious that he was too impatient to wait until tomorrow to find out. "And, will we be at the party?" he pointed to Angus and himself.

"I'm not allowed to miss it, and I'm fairly certain you both will be here. I mean, Ethan will, so you both should be, too," Anna blushed.

"You said 'here'?" Angus picked up on her subtle location reference.

Anna nodded. "I can't say anything else, so please don't ask me," she pursed her lips. "And don't say anything about it until Kila tells you."

"We won't," Brixton assured her.

"I'd be blatantly lying if I said I wasn't curious," Angus found it endearing that Anna's eyes tended to gravitate toward Brixton.

"You can be curious, just be quiet," Anna hugged Angus when she heard Brixton's laughter.

"Hey, I kept your other secret, didn't I?" Angus tugged on Anna's ponytail and waited for her to blush.

"You kept it for a few hours, yes," Anna grinned. "Let's see how much longer you can keep it."

"You're on," Angus nodded his head. "Though it might be the juiciest secret in the history of Cypress High. Does anyone else know?"

Anna gasped. "No. And you better not tell!" She squeezed

Angus's shoulder to note her seriousness.

Brixton's smile could not have looked cuter, and Anna found herself especially nervous to hug him. She rushed in and out of his arms so quickly that the embrace lasted less than half the time Angus's had. She wanted a second hug, so she could actually enjoy it, but thought it might seem odd to ask.

As if on cue, Peaches bounded through the hallway and slipped in front of Brixton. Anna took the distraction as a sign she should make her exit and try again with Brixton tomorrow. Once alone in the hallway the boys resumed their conversation.

"Today might be the strangest day we've ever had," Brixton lifted his hands. "We learned about the EmOpen. We've decided to rename and enter the band. Ethan and Maya passed through the friendship barrier. Anna's part of the group, and she's much different than we thought. We befriended a pastry chef, who's smitten with Kiki. And tomorrow night Kiki is throwing a rager, something we previously knew nothing about."

"All true," Angus raised his eyebrows, lifting his chin, "but you purposefully omitted the part that you're warming up to the idea of Anna."

"Not warming, per se, but I do find her warming-worthy," Brixton shook his head at Angus's expression. "You know, Ang, it doesn't always have to be like that with the opposite sex—there is the potential for just being friends, you know."

"You think so?" Angus eyed him, "I don't know about that."

"For the record, though, I did quite enjoy her attempt to turn you off to Reese. Then again, you never heeded my warnings, so what would make you listen to hers?"

"I know Reese is no saint. Obviously," Angus glazed over the mention of where Brixton fit into that equation. "To be forthright, what I didn't tell Anna, which I will tell you, is that I'm trying to get over her," Angus paused, "but it isn't easy. I've liked her for years. She's hard to extract from my mind. It's like she's infected it."

Brixton let down his guard. "I didn't realize it was that bad. I'm sorry I've been acidic about all of it. I'm only agitated because I want it behind you and behind us, not because I don't want to see you happy. You're worth more than Reese's maniacal games. And there are many girls at Cypress who would love to have a chance with you."

"It's alright. It'll be better for both of us when I can let her go," Angus whacked his shoulder. "She still asks about you...."

"I hope you either tell her nothing or make something up. None of the details or all the wrong details are best suited for her," Brixton forced a smile, hoping Angus was as serious as he sounded about giving it up once and for all.

Angus looked at him, "She knows nothing other than what little she knew before...."

"I wish she could know nothing about all of us," Brixton looked beyond Angus into the distance.

"No surprise that Ki feels the same," Angus watched Brixton's face. "Even without talking to her all those months, you two still somehow share the same opinions."

Brixton wasn't ready to discuss the subject of Kila with him. "I wonder how many girls will be here tomorrow night…do any of the five I named interest you?"

"Nope," Angus laughed lightly.

Brixton frowned. "But they're all LOFTY picks!"

"Okay, so they're lofty picks," Angus humored him. "Are you interested in any of them?"

"Well, no, not really," Brixton grinned, "but you have to have had a weakness for someone other than Reese in your whole life…have you ever?"

Angus kept his expression to a minimum and looked at the group of photos on the wall.

"Good," Brixton crossed his arms. "We're getting somewhere for once."

"I suppose," Angus humored him, at once relieved and embarrassed that he'd finally opened up to Brixton about his feelings, even if he hadn't divulged everything.

"So," Brixton thought aloud, "do you think this is some last-minute surprise party for Ethan? And Kiki didn't tell us 'cause she thought he'd dig it out of us if we knew?"

"I don't know, but I do know I'm not waiting to find out,"

Angus rolled his shoulders back. "We have to know the details in order to plan. Without details, we're at a disadvantage, and you know I hate being at a disadvantage. We promised Anna we wouldn't say anything to Ki, but we didn't promise her we wouldn't find out and keep it to ourselves."

Brixton tilted his head to the left and to the right, deciding whether or not he agreed with Angus. Angus hung onto the moment, waiting for Brixton's blessing. When the tilting was complete and Brixton showed the slightest smile, Angus held both his hands up.

"Proceed with your plan," Brixton gave the go ahead. "I'm guessing you already have one?"

"Yes," Angus spoke proudly. "Here it is: quick, easy, foolproof. Ki wouldn't throw a party without putting Josie on the guest list. So…I'm texting Josie."

"You have Josie's number?" Brixton smiled.

"Yes," Angus held a straight face.

Brixton rubbed his hands together. "Does Reese know?"

"No," Angus shook his head. "Why would I tell Reese I have her number? It has nothing to do with her. It's not like that between Josie and me. Even if it were, which it isn't, I told you I'm trying to get Reese out of my life anyway."

Brixton's lips stretched wider. "Why do you have her number, Ang?"

Angus huffed into a grin, "She calls me sometimes for help on her Pysch homework."

Brixton snickered. "How OFTEN does she call you for Pysch help?"

"I don't know. Before grades were submitted, she'd call me a few times a week, like three or four nights. We'd work out the scenarios together and bounce paper ideas off each other. She did call me again after grades were submitted just to thank me again, which I thought was nice," Angus failed to determine why Brixton had succumb to such laughter. "What? Why does it even matter? Stop making that obnoxious face."

"Bro. Both Josie's parents are psychologists in town. My mom knows them through the hospital," he laughed harder at Angus's annoyed expression. "Come on, Ang. Don't be mad at the girl. She likes you. Clearly. Be flattered. I'd be flattered even if I wasn't interested."

"At least I KNOW Reese plays games. Josie, too? Hell," Angus scrunched his nose, typing the message to her on his phone.

"Get over it. Most girls play games. And don't EVER compare Josie McCellum to Reese Seratine again," Brixton's train of thought screeched to a halt when he noticed the cluster of pictures on the wall beside Angus.

Kiki. Homecoming dance, freshman year. The best dancer, but afraid to dance in front of all the people she didn't know. We went together, stood by the balloons for nearly an hour, then danced alone outside in the grass to the playlists on my phone. I loved the rebellious way she kicked off her heels, destroyed her updo, fastened the hairpins to her dress, and shook her hair free. I hated the glow of the headlights when they pulled up next to us. I kept telling myself, "One more song, then I'll kiss her." Why didn't I kiss her? It's more than two years later, and I still haven't. Jacques made more progress in a few hours than I have in the span of several years. Why can't I just tell her the truth?

"Uhhhhhhh," Angus wasn't sure what to say. The reddish color drained from his cheeks leaving his face a single shade of eggshell. "Nnnnnnnnnn...Aaaaaaaaaaaa...."

Brixton tried to make sense of Angus's odd sounding murmurs. "What the hell is it?" he asked.

Angus replied, "Josie just threw a sizeable wrench at us." Unable to speak the words, Angus thrust the phone into his friend's hands.

Brixton looked down at the screen. The text was monumental. "Why didn't she tell him? We have to tell him!" Brixton shook his head. "Don't you see him in there? He'll be crushed! Flattened! Annihilated."

"It's her news to break, Brix," Angus's voice came across as somber. "I think she would have told us if she wanted us to know. Heck, Ki would have told us...I guess this explains her sudden change in behavior."

Brixton threw his hands up to keep him from raising his voice. He paced the hallway with Peaches right beside him, then acknowledged Angus had a point. Both boys recognized this would be catastrophic for Ethan's constitution. Ethan would enjoy the time with Maya until she told him, and then Brixton and Angus would be there for him. They'd always made it through everything together, and now they'd hopefully have an extra hand in Jacques. Even if Jacques couldn't soothe Ethan with his words, Ethan could wallow away some of his misery at The Hidden Meridian, consuming coco'range and gelato when his mind wrestled with dark thoughts.

Wearing a new burden, the boys sauntered down the hallway on the first floor to the guestroom. On their way, they passed the library, where Kila and Jacques remained in lively conversation. Angus hovered in the doorway as Kila took her turn reading. He admired the way she enunciated every syllable and paused properly at every grammatical sign. Wanting to be near her, Angus slipped into the room. Just as Jacques spotted him, Brixton yanked him back into the hallway. Kila, engrossed in the story, hadn't noticed either of them. Jacques, however, remained a bit confused. When he looked at the boys, Brixton waved and smiled, as if everything were fine, despite the visual of a peeved Angus standing right beside him.

"What do you think you're doing?" Angus snapped, storming after Brixton as he sped through the hall.

"YOU don't need to be in there right now anymore than I need to be," Brixton said plainly.

"Maybe we BOTH need to be in there. Why are we giving Jacques the free pass to Ki, anyway?" Angus squinted his eyes. "It's unheard of! Neither of us ever had it that easy...."

"Neither of us ever tried...," the truth in Brixton's words

singed the hole burned in his heart from seeing Kila and Jacques alone for the first time.

"We should have," Angus's words confused not only himself but Brixton as well.

Brixton sharpened his eyes. "What are you talking about?"

"Doesn't matter…," Angus exhaled. "Like I said before. I need to get over Reese and you need to open up to Anna. If Ki and Jacques are a pair now, so be it."

Brixton tried to assure himself, "They're not a pair. They're just talking."

"Yeah…for now," Angus grinned. "You do know how these things work, don't you? Maybe not for you and me, but he seems to be an anomaly. That blanket trick set me ablaze. Beyond audacious."

Brixton shook the sour feeling from his stomach and thought of Anna. *Maybe I should try…*

The guest room was pristine, as could be expected. No matter how busy Claire and Dil were, they always found time to keep the house spotless and welcome. Their hospitality was unparalleled, making the Lorens house the preferred place for holiday meals and friendly gatherings. Angus had already moved his bag of clothes downstairs after school, but Brixton realized his things were still upstairs.

"I need to grab my bag in Ethan's room—wanna work out then play some cards?"

"Entirely down. I was hoping we could talk some more," Angus admitted.

"Me too," Brixton welcomed the opportunity for more conversation.

Fact-finding was sort of his thing, and he wanted to learn more about where Angus's feelings were headed next. As Brixton passed through the living room, he glanced at the love seat. The roles had been reversed. Ethan was sleeping. Maya was awake. Brixton worked hard to avoid talk of the text and the party.

"Hey Maya," he whispered, "I'm going upstairs to get my bag. Angus and I are staying in the guest room as usual. Anna's upstairs in Kiki's room."

"Where's Ki?" she asked.

"In the library with Noah," Brixton disliked delivering the message.

"I see," Maya replied, with a grin. "Should I wake Ethan up?"

"He's all yours," he swallowed hard, forcing an impending outburst back down his throat. "I guess it's up to you."

Maya thought about Brixton's comment, overwhelmed with the possibilities. She entertained each of them until she remembered she still had one very important thing to tell him. Something that risked ruining everything that had already happened between them tonight. Something she hated, hated above all for the past several weeks. As her fears battled with the love in her heart, she snuggled breathlessly into Ethan with the resolve she would wake him and tell him once Brixton returned.

Annabelle, who had been listening to music in Kila's room, perked up when she heard footsteps on the stairs. Right at the start of **"Like Real People Do" by Hozier**, Anna opened Kila's bedroom door, allowing the tender, poetic music to follow her into the hallway.

Brixton held a hand up and nodded.

"Hey you," Anna greeted him more intimately, amused by his somewhat odd gesture.

He took advantage of their privacy. "I'm sorry about earlier, during the movie...if I seemed a bit distant," he adjusted the cuffs of his sleeves.

"I didn't notice anything," she could only spend so many seconds in his green eyes, so she turned away at intervals. "I mean, I guess I did...it's that, we all have our own struggles," she rushed to reach her point, "...and, I guess you and I at least can say we've rid ourselves of Reese, something uncommon I guess we have in common."

"Yeah, it is," he realized. "She'll never rid herself of us though, something else we share."

"She'll never be over you," Anna hoped she wouldn't share that same fate.

"I couldn't give myself to a taker. I need more. I want more than that," he worried his words had grown too intimate for a conversation with someone he had first spoken with today.

She held her words inside, tasting their sweetness. He wasn't ready for them yet.

"Probably no one appreciates what you said to Angus more than I do. He's the most stubborn person, possibly in existence," Brixton laughed, "and I know you reached him tonight. I"—he smiled at her—"enjoyed the back-and-forth you two had for a while. A bit bitter, but genuine."

"I've only known Angus from a distance, but somehow, maybe from Ethan"—her eyes pulsed at the sound of Ethan's name—"I feel like I know him."

"Does Ethan talk about Angus more than me?" He shrugged as he repeated those ridiculous words in his head. *WHY would I ask that?!*

"No," Anna responded, just as quickly, "I just think Angus is more readable than you are."

Anna didn't know it, but she had unintentionally delivered to Brixton what he deemed to be a massive compliment.

"I have to head back down," he self-consciously called to close a conversation he knew he'd revisit alone later tonight.

"Hey…wait," Anna looked at her toes, "I know Angus and I talked a bunch tonight, and I didn't want you to think I was, like…interested in him like that. I know…almost everyone else is...but...I'm not...so, just so you know," she looked up into his emerald eyes.

Brixton nodded with a half-smile, not knowing what else to say.

She took a cautionary step forward, "Can I get another hug?"

"Of course," he hoped the welcome in his voice hadn't opened the floodgates for endless future embraces.

The hug was easier to accept than he suspected. There was a lightness in the way she came in gently without cling. It was Brixton who squeezed her and held her for moments, his limbs weighing the possibility of her, his mind testing the waters.

She remained still in his arms, reminding herself to breathe as his hands pressed into her back right before he released her. Fighting against her heart was never Anna's aim. She knew it wouldn't serve her. She took from the embrace what others might take from an inspirational quote, appreciation and hope. And that was all she needed tonight.

"Sweet dreams," the softness in Brixton's own voice startled him.

"They will be now," Anna walked away without looking back, slowly closing Kila's bedroom door and melting on the other side of it.

Affection. Brixton stood reflective in place until his feelings settled. Then he rushed into Ethan's room to retrieve his bag and returned to the guest room to find Angus listening to **"I Hope You Never Call" by Indian Run**. Seeing Angus's tense face, Brixton waited to speak until the sweet-and-sour song had reached its end. At that point Angus grew animated once more. After what evolved into endless sets of crunches, squats, push-ups, and dips, the two played several hands of cards, discussing everything from Reese to Anna, to Kila's metamorphosis, to the EmOpen before eventually falling asleep. Brixton under the covers, Angus over the covers, they followed a tradition established when they were little. Only now they weren't trying to avoid girls, they were trying to attract them.

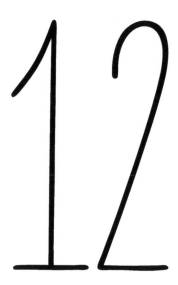

Maya struggled with her conscience, questioning how long she could enjoy Ethan before she shared her last piece of crushing news with him. In a way, she almost wished tonight hadn't unfolded in such a palatable manner. Now she knew what she would be missing, whereas before she just had a vague idea of a love that never was. It was a lesson in bravery she doubted she would ever forget.

Had she simply spoken with Ethan sooner, had she maybe hinted to him a year, a few months, or even a few weeks ago, they could have had more time together. Time to experience one another as more than friends. Time to tell him the things she had always thought but never spoke, and time to hear the things he might say. Sure, he had mentioned the word "boyfriend" in his text to her, but that was before he knew the bitter truth.

When Ethan shifted next to her, she took a long look at him.

Even with his eyes closed, the sight of him rocked her senses. *Maybe I like his hair so much because it's close to his brain.* She pushed his hair back with her fingers, working the top section up into a giant wave that curled under on one side. *I probably shouldn't have done that,* she stared at it longingly until the impulse to kiss him triumphed over the nagging of her worry.

The warmth of his cheeks was almost as inviting as the warmth of his lips. And she kissed his mouth like it might be the last time, lengthening every gesture and drawing his lips into hers. In just a few moments, he awoke in a passionate haze, clutching her waist and pulling her closer.

"I'll only be yours, if you want me," he grazed his lips slowly across her cheek, "just promise you'll always wake me this way."

When she pulled away, looking at the couch cushion, he studied her face for fear she might have changed her mind.

"Nothing's wrong," she assured him. "It's just that I...I...," the words were nearly in reach, "it's been a long time."

"Since when?" he wasn't following, but wanted to, desperately.

"Since I first wanted it," Maya admitted, "wanted you, that is."

"If you told me," he touched two of his fingers to her bottom lip, "I wouldn't have made you wait."

She looked into his eyes, just as the credits finished rolling and the screen faded to black.

Left in relative darkness, Ethan whispered to her, "Come here."

"I am here," she nuzzled her cheek against his. "If I was any closer I'd be in your lap."

"…Well…I don't see that as a bad thing…do you?" he danced his fingers along her forearm.

"…No…," the idea burned inside her, so much so she couldn't speak further on the matter.

"…Do you want to?" he crossed his fingers and closed his eyes.

"…Yes…," Maya touched her fingers to his, "but you have to kiss me."

"I was planning on it," he reached for her while biting his top lip.

She touched his hair as soon as her legs were stable. When his lips met hers, her mouth swept over them without mercy. The dark silence embraced them as they embraced each other. And Maya's insides surged with each indiscernible noise that sprung from Ethan's throat. *I'm tasting his voice,* she realized as she felt the vibrations from his words in her mouth. She remembered the sound of his vocals earlier, how his voice had played off of Brixton's while his hands had kept the rhythm on the bongos.

Ethan's body, which had remained relatively calm since the library, grew overly receptive to her affection. The steady, tender pressure of her lips untied the final knot of his reservation, and each time he felt it, he rushed in for more. She shivered in his lap, and he leaned back into the couch cushion, pressing his hands tightly to her sides. After several more minutes of continuous kissing in the dark, she gasped and withdrew her lips from his.

"Was the kissing too much?" He worried he may have crossed "the line," wasn't sure where "the line" was, and hoped she would soon clue him in.

"No," she rested her forehead against his, "you…um…gave me the chills." She laughed into his skin.

"Oh," he shifted so they sat in a more upright position, "pretty good for our first day."

"I know," she leaned on his shoulder, stretching her arms around him. *This is better each moment…*

"It was nice to see you sleep." Ethan's voice, though deep, held a softer edge, "I don't think I've ever seen you sleep before."

"I don't think so, either…," her fingers touched his shirt, wishing she could feel his skin instead. "It's sort of been a rough couple of weeks. And I still have to tell you something you don't want to hear."

Perplexed by her last comments, Ethan lifted his head to kiss her cheek. He thought it might prompt her to tell him what she'd been hiding. When she remained silent he amended that he wouldn't push it, lest it risk changing their new status, or whatever it was to be considered. *Nothing can come between us now. I don't care what it is. She can tell me when she's ready.*

He turned on the lamp next to the couch, "Maybe you need some rest? Let's get you up to Ki's room. We can always resume this conversation tomorrow...," he smiled, kissing her just once on the lips. "I'm not exactly going to make myself scarce, you know, no matter what you tell me." He touched the back of his hand to her hair, then caressed her cheek.

Maya straightened up, gathering her strength about her. *I have to do this. I promised Ki and I owe it to myself and to him. I have to find my brave. I have to tell him tonight.* She smoothed all of her hair and draped it over one shoulder. "Can I stay in your room tonight?" She looked into his gray-blue eyes.

"With me?" Ethan wanted to be sure he understood her question.

"Yeah," Maya looked away from his face, "I don't move about much, I promise."

Ethan stroked her hair and answered with a long-lasting kiss.

"So, that's a yes, right?" Maya nuzzled her nose into his when they parted for air.

"Yes," Ethan pulled her close. "I'd love to be alone with you. I didn't know if you'd want that."

"I've always wanted to stay with you, in your bed. I've...," she leaned back, smiling in his arms.

"You've what?" he tickled her, hoping she'd tell him.

"Okay," she giggled uncontrollably, feeling his fingers dance atop her ribs. "Stop! I'll tell you if you stop!" She clutched her stomach, smiling when he held his hands up in the air.

"Five seconds until I start," he warned, wiggling his fingers with his invincible half-smile.

"Alright! I've...," Maya looked at the lamp, grinning at the thought of telling him and feeling all the more bashful.

He moved his hands close to her stomach again, watching her eyes.

"I've already slept in your bed before," Maya confessed. "Not the new one you just got for your birthday, but the double you had."

"Really?" he kissed her nose twice. "With who?"

"No one! I mean, just me...wishing you were there too...," Maya felt herself blush.

With her cheeks so rosy, he didn't have to question her honesty. "Ki never told me!"

"Yeah, well, I made her promise not to. I might have also worn a shirt or two of yours as well, here and there, now and again, instead of my pajamas," she blushed again, this time harder than the last.

"How could I NOT have known? How many times were you in my bed in my clothes?" he looked at her, wiggling his fingers in threat.

"I'm not sure...," she smiled nervously, "...I guess almost every time you were over at Brix's and I was staying over."

"I'm glad I know about this now," Ethan tickled her despite her confession. "Ugh! You're making me crazy, My. Crazy."

Maya giggled and pushed him backwards into the couch cushion. *I wish I didn't have to tell him. I REALLY wish it, that we could have a night together without him knowing and with me forgetting. Just one. One perfect one. Tonight.*

"By the way, moving forward, you can wear any of my shirts without having to hide it." He grinned, "You probably look better in them than I do."

"I like the way they smell," she watched his eyes look at her lips.

He ran his fingers through her hair, leaning the bridge of his nose into her cheek, "I like the way your hair smells."

She squeezed him, closing her eyes, "I could fall asleep... right here...with you."

"Not yet," he kissed her forehead. "We should go up to my room. We'll have...more privacy...and we can...listen to music."

"Yeah...," she circled his shoulders with her thumbs, "your new bed IS pretty sweet. Anna and I checked it out after school and we could stretch into snowflakes without touching one another," she pressed her nose into his shirt, smelling the scent she loved more than any other.

"Apparently my room's been free range for a while…I think I'm going to lock my door and give you the only key," he rocked her in his arms, loving how it felt to hold her. "Come on, let's go up," he whispered. "You can change in Ki's room and then see me once you're in your pajamas. It'll be safer that way. I won't be tempted to…watch you change."

Maya cherished Ethan's words. She always figured he was a gentleman, but never pegged him for squeaky clean. "Probably a good idea…," she voiced her reply, all the while wondering if she would ever get to see him change. *If ever there was a true test of my self-control that would be it. Then again, why should I suffer to pass such a test, when failing it might actually be more educational?*

"What is it?" He called out her wide eyes and sultry smile.

"You," she laughed, standing up and pulling him to his feet.

"What about me?" He wished he knew what she was thinking.

"Everything about you," she pursed her lips, leading the way upstairs.

Alone in his room, Ethan hunted for something suitable to wear. Most nights, he just slept in his boxers, but those wouldn't be suitable tonight. He didn't want to appear too naked. While he was magnetized by Maya's body, and his hormones were no stranger to him, he also knew that they were newly seventeen, and he was more concerned about things feeling right than feeling rushed. This evening's kiss in the library was his first, and he savored the idea of talking and falling asleep together without anyone else around.

As he frantically rummaged through his dresser, he happened upon a new pair of pajamas Kila had given him for Christmas. *YES! I forgot about these. Will they work?* He smirked at the image of the mannequin-like man with movie-star hair stretched across the front of the box.

At least if these fit me, my smile won't be phony or forced. Wait...are they meant to be THAT form fitting? Oh boy... His eyes noticed the places on the picture where the striped fabric looked taut. The size of the model's shoulders, arms, thighs, and what rested in between made Ethan worry the pajamas might appear floppy on his own frame in those particular areas. *Let's hope the packaging team digitally exaggerated the bulk of his buffness.*

I can handle this. If there's too much room in the seat, I can roll the waistband down. I've had to do that with gym shorts before...not a big deal. If there's too much room in the upper arms, I can wear an undershirt to fill it out a bit more...that'll also help in the chest department.

No...wait. I can't do that! If I'm two shirts deep before I'm even under the covers, I'll be certain to sweat. Ugh. Sweating before cuddling and kissing could even come to be—THAT's not good. Sweating isn't exactly a turn-on...at least not that I know of. I've never heard Ki or any of her friends discuss perspiration in a sexy light...

Logic. These are either going to fit or fail to fit, in which case I will need a fallback...immediately. Frantically ignoring the step-by-step instructions on the side, Ethan ripped the gift box open, tearing through piece after piece of paper and cardboard until at last the clothes were free. After hastily tossing the package remnants into his recycling bag, he set the pajamas on his bed. Soft flannel with thin vertical graphite-and-white stripes, the pair consisted of a button-up top and snap-close bottoms. From first glance the sizing appeared about right, yet he worried anyway. *I shouldn't have waited this long to try them on...*

Removing all of his clothes in a nervous rush, he flew into his bathroom to clean himself up. He grinned while applying a fresh coat of deodorant. *I don't have time to shower...but neither does she...I need to hurry this up.* Splashing water on his face, he caught his reflection in the mirror and couldn't stop smiling at himself. *She likes me! And I have SOME muscles. Maybe not as many as the guy on the box who gets paid to have them, but I do work out. Not obsessively, but regularly... guess I have Brix and Ang to thank for that.* He washed his hands and forearms with the rosemary hand soap his mom had brought in yesterday, and wondered what it would feel like to lie next to Maya in bed.

After toweling off, Ethan's palms tapped in rapid succession on the countertop. *I'll teach her how to play the bongos. She can teach me how to improve my running endurance. I'll listen to her throwback music. She can listen to my emerging artists. I'll send her links to some of my alt music news. She can send me links to some of the blogs she follows. We'll work to build our tallest Jenga tower while we get to know everything about each other. And we'll kiss 'till our lips are numb...or close to...and we'll take breaks when we need to...then kiss again...*

He spun around in happiness, then sprayed a fresh round of cologne on his chest, neck, and arms. Before dashing out of his bathroom, he poked his head out to be sure Maya hadn't returned. *Why'd I go in there stark naked without the pajamas, anyway? I'm losing it...because of her...* Ethan's smile, which he forced into a smaller form, remained in place as he took a deep breath and stepped into the pajama bottoms.

Can you see my gray boxers underneath? Ethan walked to the full-length mirror next to his closet to investigate the pants. *Not bad. At least the dark outline lets her know I'm wear-ing boxers. PANTS FIT!* He fumbled a little snapping the front closed, then reached for the top, pleased that there was no need to roll the waistband down. *If the top doesn't fit, I'll just wear a white T-shirt. Easy problem, easy fix.*

Slipping his left arm in and then his right arm, he felt the seams of the shoulders hit him right where they should. *Kila, THESE are a GODSEND.* He buttoned the front closed, amused that it had a collar, and stepped in front of the mirror once more. *Chest and upper arms are looking alright...but the sleeves... they make my forearms look like POLES!*

With a slight flush to his cheeks, Ethan unfastened the cuffs, which hung loosely below his wrists, and rolled them three times up his forearms. At the new length, the cuffed sleeves hit right below his elbows, and his forearms, which once appeared boney, looked full and masculine. He exhaled into a subtle smile.

With the pressing issues of cleanliness and sleeping attire resolved, Ethan redirected his attention to the ambiance. He tidied everything in sight, from his clothes hanging half off their hangers to the pile of sneakers on the floor. Well, not so much tidy as shove it all into the closet and shut the sliding, slatted wooden doors. Regardless, the floor that could be seen looked clean for the first time in quite some time.

Fluffing his bed like he figured a girl might prefer, he tossed the three embroidered throw pillows to the floor. *Throw pillows? Don't know why, but the girls love them. Why have extra pillows on the bed during the day, only to throw them onto the floor at night? Marketing scheme if you ask me...yet, here they are, just the same, on my floor. Every day on the top. Every night on the floor...*he babbled internally, questioning which of his playlists might suit the night best. *Nothing too rushing, nothing too rough, nothing too gloomy. Ah! My "Saved It To The Last Minute" study mix. That should work... at least to start. I'll adjust afterwards, if necessary...*

He shut off his overhead lights and clicked his bedside lamp to the lowest setting. The dark shade cast a warm, amber glow about the room, and he instantly thought of Maya's lips. *When will I get to kiss them again? What's taking her so long? I hope she's not trying to look better...because...that's impossible.* He fed the music from his phone into his speakers, then acutely heard the turn of the doorknob as **"Hard Believer" by Fink** seduced every molecule of oxygen in the room.

Ethan's heart leapt in his chest as he watched the door open. Maya stepped in, adorned in a flowy cream-colored camisole with scalloped straps and matching terrycloth bottoms that cuffed at her ankles. He had seen her wear less in a bikini many times by the pool, but this ensemble sung to him—it resonated with romance. His lips, painfully waiting to kiss her, parted without his permission.

Maya grinned, "You didn't have to wait for me to get into bed."

"Waiting doesn't bother me," Ethan worked to control his thoughts.

"You finally wore the pj's Ki bought you," she gushed. "You're shaming the poor model on the front of the box looking like that."

"Good thing he's not here," Ethan noticed her pastel-pink painted toenails. "I really don't want any competition," he glanced at her face again.

"You have none. None even if he were here," Maya's hands touched the bottom of her camisole, longing to touch his hair. The fabric couldn't soothe her like his chocolate locks could. *He might never understand that.*

So I look alright in the pajamas. When can I kiss her? Though he couldn't feel his feet on the wooden floor, Ethan walked her over to the side of the bed closest to her, and unfolded the covers into a right triangle.

She watched him walk over to the other side, letting herself slide in between the many layers of sheets and covers like a swimmer might slip into the water feet first. *Better than a dream,* she was astounded at how comfortable she felt. Wiggling her fingers around the ultra-plush duvet, she excitedly watched Ethan climb in beside her. The bed was so large that no part of them touched, even when Maya stretched herself into a starfish.

His mind scrambled to believe the image his eyes took in. *Maya's in my bed trying to touch me.* He smiled uncontrollably, stretching his arm to its fullest and trying to reach her fingers.

"This mattress is too wide—I can't get to you," her face turned toward his, half of her smile hidden in the pillow.

"Might be safer this way," he winked. "My mom might have been onto something with this."

"Yeah," she scrunched her nose, "Claire always knows."

"Come here," he motioned for her to come to his side, "…I don't think I want to be safe right now."

"…Me either," she wiggled toward him under the covers, taking her pillow with her.

When Ethan's arm curved around her waist, it felt like the sun was upon her. She let herself be taken by that sensation, his energy trickling its way to her core, heating her insides from deep within. *All of his skin so close to all of my skin.* Her head sunk further into the pillow and her closed eyes helplessly conjured images of him despite his actual presence beside her.

When she felt his fingers tap on her cheek, her eyes opened to find his face next to hers. Unwilling to go without any longer, her hands began a new sculpture in his hair. Her touch washed colors of vitality over his soul.

His fingers swept across the silkiness of her camisole. "Kind of feels like today's more of my birthday than yesterday was," he let the words slip from his lips one by one, as he watched her eyes descend from his hair to his face.

"I wish I could have been there last night, for the cake in the tree house. Ki kind of reamed me out about it," she watched his eyelids close when he laughed a little.

"Ki likes to ream people out," his voice more or less mesmerized her. "You gave her good reason, though. Why weren't you there?"

"I was scared." She watched her fingers move through his hair.

"...Of me finally turning seventeen?" he propped a hand under his head, looking at her. "I'll never quite catch up to you...six weeks, you know...it's a sizeable gap...could that be the problem?"

"No," she smiled, "I don't mind being a little older...actually, I like it."

"Me too," he kissed her nose while looking into her eyes.

She kissed his lips only once, then retreated.

He looked at her in question.

"I...um...I want to kiss you for a few more minutes before I tell you what's going on. Can I?" she looked at his face.

"Obviously," he touched the edge of her nose. "You can kiss me all night until tomorrow morning, and then tell me, if you want."

"Oooo," Maya touched her lips to his intermittently, "...that's a tempting thought."

"...And those are some tempting lips," he began to kiss her like he had when they were on the couch downstairs.

Maya took in his lips as gladly as her ears took in his breathy sounds. But the minutes of kissing could not make up for her news. The news, which she had shielded from him, taunted her. Time dwindled at an alarming rate. No amount of kissing could stop the numbers from falling, yet she kissed him in vain regardless of her knowing. She kissed him in vain until the second part she had promised Kila was all she could think about.

His lips stopped moving when he realized hers had.

She sat up abruptly, rustling her hands in her hair, knowing the news had to make its way from the inside to the outside. It could no longer be prolonged, and the words, already knowing their stage time, leapt from behind the closed curtains and out of her trembling mouth.

"Ethan I have to tell you something that I really, REALLY, don't want to. I've been avoiding it for weeks, even against your sister's wishes. And, I should have told you sooner, before... or, once things started happening between us."

He sat up next to her, studying the obvious concern on her face. "What is it? Tell me—it'll feel better to let it out. I was only joking about waiting until the morning. Tell me now... you know you can tell me anything. Let go of it...come on...," he kissed her cheek.

She shook her head "no" and took several loud, deep breaths.

"You're shaking…," he rubbed his hands from her shoulders to her arms in an attempt to relax the distress out of her.

Salty water dripped from the corners of her eyes and rolled down her cheeks in steady streams. Her shoulders continued to tremble between his hands.

"Come here," Ethan pulled her in to him, wrapping his arms around her. "Tell me, My. It can't be that bad." He rocked her back and forth like he used to rock Kila when they were little and she was upset.

"It is! It is that bad!" Maya's words sounded muffled against Ethan's soft pajamas. "And you might never forgive me. I shouldn't have listened to Kila. I should have kept both parts a secret, and then you wouldn't have ever known. And we wouldn't be here right now. And I wouldn't know how right my feelings were. Or how exceptional you feel. Or how intimate you sound. Or how hot you look in those striped pajamas. I knew you'd look hot in those pajamas. I knew it right when she picked them out. I was with her," she squeezed his shoulders. "I could barely sleep that night picturing you in them."

"What could possibly be so wrong?" One of his hands reached to touch the ends of her hair. "I won't be mad at you no matter what you say. It's only been a few hours, that we've been…like this, but I want you to trust me. Please trust me," he was beginning to worry. *What the hell is going on? She's usually like a rock.*

"Okay," she pulled away from his shoulder, looking in his eyes. "I'm going to tell you. I'm just going say it—I'm just going to throw it out there with all of its blackening finality."

Ethan held both of her hands in his, hoping a physical link might make it easier for her to speak. He nodded for her to continue.

"My dad's been angling for a promotion for years. Taking on extra responsibilities. Taking trips whenever they need him to. You know my dad, he's always with that laptop and second cell. My mom told me to be supportive about his career, and I have been. So has my sister. We've all been," Maya paused to take a breath.

Ethan caressed her fingers, relieved that the issue at hand was somehow tied to her father.

She continued, "All of it finally paid off. He's been promoted, which is supposed to be a good thing. Right? But, instead of moving ONE rung up the ladder, which would have kept him in Felton, he's been pushed TWO rungs up the ladder. A double promotion of sorts; and, it should be celebration-worthy. I know. I mean, it's supposed to be, but it is BY FAR the WORST thing imaginable!"

Ethan clasped her hands, then rubbed his fingers briskly on hers. "It's alright, My. It's alright."

She shook her head "no." Breaking contact with his eyes, she looked down at the pattern in the duvet. The next words she spoke came hard, her mouth choking the sound out from her lips. The sound that rang softer than a whisper. The sound that broke off at intervals, crumbling into bits and pieces, like the shattering of her heart into his hands.

"They're posting him to Rhode Island. And, I have no choice. I have to go with them. I hate it, I hate it so much, and I don't see why we are even going. My sister just had a baby. You'd think they would want to stay near their first grandchild, wouldn't you? They've known for over a month, yet they told me only thirteen days ago. They didn't know how to. Big surprise there. And with the exception of tonight, it has unmistakably been the worst thirteen days of my life!"

She looked up to find his eyes straining to make sense of it, and she pulled one of her hands from his grip to touch his hair. As she stroked a section behind his ear, she noticed a single tear escape from his right eye.

"I'm so sorry I did this to you. I...I have to leave at the end of next week. I haven't been able to sleep. I've been sick to my stomach. Every day I'm sick to my stomach. Tonight's dinner was the biggest meal I've eaten this week. Your veggie burgers—I couldn't resist them. I didn't know if it was my last time, with them...and...with you. And, I know there's no way around it. I have to have senior year at a new school where I don't know anyone. I'll be away from all of my best friends and everything I have grown to love. I'm SO in the wrong for not telling you sooner, and that all of this happened between us tonight. I just kept thinking maybe you would find out from someone at school even though Kila was on me about it. I was afraid to tell you everything: that I'm leaving, that I like you—I've been crazy about you ever since I can remember. I know it sounds ridiculous, and that, as a girl, I'm supposedly supposed to play hard to get, but I don't even care if my admitting that I've always liked you scares you off. My feelings for you don't even really matter now, given the circumstances, do they? Perhaps what's worse is that you are, every bit, the incredible kisser I imagined you were, and now I am going to be thinking about your lips ALL THE TIME, while I FREEZE in godforsaken New England!"

The pressure inside Maya's head had reached a boil and released itself in steaming words, spinning her body into utter exhaustion. Her eyes, so full of tears, could no longer handle the sight of Ethan's heartsick face, and she moved to the edge of the bed she had climbed into only minutes ago. Her whole being ached as she swung her legs over the side and stood, preparing to make her way into Kila's room.

Ethan swallowed hard, wiping both of his now very wet eyes. The revelation had punctured a hole in the otherwise ideal evening, but it certainly wasn't Maya's fault. He knew she was waiting on him, that anything he said or did in this moment would be remembered and weighed. This was, without question, one of those critical-mass points in his life, and he would be damned if he chose not to speak up, living the rest of his life in unshakeable regret.

In his mind he attempted to calculate the distance, and it overwhelmed him. He dismissed his cognitive processes for the time being and opened up his heart to her just as **"King And Lionheart" by Of Monsters and Men** began to play. *I can't hold back. Not while this song is playing. It's too noble. Too true.*

Tears continued to stream down Maya's face as she counted the seconds without hearing his reply. She took a step away from the bed, wiped her eyes, and inhaled when she saw him step in front of her.

"The only problem I have with all of that," he touched both of his hands to both of hers, "isn't the problem you thought I'd have."

She sniffled, smiled, and wiped the new tears that seemed to keep falling.

"Hey," he lifted his right hand to caress her cheek, "you really thought I'd give up?"

Her eyes looked into his.

"You owe me. You said our friendship was over. Over. That means I can only be your boyfriend. And, believe it or not, that status is not contingent upon your geographical location."

"It's not?" her hand found its way to his hair again.

"No," he kissed her left cheek, then her right cheek. "It's going to take a lot more than a dozen states to separate us, Maya."

She touched his shoulders. "I love the sound of that, but I won't hold you to it. Starting our relationship as a long distance one…might be…," she preferred not to say the words lest they come true.

"I wouldn't exactly say we're starting our relationship," he touched his palms to her sides, pressing them into her camisole. "It started a long time ago. Maybe not like this, but…."

Her dark eyes held onto his light eyes like their next revelation held the potential to sculpt the rest of her life.

He kissed her forehead, then rubbed his cheek against hers. "I guess I didn't know how to tell you, either. As time moved along, I found myself making excuses for why I had to leave Brix and Ang earlier than expected when you were staying over. They teased me 'cause they knew, and I couldn't admit it to myself, let alone to them. I always liked to catch you after Ki tuckered out, when we would talk for hours, without anyone else around. I treasured those conversations, treasured learning about you, and treasured all the questions you would ask me. It made me hope you might be interested in more than talking one day."

"I was...and...I am," Maya touched her lips to his, in a way that wasn't desperate but let him know she cared.

He lifted his hands from her sides to her cheeks. "Your lips, good god," he kissed her slowly. "Hang on...I lost my train of thought...."

She backed away from him smiling, patting the last of her tears into her skin. When he stepped into her again, she buried her hands in his hair, grabbing as many chocolatey locks as she could fit between her fingers.

His eyes closed at the sensation, his thoughts rippling out in separate whispers, "Maya, the sound of your voice alone could keep me yours...All you have to do is call and visit when you can...We can make it work...I know it...We can brand this weekend ours...I'll do whatever you want...two full days...then some of next week...parents, band, school, whatever else, I don't care...I'll move EVERYTHING else around...I'm yours...I...I can't change that now." He opened his blue-gray eyes to see her beholden smile.

She extended her arms to him since he already had her heart, and they settled under the blankets, tangled up tightly inside the embrace of the night.

Maya tossed a little, but fell asleep with her knees over his and his hand clasped over hers. Ethan lay awake a bit longer. He planned to savor every moment in hopes that the last might not hurt as bad as he feared. Before succumbing to slumber, and deep in his thoughts, he realized he was never truly confused about his feelings for Maya—he was just frightened of them. They were feelings of love. And he hoped that love would be the lasting kind.

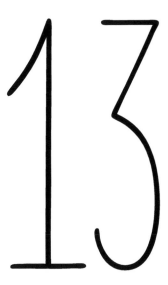

A heavenly aroma slipped into the room, and Kila wiggled her toes. *Yum,* she breathed in again, caught between wanting to open her curious eyes and wanting to drift back to sleep. Yawning, she stretched her legs. *It smells too good to wait.* Under a floral sheet and matching floral comforter, she found herself in yesterday's clothes on the daybed in the library. A neatly folded striped sheet and blanket on the adjacent recliner led her to remember Jacques and their almost enchanted conversation. *I wonder how long it took him to find the bedding,* she smiled at the thought of him opening the many cabinets recessed in the walls.

Once on her feet, Kila quietly made her way towards the kitchen. She heard mellow music but couldn't make out the song or even the artist. Pressing her ear against the door, she listened for seconds without success. *So it's like that...* she bit her bottom lip, wondering how many songs he might soon introduce her to. *Brix and I tended more times than not to find the same music at about the same time. Maybe it's because we searched together. We waited in anticipation of album, EP, and single releases, always finding a way to celebrate release days when they came. Many times, we listened in his station wagon driving up the coast. He'd say that as long as the music moved us, we should continue north; and, that one day we'd just keep driving until we reached Seattle. That never happened, but we did clink coffee cups in San Francisco a few times without Ethan or our parents finding out,* she reflected fondly, before shooing the adoration of Brixton outside her circle of focus. *That's over. This is beginning…*

Kila's palms, resting flat and even against the door, pressed forward in a gentle motion. The narrow opening she created allowed her eyes access inside. Like someone seeing the ocean for the first time, she took in the sight of Jacques. He faced the counter with his back turned towards her, the side of his face visible only for a few seconds at a time. Her eyes flashed each time she saw the slope of his nose.

Also still in yesterday's clothes, he gingerly spooned batter into the waffle iron and then began slicing a row of fruit into an array of shapes. Sunlight poured in from the French doors and windows onto the white and gray marble counter where he slid the colorful morsels onto a serving platter. His arms flowed in precise movements, his muscles appearing then disappearing under his bright skin. Tied both at his neck and his waist, a navy canvas apron embroidered with The Hidden Meridian emblem protected his cream-colored shirt while he cooked. The olive cargo pants were just as eye-catching on the second day. Now cuffed at the bottom, they revealed his sturdy ankles.

HELLO Saturday morning, she nearly sighed, pressing her tongue to the back of her teeth before sound could emerge. Releasing the pressure from her palms, the kitchen door returned to its former position. Kila then raced up the stairs to wash her face, scrub her underarms, brush her teeth, tame her bedhead, and apply a double coat of strawberry lip gloss. She thought about showering, but didn't want to forfeit an opportunity to be alone with Jacques again. After all, any of the others could wake at any minute.

Tiptoeing around her room, Kila grabbed her pastel-and-white-striped bikini, still slightly damp from yesterday, and her favorite no-fuss sundress. Annabelle lay curled up on the bed, which she had had all to herself last night, the top half of a book escaping from the canary-and-white-striped covers. *A book in place of a magazine!* Kila loved the picture before her. *I wonder which one she picked, or if she asked Brix to recommend one. Maybe she's bookish at heart like Maya and me...*

Crossing the hallway, Kila assumed she would find Maya with her brother. The door, already half ajar, allowed her a guiltless glance inside. Ethan smiled in his sleep. *He's not drooling for once!* She grinned. Peering deeper, she scanned the enormous California king bed, confirming Maya's presence by the tuft of long dark hair resting atop a mountain of blankets. *Maybe Maya's the long-awaited antidote to my brother's chronic drooling.* The thought warmed her.

Satisfied with the state of affairs on the second floor, Kila bounded down the stairs with a hopeful heart. She touched the edge of the bannister to calm her energy. *Play it cool, like I did last night. That's all I have to do.* She entered the kitchen just in time to catch Jacques setting a perfect table and hear the start of **"Only Love" by Ben Howard**.

"You're up!" he announced. "And dressed."

"Yeah, the smell woke me up...I thought I was dreaming of"—she took the song in straight through her heart—"...Ben Howard."

Jacques grinned, "...You were dreaming of Ben Howard?"

Kila giggled, embarrassed by her mixed-up words. "No," she covered her mouth, "I mean, not last night, at least."

He liked her humor, and nodded his head. "I see. Well...what do you think?" he motioned to the table.

Her eyes widened as she scanned the massive spread of breakfast platters before her. There were stacks of warm waffles, spirals of fresh fruit, pyramids of crumb-topped muffins, and a bubbling carafe of orange juice. "This is a Renaissance-like feast, Jacques," she smiled, rubbing her top and bottom lips together. Her double layer of lip gloss allowed her lips to slide easily, her mind churning with thoughts of him. She didn't know what was more attractive, the delectable spread or his ability to create it.

He grew shy but concealed it, "I guess the teenager trait of sleeping in never stuck with me. I tend to get up early, and when I woke to see you, I wanted to make you breakfast. Certainly, it would have seemed selfish just to feed you, so I made a quick trip to the restaurant to grab the ingredients and a few other things I needed."

"I didn't think that was ours," Kila pointed to the commercial-grade waffle iron, which allowed him to make six Belgian waffles at once.

He nodded with a hint of grace. Cooking had been his primary care for so long that he couldn't believe Kila stood at the forefront of his thoughts this morning. Ordinarily at this time, The Hidden Meridian was his sole focus, his uncle acting as a rare, kind dictator forcing things at the restaurant into their proper motion. While he had established this morning's pecking order before he left the restaurant, and his uncle had granted him his full blessing to cook for his new friends, Jacques stood before Kila recognizing he had, for the first time in his life, revised his plans for a girl. A girl he had only met last night.

Kila stood still, experiencing the significance of new feelings. Over the past few months, she'd received, unexpectedly, quite an influx of attention from boys. Yet, those interested never knew how to reach her; they mistakenly assumed she was like the majority of other girls at Cypress, chasing after phony status symbols like designer handbags or expensive sunglasses. Gifts of flowers never impressed her, but irked her. She felt the flowers would be better suited to remain wild in nature or still growing in a lucky gardener's greenhouse. Any gifts she received she either returned to the would-be suitors or funneled straight to her mother, Kila's father often joking that Claire was taking advantage of Kila's admirers.

Despite the humor that came of it from her brother and her parents, and that Kila initially imagined the "turn of the tide" with boys could only be a welcome thing, one question always arose in her mind about the advances from boys she had known for years but who had, up until recently, never spoken with her. *Why NOW and not then?* This question, molded in neon lights, burned her more than the silly gifts and remained illuminated in her mind as she tossed about restlessly most school nights.

Is it JUST about looks? Nearly everyone at Cypress has been dating since freshman year, both seriously and casually. No one ever asked me out before a few months ago, when I was... clueless about my appearance. When I didn't know how to pick out clothes (let alone match them). When I didn't know how to use a curling iron nor have the want to learn. And when I most certainly didn't know the difference between shiny and matte lip gloss, because I wasn't wearing any.

The more she pondered it, the more she seemed convinced. *My insides haven't changed. Sure, I've found my way into the world of clothes pairing and colorful makeup, but those aren't topics guys typically want to talk about anyway. I have the SAME personality. I'm interested in the same things. I have the same friends, with the recent addition of Anna.*

Why didn't anyone ask me out sooner? Were my outsides so unappealing that no one ever made it to looking at the insides? Will I have to live with this for life, always wondering whether someone is more interested in my outsides than in my insides? Is it possible to know? To REALLY know?

I want a relationship where the inside assumes a greater (if only slightly) assigned weight than the outside. Is it possible for both people involved to reach the same ratio of attraction? And to keep that fractioned attraction alive, in the same proportion for long-term? I don't KNOW...I don't know if it's possible. But

I want it to be…I have to believe that it is…

Jacques's gift of breakfast struck a chord within Kila she didn't know if she would ever feel, although she had read of it many times while pouring over her literature. She had, perhaps, wrongly gathered that Angus Lyr was the only one capable of making her feel this way.

"It all looks so tempting—especially the way you look in that hat," Kila let escape, though she wasn't as bashful about it as she thought she might be.

Jacques grinned. Too often he had received compliments from older women at the restaurant; those he brushed off. This one stuck with him and he replayed her words in his mind. Juggling his thoughts, he managed to continue the conversation without falling too subject to her charms. "I need a favor—are you up for it?" he questioned her.

"Of course—what is it?" she asked with full interest.

"Will you taste a piece of everything and tell me if anything needs different flavoring? You see, that's usually my uncle Horace's job…and, well, he's not here," he laughed lightly.

Kila began sampling a nibble of each item. Her eyes soon landed on the bubbling orange juice. "Mimosas?" she asked in delight.

He nodded.

She gazed at the orange again, in awe.

"Not real champagne," he watched her shoulders slump. "When I earned my last blue ribbon, I won a top-shelf bottle of champagne. I thought I'd actually get to uncork it, when my uncle locked it away in his vault and gave me this nonalcoholic instead," he smirked. "I've had it at The Hidden Meridian for a few weeks, and I've been debating what to do with it. It's sort of silly to crack it open by myself, and my close friend Clive isn't really into it. I saw it in the fridge this morning and thought...hell, why not?"

Kila looked up at him, as **"Old Pine" by Ben Howard** whisked the emotion in the room. "I've never had any type of mimosa, so I guess I won't be missing the alcohol, anyway."

"I've had some alcohol, but that's only because I have to know enough about it to cook with it. Trust me, it's not exactly as exciting as everyone makes it out to be," he paused to smile at her. "I mean, there are some really great tasting wines and specialty liqueurs, but I've seen some people at The Hidden Meridian sip wayyy past the point of moderation. It's usually not an attractive sight."

Kila raised her eyebrows. "Yeah, my dad's coworker had to spend the night here once, because he went too wild with the bourbon at their company's holiday dinner. He's still in his twenties, but he looked REALLY old that night," Kila shook her head for emphasis. "So, did your uncle take the champagne for himself, or is he keeping it until you're old enough?" Kila couldn't help but ask.

"He's saving it for me. He has enough of his own, anyway," Jacques grinned. "The real question is whether I get to have it when I turn eighteen, or whether I have to wait until I'm twenty-one to collect."

Kila tilted her head.

"You can buy liquor at eighteen in France," Jacques explained. "My uncle has yet to decide which rule we'll be following inside our house."

"My fingers are crossed for you," Kila held her hand up to show him. "You know, that champagne will only taste better then."

"Thanks," his warm eyes fell upon her face, "I liked last night."

"Me too," she found herself wishing she could somehow eat the air that contained his freshly spoken words.

"We stayed up fairly late, and we debated pretty hard," Jacques touched his hand to the table. "Next I knew you were sound asleep. Turns out you're even more beautiful with your eyes closed."

Kila's mind tensed at the fear of falling for him. Her eyes panned across his face, connecting the dots of his freckles.

Jacques looked at her bare shoulders. "I pulled some blankets from the cupboard and covered you up, in case you were cold. I couldn't tell. I hope you don't mind."

She shook her head to let him know that it was alright.

He wondered when she would speak next and he felt the need to fill the void. "I worried you might not be comfortable where you were. But, since Anna and Maya were nowhere in sight, and neither was your brother, I wasn't sure what else to do."

"You shouldn't have worried—I slept really well," Kila beamed, pondering what twist of karma had translated into this fortunate turn of events for her. She playfully tugged at the neatly tied bow atop her shoulder on the linen sundress, hoping he'd continue.

"And," Jacques was relieved she had spoken, "it was a little selfish of me, I know, but I did stay in the same room on the recliner."

"You should have stayed on the daybed with me," Kila blushed as the words slipped from her mouth. "There was plenty of room."

"I couldn't do that unless you asked me to," Jacques's wide grin revealed a small set of dimples.

Kila caught her mind's trajectory like she would catch a fly ball. "I guess I'll have to remember that rule moving forward," she felt more mature having spoken the words than she would have had she merely kept them inside.

Jacques touched his hand to the table once more.

"I'll try the rest," Kila sampled the food she hadn't before and found herself wishing for the night. *Will he be here?* She wondered, *should I ask him to be or let things fall into place of their own accord? I bet he has to be somewhere else tonight. Surely he does—it's Saturday night! He has other friends, other obligations.*

He handed her a small glass filled with mimosa, and she swallowed a swig. The bubbles tingled from her lips to her throat to her stomach, and she remembered how she felt under the blanket with him during the movie. How her fingers felt alive locked between his. She tipped the glass up, guzzling the liquid until only sprinkles of fresh pulp remained.

"Killer, slow it down—I'll feel responsible if you get a stomachache."

She looked in his espresso-colored eyes, "Say it again."

"Why?" he smiled nervously. "Did one of my words sound funny because of my accent?"

"No," Kila set her empty glass on the table. "Say 'Killer' again."

His eyes gazed at her suspiciously before giving in. "Killer," he said it as fast as he could.

"Will you call me that?" her bright eyes prayed he wouldn't refuse.

"Like a nickname?" he asked.

"Yeah," she gasped, realizing he hadn't committed to it yet.

"Okay. I will," he lifted his shoulders, sensing this somehow made them closer. "So...I take it, you're into nicknames. I know about 'Kiki.' That's Brixton's only, as I was informed last night. And Angus referred to you as 'Ki' but that one doesn't seem as restrictive."

Kila nodded with a complete smile.

"How many do you have?" he took a sip of his own mimosa.

"Quite a few," she admitted, "the worst of which is 'K. Bear'... given to me by E when we were super young. I do admit that I loved it back then, but now it's just...unbearable." She rolled her eyes when Jacques laughed. "He still says it when he wants to tease me! But, I really, really like 'Killer,' and I'll grant you exclusive rights to it, IF you want them," her cheeks beamed, a velvety shade of rose.

"Who can say no to exclusivity?" Jacques lifted his glass.

Kila pursed her lips, feeling quite pleased, and touched her glass to his.

"Alright Killer"—he emphasized the new name—"how would you rate the breakfast? Be honest. My chef feelings are not delicate, you know."

"The food? It's all the best I've ever had. I feel like I'm on vacation somewhere but I'm actually just at my house."

"Are you sure?" Jacques thought about Ethan in particular. "Do you think the others will like it?"

"YEAH...I don't know what you're doing in Felton," she smoothed the folds of her sundress with her fingers, "but... please don't leave, if you can help it."

"Something tells me it would be hard for me to leave now," he touched Kila's shoulder, in disbelief at how soft and smooth her bare skin felt beneath his fingertips.

She warmed to his touch and her thoughts drifted to Angus. *No,* she redirected her mind, *Angus only has eyes for Reese. I can't waste any more time on him. I've wasted enough time already.* "Should we wake the others before it gets cold?" she asked. "It'd be a shame for them not to enjoy it like this."

Steam still rose from some of the plates and Kila glanced at the clock above the stove. She had assumed it was about 9 a.m., but it was almost 10:30. "Oh NO, I hope Anna's not in trouble. She was supposed to help her father today, and she's already OVER an hour late."

"Can you get her out of trouble?" Jacques watched Kila's eyes dart back and forth in thought.

"I don't know, but, I'm sure as hell going to try," Kila touched her hand to Jacques's upper arm before leaving the room.

Claire and Dil frequently traveled for business, but this marked the first full weekend Ethan and Kila had been left home without their grandparents. With a practiced delivery, the siblings insisted to their parents that it was time to be trusted at the house without supervision. And Ethan, having reached the "age of seventeen" milestone, at last sealed the deal with his father via a handshake and a hug this past Thursday morning before leaving for school.

After a short hunt, Kila found her phone in the living room and called Mr. Delancy. When he voiced his approval for Anna catching up on her sleep and stated he was perfectly capable of running the errands on his own, Kila thanked him to the point that he laughed. For a few brief moments, Kila missed her own father and hoped that her parents were enjoying Houston.

Guessing someone else might be pleased to learn about Anna's change in availability, Kila rushed down the hallway to the guest room. In somewhat of a fever, she swung the door open to find Brixton and Angus sprawled out on the bed like two bears who fell asleep fighting for more space. She took a few quick strides and launched herself on the bed to shake them up.

Angus's eyes shot open during the disturbance. When he realized the hand touching his arm was Kila's, his whole body hardened. "My God, Ki," he scolded. "Don't you know I'm near to naked?! We're not kids anymore...."

As he rolled himself off the bed, Kila huffed and closed her eyes. She opened her lids seconds later, though, to see exactly what it was he was or wasn't wearing. "You're not naked," she whispered.

"One garment away," he snapped.

"So what?" Kila looked at the wall. "It's the same thing as a bathing suit."

"No...it's not," he bent down to grab his bag from the floor.

Her eyes, growing tired of the wall, leapt to his exposed back, shoulders, and arms. "I'm sorry," she wasn't quite sure why she was apologizing. It wasn't for the reason Angus assumed.

"It's okay," his eyes met hers.

Kila couldn't think of a reply. Her eyes were too busy admiring the symmetry of his face and questioning why his presence could do such things to her.

"Kiki," Brixton mumbled through his half-asleep mouth. His hands rubbed his face and he turned toward her, further tangling the blankets about himself.

"Guess I'll leave you to your BFF, then," Angus glared in Brixton's direction, then left the room with his mailman bag strategically placed in front of his boxers.

Damn him and his...his existence. How can he still do that to me? Kila placed a hand over her chest. Her heart, having blatantly refused to heed her direction, danced wildly beneath it. *Oh, never mind him. He's almost in the past,* she resorted to lying. *Maybe it will take root and I can fully invest myself in Jacques.*

Changing gears, she turned to Brixton and the mess of covers surrounding him. "Still? Still with the blankets like this?" she laughed, then attempted to unfold them, making sure her hands didn't come too close to his body.

"Are you pleased or displeased by the fact I haven't changed?" Brixton stuffed a second and a third pillow behind his head to prop himself up.

After the bedding lay flat she sat atop the covers near him. "Are you mad that I came in here while you were sleeping?"

"You didn't answer my question," Brixton realized they were alone at last. *This feels perfect.*

"You didn't answer mine either," Kila crossed her arms. *I miss arguing with him.*

"I asked first," Brixton nudged, "so you answer first."

"I'd go along with that if you hadn't ditched me," Kila scrunched her nose.

He opened his mouth in exaggerated surprise.

"Hey," Kila held her ground, "if you want my answers, you have to answer first."

"Fine," he pulled his arms outside the covers, his chest and shoulders emerging at the same time. "I don't care that you're in here—it's your house, Kiki."

She squinted her eyes in thought, "And you don't care that you're only in your boxers?"

Is she playing with me? "No," he watched her face, "I don't care if you don't care."

Her eyebrows moved in thought. "I'm pleased you haven't changed."

He reached for his phone on the side table when Kila caught his eyes.

"Shuffle," they both mumbled in unison.

While Brixton tilted his head, Kila smiled wondering what would come first.

"If You Ever Want To Be In Love" by James Bay filled the room with a tender ache.

Kila closed her eyes and folded her legs atop the covers. She remembered all the times they had spent together with a nostalgia that nipped ceaselessly at her heart. *Music is so different with Brix. I don't understand why...*

A piece of Brixton died in that moment, while another piece was born. "Hey, let's go to Lazy Tortoise and get breakfast, like old times...my treat," he pinched her elbow to open her eyes. "Then we can take a short drive and catch up. You down?"

"God, that sounds good, but, we already have breakfast," Kila smiled. "Jacques made a feast for everyone—that's actually why I came in here." *He hasn't asked me to breakfast in ages...*

"Oh," Brixton sat upright, "I guess that sounds good, too." He faked a smile. "By the way, how was last night? Angus tried to burst into the library, but I wouldn't let him." *Did I just incriminate myself?*

"What?!?" Kila laughed. "When? And why?!"

He chose his words meticulously. "After the movie was over. He was worried about Jacques getting too close to you," Brixton touched his hands together. *Not.a.lie. I'm safe.*

"No need for concern," Kila shook her head with a hint of a

smile. "Jacques tried nothing. And I mean noth-ing. He slept on the recliner. He didn't even stay on the daybed with me...."

"Did you want him to?" Brixton spoke too soon to change his mind.

"I don't know," Kila blushed, "I mean, I just thought by now, almost being a senior and all, I would have at least slept in the same bed with someone, even if nothing else happened. I just...want that, I guess," she felt vulnerable for the admittance.

"Someone as in anyone, or someone as in one person in particular?" Brixton watched her look at the ceiling.

"I don't know, Brix. You just...I mean, you can't just expect I'm going to tell you all of my secrets again," she touched his forearm to take the edge off her words. "Anyways," she softened her voice, "I think you should wake Anna up. She's sleeping in my room...."

"I think I should brush my teeth," Brixton spoke aloud, wondering why Kila had covered her mouth. "What is that all about?" he pointed to her wide smile.

"You kissed her, didn't you?" Kila bounced off the bed and proceeded to jump up and down in silent celebration.

"What? No!" Brixton kicked his legs to the side of the bed. "Sorry to disappoint," his eyebrows crunched together in an unusual expression. He rubbed his thumb and index finger across his brow amidst his own aggravation.

"Did something bad happen?" Kila asked in concern.

"No, not at all," he thought of all the knots that never seemed to loosen inside his chest. "I'll wake her up if you want me to...I just think I like things to move at a much slower pace than you do."

"I respect that," Kila nodded. "I'm not pushing you into anything, don't worry."

"Good," Brixton stretched his arms and stood up. "I want to feel like we're on the same team again."

"We are," Kila held up Brixton's maroon backpack in her hands.

He nodded to the question that need not be asked.

Their former means of communication had just been resurrected, gestures at times taking the place of their would-be words. In the past they had crowned whole afternoons by speaking without speech. Between their gestures and their playlists, they had vowed they needed nothing else. Brixton turned away from Kila and made the bed, so she wouldn't see the emotion on his face.

Kila unzipped his bag. *He always looks best in the morning,* she paused to admire him. His golden curls, a beautiful mess. *Anna couldn't hope for a better alarm,* she exhaled and rummaged through Brixton's bag, searching for an outfit to dress her former doll in. A half year ago, when they were practically inseparable, Kila spent many afternoons clothes shopping with him. Back then, she could never find anything that fit her as she wanted it to. Brixton, on the other hand, was true to size—everything always fit him the way it should, as if he were a mannequin come to life.

"So do you think I really upset Angus by barging in here this morning?" Kila hadn't planned to ask the question, but remained inquisitive even after saying it.

"Nah," Brixton assured her. "He'll be fine...you caught him off guard. That's all."

Kila rolled her eyes.

"Come on," Brixton half-smiled, "you know he's super self-conscious about his appearance. He likes to feel put together before seeing people."

"If he's super self-conscious, it's only because of Reese. Everyone else finds him gorgeous beyond measure. It's not my fault that she's lost her mind. That being said, I never told you how ecstatic I was that you turned her down," Kila flashed her piercing eyes, tossing a V-neck dark-gray T-shirt and a pair of linen shorts his way.

"You were?!" he conjured up memories with a swiftness he rarely exercised. "You didn't tell me at the time."

"Yeah. I would have...if you would have returned my calls or messages," Kila countered playfully. "I picked up on your subtlety, Kading, don't worry."

"It wasn't that I didn't want to," Brixton saw the trap around him. *Why? Why now?!?*

"I get it. It made sense. We had grown too close. Maybe it wasn't healthy for either of us. Anyway, Ethan was close to snapping over his term paper, and he needed you more than

I did…at that time." Kila recalled the vast pain of losing him, but refused to feel it. *At least trust me on this one,* she begged her heart.

Brixton couldn't believe this conversation was happening right when he was least prepared for it. He sized himself up in the mirror, irritated by his inability to craft an appropriate response. "Kiki, you don't get…it's not how you see it…," his limbs tightened in aggravation. "I wanted to talk to you last night. This keeps happening," he looked out the window.

"Brix. Focus. Anna," Kila smiled, changing the subject skillfully as she often did. "Please, oh please try to talk some sense into Angus this afternoon when you are alone with him. Reese is going to be here tonight, and I cannot bear to see him bow to her as if she were a queen and he were her loyal guard," she made the gag sign.

"Yeah, well…," Brixton paced a little, "I'd think about it if I hadn't had to find out from someone else you were throwing a party here tonight. Not cool, Kiki. Not cool. You should have told us," he looked at her lightly, "or at least told ME! You used to tell me EVERYTHING. Now I have to find out third-hand from Josie to Angus?"

Kila closed her eyes in place of a reply when **"Feathery– Slow Version" by Milky Chance** tempted her senses.

In his mind, Brixton imagined playing the song for her in his room away from Jacques and away from Angus and away from everything that always seemed to stand between them. *They don't understand her. They don't know who she is…what she wants…I should tell her that I do…that we could spend* *every night together in the same bed if she wanted to...I'd make musical love to her mind...*he noticed his chest rise and fall from his heightened thoughts.

Kila opened her eyes, then forced their focus away from Brixton's shirtless, well-built frame. "I could just pinch Josie—I specifically told her not to tell anyone, especially Angus. I should have suspected she would cave to him. How'd he finally get it out of her?"

"By text. One text to be precise," Brixton found this hysterical and he appreciated the release. He touched his stomach, "I was with him and he certainly didn't pry at all. The response came not more than a minute later."

Kila rolled her eyes, "Hopeless. Josie is absolutely hopeless." Still poking through Brixton's bag, she tossed him a pair of jeans.

"Wait, I thought I was wearing the shorts?" He grabbed his knotted rope bracelet from the dresser and slipped it over his right wrist.

"No—wear the jeans, trust me."

"Why? What's the difference?" Brixton itched to know. He hoped Kila would reveal her new intricacies of dressing to him.

"Well," Kila looked across the room and whispered, "your backside looks so much better in the jeans. They are, without question, your best pair of pants."

Brixton was delighted that his backside looked good in anything. When he had more time, he planned to ask Kila to provide more of these details. Unlike Ethan, he wasn't fearful of a clothing critique. "Thanks for the outfit assist. How bad was I without it?" he took the clothes into the adjoined bathroom and reached for his toothbrush.

The door remained open, and Kila looked inside. "Not too terrible, don't worry," she teased him. "You did tend to buy things a tad on the larger side for a while."

"I grew into them, though," Brixton countered. "I had a bunch of extra time to work out."

"Yeah, I hope it was worth it," Kila looked at the ceiling, misinterpreting his intentions.

"I didn't mean it like that…you never kept me from working out," Brixton's hands clutched the sink's stone countertop. "You never kept me from anything," he tried to make amends for something she misunderstood.

"Make sure to tell Anna it's alright that she slept in. I've already spoken with her dad and he said she can stay here until tomorrow afternoon," Kila walked towards the hallway.

"Kiki," he caught her attention before she left the room.

"Brix. It's okay. I said it was okay, and it's still okay. If you want to be friends moving forward, let's be friends. Six months shouldn't put such a strain on two people who used to be friends, who still want to be friends…at least for my part," her words seemed calm but she couldn't look at his face.

The knots in Brixton's chest tightened. "For my part, too... friends," he managed to speak those five words before his senses flooded with thoughts of inadequacy. *Maybe it's not working because it's not supposed to work...why can't I want someone this badly who wants me this badly?* His hands ached from wanting to touch her. *She'll never let me. I damned myself six months ago.*

After a brisk lap around the hallway, where she could still hear Brixton's music, she attempted to cleanse her mind. *If I could go back, would I? Would I trade all the things I am now for who I was back then? For the time I had with him? For the adventure and for the music? He still hasn't told me why he ended it, and I've too easily fallen back into wanting to share my life with him. I mean, friends don't break up like girlfriends and boyfriends do, so why does it feel like we broke up? Why does it hurt like this?*

Kila returned to the kitchen, startled to find Jacques and Angus deep in conversation. Jacques greeted her with a warm smile. Angus poured himself a generous glass of mimosa and opened up the French doors to the veranda. He led Jacques along with him into the sunlight.

Kila trailed behind them, eyeing Angus. While his longish hairstyle looked modern, his features appeared more old-world, an unforgettable grade of dark and handsome. Yet, unlike the others at Cypress pining for this boy, Kila knew Angus's mind, not his body, was the real gem.

Through Brixton, Kila had learned that Angus had achieved near perfect SAT scores. And because of it, his teachers incessantly encouraged him to compete in academic electives like the debate team. One day after school, Kila had even overheard the honors faculty discussing Angus's writing aptitude as if he were destined for greatness. However, Angus kept all of this hidden from his other friends and classmates, and Mrs. Lyr fully respected his wishes, tactfully brushing off the sometimes pushy recommendations from his teachers.

While Angus recognized the importance of academia, he was neither interested in nor compelled to tout his abilities in public. Kila adored this, above all, about him. He was in such contrast to the other boys at Cypress, alarmingly bright and dangerously attractive. *No wonder I haven't been able to get over him.* She inhaled deeply when he spotted her on the deck.

"What took you so long?" Angus teased her in front of Jacques. "Did you dress him too?" He delighted in the momentary panic on Kila's face.

"I wasn't long. I was quick. You're the one who spent the whole night with him," she retaliated triumphantly.

Jacques laughed, instantly partial to Kila's ability to turn sharp. He hadn't seen that yet.

Satisfied with his instigation, Angus returned to his dialogue with Jacques.

Kila turned inward to her own thoughts. After all this time, she was still furious with the way Reese had handled the state of affairs between Angus and Brixton. When the long string of unmentionable events began to unfold a little over a year ago, Kila was secretly crushing on Angus. Reese was the only one who had known. And Reese not only drove a wedge between Brixton and Angus, but she also crossed Kila, who had historically looked out for everyone, including her.

Kila hadn't planned on inviting Reese this evening, but Reese had heard about the party from others at school and called to ask if she could come. She had apologized to Kila specifically and begged for her forgiveness, stating her want to put the past behind them. Kila believed there was good in everyone, and, though she was no longer particularly fond of Reese, she thought it might be cruel to ban her from the party when many of her other classmates would be present.

Studying Angus, who looked better than ever, she wanted to believe that Reese had changed her ways. But Kila's instincts warned her otherwise. *There's just so much MORE to Angus than what he looks like.* Kila felt a hand on her arm. She touched it with her own.

"You alright?" Jacques whispered.

"Of course," she spoke softly. "Brixton's about to wake Anna, and I just messaged Ethan to let him know about breakfast," she smiled wide. "He was alone with Maya last night."

"Nice," Jacques's lips formed a slight grin, "seems like there wasn't much for him to worry about, then."

"Ethan was worried?" Kila looked surprised.

Jacques nodded, placing a finger to his lips. He found himself in an awkward situation, wanting so much to give Kila details that Ethan might not wish her to have.

"It's okay. I don't need to know," Kila assured him, sensing his position. "I'm ecstatic the two finally came to their senses and coupled up."

He gazed at her, wondering if and when he would ever get to spend the night in the library with her again. "Angus told me you're throwing a party tonight." He rubbed his hands together quickly, "Any chance I'm on the guest list?"

"Yes," Kila replied energetically, "moving forward, you can just assume you're on the guest list. That is...whenever you want to be."

Jacques looked deep into her blue-gray eyes, thankful for her reply.

Kila felt her insides melt into a warm chocolate-like fondue.

"Uh—you guys, can you knock that off?" Angus huffed, "I'm right he-re!"

"I hope your manners find their way back to you tonight," Kila scrunched her face at Angus. "Josie's been asking about you, and I fully intend to tell her you're a mannerless snake if you don't come around and be nice."

"Good! Tell her that, Ki. I don't care what she thinks," Angus roared, then suddenly remembered something. "Wait. She said that Reese is coming. Is that true?"

Kila lifted her shoulders noncommittally.

"Did Reese RSVP?" Angus asked the question directly.

"Hmmm. Let me think," Kila delivered the last part in a childish sing-songy type tease. "Mayyy-be she di-id. Mayyy-be she di-dn't."

Angus, galled that Kila held a greater power to taunt him than he did to taunt her, lunged toward her. She jumped backwards. He proceeded to chase her across the veranda and around the pool as if his happiness hung in the balance.

"Angus! Stop it!" She laughed and lifted her floor-length sundress from her feet to her calves while she ran.

He ignored her plea.

"Angus! Come on!" Kila sped down the steps to the pool, too afraid to look over her shoulder.

Closing in on her, Angus reached for the back of her sundress. Once he had ahold of it, he maneuvered her to the edge of the deep end.

"Get 'em Killer!" Jacques roared, "Don't let him win!"

"Come on, Ki, just tell me," Angus whispered. His crimson lips twisted into in a mischievous smile, pleading with her in his irresistible way.

"No," Kila spoke with an air of finality. "You text with her enough. It's your problem if she doesn't air her comings and goings to you. You can play her games if you want to, but I REFUSE to," she said firmly, remaining steadfast even as she felt Angus's foot slide underneath hers.

Before falling, Kila managed to grip Angus's shirt so tightly with both her fists that he tumbled in with her. His arms wrapped around her back as they plunged deep into the water. He held her tightly the whole way down and the whole way up, releasing his arms only when they returned to the surface. As soon as their wet heads emerged, the quarrel continued.

"Angus Lyr! I CAN NOT believe you did that!" Kila swam away from him. "Ridiculous!"

"Kila Lorens! Let this serve as a reminder NOT to meddle in MY relationships," Angus barked loudly.

Jacques, fuming that Angus tripped Kila into the pool, felt compelled to say something. However, the crossfire hadn't ceased and he thought it might be rude to interrupt. The predicament reminded Jacques that he was still more of a stranger than a friend to them. And he wondered what type of history might exist between Angus and the girl in question.

Ethan and Maya emerged from the house holding hands, Anna and Brixton close behind them. They moved next to Jacques and tried to piece together why Kila and Angus were thrashing about in the deep end of the pool, fully dressed. The argument ensued.

"Your relationships? What relationship? You are not IN a relationship with Reese. She used you to get closer to what she really wanted, and to her eternal damnation, Brixton didn't even want her! You're a remainder to her, an insignificant part of her equation. The quotient was ALWAYS Brixton, yet you waste your time on such a waste of time," Kila shook her head, reeling inside.

She hadn't meant to take it this far, and Angus experienced the pain in her words. It killed her that she hurt him, and she didn't know what this outburst might cost her. "I—I just can't bear to see it happen again. She is embarrassingly incapable of knowing what she could have had, what she most obviously overlooked," she gazed into his eyes purely and sincerely, hoping he wouldn't hold this against her.

His dark eyes, full of an emotion Kila was unfamiliar with, looked back at her without revealing his thoughts, without even hinting at his reaction to her last admissions.

Fearing she might shed tears at any second, Kila climbed the ladder with the graceful disappointment of an Olympian who finished without a medal. Recognizing only now that her comments had been heard by all her friends, she excused herself quietly and went into the house to collect her thoughts in the privacy of her bedroom.

Ethan had never, ever seen his sister deliver such a series of blows. He'd also never seen Angus appear this sorrowfully introspective. The whole group had always danced around what had transpired between Reese, Angus, and Brixton. *I thought I made it clear last night we shouldn't discuss her,* Ethan fumbled with his thoughts at the sight of Angus's twisted face. As only a true friend would, Ethan kicked off his flip-flops and dove, fully clothed, into the pool where he tossed Angus's body into the air.

Angus finally cracked a smile as the two began thrashing around. After making some quick mental notes to revisit later, Brixton joined in the fun himself. Anna gasped as he dove into the water, jeans, T-shirt and all. Soon afterward, Maya tugged Anna inside to find Kila. They hoped they could bolster Kila's spirits and uncover the truth behind her emotional volley with Angus.

Jacques walked toward the edge of the pool to remind the boys about breakfast. He patiently waited for Ethan and Brixton to enter the house before approaching Angus on the veranda.

"I admit that I don't know who Reese is, but I also don't think you should have pushed Kila into the pool," Jacques spoke point-blank.

"I know," Angus lamented. "I need to talk to her about it. I'll tell her."

"Good," Jacques tried to relieve the growing tension, "because I don't let tyrants eat my waffles."

Angus laughed.

Free of their wet clothes and with towel-wrapped bottoms, Ethan, Brixton, and Angus made their way back to the table, which had already been set by Jacques an hour before. Maya and Anna returned with a freshly composed Kila, who refused to speak further about the Angus incident. She chose her place at the table with precision, two seats down and on the same side of the table as Angus, so she could minimize their interaction. Jacques sat beside her.

Over a rich and hearty breakfast, three important details were shared. First, Maya was moving to Rhode Island next weekend. Second, Maya's farewell party was taking place at the Lorens house tonight. And third, Reese had, in fact, RSVP'd.

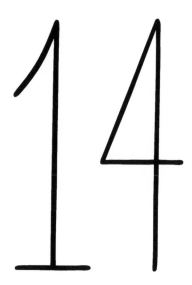

Right after breakfast, the girls raced upstairs to review the order of events before the party. The elaborate "to do" list Kila held in her hands included both words and shapes. While Maya assumed the squares, triangles, and hearts were merely doodles, they were really additional action items. As Anna took the list in her hands, studied it in detail, and looked to Kila with fretful eyes, Maya couldn't understand how the time remaining posed such a significant problem. When Maya asked the question aloud, Kila smartly switched subjects, asking her about her night with Ethan. And Anna, in an effort to keep Maya distracted, commented on each and every one of Maya's tiniest details.

Ethan, Brixton, and Angus remained downstairs, cleaning up the kitchen and dining room. Though Jacques offered several times, he wasn't allowed to assist with the dishwasher. Nor was he allowed to clean the countertops, pans, or waffle iron. Ethan stood firm in his resolve that if Jacques cooked for the group, he should be exempt, without question, from the cleanup.

"Guys, I really don't mind helping," Jacques insisted. With his hands in his pockets, he felt foolish standing in place while his three new friends scurried around him with sponges, cleaners, and towels.

"You can't do everything, bro," Angus tried to appease him. "You woke before any of us, you brought the ingredients, you cooked AND you served us. Let us handle the last part...."

"Seriously," Brixton added, "as far as I'm concerned, anyone who makes waffles like that should never have to clean another dish in his lifetime."

Jacques smiled, "Those weren't even close to my best waffles."

Ethan stopped wiping the table to look at him, "On a scale of one to ten?"

"Probably...a seven point five," Jacques admitted with honesty.

"Only a seven point five," Ethan mumbled, "how can that be...?"

Brixton laughed and addressed Jacques, "Was it because you were in a new kitchen?"

"No," Jacques answered Brixton and turned to Ethan, "I was a little nervous...about your sister, and all."

Though no one noticed, Angus began washing the same spatula a second time.

"You SHOULD be nervous, Noah," Ethan tried to appear serious but failed. "Everything's cool. You don't have to worry."

Jacques shook his head, smiling, "I need to report to The Hidden M. for a few hours, but, I spoke with my uncle, and, I can definitely make it back tonight."

"Niiice!" Ethan applauded without hesitation. "It'll be good to have you here." Shortly afterward, he wondered why he had been the only one to celebrate the good news.

Jacques maneuvered through the absence of Brixton and Angus's replies. He continued speaking with Ethan. "Kila told me she was thinking of picking up some premade cupcakes from one of my competitors, but...I'd prefer that not to happen," he smiled, shaking his head. "It's an occasion that calls for more than cupcakes. I'd like to make a worthy sendoff cake for Maya, something artistic—would that be alright?"

"YES!" Ethan cupped Jacques's shoulder in gratitude. "What do you need from us to make it happen? Money? Supplies?"

"No," Jacques smiled.

"Don't say Kiki," Brixton tested Jacques, "she's not a bargaining chip."

Jacques tilted his head, looking at Brixton, "Killer makes her own decisions. You should know that by now."

"I do," Brixton half-smiled and half meant it. "You know, I've known her for a long time." He mulled over the new nickname. *Killer. How'd that happen?*

Ethan's hands came together. Despite his awareness of the readily developing friction in the room, the greater part of his attention remained on Maya. Memories and wishes of her, in lucid form, overtook the sea of infinity that contained all of his other thoughts.

Angus proceeded to wash the same spatula a third time without realizing it. Peering out the window, he watched a single monarch butterfly take a rest in the bed of the flower planter and stretch its wings. Another monarch joined the first shortly afterward. The difference in timing and the grace with which each folded and unfolded its wings led Angus to contemplate the nature of their silent communication. He couldn't help but smile as the two took flight together, dancing playfully until they reached the entrance to the woods in back of Ethan's house. Straightening his stance and rolling his shoulders back, Angus at last placed the ultra-clean spatula in the drying rack.

Jacques thought it odd the conversation had slowed. He attempted to move it along again. "Listen, all I need to know are Maya's flavor preferences. What are the desserts you already know she likes? If I know those, I can include those elements and create a new, layered flavor combination."

"Make it taste like Ethan," Angus flicked soapy water at Brixton.

"Ewww! Do NOT make it taste like Ethan," Brixton's face twisted as he wiped the suds off his nose and neck. "I like him…but, not enough to allow that. Plus, if the cake tastes like Ethan, Maya may no longer need the real him. And, it's our job to get across his uniqueness. His mouth should be the only place she can indulge in that taste."

"Now that that pointless discussion has been had," Ethan shifted in place uncomfortably, "Maya loves carrot cake. I know it for a fact. I'm pretty sure it's her favorite, or at least in her top three. But, she likes most desserts with the exception of one. She LOATHES pound cake," he laughed.

"I don't blame her, I stay away from the pound as well. I'll bake it if my hand is forced, but I always make my uncle do the testing. I can't handle the consistency of it," Jacques puckered his face.

"Yeah. I've never been sure what the pound's all about. Maybe we'll all like it when we're old," Angus thought aloud. "You always seem to see it sliced thickly and proudly, elevated on glass pedestals on the tables of the well-aged."

Brixton smirked at him. "Make time today for some writing, will you? Put those word-pairings to use."

Angus grinned, lifting his head in Brixton's direction.

"…So a writer stands among us…," Jacques also lifted his head in praise.

"Yes. Believe it or not," Ethan looked proudly at Angus, "he's not as biting as he seems." He took a loud breath, "I guess tonight will be bittersweet. I'm glad you'll all be here."

Jacques saw a sadness sweep over Ethan's face.

"This weekend's FAR from over," Brixton reminded gently. "There's plenty of time to enjoy the sweet before the bitter takes hold."

Angus smiled in such a way that Brixton supposed he was thinking of Reese.

Jacques brought Ethan's thoughts back to the cake. "If carrot is the closest to her favorite you know, then carrot she shall have. Only I'll make it better. I'll make it memorable," Jacques rubbed his hands together, already figuring the ingredients, the timing, and the message he would scribe across the top in colored icing.

"Seems like everything changed once we hit up The Hidden Meridian," Brixton pondered aloud.

"Yeah," Ethan realized, "it has."

"Not for me—yet," Angus sounded strong-willed. "I aim to change that, though."

"Good," Brixton commended him.

"Well," Jacques wrapped up his part, "my next change is a change for cleanliness sake. I need a shower before I can return to work. Do you mind if I shower here?"

"No! You've baked yourself into the group," Ethan laughed, "and, as part of the group, you now have access to all the showers...less Kila's," he added to Brixton and Angus's approval. "So, there's two upstairs, one downstairs, and one by the pool."

Jacques stepped out to his car to retrieve the uniform he had packed the night before. Then he made his way back to the house. The bathroom on the first floor was already occupied, so he walked upstairs to find one of the two remaining options. In the hallway, he bumped into Maya, who scurried away with a sense of purpose. Seconds later, Kila emerged from one of the doors eyeing him.

Having been summoned by Maya in the middle of changing, Kila stood only in her bikini. "What are you doing up here?" she teased.

"I was hoping to find an empty shower," he pointed to his work clothes. "I'm headed into work for a few hours, but my uncle gave me the night off, so I can return." He pulled Kila aside, whispering the next part close to her ear, "And, I am going to make her a giant cake. Ethan told me that carrot is her cake of choice. As her best friend, can you confirm or deny this, Killer?"

Kila, delighting in the sound of his every word, especially her new nickname, responded, "Complete confirmation on the carrot. You can shower down the hall. Come on, I'll show you."

In a trance, Jacques followed her, studying the deep groove in her back, which ran the length of her spine. Inside the bathroom, she reached into the closet and pulled out an oversized fluffy white towel for him. "Here," she placed it in his hands, feeling the smallness of the room.

"Thank you," his fingers closed around the pillowy fibers. "I've had a nice time...this morning, and...last night."

Kila simply nodded her head. Her thoughts had run rampant, scurrying to places she knew they didn't belong. Glancing down, she noticed the bare tub ledge. "Hang on," her words startled him, yet she continued without hesitation, "there's no soap or shampoo in here, I need to grab you some. What type do you like?"

"I don't usually have a choice," Jacques grinned. "My uncle does all of the necessity shopping."

"Well, I'll make it easy," she leaned back on her hands, which rested on the vanity. "Do you want something floral, fresh, or spicy?"

"Hmmmm," Jacques asked flirtatiously, "what would you have me smell like?"

She wrapped a few rogue locks of her hair behind her ear at his last comment. "I think the fresh category will suit you nicely. If you travel the spicy route, you might entice the female clientele at the restaurant a little too much today," she bit her tongue to bring herself back to a level of boring, familiar comfort.

"I'll be fresh for you, then," Jacques caught her eyes though they tried to look away.

Her hands began to throb against the countertop from applying more and more weight to them. In an effort to relieve them, and also not wanting Jacques to be late, Kila rushed down the hall to her room to retrieve the soap, shampoo, conditioner, and lotion she thought would complement him best. To her surprise, she saw Angus loitering in the hallway near her room. Nodding nervously, she stepped past him, assuming he was on the hunt for Ethan.

He wasn't.

"Ki, can I talk to you really quick?" Angus eyed her with focus.

She kept moving, so he wouldn't sense her panic. "Yeah. What's on your mind?" she zipped into her bathroom to retrieve the toiletries. Her arms, within an instant, grew full of small boxes and bottles.

Angus hadn't seen the inside of Kila's bathroom in quite some time. It now reminded him of an alchemist's lab, with jars of creams and tubes of serums perfectly positioned on the shelves and neatly tucked away in drawers. He tried hard to order his thoughts, but they jumbled against the fabric of her pastel-and-white-striped bikini.

"I just—wait," Angus breathed, "where are you going with all of those? Do you need a hand?"

"No, I have 'em. It's okay...," Kila explained, "they're for Jacques. He's about to shower down the hall."

It was evident to Kila that Angus seemed out of sorts, and she couldn't help but recall the words she had uttered in the pool to him. *How could I have spoken to him like that? In front of EVERYONE?* She chided herself, issuing a comforting glance. "Hang on, I'll be back in a moment. Don't go anywhere."

"Okay," Angus's eyes issued such a look of intensity that Kila paused. He smiled warmly, "Just don't forget about me."

Kila forced the words from her mouth. "I won't," she nodded to him.

Feeling more at ease, Angus took a seat on her bed and watched her disappear down the hallway.

By the time Kila returned to the spare bathroom, Jacques had already removed his shirt and shoes. He stood in front of the shower curtain somewhat proud and somewhat embarrassed. At the sight of her, he crossed his arms, questioning why he felt self-conscious.

Kila's eyes glued themselves to his skin. *Oh...why? Why right now? I can't think about it. DON'T think about it! I can't stop looking...*

The shock lay in the reality that Kila hadn't really given much thought to what Jacques might look like underneath his clothes, since he had already looked so good inside them. While she had guessed he was fairly fit, she was stunned to see such muscle definition on his lean frame. Issuing glances that grazed the structure of his arms, the ridges of his stomach, and the plates of his chest, Kila felt her body temperature rise.

"How'd you get so athletic?" she blushed as the words came out.

"I've been asking myself the same question about you," Jacques's tiny warm smile assaulted her heart.

She'd kept it so guarded since last year. Yet, here it was clamoring to see what lay beyond the stone walls, which had framed it in a stale fortress of safety. She found herself counting his innumerable freckles to keep her mouth from confessing her budding affection for him.

Growing bashful, he grabbed the bottles from her arms, lining them by height on the shower shelf. Once her arms were empty, he reached for one of her hands and gently wrapped his fingers in hers. Like last night, he squeezed her hand then released it.

Kila managed to click the door shut behind her just before her eyes closed and that weak feeling stung at her thighs. Resting her head and back against the wall, she heard Jacques remove the remainder of his clothes, wondering just how improper it would be if she opened the door once more and hopped into the shower to assist him. *Calm down!* she ordered herself, confused at how heavy those last few minutes had felt.

I'm no better than the boys I despised, am I? No, wait. I'm worse: a total hypocrite, drooling over every cute boy I see, clothed, or, in this case, shirtless. Have I lost it? REALLY lost it? I can't let this happen to me. It just isn't sensible. It's UNsensible, actually. And really...unbecoming.

Looks are so fleeting, so CHANGEABLE, so deceiving. I wish there was a way to see the inside first. Now that would be something. To avoid a boy's outside, to look beyond his aesthetics until one is absolutely positive that the boy's inside is what she really likes. And, at that point and ONLY at that point, some form of tasteful drooling could potentially commence...

...I think that's my answer: "Insides only" until I know how I feel. "Insides only" before I can look. Insides only. Insides only. Insides only. Kila repeated her new mantra over and over again until she felt grounded. At that point she gasped, remembering that a possibly still angry Angus awaited her. *God, I bet he's still ticked at me,* she reeled. *I cannot believe I said what I said. I'd be ticked at me, too, for a looong while,* she thought, feeling woozy from swinging from one end of the spectrum to the other so quickly.

Entering her room, she was startled to see Angus perched on her bed. There were so many times she wished he had been there, dreamt of him being there, and so many feelings she had kept tightly locked away from him. After the Reese incident exploded last year, he was no longer an option. She forced herself to put him out of her mind; and, for the most part, she had been mentally successful at doing so...that is, up until last week.

"Is he happy with his soap?" Angus inquired emotionlessly.

Kila nodded without expression.

"Would it be alright to close the door?" he asked.

"Yeah," she pushed it shut, fearing he might tempt her across a minefield. "What's going on?" She took a seat next to him on the bed, realizing with her whole self this was the first time they had ever been in the same room alone behind a closed door.

Angus rubbed his hands nervously, then ran one along the side of his dark, still damp hair. "I need to apologize."

"No," she interrupted, "it's me that's sorry...I shouldn't have said...all...of...," she sank into his deep eyes, unable to complete her thoughts.

The distress on her face revealed a hint of a clue he never thought he would see, and the magnetism that overtook him when she pulled him into the pool returned with a vengeance. "My tripping you into the pool was COMPLETELY out of hand. It was wrong of me. I did like falling in with you, though," he grinned helplessly. "That iron grip on my shirt...was...pretty intense."

Kila lightened, "Well, I was ticked at you!" she admitted at last, smitten by his smile. *What I wouldn't give to live inside those crimson lips*, she reflected. *Damn you, Angus,* she blamed him for something he couldn't possibly help. He was who he was.

"All joking aside, Ki, I want to thank you for what you said," he placed a hand on her knee.

She looked at him in question.

He continued, "I needed to hear it. You were right. Reese totally played me...the whole thing...and, the worst part is that everyone knew it."

"It's okay," she wanted him to know that it was, but didn't know which words to say.

"No," his voice wavered, "it's not. Everyone found out, and I...I looked ridiculous...the...unrecoverable type."

"It's alright," Kila touched her hand to his and two of his fingers clamped onto two of hers. "It happened, but, because it did, that means it's also in the past," she whispered. "I mean, it's done if you want it to be."

"It should have been done a long time ago. It should have never happened," Angus looked at Kila's face to find her looking straight ahead at the wall. He decided to look at the wall, too. "You know, I wasted so much time thinking about her after that and I never knew why." He paused for a few moments. "It wasn't because I wanted her...somehow I knew I didn't...," he side-eyed Kila, but her eyes hadn't budged from the wall. Pressing his hand upward into hers, he continued, "Ki...she rejected me, so...heartlessly and... pointedly...and, I wanted to prove to myself I could make her want...me. That...uh...that...nothing was wrong...with me."

"Angus," Kila's sudden gaze washed upon his face, "listen to me. There is NOTHING wrong with you. NOTHING. Nothing as in zero, true zero, no decimal...."

As he weighed her statement, his chest rose and fell, questioning its sincerity.

"I mean it. Don't second-guess my words this time. Please," Kila pressed her hand down onto his, floored by his unexpected emotional outpouring. She felt the strings of her heart unlace and recognized how vulnerable she had voluntarily rendered herself in this moment. "Reese doesn't presently possess the capacity to understand who you are."

"I know...I don't even like Reese, Ki," he pulled his hand out from underneath hers, "and the very thought of her is beginning to make me ill. I just want everyone to know it's over. Broadcast to the masses. The whole ordeal ended, so I can move on with my life and pay attention to the people that actually matter."

Kila inhaled.

He shook his head in self-aggravation, massaging his forehead with his hands.

It tore Kila in half to see him this burdened. *How had Reese not wanted to be close to him? I would have touched his face the very first chance I had. I would have told him how intelligent he is, how his mind perpetually astounds me, how I always wanted to touch him, even before I think I was supposed to have those thoughts.* Those truths overtook her, and she knew without further reservation that she had to touch him herself, to feel his skin, to sense his pulse, to give into the craving, just once.

Her fingers stroked his, and she pulled his hands away from his face and down upon the bed. His bloodshot eyes watched gratefully as she moved herself inside his arms. Sensing his pain all the more now that her body rested inside his, she clung to him.

He didn't know why, at first feeling undeserving and then feeling indebted.

"It's alright," Kila spoke softly, stroking her fingers through his wet hair for the first time. "I mean, I think we all have to go through that feeling of being rejected by someone at least once in our lives. It's like you spend so much time thinking about them, dreaming about them, and wishing for them. You love every moment of it, the holographic idea of them you have created in your mind. The hope of potentially being together, of that person being happier with you than with anyone else. But when you breathe reality in, and logic crushes the walls of your emotion, you realize that person doesn't really think of you like that. I know…I really do know Ang, and it just ACHES…aches without end." She squeezed his shoulders at the irony of this unfolding, ordering herself not to cry.

Angus, listening intently to her words, unclenched his hands and spread his fingertips across her back. Having Kila's chest opposite his revived his heart. It awoke with a clear understanding of how to release itself of the pain. After the last of his torrid emotions for Reese drained from his limbs, his senses, having been flushed clean, felt more pure and alive than he could ever recall. In the midst of holding Kila, he realized he didn't want to let her go. He let his palms press into her back and descend slowly, enjoying the sensation of her skin underneath his.

Kila strained to ignore the feeling of his hands on her back, but she simply couldn't. He was so close and she was wearing so little. In her mind, she worked to calculate the percentage of her bare skin touching his. For her, it was substantial. She imagined touching her hand to his neck and running it down the back of his shirt and along everywhere else Reese hadn't touched; but, fear gripped her chest, and she only leaned into him further. Letting her head rest on his shoulder, she closed her eyes and listened to him breathe.

"Ki, this is…," Angus whispered, touching one of his hands to the back of her hair.

"Am I too close?" She quickly drew away from him, studying her knees. "I shouldn't have leaned, I'm sorry, I…didn't mean to make you uncomfortable."

"No, I—I wasn't, at all," he reached for her again.

The door swung open.

"Can you hear that?" Maya burst into the room, jumping several times in excitement, "Jacques can sing—REALLY sing—he's the handsomest, most talented chef you've ever laid eyes on, and he is singing one of your all-time favorite songs, NAKED in the shower down the hall. If ever there was a jackpot weekend, this is YOUR JACKPOT WEEKEND!" Her expression morphed from wild to timid when she grasped that Angus appeared not only upset, but also rather uncomfortable. "I'll be down the hall if you need me," Maya mouthed, nearly inaudibly, before she turned and slipped from the room.

Kila's heart pounded like a sledgehammer in her chest, and her mind, throttled by the interruption, throbbed to process everything all at once. *Am I hyperventilating? What was the last thing he said? Don't pass out. Not now. Oh god, not before it's understood!* Jacques's velvety voice echoed down the hallway bounding into her ears. She forced herself upright and toward the door, pausing only for a moment to take in **"Like A Stone" by Audioslave** before clicking it shut. Jacques's voice grew faint, but she could still make out the lyrics. *Start of the second verse…*she mumbled in her mind.

"She didn't know you were in here," Kila felt the need to explain Maya's entrance even though it was unnecessary. The time between each step back to Angus felt like an eternity.

What a minute ago seemed like hyper-speed, at present felt like slow motion. Neither tempo pleased her, and she longed to feel time move as it should. Aching inside, she took a seat on her bed, her feelings forcing their way from her chest into her throat.

Jacques's singing had aggravated Angus but solidified his intentions. "Ki, you...don't understand," he mumbled, trying to make his mouth say something sensible. "Let me explain...," he agonized over wanting to speak his mind, yet feared it would go without comprehension. He had spent too much time tangled up in something foolish for her to take him seriously.

"Keep talking about it," she placed her hands on her knees to prevent them from touching him, "I don't mind."

"...I need you," he watched her face.

"I won't tell anyone," she promised him. "It's best to let it out."

"No, that's not what I mean," he took one of her hands and turned it so her palm lay flat against his.

The heat from his hand transferred into hers, and the warmth traveled up her arm, into her heart, and swelled up in her eyes. *He's torturing me and he doesn't even know it... I can't take it.*

"I mean it...in its purest form...I...," he moved to the edge of the bed and knelt on the floor in front of her. Seeing her look away, he placed his hands on her knees, using his thumbs to caress them. "I thought you asked me to the Sadie dance last year because you felt bad about what Reese did to me. That's why I told you to ask Brix. I knew he wouldn't refuse you, and I also knew it would enrage her."

Kila exhaled and looked away from him.

"I remember being so rude to you when you asked, and how upset you seemed when I said 'no,' and...I thought you only asked me because you wanted to help me, so I didn't look so bad in front of everyone, and...I couldn't bear the thought."

Her eyes fell upon his cheeks. Never before had Angus been this intimate with her, and she wondered if it truly was an unquenchable thirst that she harbored for him. Moisture gathered in Kila's eyes as the pain of her repressed rejection threatened to surface in the form of unending tears.

"Angus! You in there? I'm coming in!" Ethan barged through the door mid-delivery, "I'm pretty sure the second singer is already among us. We need to devise an angle and LOCK JACQUES DOWN!" At the sight of Angus on his knees, Ethan raised his shoulders and looked to Kila. Confused, he nodded just once to Angus then disappeared as immediately as he had entered, pulling the door until it clicked shut behind him.

Angus stood and exhaled loudly, touching his hand to his forehead while his heart raced. This time, Kila sprinted to the door and locked it. A silence filled the air that seemed to thicken by the second. Kila could barely breathe. Anxiety cradled her like a mother to a child—she feared she wasn't getting enough oxygen.

"Can you put some music on?" Angus asked as soon as the thought came to him.

Kila rushed over to her laptop, panic a mere moment away. "Yeah...what do you want to hear?" *The first song will make or break this. I know it...I feel it...he needs to pick.*

"Anything. One song, on repeat—that's all," he continued to breathe audibly, stretching his arms out for some unknown reason.

*I can't believe I have to pick the song! Why didn't HE pick it? Is this some kind of test? I bet it will be the only one I've ever failed. God. This is a make-or-break situation. My future happiness lies at the mercy of the digital code of the track I pick. I have to go for strength. For certainty. For a no-fail-no-matter-what-the-circumstance-vocalist...*Kila racked her brain like the answer mattered more than all else. *There is only one...*she smiled despite the mess in her mind. Programming the single loop, she queued up the track.

"Shake It Out" by Florence + The Machine came on gently and sweetly. Kila looked back at Angus to see if he approved.

He grinned, "Louder."

She raised the volume and she felt weightless. The oncoming rush of the song directed the varied group of emotions in the room like a conductor leading an orchestra. Knowing the song wouldn't change, she rested inside it, listening to the words as she never had before, trying to determine if this would be the day she released him from her heart or caught him in her arms. Both options seemed to offer promise and hurt. The first with the hurt up front, and the second with the hurt at the end.

Does he know how I feel from what I said? What is he trying to say to me? At once, Kila caught her reflection in her bureau mirror and saw she was still in her bathing suit. Flushed and flustered, she grabbed the chartreuse shawl on her dresser and wrapped it swiftly around her waist and neck to create the likes of an elegant cover-up. Once the fabric was secured, she turned around to find Angus back on her bed.

Angus found himself mesmerized by the combination of her movements and gaze.

She stood in place until he motioned her to sit beside him.

He moved closer the second she sat. "I don't want anyone else to hear our conversation...I hope that's alright," he whispered.

"Yeah...it's good," Kila's lips felt numb. "No one can come in, and no one can hear."

"You know," Angus confessed, "I never saw Reese outside of school, except for a few events lots of people were at. She wouldn't even speak to me in public unless it served her. But she called and texted me daily. I never had that connection with anyone...like the way you and Brix would talk and text all the time."

Kila nodded, pain threatening to set in from all angles.

"It was misdirected, though. My feelings. I started to wonder about that when I saw the pictures from the Sadie dance last year."

"The Hawkins dance is miles behind us. Besides, Carter was so drunk he could barely dance," Kila rolled her eyes. "When he attempted, it was more often with other girls than with Reese, and he spent the majority of the night asking if anyone had any more rum. Plus, he nearly threw up on Delaney. And, despite how good Reese looked, she was alone most of the time."

The loudness of the song and the required closeness in order to hear one another established a new level of intimacy between them.

"I wasn't talking about Reese," Angus corrected, "I was talking about you...I never saw Brixton look as happy as he had in those pictures."

Kila's eyebrows stretched together. *Where is he going with this?*

"I don't know why I'm talking about Brixton. I'm not talking about Brixton," Angus huffed at his own clumsy words, "I mean, I'm only talking about Brixton because the pictures made me realize I should have gone with you. I should have said 'yes' the millisecond you asked. You're...fun."

Kila's eyes narrowed and her mouth opened in confusion. *If he thinks I'm fun, this is going nowhere. Nowhere. Just. Like. I. Thought. He doesn't even see me as a female. I'm Ethan's fun little sibling—that's all.*

"Fun wasn't the best descriptor for you," Angus realized aloud. "I shouldn't have said fun. Fun is…deflating. I get it now," he mumbled into a whisper looking in her blue eyes. "It's clearly more than fun. You. Who you are," his hand touched her hair.

She double-blinked. *So what if Reese's mind games have caused him to act irrationally towards me? The world doesn't always operate on the best terms and the most ideal circumstances. Would one be damned if, on a very limited basis, she took advantage of such an irregularity?* Kila pondered her next move as she felt his other hand tap her chin.

She wanted to tell him everything: that she loved him desperately, but couldn't bear to risk an ill-fated return from a Reese rebound. *This can only end badly*, Kila's mind fought valiantly to protect her heart. *He might not be over her yet. He might never be over her. "Reese" could be his "Angus,"* she wrestled with her conflicting thoughts, ultimately switching gears.

"SO much has changed since last year. You don't have to feel bad about it anymore," she pulled his hands out from her hair softly with her fingers. "…I think what's happening is that you're really emotional right now. You've grown confused… and, then, that's confusing to me, and I—"

His eyes paralyzed her. "It's okay, Ki…," he assured her.

Somehow she stood.

He rose right next to her.

She swallowed the lump in her throat as his arms encircled her body.

"I know there's a lot we don't know about each other," he whispered in her ear. "There's pain we both carry. Different things that have happened to us at different times...like losing my dad...your friend-split with Brix...this whole Reese disaster...which almost broke up the band...."

Her arms pulled him closer and she leaned in, cherishing the embrace. To Kila, Angus represented a glimpse of something greater she would never reach. Something unattainable. Unattainable even while her body presently rested in his arms.

"You don't have to tell me anything you don't want to...I won't pry," he confessed to her. "I just want to be near you."

She withdrew from his embrace, fearing the ultimate risk of another broken heart. "You can be near me, but I know you're still confused...you are," she repeated, "and until we're both not confused, we should be...careful."

He knew she'd retreated, but he didn't want their closeness to end. He wanted it to loop like the song, over and over again. "I can be careful," he stroked his hand through her hair just once. "I'll show you."

Pressing up on her toes, she kissed him softly right between his full eyebrows, letting her lips linger on his skin.

His eyes closed, drinking her in, and Kila allowed herself to do something she had always wanted to: outline his thick cheekbones with her thumbs.

He enjoyed the feeling.

"I wish I had your cheekbones," she whispered when his eyes opened.

"You can have them," Angus touched her chin, "if I can have your eyes."

"Why would you want mine when yours are dark and brooding?" she touched his nose.

"Because I'm tired of brooding," Angus laughed, "...and besides that, I like them." He placed three of his fingers on her shoulder and began fiddling with the part of her cover-up that wrapped around her neck.

Feeling his fingers slip under the cloth near her collarbone might have been the best sensation Kila had experienced. She was scared to close her eyes, yet also scared to keep them open. She looked at the wall until she felt his other hand on her other shoulder.

"Thanks for bearing with me today," his fingers stopped moving on her skin. "I think I finally know what I needed to."

"Good," she backed away from him, knowing both that she should, and also that she would hate herself for it later. "Don't worry," she assured him. "Once word gets out that you're over Reese, they'll be lining up to get a chance with you," she smirked. "And this whole conversation will have been merely a transition to your new life."

"Will you be in my line?" he asked boldly. His lips parted

before he smiled at her.

"Not…a…chance," she forced an eye roll to fake authenticity, "but, I want you to know that you have my vote for anyone but Maya. And if I can help in any way, with girls," she bit her tongue to maintain composure, "let me know."

"Maya's not my type—she wasn't even before she was off limits," he replied, "but I may take you up on your offer. We'll see how it goes," he nervously touched his hair, "when we're alone again, being careful and all." He watched her eyes, but they no longer met his.

Kila's mind busied itself seeking logical ground. Within moments, she had deemed it inevitable that Angus would soon invest his attention elsewhere. The past few minutes they shared in private could very well turn out to be the closest she would ever be to him. Swallowing that dose of reality, she stopped the music and continued the conversation as though nothing out of the ordinary had just happened between them.

"Clean yourself up for the party. All the girls will be looking to dance. Anna handpicked Ethan's shirt so he'll match Maya. She doesn't know it yet, but we bought her a dress," Kila tried to slow her words, but they tumbled out without change. "Tonight's shaping up to be perfect," she patted him on the shoulder.

"I hope so," he laughed at all the details she'd provided in only one breath. "I could use a perfect night."

Kila unlocked and opened the door.

Anna jumped at her frantically. "Finally! What were you two doing in here?"

Angus raised his eyebrows.

Anna's eyes darted to Kila's face.

"We were TALK-ING!" Kila had, against the odds, avoided blushing. "Can't two people of the opposite sex have a conversation behind closed doors without everyone assuming they're going at it?"

Anna, without answering the question, looked again to Angus in hopes she might find traces of lip gloss on his mouth. When she saw nothing determinable, she turned back to Kila. "Yes. Sorry, it's just that the day is escaping us. We still need to drop Maya home, run to Mayberry, pick her back up, decorate the backyard, get her dressed, give her the gift, and get her ready!" Anna attempted to catch her breath, while she watched Angus close in on Kila.

Kila found Anna's unusual nervousness hilarious. She turned to Angus to tell him, but that thought dissolved against his body. *He's close again...*

Angus danced his dark eyes across her face, alluring her. Without words, he pressed his nose into her skin, kissed her firmly on the cheek, and dashed down the stairs.

She wanted to sprint after him and kiss him everywhere, and she didn't care how absurd it might seem to Anna or to anyone else. *I want him, and I've wanted him as long as I can remember...I should calm down,* she instructed her senses, *it's just a kiss on the cheek...in front of Anna. A very minimal advance, if you could even call it that. From a confused and brokenhearted boy. After all, I just kissed him on the forehead. Maybe he felt like he needed to return the gesture.*

"What was that all about?" Anna scrambled to dissect Kila's ever morphing facial expressions. "Does Angus get lovey on the weekends or something?"

"Yeah, I guess. I mean, I have no idea," Kila thought she spoke convincingly, until she felt her hand touching the cheek he had kissed.

"I don't exactly believe that...he was locked in your room with you with the music jacked to make-out level," Anna whispered the last part, "and Maya felt fully convinced she barged in on something."

"Shhh! Anna, oh my gosh," Kila whispered back. "Noth-ing is going on. Trust me. I wish I could say otherwise," Kila blushed. "Really...."

Anna raised an eyebrow and a smile, wanting desperately to pry for more details. However, Kila's prompt showing of crossed fingers signified the subject's secretive nature, and Anna knew this meant she wouldn't be receiving any further details on Kila's tendency toward Angus anytime soon. Still, she felt pleased to know about it.

Instead of prying, Anna took the opportunity to gush to her about how she thought she might be falling for Brixton. It was the first time in Anna's life she did not want to rush anything. In fact, she didn't even want him to know how deeply she felt.

The idea of Brixton, Anna explained while Kila switched outfits, had changed her mind about what she identified as meaningful. She found herself wanting to read philosophy and history and topics with depth. She yearned to speak with him at length about such subjects. And she wasn't wasting any time. "Operation Information Overload" launched just last night, Emerson acting as her first guide. Anna found his writing at once simple to read, but then dense in dimension. The same paragraph could be read multiple times in a sitting and each time provoke a deeper thought. Fixating on her appearance, Anna declared, would soon take a back seat to her new plans. She had things to learn. Things of importance.

The vibrant trio of girls proceeded with their errands, music blaring in the car, first dropping Maya home to see her parents, then to Mayberry to pick up Maya's surprise present, her dress for this evening. Kila had tactfully designed the invitations, requesting that all guests wear pants or shorts. Maya would be the only one donning a dress, a rare occasion for her. Kila and Anna had plotted secretly to buy this dress for weeks, ever since Maya had cooed over it, hanging perfectly in their favorite boutique downtown. It took some skillful savings on Kila and Annabelle's part, but they both agreed it would be worth every penny to see the look on Maya's face when she unwrapped the box. The other perk, of course, would be the look on Ethan's face when he saw her in it. And Annabelle was better than anyone else at making a girl feel her best. They sighed over the very thought of it, and wanted more than anything for this to be a dreamlike night for their closest friend.

While Anna continued to elaborate on her feelings for Brixton, Kila found her mind ping-ponging from Jacques to

Angus. *Why am I doing this to myself? Either would surely prove disastrous. Even IF Angus likes me in SOME way, he can't possibly feel the way about me that I feel about him. An imbalanced nightmare would prove insoluble. Even in his arms.*

And Jacques—how can I even venture down that path when I know I'll probably never be over Angus? Ugh! What if this carries into college, and I STILL can't get over him, when he's not even around? There are only so many A's one can accumulate without experiencing a good make out. I SO want a good make out, or at least a good kiss. I haven't even had ONE. No one has tried! Wait...Ollie...

In the whirlwind of last night and this morning, Kila had neglected to check Nektir for Timothy's update. She couldn't check while driving and wouldn't when Anna might see, so she waited. When they were standing in what felt like a mile-long line at the coffee shop, Kila suggested Anna check out The Rocking Horse, the antiques store next door. She told her where to find the sections of old books once inside. And Anna gladly took her up on the offer, instructing Kila to head over once she had the drinks in hand. With a hesitant feeling, Kila pulled her phone from her bag and opened the Nektir app:

Received last night at 10:05PM

‹ **1HighKite**: Aurora. Are you there? (I just stole my phone back from Vik while he was flirting with Gretchen.) ›

‹ **1HighKite**: Those two already seem hot 'n' heavy. Not sure how I feel about that OR how I feel about Jocelyn. Definite mixed feelings. The conversation's a little muddy, but she's looking at me like she wants me. ›

‹ 1HighKite: PS, I'm hungry because I had to eat the damn garden salad, and Vik is insistent on walking the beach despite that he knows I'm more or less on empty. ›

‹ 1HighKite: I'm wondering if anything explosive happened on your end. If it did, would you tell me? ›

Received today at 12:45AM

‹ 1HighKite: I just realized you haven't responded since yesterday afternoon. I should probably stop messaging, but this thread has become a bit of a diary for me, for better or for worse. ›

‹ 1HighKite: I'm curious about what's going on with you. Your music feed is all over the place. Impossible for me to piece it together. ›

Received today at 9:21AM

‹ 1HighKite: She kissed me this morning (in public) when we all met back up for breakfast. It felt aggressive, and I think she thinks I play rough. (I don't & I'm not into that.) I cut out of breakfast early under the guise of having to prepare for tonight's show. Vik seemed unamused, but it was necessary on my part. Wicked hoping to get your advice. I will be singing one of the new covers you recommended. I've narrowed it down to two, but I'm not telling you which ones. Hit me up. ›

After reading the new messages three times, Kila looked up from her phone to check the length of the line. Nine people remained ahead of her, so she jumped right into her replies:

‹ **K.Lorens:** Ugh! Ollie. Sorry I didn't see these sooner. It's only been a day, but it feels more like a week. Things have been crazy over here. Too crazy, in fact. Can't say I've been kissed yet, though, and you've already been kissed AGAIN. What.the.hell?! ›

‹ **K.Lorens:** By "aggressive" what do you mean? Maybe she's super into you. Is that a bad thing? ›

‹ **K.Lorens:** PS, wish I could be at Bitters tonight. Might make more sense to me than my current predicament. Plus, SforS rocks. ›

‹ **1HighKite:** AURORA! There you are. ›

‹ **K.Lorens:** Hi! I'm in line at the coffee shop, and Anna's next door. Not sure how long I have. If I disappear, I'll check again as soon as I'm able. ›

‹ **1HighKite:** I'm just glad you've surfaced. What coffee shop? ›

‹ **K.Lorens:** Teegan's. ›

‹ **1HighKite:** Ahhhh. I'm not too far from you—I'm over at Casper's checking out the new Audeze headphones. Love at first listen. To be honest, I don't want to take them off. Hey, what song's playing at Teegan's? I'll play it in these headphones, so we can tandem again. ›

‹ **K.Lorens:** Ooo. Keep 'em on! Let me listen. One's just starting. ›

‹ **K.Lorens: "Someone To You" by BANNERS** ›

‹ **1HighKite:** Got it. (NICE one.) Aaaaaannnd…we're (nearly) tandem! ›

‹ **K.Lorens:** (Yeah. Love it.) Awesome. ›

‹ **1HighKite:** By aggressive, I mean forceful. Her nose kept slamming into mine—not in a cute way. I don't know how to describe it. Everyone was looking at us, and she was all about it. It was like she wanted people to see her kissing me MORE than she actually wanted to kiss me. Does that make sense? I'm really attracted to her, but…I thought it would feel different. Kissing's a private thing. Like, a closed-door thing, at least to me, anyway. And she keeps bringing up the band. I get that that's how she knows me, but I'm more than that. Does that sound superficial of me, or her? ›

‹ **K.Lorens:** Whoa…I don't know. I mean, on one hand she could be this forcefully affectionate fame monster, but on the other hand she could just be trying too hard or feel so nervous that her personality is coming across in all the wrong ways. You're an incredible singer, so I don't blame her for wanting to talk to you about that. I mean, I also get that you don't want SforS to be the topic of EVERY conversation. You have other interests. Other things you like and do. Unless Vik briefed her, she doesn't know that yet. My vote is to give her a chance. Some more time. You can also gently tell her you're not into the PDA thing, but that you ARE interested in some alone kissing. Has she hugged

you or touched your face or held your hand or anything
when she wasn't kissing you? ⟩

⟨ 1HighKite: No!!! She hasn't done any of those things, now
that I think of it. And when we're not in a public place
she's more distant. Checking her phone or refreshing her
makeup. Who the hell kisses someone before touching them
anywhere? In public? Now, I'm more concerned... ⟩

⟨ K.Lorens: Don't be. Focus on the show tonight. That's
more important. Figure out the rest later. (You'll probably
want a celebratory make out after you guys kill it,
anyway.) ⟩

⟨ 1HighKite: Good advice. Maybe on the post-show make
out, but...maybe not with her? ⟩

⟨ 1HighKite: By the way, I already mentioned I might have
to see Naomi after the show (I don't), so that I can avoid the
whole double-date thing again if I need to. Maybe I'll just
sneak into the party for a quick bit, that is, if it wouldn't be
too weird. ⟩

⟨ K.Lorens: Come if you can, but I won't be upset if you
can't. (It wouldn't be weird.) ⟩

⟨ 1HighKite: I think we both know it would be. ⟩

⟨ K.Lorens: OK. People would think it was weird, but I want
you to. You satisfied now? ⟩

⟨ 1HighKite: Yes (and no). ⟩

‹ **K.Lorens:** I see you've brushed up on your flirting. ›

‹ **1HighKite:** Swam in a sea of boredom more than anything else. ›

‹ **K.Lorens:** Dissolve the drama. A forceful public kiss is still a kiss and I haven't had one. So you'll get no sympathy from me. ›

‹ **1HighKite:** Hey. I offered yesterday. I risked a detention to court you outside your class, but you opted for a dead Oscar Wilde instead. ›

‹ **K.Lorens:** Please. You weren't serious. Plus, it would have been a public kiss, and you're not into that. ›

‹ **1HighKite:** I was serious. I told you that. And, it wouldn't have been a public kiss. I have the key to the art storage room by the gym. That's where I would have taken you. ›

‹ **K.Lorens:** Whoa ›

Kila regretted her last reply the moment she sent it. She hadn't actually meant to type it. Her mind and fingers had aligned too quickly, and she nearly jolted when the barista spoke to her. She pictured Timothy Cardiff the entire time she recited her order, and resumed the Nektir thread the instant she was waiting for the three drinks.

‹ **1HighKite:** What did you mean by whoa? ›

‹ **K.Lorens:** ? nothing. It's an expression. ›

‹ **1HighKite**: Aurora. I think you know what I'm asking. ›

‹ **K.Lorens**: Ollie. We're both already in complicated situations. ›

‹ **1HighKite**: What happened with you? ›

‹ **K.Lorens**: A couple things. ›

‹ **1HighKite**: Emotional things? ›

‹ **K.Lorens**: Yeah. Nothing determinable yet, though. ›

‹ **1HighKite**: So we're basically tied, less the kissing thing on your end. ›

‹ **K.Lorens**: Pretty much. ›

‹ **1HighKite**: Cool. Well, if both our potential hookups go south, I think I'll throw down on an Oscar Wilde poster, so we can both take turns kissing him. ›

‹ **K.Lorens**: Oh. I'm so down that I'll split the cost. ›

‹ **1HighKite**: Right on! ›

‹ **K.Lorens**: Hey. My drinks are ready, and I need both hands to carry. Rest your voice, so you can stun them tonight. Can't wait to watch the whole show online with Maya tomorrow, and see you late night tonight—maybe?!? (You can take your crew, you know. I expect a good crowd, based on the RSVPs.) ›

‹ **1HighKite:** Thank you for the support, Aurora. Means much. If I come, I think I'll show solo. But, we'll see how it shakes out for both of us. (I'll look up hot Oscar Wilde posters during intermission, just in case. Tell no one.) ›

"WHAT are you grinning at?" Anna asked, noticing Kila bite her bottom lip. "Our drinks are sitting at the counter. Did you even notice?"

"YES!" Kila overcompensated in her reply. "I did notice. In fact, I was just about to grab them."

"No, you were standing here looking…fabulous and flirtatious," she touched Kila's blushed cheeks. "Did someone talk to you in line? Ooooooh, was it that guy?" Anna pointed to a slim, bearded hipster in bright athletic sneakers carefully pouring almond milk into his coffee.

"No! He's cute but too old. What's wrong with you?" Kila laughed nervously, "I just saw the new Bates poster."

"Your face didn't look like a 'cooing over Bates' face," Anna eyed her.

"Alright, alright. It wasn't Bates. It's just that SO much has happened in the last couple of days," she truthfully relayed her thoughts in an ambiguous manner to Anna.

It wasn't that Kila didn't trust Anna. She did. It was just that if she relayed in detail the truth about her mercurial feelings she would know that someone else knew, and it would make it even harder for her to be around either Jacques or Angus back at the house. And even more awkward if Timothy did make a cameo at tonight's party. So, like she often did, Kila internalized things.

"Enough about me. Tell me about that book you're holding, and then let's talk about Brix again," Kila grinned, this time in relief. "I know you want to."

"No," Anna laughed. "It's probably boring to you. I'm probably not telling you anything you don't already know."

"It's not boring," Kila lifted her coffee cup. "I'm excited you're reading. You have my full backing on the Brix front. He's absolutely one of a kind and will probably make the greatest boyfriend ever."

The goofiest smile plastered itself on Anna's face. "If that's true, how come YOU never entertained that idea?"

"He doesn't think of me like that," Kila explained. "He's almost like another brother to me." *Plus, we had a six-month dry spell, which I have yet to understand...*

* * * * *

Maya's parents, having no idea their daughter was about to leave for her farewell party, were waiting outside on the porch with her. They hugged Kila and Anna and shared sentimentalities, but Maya grew impatient halfway through her iced Americano and broke the conversation short, anxious to return to Ethan. The hourglass of dwindling time had become almost tangible to her, and she wanted to spend as much time with him before she left as possible.

Once they returned to the Lorens house, the girls headed straight for the backyard. They stood together in awe of the deck and lawn, which had been transformed into a dazzling dream. Endless strings of lights and lanterns led to a farewell banner for Maya, where guests could leave personalized messages and artwork. For easy access, the boys had separated the many different markers into Mason jars by color and width. The girls turned toward one another and conversed in facial expressions only. Maya spotted Ethan on a ladder hanging extra speakers, while Anna found Brixton hanging perfectly spaced citronella lanterns around the pool.

As Kila peeled around the corner to look for Angus, she heard the start of **"40 Watt" by ELEL** and found him studying a playlist on Brixton's laptop. *He looks...different from when I left. He fixed his hair,* she inhaled, trying to admire him without staring. She began at the top and worked her way down. Dark strands spilled all around his face, their ends turning off in different directions as they reached his neck. Wearing a navy Henley that hugged his frame, he stood barefoot, his vintage washed jeans cuffed just above his ankles so the hems didn't drag on the ground.

"Wow," she stepped close enough to watch him scroll through the songs, "I had no idea you guys planned to take care of all of this."

"We didn't either," Angus admitted, "but when we came outside to work out, we found the heap of decorations against the garage." He grabbed the cloth bags from her hands and set them on the corner of the deck. "You always said an artistic challenge is a worthwhile challenge. Plus, I told your brother he'd get to dance with Maya pre-party if we hung them so you didn't have to," his eyes studied her reactions to his words. At the first start of a smile he asked her to dance.

"Would you like to grind with me?" he offered her his hand.

She erupted with laughter. "No! There will be no grinding," she looked up at the sky, shaking her head with a smile. "At least not here," she bit her bottom lip.

"Come on," he grabbed her hand. "It'll be great. Let's freak your brother out."

"No," she laughed again. "He has enough to worry about already."

"You're right," he pulled her closer, "let's almost grind, then."

"K," she gave in to his delight, gripping his shoulders and following his lead.

He swept her into movement. "So...does this count as careful?" he pushed her away, then pulled her back quickly. Their bodies collided and he grinned.

"I don't know," she leaned in to whisper, "I'd say it's borderline at best." She changed up the dance.

He struggled to keep up with her fast movements, "...But the careful requirement was only enacted due to your thinking I was confused, and since I've since determined I'm not confused, we might not need to be as careful, right?" He pulled her into him again, slowing the pace to keep her body close to his.

Their eyes met and it took her longer than she had intended to reply, "Yeah, but...now I think I might be confused." For a split second, she thought of someone else. Then, she recalled the hundreds of nights she lay awake in bed thinking of Angus, and only Angus, and added, "I didn't...mean it in a bad way...I just...need a little time to think about it." She ran her hands along his upper back to convey what her words simply couldn't.

"Good. I want you to think about it. Actually, I want you to think about it a lot," he said softly, dipping his head to kiss her cheek.

Her eyes widened.

"I made sure no one was looking. Don't worry," he grinned, touching her hair.

I shouldn't allow myself to enjoy this. If I do, I'll only want more. Kila's eyes closed when his palm slid under her hair and he touched the back of her neck. She squeezed his upper arms and he flexed them, winking at her.

"I told you we should grind...I know you want to," he laughed before she did.

Rolling her hips into his, she indulged her imagination despite what she previously perceived to be her better judgment.

"Hey! Look who's not being so careful, now," Angus rolled his hips back into hers.

"Okay," Kila pursed her lips, trying to tone down her

excitement, "let's stop now that we're even."

"I'd like it better if we were uneven though," he laughed in her ear, "because then we could do it again to get even." He drew in a long breath of her vetiver perfume and his eyes lifted with his thoughts.

She pulled him closer, feeling something new take hold. "Do I need to warn my friends you're in rare form tonight?" She tested him, "maybe I should send a mass text...."

"Why?" He kissed the same cheek again, "It's not like I'm going to grind with any of them."

"Yeah, well...we'll see," she replied with equal hints of question and flirtation.

"You could send them a mass text to let them know that we just grinded though," he pressed into her. "Uh-oh, you better tell them we're uneven again," he winked.

She felt his hair in her hands, questioning why she was suddenly able to.

He held her as close as he thought she would let him.

On the other edge of the deck, Ethan twirled Maya in loops and prevented her from twirling back out once she reached him. She was captive in his arms, but a happy prisoner she made. His blue eyes glistened as he kissed her hands, then kissed her mouth, riding a dizzy, emotional wave.

By the pool, Anna patiently handed Brixton the last lantern.

She asked him to dance the same moment it was secured. Expecting him to dodge her, she blushed when he took her hands without the need for further coaxing. Anna had no idea Brixton was the best dancer of his friends, and it didn't even appear as though he was trying. She mimicked his speed, giving him space, and tried not to smile too widely.

"What if we don't stop dancing?" Angus barely spoke the words in Kila's ear.

"What do you mean?" she asked, pulling him just a little tighter.

"We refuse to stop. Quite simple," he touched his nose to her cheek.

She traced his left cheekbone with her right thumb, and replied, "Everything would change around us."

"Exactly," Angus exhaled, "and that would be nice."

Kila pressed her cheek into his, imagining it through closed eyes while her anxiety drifted away.

When the song drew to a close and **"Promises, Promises" by Incubus** began, Brixton spotted Angus holding Kila. The two were leaned against each other, cheek to cheek, hardly the positioning Brixton had expected to see. *Why isn't he teasing her? Why are her eyes closed? And where the hell is Noah when I actually need him?* He swallowed the sight of Angus's hand in Kila's hair, wishing he had some water to wash it down. It lingered in his throat, like the acidic taste of vomit.

Unable to watch any longer, Brixton turned his head back to feel Anna's hands greet his face. He welcomed her soothing fingers and knowingly embraced her presence. The slopes of her face and neck were foreign to him, but his thumbs explored them for the first time. She silently assured him with her eyes. He stretched his emotions, questioning their elasticity.

But Anna inched too close for him to finish his assessment in comfort. The change in her eyes and the arch in her spine prompted him to take a mental step back. No stranger to unrequited admiration, he wanted the moments he spent with her to add up to more than an elegant distraction. When she looked the other way and rested her head on his shoulder, he pressed his hand into the back of her plush, sun-kissed hair, wishing he could bring himself to give her the chance he knew she deserved. The chance that could also bring about his own happiness.

*I fell for Kiki, didn't tell her, abandoned her friendship, and am now plagued with watching Angus get closer to her than I ever will. Jacques is different. Jacques I can handle. Jacques makes sense...*Brixton began identifying and arranging all the variables in his mind. Every so often, he found himself distracted by the floral scent of Anna's hair. *Is that geranium?*

By this time, Kila had fallen irreversibly subject to the song's allure and Angus's swaying. Amidst the lyrics, which had always captivated her, his body seemed to ease every worry she ever had in her life. She wanted to tell him but knew that she shouldn't. And she feared if he asked her anything, she would confess her most guarded thoughts to him. Each time he kissed her cheek, which grew more and more frequent, her hands pressed further and further into his skin. *He's trapping me and I've offered no objections...* she opened her light eyes to find his dark eyes only a few inches away.

"Thanks for letting me dance with you," he whispered, "I didn't know if you would."

She couldn't speak, so she nodded.

He assumed she was playing it cool.

"There's going to be a lot of people here tonight, huh?" he continued looking at her.

She nodded again, speaking this time, "Anna and I figured if we invited forty, about a hundred would show—you know how these things work...."

"Yeah," Angus exhaled. "Unfortunately, I do...," he leaned down, about to kiss her cheek again, when he felt Brixton's lingering glance and decided against it.

Kila studied the smoothness of Angus's cheeks, wondering how they would look in a few years with facial hair. *I couldn't handle it. I couldn't even pretend to.*

"What?" he grinned.

She blushed, shaking her head.

"What were you thinking?" he touched a section of her hair.

"I was thinking," Kila circled her hands around his shoulders, "that you've given me a lot to think about."

"Can I see you before everyone arrives?" he asked suddenly.

She looked over his shoulder at Ethan and Maya before she replied, "…You already are."

"Not in the way I want," Angus explained. "Can I take you somewhere?"

Kila felt her heart swell, wishing it was yesterday and she could say "yes." "I have to stay here—Anna and I have to get Maya ready. Are you going somewhere?"

"No," he whispered, "I just thought it might be nice to talk without everyone watching…."

"Who's watching?" Kila whispered, feeling anxious.

"Everyone here that's not us," Angus regretted mentioning it.

"Oh," Kila opened up the space between them and pulled her arms off his body. "That's probably better," she attempted to look serious.

"Not for me," Angus admitted. "They're approaching."

Kila asked Angus something that wouldn't be deemed intimate. "Did you put the music together?"

"I wish I could take credit," Angus churned his delivery out like a practiced actor, "Brix was the real mastermind. We spent over an hour after our workout compiling the most badass playlist Cypress has ever seen."

"KiKi," Brixton chimed in behind her, "it's the dance party playlist to END all party playlists."

"I'm definitely into it," Kila spoke honestly. "Your playlists never disappoint."

"Just wait until tonight." Brixton half-smiled, "…Nothing can stop it once it's in motion." He lowered then raised his right shoulder slowly.

Excited at the prospects, Kila jumped to meet his raised hand for a flying high-five.

"Nailed it," Brixton exclaimed. "You always nail the air hi-fi, Kiki. It's a rare gift. Seriously."

"You guys creep me out," Angus shook his head, noticing Anna's eyes on Brixton's backside. "We need to get some secret gestures of our own, Anna. We can't let them have all the fun."

"Yeah," Anna pursed her lips into a smile, "I guess you're right."

"Leave it to me. I'll come up with something just as rare and just as serious. Oh, I know!" Angus teased Brixton, "Anna, when you touch your nose, I'll walk around like a stork. No one will ever know what it means, and we can laugh like we have superpowers while the rest of the group is left to guess."

"Who's guessing about what?" Ethan reached the circle with

Maya hooked to his side.

As if she were about to scratch an itch, Anna touched her nose.

Determined to impress, Angus lifted one leg high. Crouching into a squat with both arms bent at his sides, he walked around, imagining he possessed stork-like legs.

Maya's giggles caused the others to laugh, too.

Before Angus ceased his antics, Brixton caught Kila's eyes. He made a circle around his left shoulder with his index finger to indicate that Angus had been jealous.

Kila double-tapped her right eyebrow to convey the message "I know."

While everyone else's conversations had stopped, Ethan correctly suspected that Brixton and Kila's had not. *They don't realize how rude that is. They never did.* He pulled everyone together, "Bird dance aside, I'm proud of Angus's success. He focused on one task for several hours today WITHOUT texting." He beamed, "I hope this is the dawn of a new era."

"Bite it!" Angus snapped.

"Make me," Ethan countered, motioning Angus to come closer with raised fists.

Anna, noticing the clock on the deck, knew she needed to speed things along or there wouldn't be enough time to ready Maya in the way she and Kila had planned. As the boys engaged in some sparring, Anna corralled Maya in her arms.

Kila reluctantly followed the two toward the house, but she turned back to seize one last glimpse of him.

Angus met her gaze head-on, causing him to fall victim to a joint lift and toss from Ethan and Brixton. Dusting himself off in the grass, Angus laughed and winked at her. Kila held up a hand and pulled her bottom lip into her mouth. He winked again and she turned forward, touching her hand to her face so Anna and Maya wouldn't see her telltale smile.

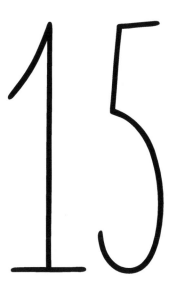

Convincing Maya to take a twenty-five-minute catnap was a bit of a challenge. She stood, plastered to Kila's window, gawking at Ethan on the lawn, and pouted pitifully when Anna pulled her away and pushed her onto the bed. In an attempt to entrap her, Kila tossed a blanket over her body.

"I know what you're trying to do, and I'm not going to sleep!" Maya protested. "My time is limited, and I don't care if I sleep another minute in Felton. I'll sleep in Rhode Island, when I have nothing to do but cry and dread the winter."

"Ma-ya," Anna whispered, "don't talk like that."

"Why not?" Maya pouted. "It's the truth...and...until then, until I leave, let me look at him. He's playing baseball...and... he looks so good when he plays. Go see for yourself," she pointed and smiled in a way that melted more than half of Anna's determination.

Anna walked over to the window, looked at the three boys, and raised her eyebrows.

Kila inhaled, nodded in sympathy, and made a noticeable fuss over fixing the pillows under Maya's head. "You'll see him soon, and while you cannot think straight, you should trust us. All we're asking for is twenty minutes of downtime. I don't think that's unreasonable," Kila caught Maya's eyes. "You can stay up all night alone with him after the party if you want…but, you'll be more likely to keep your lids open later when it counts if you bank a little sleep now." She touched Maya's forehead, and Maya's eyelids flickered up and down. "Aha," Kila smiled, "you do need sleep. That iced Americano couldn't even save you."

Maya huffed; nevertheless, her eyes remained closed.

Anna pointed to the clock on Kila's bureau.

"Go shower," Kila directed. "I'll take care of this."

Anna looked at Kila skeptically. She then glanced at the bed to see Maya's toes moving anxiously beneath the blanket.

"Trust me," Kila whispered. She rose to dim the lights and fed **"Follow Me Down" by Lydia** from her phone to her speakers.

Anna waited for the lyrics and tilted her head when they rose through the air.

"I told you you'd like Lydia—wait 'till you hear their whole discography. You will be wooed with words," Kila gushed.

"Oooo," Anna softened, "I could use a little of that."

"Go," Kila motioned her to the shower.

"Alright," Anna conceded at last, "but you know the consequences if you fail."

"I'm not going to fail. I have a secret weapon," Kila winked.

Once the door was closed, Kila eyed Maya. Her dark eyes had opened and they looked at Kila in a pleading way. Without words, Kila warned her to stay in bed. Maya obliged, though she clearly would have preferred otherwise, and watched her best friend walk out the door. Left alone, she listened to the lyrics of the song, but they only made her long for Ethan. She lay on her back, looking up at the ceiling, imagining the feeling of his lips and what it felt like to fall asleep beside him last night.

Inside Ethan's room, Kila rummaged through his drawers and closet, looking for something that would help Maya sleep. A sweatshirt would be too heavy, a button-down would get too wrinkly, and sweatpants would be too silly. There were no pajama tops she could locate. *Aha!* She spotted a well-worn, heather-gray, long-sleeved thermal shirt on the top shelf of the closet. As fast as her limbs allowed, she dosed it in his cologne and returned to her room, flustered to find Maya staring out the window again.

"Ab-so-lute-ly ob-sessed," Kila scolded, "and here I was about to let you wear his thermal for your nap...tisk-tisk. I shouldn't have even grabbed it."

Maya turned away from the window to gaze at the gray waffle shirt in her friend's hands. "Wait! That's the shirt he wears to Brix's to play drums. Give me that," she yelped. "Please? I'll sleep. I promise!" She raised her hand to signify the seriousness of her oath. "I promise I'll sleep. I'll be your sleeping angel," she forced the sweetest face she could muster.

"I thought you might change your mind," Kila remarked triumphantly, pointing to the bed.

This time, Maya climbed under the covers without objection. When Kila was satisfied, she surrendered the thermal, and Maya slipped it over her head lovingly.

"It still smells like him," Maya snuggled inside the fabric.

"Yeah," Kila crossed her fingers behind her back, "I think he wore it the other day." She hoped that this slight shift in the truth wouldn't come back to haunt her, but she was willing to assume the risk for the sake of securing Maya's surprise.

When Kila felt confident Maya was asleep, she dashed out to her car to remove the box from her trunk. Although Kila knew the box rested safely under a small pile of sweatshirts, she still held her breath. There was no real reason for it, but she worried just the same. No one else had known the dress was there, and no else had a key to her car except for her parents, who were in Houston. Odds were more likely that someone would want to steal Kila's car than to steal Maya's dress, which remained in the same space where it had been placed hours ago.

Ahhhhh! Kila exhaled when her hands found the edges of the box. *Still here...* In somewhat of a habit, she neatly folded her sweatshirts before closing the trunk. *Two hours left. I have to make sure we don't forget anything.*

On her way back to the house, she heard **"The Business of Emotion (feat. White Sea)" by Big Data, White Sea** blast through the backyard speakers. *I should have known Brix couldn't play baseball without music. He must have fallen for Big Data, too. So...ridiculously...necessary...*Kila knew she had energized herself, but given tonight's festivities, she chose not to calm herself down. *Music is the ultimate high. Why don't more people understand that?* Her body moved to the beat.

Angus jumped in front of her, jarring her thoughts. "We can dance some more," he studied her eyes, "if you want."

Kila found his face irresistible. He'd talked to her more today than he had in the past month, and that granted her the ability to speak with him more freely than she had ever imagined. "You're sweaty," she watched several beads of water gather in his hairline and trickle down the side of his face.

He had swapped his jeans and Henley for maroon jersey shorts and a white form-fitting athletic T-shirt. "If you won't dance, then come play," he begged with his eyes. "We need a fourth for even teams."

"Rain check?" she asked, lifting the top of the box.

His wet eyebrows stretched together.

"Maya's dress for tonight," she explained.

He nodded and moved closer.

She was drawn to his full, dark lashes, and watched as they lifted and closed over his coffee eyes.

"I keep thinking of you," he spoke quietly, "...tell me that doesn't bother you."

"It doesn't," Kila's lips moved but her heart's pounding kept her from hearing her voice. She focused on holding the dress box, but her eyes fell subject to estimating the angles of his face.

"There's so much I want to tell you," he lost himself in her light eyes.

"Oh yeah?" She felt her whole body vibrate, despite that she remained in place. "Tell me, then."

"I will," his voice took on a deeper tone, "if you see me. Will you? We can keep it quiet...."

Kila attempted to process his words when she heard Brixton shout.

"Watch out!" Brixton warned as a baseball came hurdling over the garage in their direction.

In an instant, Kila covered the dress box and pivoted to the left, narrowly escaping the ball.

"Dynamite, Kiki—absolute dynamite," Brixton sprinted towards them and swiped the ball from the grass into his mitt.

"Your brother's a bit preoccupied. That may have been his most awkward hit since T-ball," he laughed, eyeing Angus.

"Doubtful," Angus smirked. "You obviously don't remember his T-ball days."

Kila giggled at the recollection.

"See? Someone knows what I'm talking about," Angus grinned. "I'll be back in a minute," he spoke to Brixton, "I was just helping Ki with the heavy box." He lifted it from her hands.

"It can't be that heavy if she was able to slide sideways and hold onto it with one hand," Brixton countered. "Then again, she does seem to possess some unnatural athletic abilities," he looked at her.

"Up for debate," Kila laughed. "The good news is you only have to keep E busy for another couple of hours," she rubbed Brixton's shoulder.

Angus hardened.

Brixton shifted in place, removing, then tossing the ball back into the mitt a few times. "We still need to talk later. Don't forget."

"Hey," Kila reminded, "I'm waiting on you, remember?"

"Not for long, Kiki," he continued tossing the ball into his mitt, his thoughts growing heavier by the second. *I should just tell her I'm in love with her. Quick and direct...and see what she says...*

"Three minutes," Angus waved to Brixton but received no reply.

Kila began the walk back to the front porch, which should have seemed short but felt much longer given her mounting jitters. When Angus rushed to open the door for her, she acknowledged the significance of the situation. Inside the landing, she tried to prepare herself for anything that might unfold.

Brixton watched their interaction from the front lawn, his view semi-obscured by the light reflecting off the front door. *I shouldn't have pushed so hard to get him off Reese. I may have been a day premature, and that one day may have cost me everything…*Brixton fretted. *Doesn't he know I love her? He HAS to. Maybe not. Who loves someone, then refuses to see them for six months? I don't even know if music can save me now. Dammit, Angus.*

"Thank you for delivering me safely to my house…," Kila rolled her eyes, breaking through the prolonged silence. "I was worried I might not make it."

Angus opened his lips, "It won't happen again, so remember it fondly."

"I will," Kila touched her hair, "with profound fondness."

Angus grinned.

"And sincerest gratitude," she continued, hoping his grin wouldn't fade.

Angus stood tall, concentrating on his posture. "What does he have to talk to you about?"

"I don't know," Kila shook her head. "I guess I won't know until we talk," she smiled slightly.

Angus wondered if she was telling the truth, given how close Kila and Brixton once were.

"I'm sure it's nothing major," she kept herself from rambling. *Button this up!* "Probably Anna-related." *Don't SAY anything else...*

"I see it like you do...but I know Brix doesn't see it yet," he winked and returned the box to her.

"Maybe he will tonight," she noticed a pair of large, discolored handprints stretched around the box sides.

"Ugh," Angus fretted. "I'm sorry," he shook his head.

"It's okay," Kila assured him, amazed that he had grown self-conscious. "I have to wrap it anyway."

A few seconds passed in quiet while she touched the edges of the box.

Angus studied her. "I didn't plan on getting this sweaty," he hoped she'd look up from her box-fiddling, but her eyes hadn't yet risen above his chest.

Kila thought aloud, "You know you guys can never do anything without taking it to the full-out extent...remember the midnight bocce suicide tournaments?"

"Yeah," Angus laughed.

"Running and bocce, together at last, together forever," Kila giggled. "I'll never forget Ethan's tagline."

"And how it blew up on social media and we had like thirty guys competing here on the weekends as if it were a meaningful and legitimate sport?" he smirked.

"My dad thought it was hysterical! Brixton TORE the backyard up," she recounted, "although Tyson would probably take the win now. He wasn't at Cypress back then."

"You're probably right," he finally felt her eyes on his. "Hey, do you know when Jacques's coming back?"

"No...," she thought back to earlier in the day, "I was with you when he left, remember?"

Angus grinned, "Oh yeah, that's right. Too bad we had to leave your room...."

"I know...," Kila worried she revealed too much. "I need to get back up there," she whispered.

"I can't believe I got so sweaty," he realized only afterwards that he had repeated himself. "I'm definitely going to shower after we finish playing, so I don't look like this tonight."

"I was only teasing you about it," she smiled at his heavy eyes. "Stop worrying so much. I have to shower before I get ready, too."

Angus rubbed his palms on his jersey shorts to dry them. "In that case, can I have a hug?"

Kila smiled and set the dress box on the edge of the stairs. When her hands were free, his arms opened and motioned her closer. She rushed into his embrace, feeling a little awkward for it. He squeezed her against his chest and closed his eyes, basking in the tenderness.

She stayed in his arms until she heard Brixton calling for him. "Guess we both need to go, now," she slipped from his embrace.

He eyed her.

She wanted to hear his voice, but he remained quiet, despite his knowing she needed to leave.

He touched one of his hands to her shoulder, caressing her skin as he had earlier when they had been alone in her room.

With dreamlike eyes, Kila stretched up to his face and returned his affection from earlier. Although she executed her cheek kiss seamlessly, the thoughts that followed turned her insides around and she realized that her lips were moist with the sweat from his skin. *That crushing smile,* Kila glanced at it willingly. She instructed herself to begin the ascent up the stairs the moment she held the dress box in her hands.

"Ki," Angus called after her suddenly.

She turned back, struck by the sound of his voice.

"Will you make sure you have your phone on you at the party?" he touched his hair.

"I'll probably have it," Kila spoke, distracted by his hair tousling. "Anna wants me to take a million pictures...why?" she examined his face but couldn't make sense of his expression.

"Just...," he rubbed his hands together, "will you promise to have it?" he asked as directly as he could.

"Yeah," she nodded her head, finally giving into the urge to lick his salty sweat from her lips.

"Did you just...?" Angus looked up at her in a fever, then stopped short, thinking better of it. "Never mind...have fun dressing the bride," he grinned, touching his hand to his neck.

Before she risked embarrassing herself, Kila ran up the stairs. As soon as she reached the top, she bit at her lips, indulging in the taste of the salt from his skin. *How can he do this to me? I feel wild. WILD.*

In her parent's bedroom Kila at first quelled her dangerous thoughts and then found her mother's impressive stash of gift-wrapping supplies. Carefully, she pulled a few pieces of pale yellow-and-white-striped tissue paper away from the rest and chose an almost matching yellow-and-bright-blue polka-dotted ribbon. *Wrapping presents is more fun than opening them. It's an art, after all. If a present doesn't look like a present, who will want to open it?* Kila thought back to when she was younger and her dad would wrap her birthday presents with the comics section of the newspaper. She'd spend as long as necessary flipping the boxes around to read all of the funnies she could see, before tearing the gift open with wide eyes.

When the yellow-and-blue bow appeared nothing short of fabulous, Kila returned to her room. Seeing Maya's closed eyes, she soundlessly slipped the box into her closet. To relieve Anna of her concern, Kila tiptoed into the bathroom, whispering at the shower curtain that the present now rested in its final hiding place. Figuring she probably shouldn't wait for Anna to finish, Kila strode into Ethan's room, latching onto his sweat-soaked shirt when she spotted him with towel in hand.

"Not so fast!" Kila squeezed his arm. "Use mom's, pretty please? You know that glass door freaks me out," she pleaded, making a cute face when he looked like he might protest.

"Ugh! Al-riiight," he gave into her, "but lock both doors—I don't want Brix or Ang or anyone else barging in on you accidentally."

"Done," Kila scooted him out of his room, locking his bedroom door, and then the bathroom door. She carried only her special-occasion toiletries and a towel, and the thought of bumping into Angus in the hallway without looking ideal scared her enough to soap and shampoo at what seemed like the speed of light. When she was safe in her room, she relaxed again.

"I peeked in the closet," Anna spoke softly, "the ribbon is perfect!"

"Took me a few times to get it that full," Kila confessed.

"It was worth it," Anna smiled. "I think it's time to get her in the shower."

"Agreed," Kila moved towards the bed. Gently, she tapped on Maya's shoulder and rubbed her arm.

Maya awoke dazed but docile, and she moved toward the shower without a fight. "It smells sooooo gooooood," she sniffed Ethan's gray shirt once more before taking it off. "I'm keeping it!" she announced proudly to Kila, hugging it like a child might hug a teddy bear.

"Go for it. Just get yourself in the shower," Kila shut the door to the bathroom. "I don't think that shirt even fits him anymore," Kila whispered to Anna. "He hasn't worn it in months."

"She doesn't need to know that," Anna teased. "At least she's over the window."

Kila laughed. "That, or she realizes there's not enough time for further delay," she straightened the bed and pulled her clothes and shoes from the closet thinking of Angus. *How much of what I think happened today actually happened?*

Anna, already dressed, stood blotting the excess moisture from her hair with a small towel. "Would you let me do your makeup?" she asked Kila. "Truth be told I sort of have a vision for us. Light and cheery…and, I really want Maya's to stand out."

"In favor," Kila smiled, adjusting the hem of her pants around her platforms.

"You're so particular about that," Anna teased.

"You're particular about makeup," Kila pursed her lips, "can't I be particular about having my pants graze the ground?"

"Yes," Anna let up, "Kila Lorens, you are your own style maven."

Kila curtsied with a forced air of stateliness, then debated what song to play next since her last playlist had reached its end. *I didn't loop it, but maybe that's a sign. A sign I should play something new.* She thought about asking Anna, but then thought better of it, given her fluctuating emotions. *Something to ease this constant ache of wanting him...I know,* she scrolled to one of her playlists and selected **"Hunger Of The Pine" by alt-J**. While she proceeded to participate in the pomp and circumstance of getting ready, her mind flooded with electric thoughts of Angus. *He's irresistible... wholly irresistible...he always was.*

The girls had flawlessly matched their outfits while maintaining their individuality. Both wore merlot-colored corduroys. Kila opted for hip-hugging bell-bottoms and Anna opted for hi-rise skinnies. They each wore variations of the always "in" clean white Tee on top, perhaps the best route to take when under-dressing for an outside party. Kila's was longer both in length and in the sleeves, and had a deeper V-neck, showing off her tight torso and athletic curves. Annabelle's had shorter flutter sleeves and a ballerina neckline, to highlight her porcelain arms and swan-like neck. Both wore only one piece of jewelry: Anna a glass-beaded bracelet from her dad, and Kila a silver thumb ring.

When they were ready for their makeup, Kila applied a thick moisturizer to Anna's face and then applied the same to her own. Anna worked some minimal foundation onto Kila's skin, careful not to cover the freckles on her nose. Dusting only a hint of bronzer here and there and dabbing a pinch of creamy peach blush on the tops of Kila's cheeks, Anna quickly accomplished her goal. Kila's face seemed natural and bright. In a flash, Anna copied the look on herself, then handed Kila a new lip gloss from her storied makeup bag.

"Al-right! A new one! Thank you," Kila ripped the wrapper off the tube. It was a super-sheer soft pink without the pesky shimmer. Dipping the wand several times back into the tube, Kila layered the gloss onto her lips until they felt full and juicy.

"I thought they'd look like that!" Anna declared proudly. "It's close to the consistency of the strawberry gloss you always wear, but in a lighter shade that brings out your eyes. What do you think?" she asked.

"Honestly?" Kila smiled, "I never would have picked this one up myself, but I'm glad you did, because I love how natural it looks."

"Yup. And if the night moves in a way you like, you can always layer your strawberry one on top to tempt a certain someone," Anna winked, as she dabbed an even lighter pale-pink gloss onto her own lips. "How's mine?"

"You look like a stylish philosophical apprentice," Kila complimented her friend, "who's in the midst of traversing the literary world."

Anna blushed and pulled Kila in for a hug. "It seems like your mind is set on Angus, but please don't forget about Jacques," Anna whispered politely. "Angus is a known entity; Jacques is uncharted waters, uncharted not only by you, but also uncharted by Reese."

Kila's face twisted in thought.

"Lyr's charismatic, I get it...but Jacques seems more... refined...and...mature," Anna suggested.

"And what are you two whispering about?" A towel-wrapped Maya crept close to them, "Sharing secrets without me, I suspect."

"No secrets, just boy stuff," Anna squeezed Maya's shoulders.

"But boy stuff is usually the secret stuff!" Maya touched Kila's hair. "Jacques?"

"Maybe," Kila responded famously.

"Hmmm...I like his voice," Maya jumped in place, pouting her lips, "it's spellbinding."

"No joke. Even Ethan fell in love," Anna laughed.

"Yeah, he and Brixton pretty much swooned together," Maya jumped in place again. "Speaking of swooning, or in this case of wooing," Maya pinched one of Kila's cheeks.

Kila looked at her nervously, "What?"

"You know WHAT!" Maya giggled, "You skillfully switched subjects in the car, but I have NOT forgotten to ask: what exactly was Angus Lyr doing in here a few hours ago ON YOUR BED?"

"Maya!" Kila pushed her backwards onto the mattress, preparing her for Anna's elaborate makeover. "He just wanted to catch up, not much else to note."

"Not much else to note?" Maya screamed excitedly. "MIGHT I remind you that your door was shut and he was trying to get close to you!"

Anna divulged, "Plus, he kissed her on the cheek right after he left her room."

"And," Maya held her hand up, pointing to Kila, "I saw him kiss your cheek at least five times while he was dancing with you...I wasn't going to bring that up IF you had answered my first question with honesty." She placed a hand over her mouth to keep her high-pitched voice under control.

"I saw his nose on her cheek, but not the kissing of her cheek," Anna gasped and touched Kila's forearm. "How many times did he kiss your cheek on the deck? Wait! Did you receive more or less than ten cheek kisses in total from Angus Lyr today?"

Kila, quietly looking at the wall, bit her top lip and attempted to limit her expressions.

"Oh my gosh," Maya spoke quickly, "Angus never dances. He was dancing with you, right up against you, and it looked... intimate...like something was about to happen...something pivotal." She fanned her face, then screamed in delight, "Did Angus Lyr kiss your mouth?"

Anna's eyes practically doubled in size.

"No," Kila laughed, "he hasn't."

"Okay, well, that might not be a bad thing…," Maya placed her hands on her knees and wiggled her toes, mining for gold in another cave. "Did Jacques kiss you last night or even try to?"

"No," Kila exhaled, thinking of Timothy for a passing moment. And then again for another passing moment. "We just talked in the library, but it was nice…you guys don't have to be ridiculous about all of this," she pleaded.

"We're not being ridiculous," Maya huffed. "We just plan to pester you until we find out whom you like most."

Anna grabbed Maya's arm and linked it in hers.

"How am I supposed to provide you with an answer if I don't yet know myself?" Kila shrugged her shoulders. *I want to hear his whisper…feel his embrace…and be alone with him again…*

Anna's giggles interrupted Kila's spiraling thoughts.

"SO BAD!" Maya pressed her laughing face into a pillow then tossed it at Kila's head. "You are ALL THE WAY GONE. I wish I knew what you were thinking," she beamed in that best-friend sort of way.

"She'll tell us," Anna smiled with certainty, "later tonight."

"How do you know?" Maya asked.

"Because there's no way she'll be able to hold out on us once something of consequence happens," Anna smirked. "And something of consequence is sure to happen tonight. It's a party, after all," she raised her eyebrows and issued a charming look at Kila.

"You guys," Kila touched Maya's hands, "you're making me awfully nervous, and I'd much rather focus on you."

Maya grinned.

"It is her night," Kila reminded Anna.

"She's right!" Anna snapped into full beautician mode, eyeing Maya, "And you'll be forced to endure all of the preparations that go along with it!"

"But…," Maya issued her last protest, "can we pester Ki afterwards?"

"Absolutely," Anna rubbed Maya's shoulders, "…I'm just as curious as you are."

Maya exhaled into a grateful sigh.

Kila, ecstatic that the spotlight had shifted to Maya, served as Anna's assistant.

Their first order of business was moisturizing every inch of

Maya's skin. Anna opted to use Kila's coconut oil, since it was nearly unscented and long lasting. It was warmed in Anna's hands, then glazed over Maya's skin from the neck down like a thin sheet of shine. They waited a few minutes for it to soak in and for some of the sheen to disappear. Then, while Maya laughed, Kila buffed the remnants in with tiny circular motions.

Next came the facial moisturizer, also nearly unscented. This was Kila's specialty, and she swiftly plastered the natural cream onto Maya's forehead, nose, cheeks, and chin, paying special attention to the delicate skin around her eyes. Like she had with Maya's body, she allowed a few minutes to pass before patting the remainder gently into her skin.

Using only minimally scented, natural moisturizers ensured that Maya's perfume would remain pure. Anna had learned from her grandmother's beauty column that a lady should avoid mixing multiple scents, since competing aromas hold the potential to mix and create something less than favorable. To be memorable, her grandmother had written, was to exude a single scent, the same on every occasion— one that synergizes with the wearer's personality and makes the wearer feel like her strongest self, so she behaves like her strongest self.

"I feel like a slimy jellyfish!" Maya touched her arms.

"Don't touch!" Anna ordered, reaching for Kila's nail-polish stash, "It'll absorb more."

"You're the sweetest jellyfish ever," Kila teased, poking at Maya's knees.

"Okay, Ki—which one?" Anna presented two bottles to choose from. One was a sea-foam green and the other was a glittery ivory.

"The glittery one! It's the perfect shade for her dr...," Kila stopped short.

"Dark pants. It'll look glam with her dark pants," Anna added nervously, grabbing the bottle from Kila's hands.

"Base coat first," Kila corrected, reaching into a separate compartment to retrieve that, along with the topcoat.

Maya, surprisingly patient, sat still during her manicure and pedicure. She had never received the deluxe royal treatment from Anna, and she fully indulged in it. The three girls reminisced about the last few months. Then, they took turns revealing to each other what they hoped might happen this evening. Anna spoke of Brixton, which prompted Maya to ask how long she needed to stay outside before she and Ethan could venture inside.

"Ma-YAH!" Kila laughed, "Until all the guests leave."

"Can't we kick them out early?" Maya asked semi-seriously.

"One. Track. Mind," Anna laughed. "I don't blame her though...," she lined her makeup brushes along the bureau in the order she would be using them.

Kila thought about what Anna said and filed it away. "I kind of just want to dance again," she admitted. *With him, alone in the dark,* she mused as **"Overdose" by Little Daylight** began to play.

"Appropriate song," Maya touched Kila's hand, "how do you and Brix do that? It's like some magical thing you two possess...."

Kila smiled with her lips and her heart, recalling how excited she was when Brixton taught her how to build playlists. *I didn't sleep at all that weekend. We built twenty-five in two days, arguing and laughing the entire time.*

"I want you to exercise some restraint when you see Ethan," Anna spoke to Maya mid-makeup application.

Maya looked at her suspiciously.

"Don't run into his arms right away. Walk slowly toward him, to amplify the longing," Anna met Maya's giggle with some seriousness. "Hey, you can do whatever you want once you reach him," she amended, "just make sure you do the timed walk on your way to him. I promise you won't regret it."

Kila nodded at Maya in agreement.

"Alright," Maya inhaled and consented, "I'll do it."

Kila high-fived Anna.

The girls shared an embrace, and Anna applied a generous coat of tropical-punch-hued gloss to Maya's lips. "I picked this one out just for you," Anna smiled. "Keep it."

With heavy thoughts, Maya took the glass pot in her hands.

Anna hoped more words would calm her, "I'll ship you any other items you might need once you're away. I imagine you'll need more than a couple weeks to figure out where to get the trusted not-so-necessities in Rhode Island." She touched Maya's chin.

At the thought of Maya's leaving, Kila wrestled back tears. She dabbed the moisture on her cheeks with her fingers while grabbing the hairdryer and other potions needed for Maya's blowout. When Anna confirmed she had all the bottles and jars needed, Kila set up her tourmaline curling wand and hair clips. Thankfully, by that time, her eyes had dried and neither Anna nor Maya saw traces of tears.

"I wish my blowouts were half as good as Anna's," Maya touched her knees. "About a third of the way through, my wrists usually feel like they're about to snap in half."

"You need to get stronger, then," Anna offered. "A little more muscle wouldn't hurt you."

"But I already have more muscle than you," Maya explained.

"Hush," Anna laughed, plugging in the hairdryer.

The persistent hum of hot air prevented any further conversation. While Anna worked the round brush through Maya's dark, shiny hair, Kila held onto Maya's hand. The thought of Angus moved to the edges of her mind, which now became riddled with the anxiety of Maya's departure. *I don't want her to leave...I've never been without her...ever... not like this...*

Kila already sensed everything would change when Maya left. Even Ethan wouldn't be the same. Soon, she would be tasked with having to cheer her brother and herself up at the same time. *At least Ang and Brix will keep him busy, and possibly Jacques, too, depending on how all of that shakes out. I'll still have Anna, even though seeing her without Maya will be difficult. She doesn't understand me the way Maya does, but maybe we'll grow closer in time. Does Brix really want to be best friends again? He did ask me to breakfast...*memories of Brixton rushed through her mind, as she continued to hold Maya's hand.

"Look," Anna whispered.

Surfacing from her thoughts, Kila watched Maya's last curl fall from the tourmaline wand. *She's almost ready. It's almost go-time,* Kila realized.

While Anna vigorously ran her fingers through Maya's curls to soften them, Kila snuck the large wrapped box out of her closet.

"Maya, my sweets, we falsely led you to believe you'd be matching us tonight," Kila held the gift in her hands, "but the time has come to show you your real outfit."

Maya, who loved presents, leapt off the bed in anticipation. With eager eyes, she loosened the bow, tore through the tissue paper, and opened the box. Anna tossed the top of the box onto the floor. Maya placed the bottom half on the bed with her mouth open in excitement. Kila parted the inside folds of tissue paper to reveal the dress, and Anna began taking a series of photos on her phone.

"This—this was a MASSIVE secret, you two!" Maya gasped, running her hands along the textured, organic ivory fabric. "I love it—come on, you know I love it! I can't believe it...."

"See why I made you pack your strapless?" Anna teased, as she pulled the beige lace bra from Maya's bag and tossed it over to her.

Once Maya had her bra secured, Kila lifted the one-shouldered dress over Maya's head. Anna twisted and positioned everything in place while Kila held onto Maya's curls, so they wouldn't flatten. Maya looked at Kila with a set of grateful eyes.

"Ummm," Kila gasped, "maybe this wasn't such a good idea." She smiled dramatically.

"Why! What's wrong?!" Maya grew concerned. "Does it look weird?"

"No!" Kila walked around her, "It's just that...I'm not so sure my brother's going to be able to...keep cool...around all of this. You better be on your best behavior tonight, young lady," Kila giggled uncontrollably as Anna whistled wildly, the three friends collapsing into one giant hug on the bed.

"Wait! Her orange ginger," Kila remembered. "Where is it?"

"Here," Anna grabbed it from the side table, covering her hand over Maya's eyes and dosing her in it.

"No! I never wear that much!" Maya coughed into a laugh. "Is there any left?"

"Yes," Anna assured her. "Plenty. You needed a lot since it's an outside event. I don't want it to fade."

"He likes the smell, you know," Kila put her arm around Maya, waiting for her inevitable "coo-face" to appear.

It surfaced on Maya's face just as Kila knew it would, and she squeezed her hand.

Anna had undeniably lived up to her trusted reputation. This was, by far, her most impressive transformation. Maya looked like herself, only with an earthy, free-spirited edge. The matte-ivory dress included a lace panel at the asymmetrical shoulder line and two tiers of ruffles at the matching asymmetrical hemline, where Maya's beautiful legs spilled out into a bronze waterfall. Kila and Anna admired their creation in awe as if their friend had become ethereal.

Kila struggled to keep her tears at bay again. "Breathtaking, Maya. Truly. I really can't believe we'll be...without you...so soon."

Moisture gathered in Anna's eyes, and she dabbed at the corners, hoping neither of her friends would notice.

"I'm here another week, you guys. Don't do this to me NOW!" Maya pleaded, feeling more flooded with love than she ever had in her whole life.

Anna and Kila were family, and no amount of distance could change that. The thought alone made Maya feel more steadfast. *Maybe the move won't be as devastating as I've been making it out to be,* Maya pondered. *Maybe it'll be more like*

an adventure—a test of my ability to be away from the people
and places I have grown to love most.

All at once they noticed it had grown dark. Two hours had
passed like one, and from the windows they could already
see guests accumulating in the backyard. Kila counted the
bodies in her line of sight. *About…thirty-ish so far, but it*
doesn't look lively yet. We need to get out there. I wonder how
E's holding up…I hope he's wearing the shirt Anna picked out.
She spied Ethan by the pool with Brixton, nervously tossing
a tennis ball back and forth, donned in what appeared to be
the right button-down shirt.

Where's Angus? Kila took a deep breath. As **"Lovesick" by**
Banks began to play, she scanned the area she could see
again in full without finding him. *My phone,* she remembered,
grabbing it from her nightstand. She slipped it into her back
pocket. *I wonder why I need it…* She bit at her lips, searching
for the saltiness. The recent shower and the fresh lip gloss left
no traces of it. Just the same, she closed her eyes, wishing
for him.

"Angus, isn't it?" Maya touched Kila's nose.

Kila nodded without words, fixing her hair anxiously.

"It's perfect," Maya whispered. "Stop fiddling with it."

"It's time," Anna announced, the two words feeling heavier
than she had expected.

Maya grabbed her phone and held it out awkwardly to take a
photo, or more like five. The girls argued over which image

was the best, deleting the others and keeping only one. After another heartfelt hug, they slowly descended the stairs, walking hand-in-hand, step-by-step, in their matching pairs of blush faux-suede platform sandals.

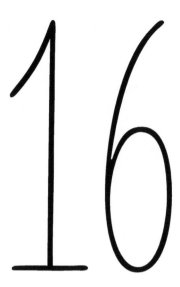

Under the enchanting glow of the moon, the party decorations assumed a life of their own. Like floating diamonds, the crisscross strands of sparkling lights painted a soft luminance onto the deck and lawn. Hanging high and proud, the citronella lanterns cradled flames that stretched high, retreated, and then stretched again. The elastic blazes cast bright shadows that danced with one another across the glass surface of the pool. In small clusters, the silhouettes of the real guests were scattered, some talking, others eating.

Behind the cover of the doors, Anna tugged on the long side of Maya's hem, making one last adjustment to her dress. Maya's nervous eyes watched Kila press her fingertips to the window. The three girls, nearly in unison, breathed in and looked outside. At Anna's cue, Kila opened the French doors, feeling more like a palace guard than a love-struck teenager.

Anna's face welcomed the night air much as her heart

welcomed the fate of the night. The first to pass through the doors, she walked just a few paces, then stopped, waiting to catch Ethan's attention before walking any further. The wishful look in his eyes when he realized Maya would soon be near caused Anna to suffer a momentary lapse in reality. She held onto the impassioned gaze of his grayish-blue eyes long enough for him to question the delay. As he tilted his head and smiled, she signaled to Kila. **"Electric Feel" by MGMT** tickled the outside speakers just as Maya appeared in the light.

When Ethan saw her, the tennis ball, which had occupied his hands for the past hour, fell free from his grip. No longer needed, it bounced five times across the stone pathway, dropping at last into the cushiony embrace of the pool. As he stood feeling numb, his bottom lip brushed against his upper lip, anticipating their next kiss.

Maya, wanting so badly to run into his arms, walked as slowly as she had promised Anna. Despite almost laughing, she placed one foot in front of the other and extended her hips, trying her best to look reserved. The hem of her dress swayed exactly as Anna swore it would, and after only four steps she decided to issue a never-before-practiced smoldering gaze.

Magnetized, Ethan moved toward her.

As her brother approached, Kila pulled Anna to the other side of the walkway. Together, they watched in silent awe. Brixton stepped close to Kila and placed a hand on her lower back. Kila, nodding to him with a warm smile, wondered where Angus might be.

"So you've decided to rub it in," Ethan tilted his head,

"...everything I'm sure to miss while you're away?"

"No," Maya's hands touched his collar, his face, and his hair, "I'm just trying to match pace with you."

Neither could wait a moment longer, and their first kiss was seen by the whole crowd. When several of the guests cheered, Maya buried her smile in Ethan's shoulder. Not wanting an audience for his affection, Ethan pulled Maya behind the cover of the pool house to continue the next round in seclusion. There would never be enough time for him to kiss her as much as he wanted to. And he fell deeper and deeper each time her lips met his.

With the new couple out of sight, Brixton lightly touched the hair near Kila's ear. "Your brother pulled that off surprisingly... well," his words crumbled when she collided with him.

"Yeah," she spread her arms around his shoulders, "makes me want something like that for myself."

"I know," Brixton pulled Kila's body into his. "It's almost painful, isn't it?"

She nodded into his shoulder. It had been months since Brixton had embraced her in that way, and she missed his friendship or whatever element had previously rendered them inseparable. From morning until moonlight, they had spent countless weekends without a pause in conversation; but, Kila sadly gathered, those marathon outings would never see a revival.

Something had changed between them, or perhaps time had

simply stepped in. His body felt different inside her arms, and she wondered if she felt different to him as well. She loosened her hold on him, not because she wanted to, but because she noticed Anna's bright face patiently waiting for her own hug. *Things ARE different now,* Kila talked herself into letting go, *and I have to let them be. Natural progression. Forces of nature. Evolution. And so forth...*

Brixton sensed Kila slipping away and moved in again.

"The first wasn't good enough?" Kila teased by means of whisper, curious to hear his reply.

"No, it was legendary," Brixton whispered nervously, "... that's why I need another." He stroked her hair with one of his hands. "Hey...," he spoke near her ear, "can we talk now? At this point it's months overdue, and I'd really like to set some things straight...."

"Now is good...but not here," she squeezed him tighter and closed her eyes. *Is he FINALLY going to tell me what happened, why he so abruptly and obnoxiously withdrew from my life?*

"Would the tree house be alright?" he asked, careful to keep his voice down.

"Yeah," she opened her eyes to find Anna's bright smile hovering above Brixton's shoulder. "Text me when you're ready, so I don't rush...anything...," Kila, without giving Brixton the chance to agree or protest, rotated his shoulders toward Anna.

Brixton extended his arms, acutely aware of each step Kila

took away from him. As Anna crashed into him wildly, the strain in his face relaxed.

It's happening, Kila exhaled, her heart warming at the sound of Brixton's laughter. *I missed that sound. He likes her. Time to leave them alone for a while.* Scanning the crowd by the pool, she verified with delight that the girls had complied with her request to remain casual. Josie, especially well-dressed, stood in a lilac, high-collared, kimono-sleeved top and scalloped organic-linen shorts. Kila grinned, watching her friend stack mountains of sliced carrots, celery, cucumbers, and heirloom tomatoes atop a bed of seed crackers already smothered in vegan cream cheese and sunflower sprouts. *I always loved her appetite.*

Kila walked toward Josie but stopped midway when her phone vibrated. Hoping it was Brixton, she glanced back at the deck. He and Anna, faces spilling with emotion, appeared entirely engaged with one another. *Maybe we won't be meeting in the tree house until later. Oh well. What's a few more hours of not knowing? I've waited six months already,* she squinted in confusion. *Who sent the text?* **"Wake Me" by Bleachers** kindled the crowd as she curiously pulled her phone from her pocket.

The screen displayed a text from Angus:

[Walk to the left]

ANGUS!!! WHERE are you? She looked to her left, scouring the lines of every face she could see. They all came up short and her heart skipped a beat. She shuffled through the faces once more, her heart pounding in question. *What...is...going...on?*

She walked a few paces but still didn't see him anywhere, so she stood in place. *If he's hiding and laughing at me, he's in for it!*

Another message appeared:

[Come on, Ki. Don't you trust me?]

The phone shook her hands, yet her feet remained still. *Do I tr-rust him? TRUST is a strong word. Do I trust anyone? A few people, I suppose. But, is he one of them?* Kila thought, really thought, about his question, wanting to respond "yes" but feeling conflicted about it.

The third message interrupted the internal quarrel that the second message had spurred:

[Forget about the last text. We'll work on that one. Just keep coming left.]

She laughed and looked up from her phone. *Lackluster does not exist in his world. It never did. Where is he?!?* Staying left, she noticed her feet leading her into the woods behind her house. *What if I'm walking to my doom?* A scene from *Camp Fright* flashed in her mind. *What if someone STOLE Angus's phone and I'm about to end up zip-tied in an unmarked van? Could I take an assailant? I'm fairly fast. I should have taken that self-defense class with my mom two years ago. Must resurrect that on the to-do list. Then I can walk around in the dark at least semi-fearlessly looking for Angus without the thought of death paralyzing me.* Her strides shortened in length as fear slowly consumed her.

Her phone vibrated again:

[It's ok. I'm leading you to me. Walk to the trail.]

Although I like the way this sounds...I'm still ALONE in the dark...is he testing me? She felt her feet hit the pebble-strewn pathway, but her eyes couldn't see much past a few feet in front of her. She stopped walking and debated whether to remain in place or head back the way she came. That's when his body emerged from the woods, and his warm hands fell upon her shoulders.

"I thought you might get a little scared...I'm sorry," Angus confessed. "I wanted to see you somewhere I knew no one else could see us," his eyes stayed above her neck, admiring the curves of her face amidst nature's shadows. "There's more people than I thought...I had planned to wait for you to come out, but people kept filing in and trying to talk to your brother, and Brix, and me...and I really wanted...all I could think about was dancing...with you...again," he looked in her eyes unsure of what truths he might find.

"...Since when do you like dancing?" Kila teased, feeling the softness of his collar.

"Since this afternoon," Angus replied without a second thought.

"...So...you want to dance here?" she blushed, but he couldn't see it.

"No," he laughed a little, "this isn't the spot. You'd never find the spot just by means of my text directions."

"Oh," Kila's smile spread wide, but she didn't let herself worry over it. "For the record, you are hysterical."

"Call me whatever you will, but I had to find a spot that was away from the party, where you could still hear the music, and which had ample moonlight," Angus exhaled acknowledging he had already revealed more than he had planned to. "May I take you?" he extended his hand.

"Yes," she looked at him in disbelief as she felt his fingers wrap about hers and her feet move of their own volition. *I hope I never forget his last question and the way this feels right now. I hope I never forget. Ever. Even if it means I have to forget something else to remember this, I'm open to that.*

"It's not that far," Angus spoke as he led her along, "you just have to duck right...," he pulled his phone from his pocket to light the way for her, "right over here...."

Kila pulled her hand from his when she cleared the low branch and took note of her surroundings. "I can't believe I've never been back here in the dark...," she marveled at the beauty before her, the breathless wonder of standing in the center of a ring of redwoods.

"...It's a cathedral...," he whispered from behind her.

"I know...," she turned to face him, his skin illuminated by rays of moonlight. *I MUST be dreaming. There is no other explanation...* "Do you still want to dance?" Kila filled her mouth with safe words before the dangerous ones found their way out.

"Yes," Angus looked at her mouth, unable to disguise his bright smile. He extended his arms to her then panicked as he realized the music had stopped.

"Give it a moment or two," Kila laughed, cupping her hands around his shoulders. "Someone, most likely Maya, is fighting with Brixton over the song order."

Angus grinned, "You're probably right." He held his hands at her back hoping the next song would play soon.

A minute and a half passed without music, and the combination of the quiet and his proximity left Kila feeling high. She inhaled and looked up at the moon. His hands lowered and bent around her sides. The warmth from both his palms traveled inward toward her belly button. She felt the weightlessness she experienced in her last dream of him.

"I like to watch you do that," he whispered.

"Why?" she grinned, feeling small and silly for it.

"You respect the infinite," his fingers touched her cheeks.

She closed her eyes.

"I feel something when we're alone, do you?" he asked.

She squeezed his shoulders.

He brushed his nose against hers, and stretched his lips to her cheek. "It's not the first time we've been alone in the woods," he touched her hair. "Do you remember?"

"Yeah," Kila recalled the scene from Big Sur. *He smells the same as he did that night. His dad's cologne. Almost a decade later.* She opened her eyes.

"I bet I've thought about that night more than you have. That sleeping bag," his warm words waltzed across her cheek. "We should find it."

She heard two heightened sets of inhales and exhales but couldn't determine which was hers.

"The forest looks better with you in it," Angus whispered. "I'm longing to memorize something I never want to become a memory."

She waded through the meaning in his words.

Each time he caressed her cheeks, he felt more certain of his feelings. An ache grew inside him, and his lips finally found their way to hers.

Kila's lips froze against his, right at the rushing start of **"Oh My Heart" by Night Riots**.

Angus retreated as unexpectedly as he had leaned in, studying her from a comfortable distance with his hands at his sides.

Kila's eyes pulsed. The vastness of the thousand-plus-year-old forest; the luxury of the clear, glittery, starry night; and Angus—the faded-slate corduroys, the slim plaid shirt, the dark, textured hair, spilling carelessly from his deep-indigo beanie—all converged to create an unending want, a want she was no longer able to wait patiently for.

"If it's Jacques, I…it's okay…," Angus tried to fill in the dialogue so she wouldn't feel awkward supplying the words herself.

"It's not, and…I agree. We should…find the sleeping bag," Kila stepped toward him, feeling the rush only a crush can bring.

"Our parents keep everything," he touched his hands to her sides, feeling his chest rise and fall, "it's either…at your place…or mine."

"Must be," her lips quivered when her nose brushed against his.

His eyes gazed at her in question and she bit her tongue, all at once remembering she was supposed to be shy. *Not tonight. I'm not shy tonight. I just need…a little…improvisation.* She slipped her fingers inside the upward fold of his knitted hat, and slowly rolled the fabric down over his eyes. *I won't be so shy if he can't see me,* she realized, running her index finger down the slope of his nose.

His full crimson lips stretched up on one side, an irresistible half-grin.

She kissed him that moment, because she knew she'd regret every additional moment she let pass.

A flame ignited inside Kila she couldn't quell—not by stopping, not by kissing. She massaged his lips rhythmically, just as she had read in a rare, vintage how-to-pucker-up book she'd sneakily purchased at The Rocking Horse last year. The book, she had previously thought, had wholly prepared her for this night. Yet, Kila realized in this moment, it had only offered instructions. No combination of words, no author, in any place, living at any time, could possibly explain such a feeling to her or to anyone else. And she let that truth sweep through her veins. The intimate feeling of Angus Lyr's mouth caught up in her own.

She thought about the sound of his voice, about his ability to sing in heightened emotion, about his intelligence and how it hooked her. For years it had hooked her. Her hands roamed his body, squeezing his shoulders, pressing his chest, and caressing his cheeks. Every inch was irresistible. Every inch burned her worse. She yearned for more, that ambiguous and impossible figure that implies that no amount, no matter how immense, could possibly be enough. Her rib cage expanded and contracted as if it was taking in and expelling helium. She feared she might drift upwards if she didn't exhale fast enough.

For several sensational minutes, Angus kept pace with her, his lips sandwiched between hers, his fingers clasping her waist tighter and tighter. She tried to calm down, to relax the kissing, but the sounds of his rapid inhales and exhales leveled the barrier of her self-control. She walked him backwards until his back touched the striated bark of the nearest redwood, then pressed her body against his.

He couldn't believe what was happening and lifted his hat back up to be sure he was partaking in reality.

At the first sight of his eyes, she ceased the kissing. "Too much?" she asked, taking advantage of the break to catch her breath.

"No, definitely not," he feverishly pulled his beanie back down, obstructing his eyes. "I'm ready whenever you are...," he rolled his shoulders back into the rough bark of the redwood, waiting and wishing for her affection to return.

Grinning, Kila leaned on her toes and into his lips, unforgiving this time that she still wanted more. Anything other than more seemed unsuitable. For years she'd dreamt of him, longed for him, hungered for him. And now his tongue was in her mouth.

French kissing. Here. We. Go. She touched her tongue to his and couldn't help but laugh and retrieve it. *Am I tasting his toothpaste or mine?! Maybe he had a mint? Should I have had a mint?!*

"Did that gross you out?" Angus laughed against her mouth. "I can't see you, remember, so you have to give me verbal cues," his words tickled her lips.

"No, I—I don't know how I taste," she laughed nervously touching her hair. "I never thought about it, I guess, and you happen to taste so minty...."

"You taste minty, too," he touched his lips to hers again. "I bet we even used the same toothpaste. I showered in your brother's room right after you did."

"Oh," she released her worry and imagined him showering. "We did use the same...."

"Ki...," he continued kissing her in between words, "I don't care...how we...kiss...just...that...we kiss."

She suddenly felt more determined. *It's supposed be an art... maybe it takes some getting used to.* She slowly let her tongue escape the barrier of her lips again and his tongue met hers in polite conversation. *Aha! This explains some things.*

Coordinating the timing of four lips and two tongues left no time for either to second-guess themselves, so they settled into a natural flow. Just as Kila began to relax into it, Angus switched to single-lip kissing and locked onto her bottom lip. She enjoyed it so much, she bit at his top lip.

The way his fingers gripped her cheeks, the way his mouth held onto hers, and the way he inhaled her exhales all changed her. She forgot about the party. She forgot she was almost sixteen. She forgot her name. She traded her former identity for her future identity. And she feared she'd do it again with him, gladly, if offered the chance.

Free from herself, she moved a hand up the back of his neck, inside the edge of his warm, indigo beanie. Her fingers caressed his hair in descending semi-circles. A series of incoherent sounds tumbled from his lips. Minutes passed in similar fashion. The thought that the kiss would eventually end plagued Kila. She pushed it to the farthest corners of her mind, wishing against his lips that time would slow or stop entirely in this moment just as he had alluded to earlier.

Off in the distance, her brother called her name. She ignored him at first, but he persisted. With great reluctance, she retrieved her lips and peered through the gap in the trees. Ethan stood at the edge of the lawn, close to the path, looking anxious.

"Angus—we, I—Ethan's coming," she shook, panicked quietly, and lifted up his hat.

He opened his eyes at the first notes of **"Fallingforyou" by The 1975** and pulled her close again. "...He's not here yet...," Angus spoke as he took in the sight of her.

He reached to slide his beanie back into "make-out position" but Kila prevented him, ultimately losing herself in the double-dark abyss of his eyes.

"Make me yours," he whispered, "I won't tell anyone...."

It was possible Angus had more to say, but Kila's lips blocked any further words from forming. In a passionate return of affection, she rotated through her entire portfolio of studied kissing styles in a cool three and a half minutes. She knew, however, that Ethan might soon make his way down the path, and, already filled with longing, she pulled her lips from his.

His eyes stared at hers. "Can we...meet up again later?" he asked, feeling the weight in his words.

She nodded her head "yes" and leaned on a nearby branch to return to her senses.

Tilting his head back into the redwood bark, he gazed upward, thanking the stars for her reply. "There's somewhere I want to take you next Saturday night. It's somewhere I know you'll like. More or less a no-fail sort of outing. Will you let me?" he requested softly. "Please?"

That combination of words in his voice dazed her, and she

attempted to ease her breaths. "I suppose," she whispered, dragging her blush platform sandal along the protruding curve of a thick root. Her former identity, her shyness, had found its way back to her.

"I'm not telling you where, because I want it to be a surprise," he clarified, although she hadn't asked him to.

"KILA!" Ethan's voice grew louder. "Are you out here?"

A sharp beam of light cut a thick line through the trees.

"His camping flashlight," Kila gasped and covered her mouth. "The beam distance on that thing is unreal."

"I know," Angus smirked. "It's my fault. I bought it for him."

At a loss for words, she looked at his face. He clasped her hand and led her a few tree rows deeper into the woods. The earth took kindly to their needs, allowing them to tread without much sound. When Angus deemed they were shielded enough, he leaned his back against another redwood, reaching for her with open arms.

I could kiss him all night long and still want another, Kila realized as her hands touched his cheeks and his lips met hers again. Just the feeling of his nose next to hers was enough to make her mind tingle. She smiled against his mouth and thought about what might happen later. *Will he want to meet at the path again or somewhere else? What if he changes his mind? STOP!* She hushed her mind and fiercely tended to his lips, inhaling his exhales as he inhaled hers.

Angus pulled away only when he realized Ethan might find them at any moment. He touched his nose to hers, wishing he knew for certain the nature of her feelings before the opinions of Ethan and their other friends were brought into the mix. Opinions, as he had known them, carried the potential to sway things. He questioned whether Kila's mind could be swayed on the subject of him, but he didn't know the answer. And it vexed him. The last thing he wanted was one or two of their closest friends—or even worse, her brother—advising her he wasn't a good idea.

Despite his unresolved mind, he spoke with clarity, "It'll be riskier to hide out here once Ethan notices I'm missing, too," he held his hands on her cheeks, wanting to kiss her, but sensing he shouldn't.

"You're right," Kila whispered. "You go first and slip back into the party. I'll head back the other way, so I emerge in the front near the garage. I'll pretend I needed something in my car," she gazed at him, feeling wilder than before.

"Ki," he brushed his nose against hers, "...I'll figure out a way for us to reconvene as soon as circumstances allow." His lips sealed the remainder of his thoughts silently onto the apple of her cheek, and he left her side at last.

She turned to follow the plan but stopped short. *Did that REALLY just happen?* She touched her lips and watched him slip through the trees covertly in the opposite direction. What she really wanted to do was run after him and tackle him to the ground without reservation...but he was no longer in sight. The sound of his strides grew increasingly faint until she no longer heard them at all.

Biting her bottom lip, she straightened up, stretched her arms against the bark, and made sure both her platforms were fastened tightly. Preparing to run, she pivoted outside the cover of the redwood when she heard the faint crunch of footsteps. Stealthily, she backtracked, leaned her back against the bark, and crossed her fingers. *I really wish I wasn't wearing white right now. If Ethan comes even remotely close he'll see me. How can I possibly explain being back here by myself? My brother will think I've lost my mind. Can I tell him about Angus? No. I can't. Why should I? He'd probably scold me for it. I'd rather E thinks I'm crazy if I get to kiss Ang without issue again. I'd rather no one knows. No one needs to, at least not at this point.*

She closed her eyes praying the sound of steps would diminish, that Ethan would turn back and look for her elsewhere. The crackling noises increased, and she feared the bright light would hit her at any moment. *That award-winning flashlight. Damn it and its whole design team.* She held her breath for seconds, until she noticed Angus in front of her. She blinked twice to make sure her eyes hadn't deceived her.

"I saw E head back to the house…," Angus pulled his hands from his pockets. "And I…thought…," he asked the rest of his question with the emotion in his eyes.

Too shy, Kila merely smiled this time.

He moved toward her.

"It's a good thing you came back," she pointed to his mouth, "we forgot about this." She used a few of her fingers to wipe away the shiny pink gloss that had transferred to his lips.

"I don't mind it," he touched the bottom of her T-shirt, lifting part of it until his fingers reached the top edge of her corduroys. "As long as it's yours…."

Her stomach tightened when one of his fingertips hit her skin and the track skipped to **"All Eyes on You" by St. Lucia**. She stumbled into her thoughts, intoxicated by the luxury of his touch and the enchantment of the music. *Not this…this sweet perfection…this song will end me. An inevitable end to an unforeseen beginning. An unbearable desire to be raw and to be conscious of it.*

Wait…

…just because I want to unbutton and unzip everything he's wearing does not mean that I should. Even though I really want to. This is merely a chemical reaction inside my brain that's telling my body what it wants to do. It's up to me not to run wild with the idea, even though running wild seems like SUCH a NOVEL idea right n—

Angus's mouth put Kila's thoughts to a close, and since she was too shy to tell him in words, she told him how she felt by the way she kissed him. She bit at his crimson smile and squeezed him through the softness of his plaid shirt, which she hoped might hang on the back of her desk chair in a few hours.

"Ki…we have…to meet up…later," he spoke without leaving her lips. "I'm…ser…i…ous." He touched her neck, gradually slowing the pace of his mouth though it pained him to do so.

She pulled her lips from his, glancing at the outline of his jaw.

"Find me, then, when everyone is about to sleep," she used her thumb to wipe the remnants of the shiny gloss from his lips.

"Don't do that, yet," he grinned and rubbed his nose into her cheek. "That means I have to wait until later...I wasn't your first, was I?" he closed his eyes against her skin.

"You were," Kila giggled. "Who else would I have kissed?"

"I don't know," he kissed her cheek three times since her answer pleased him so much. "I don't want to think about that. I just want to know how you knew how to kiss."

"Kissing is pretty...instinctual," her eyes closed at the surprise feeling of his embrace.

He held her somewhere in between lightly and firmly, and she loved the way his body enveloped hers. She wrapped her own arms around his back, realizing they had come a long way from the fallout in the pool this morning.

"Plus," she kissed the apple of his right cheek, "I will confess I've spent some time researching it and thinking about it... schematically."

His full eyebrows rose at the word. "What else have you thought about schematically?"

"I'd rather not say," she laughed against his shoulder shaking her head.

"I have an idea. Let's stay here. You can show me," he

gathered the ends of her hair into his hands like a bouquet and lifted it to his lips. "Better yet, come to my house. We can take the Jeep to the cliffs and I can tell you how deep I'm falling for someone I should have fallen for already. And you can tell me whether or not you think I have a chance with said someone."

"Both sound…infinitely tempting," Kila's hands slipped inside his beanie, "but I have to be there for Maya tonight. It's one of the last times I'll see her outside of school…," she never dreamt her words could produce such an effect on his facial expressions.

Angus rubbed his nose against hers in silent protest.

"She'll be in Ethan's room later, though," Kila traced his cheekbones with her thumbs, "and then you can sneak into mine if you want."

"Just tell me when," he gazed at her with untamable interest.

She shut her eyes and rubbed the back of his neck with both of her hands. Her fingers dipped inside the inner rim of his collar, feeling the skin of his upper back.

"Your touch…," his lips edged towards hers, "ends and awakens me in tandem…."

Her mouth opened and he caught it, holding her lips as sweetly as he knew how.

When they stopped to speak, Kila wiped his lips once more.

"Come on," Angus breathed into a grin, "there can't be much of it left."

"There was," Kila assured him.

His hands slipped into hers, "Message me the moment Maya escapes with Ethan."

"I will," she stroked the left side of his hair, adjusting his beanie so it looked as it should.

"To be honest, I'm not sure I can wait that long," his thumb touched her bottom lip. "And, rest assured, we will find that sleeping bag."

Kila's heart swelled so much she dared not speak, but instead kissed him in her favorite spot, right between his thick eyebrows. Every breath of air she inhaled near him smelled better, as if the leaves of the tall trees had released a new wave of scent just for the occasion. She squeezed his shoulders and his arms before backing away.

He grinned, raising one hand to wave to her. The truth of his brother's promise, that a kiss could dramatically change the world he knew, made sense to Angus now. He anticipated Kila's pivot even before she made it. And the clock in his mind, which always busied itself with calculations, began to count the time until their next meeting alone. Before turning back, he looked up at the dazzling night sky to thank the stars once more.

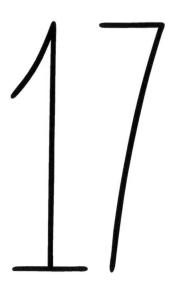

Kila's mind danced at the dawn of **"Magnets" by Disclosure, Lorde**, which she felt could not have aired at a better time. As she wove in and out of the trees, she spoke to herself to affirm what had taken place only moments ago. *Angus Lyr kissed me, without prompting, in the woods in back of my house. He kissed me several times, several ways, wearing corduroys.*

I'm not imagining it. It actually happened. And it trumped the description in that silly sought-after book.

She crept through the garage doorway, undetected, and attempted to dismiss the grin from her face. *Those full crimson lips...struck me like lightning. I never liked lightning, but I do now. I hope they strike again later. I'll be ready...ready for anything.*

Rummaging through the things in her car, she hoped to find

something she could attach some importance to; or rather, that Ethan would believe she had attached some importance to. Her eyes darted from the front seats to the back seat, then locked onto the black velvet pouch resting in the center console. *Ah! My copper cuff...all polished after my visit to Anna's the other day.* With her alibi in hand, Kila entered the house.

"There you are!" Ethan flung his hands in the air. "Hang on...," he took note of her unfamiliar expression.

"Why?" she nervously touched her hair.

"I don't know....exactly," he continued to evaluate her appearance.

She adjusted her white T-shirt against her merlot corduroys.

"What's in your hand?" he asked.

"Huh?" Kila glanced down to see what she was holding. "Oh! This? It's the copper cuff mom gave me. I've been looking for it...for the last twenty-five minutes or so...," she gulped and hoped he hadn't heard it.

"Ah," Ethan nodded. "No wonder I couldn't find you."

"Yup," Kila spoke though she had merely planned to nod. "THAT is exactly where I was," she shifted her weight from one blush platform to the other.

"We have problems," Ethan spoke swiftly.

"We do?" Kila gasped, wondering if her brother somehow already knew about her and Angus.

"Rather," he amended, "I mean one large one: Reese."

Kila's eyebrows lifted, tightened, and twisted. Her stomach followed a similar course.

"She doesn't seem as amicable as you'd hoped," Ethan touched a hand to the back of his head, "and we need a new game plan. Like now."

Flares ignited under Kila's cheeks. She grabbed Ethan's arm and dragged him upstairs to their parent's bedroom. While they walked, she muttered, "Reese promised me she'd behave, E. She PROMISED me. She can't ruin the party. I won't let her...."

"I know what you're thinking with the view," he looked at his sister cautiously, "but she's not hard to spot."

Kila gnashed her teeth, "Why?!"

Ethan chose his words carefully, "...She...uh...sort of, um... stands out."

Squinting in frustration, Kila stepped onto the dark balcony. Seconds later, she covered her mouth.

Reese, radiant like a celebrity basking in adoration, practically glowed in a white bandage dress. The dress, which looked more like a slightly elongated tank top, was inarguably several sizes too small. So little was left to the imagination that she might have appeared more clothed had she actually worn nothing to the party. Her newly rose-gold hair, studded with pearls and rhinestones, rolled like sun-kissed waves all the way down to her hips. Her legs, in endless length, stood polished and proud in a pair of silver sequined heels.

"Ohhh...she's like a rare, cruel form of perfection," Kila's spare hand touched her stomach. *I don't stand a chance.* "I don't stand a chance," she whispered aloud thinking of Angus.

"Against what?" Ethan whispered back.

Kila never replied.

The two studied the scene like meteorologists, as if a natural disaster were about to unfold in their backyard. Damage seemed unavoidable, but they sought to minimize its reach.

"Is she looking for Brixton or Angus...or her pants?" Ethan finally asked.

Kila laughed uneasily. "...I have no idea...I should have told her she couldn't come. I should have been firm and stood my ground. There's no reason we can't just ask her to leave, right? I mean, it's our house and our party," she spoke, growing more resolute by the moment. "We HAVE to get her out of here." *What was I thinking?*

They followed Reese's trail as she wove in and out of the guests, accepting compliments and stares with equal gratitude. After a while, it grew clear she appeared to be looking for someone in particular. Sporting an all-too-familiar grin, she approached Maya.

Ethan tensed.

"Wrong choice," Kila whispered, "I'm going in." Without further comment, she left the balcony and rushed away.

"Wait! We need a plan," he took off after her. "WAIT. Hang on, Ki!"

"There's no time to plan," she directed over her shoulder, "Reese is going to fire, and we're going to brace for impact."

Ethan clenched his fists. *Not tonight. Not Maya. It's NOT happening.*

The two reached the deck to find Reese in mid-speech. With a blue-glass bottle of sparkling water in her right hand, she showered Maya with half-pint pleasantries.

"...I'm not sure who will miss you more, Ethan or Kila," Reese conjectured. "Probably Kila. She loves you, you know, whereas Ethan might not feel that way, yet. Right? You know what I mean, with guys," she grinned slyly and sipped from the blue bottle.

Maya inhaled and exhaled more or less waiting for Reese to move along and torment someone else.

"Oops," Reese wiped some sparkling water from the corner of her lips. "Better be careful what I say. He's found you again," she looked at Ethan. "I heard I missed a kiss. A good one, too. Benji will be upset about that, Maya. Are you going to tell him or should I?"

Maya replied hotly, "Reese, it's neither your business, nor Benji's, WHOM I kiss!"

Confused, Ethan looked at Kila. *Benji Milton? Is that the Benji in reference,* he wondered.

Kila rolled her eyes to classify Benji as a non-issue.

Eyeroll. She can't fake that, Ethan accepted her sister's explanation. *She'll fill me in later. With details.* He smiled at Maya like he had this morning when they woke up together under the same covers.

Maya gazed back longingly as though no one else were present.

Reese appeared dissatisfied. And she growled, "You WILL tire of Ethan over time. He's no Benji. It's sad you don't see it," she shook her head at Maya, "but, you will…soon. Maybe in a month or so."

"No," Maya spoke unmistakably, "I KNOW Benji. I've known Benji forever. He's great. He's smart. He's spontaneous. He's bursting with energy…," Maya paused to look Reese right in the eyes, "but you have the names in reverse. Benji's no Ethan!"

Ethan, having braced himself at the start of Maya's reply, sighed in relief at the close.

"Ethan is boring," Reese concluded flatly. "Thankfully, Benji will be here later. I hope he's wearing one of his base layers…," she raised her eyebrows and winked at Ethan. "No shortage of body on him."

Maya lifted her chin in agitation. "WHY is Ben coming here?" She glared at Reese, "I didn't invite him."

Ben? Maybe it's NOT Benji Milton. I've never heard anyone call him Ben before…, Ethan's mind spiraled again.

"Yeah, but I did," Reese grinned. "Come on. He WANTED to see you. He's only going to stop by for a spell before he leaves for Yosemite. He and his boys have a date with El Capitan, remember? I know you know, because he told me he spoke at length with you about it. That…and the future. Now you'll get to see each other AT LEAST one more time before you're both in Rhode Island. I'm not sure if he'll be there first, or if you'll be there first, since it's all happening in a little over a week. But you'll practically have the whole summer together. It's CAH-Razy how SMALL that state actually is!" She laughed and looked right at Ethan. "Benji's bringing a gift for her. I know what it is, and I think it's ULT-imately dreamy. Did you get Maya anything yet?"

"Yes," Kila answered to her brother's relief. "He has. It's a secret, so…can't talk about it here." She rubbed her hands together briskly, warming up for the showdown she knew for certain had just begun.

It IS Benji Milton, Ethan realized. *He climbs. And he's going to college there. In Rhode Island. Benji Milton. The most irritating senior at Cypress…irritating mainly because he has no obvious flaws. How well do they know each other? I guess well enough for her to call him BEN. Ugh. It doesn't matter.*

We're together, and this isn't an issue. We have to have friends of the opposite sex, and anything else is unhealthy, Ethan resolved, speaking in turn right after Kila. "I have no issue with Benji. He can stay as long he wants, even if he thinks I'm boring, too."

Kila and Maya smiled in unison right at the punchy start of **"Get Out" by CHVRCHES**.

Ethan felt pleased with the way he had handled himself, and planned for the future. *I need to be more exciting than Benji. Some extra workouts with Brix might be in order.*

"...So where's Angus?" Reese switched gears without warning. "No one really knows, but we're a...real sorta thing, you know?" she raised her eyebrows and puckered her deep-fuschia lips for emphasis.

They're a...couple? Kila's chest ached the moment she processed those words.

Reese twirled her hair obnoxiously. "You're kidding! Angus didn't tell you? We've been together for MONTHS."

"Months of what?" Kila exploded. "Toying with him? Stringing him along? Never actually seeing him?"

Ethan and Maya traded glances.

"There was a little of that," Reese admitted with obvious pleasure. "I had to test him...but, there was a lot of other things that happened, too. Other things I shouldn't talk about. Things that should remain secret."

"Why?" Kila whispered through her teeth, "You don't even like him."

"I actually do," Reese continued with a shallow smile, "that's why I'm here. I want to be with him. Alone, in public, and everywhere in between. And I'm here to prove it HOW-EVER I need to."

The phrases, which Reese had spent hours structuring and sharpening, had pierced Kila's skin. Terribly punctual, the pain arrived right at requested time of delivery. An expression of betrayal, of deep agony, projected through Kila's pores.

Maya leapt into the conversation, determined to facilitate its end.

"You might be able to fool everyone else here, including Angus," Maya pursed her lips, "but Ki and I, and even Ethan, KNOW how you feel about Brixton. You can't fool us."

"I'm not trying to fool anyone," Reese hushed her voice. "I'll be the first to admit it, Angus wasn't my original choice; but he's my final choice. I want him now and I won't change my mind again. I'm devoted to him."

Kila looked down at her hands, which had held his cheeks minutes ago. *Will he want to be with her now that she wants to be with him? So openly and in public, just like he wanted all those years. Will I mean nothing? Will we never kiss again?*

Reese watched Kila from the corners of her eyes while she continued to inflict pain with her words. "When I discovered how cunning and wild he was I amended my plans. Angus became my focus. Not Kading. And, let's face it, Angus's body is pretty ridiculous…, right, Kila?" she turned her face to Ethan. "That's what your sister said to me freshman year, at least."

Maya held a hand over her mouth disgusted by Reese's shamelessness.

Kila shook her head, her words emerging as whispers, "HOW can you…be…like this?"

"Because Ki-LAH," Reese snapped, "to him, intelligence ISN'T everything, and I got to him first."

"Maybe…," Kila reached deep inside herself for some strength, "but…he also might be over you."

"Yeah right!" Reese reveled in a laugh. "He'll NEVER be over me, and I'll never let him be," she took it upon herself to gloat. "Before I committed to the relationship I asked him what he thought about you, because I refused to go down THAT road again. I had to make sure I was safe. And I was. He said he thought you were cute, in like, a little-girl, tomboy kinda way…and, obviously, he, well…you could say he thinks of me QUITE differently," she took a victory swig of sparkling water. "Personally, I think the main ish is your refusal to forgo pants more often. Angus digs dresses and finds them totally delish. That's why I had to make an exception tonight, despite the invitation and our little phone call. I didn't think you would mind once you knew the truth."

"Mind? Oh, I MIND," Kila swallowed hard, "there's quite a bit that I'm MIND-ing right now!"

She decided to strike Reese with a few choice words of her own, but then noticed she could no longer see her. The backside of an ivory brushed-cotton button-down and dark-walnut slim-fit corduroys had blocked her view. Her eyes traveled upward to his semi-organized mess of golden curls.

"I assumed even you knew better than to insult the host of the party," Brixton greeted Reese, the most serious look on his face Ethan had ever seen. "It's not polite. Since you didn't know, I'm telling you now. How about we have a nice, long, intimate talk on the deck and settle things between us?" he asked. "There's really no reason to involve anyone else."

"Get with the times, Kading," she smirked, brushing off his invitation. "I'm not here for you, I'm here for Angus."

"That's funny," Brixton delivered promptly, "because he's not here for you."

Reese's face winced at his bitterness, but that same bitterness strengthened her motive.

Kila, fine-tuning her thoughts, wondered why Brixton, who ordinarily avoided confrontation, had stepped up to the plate this evening.

Maya looked on with concerned eyes.

Ethan placed a hand on one of Maya's shoulders, caressing it with his thumb.

Anna, after witnessing the abnormal interaction on the deck from the lawn, called to a close her conversation with Josie and rushed up the short set of stairs to join the group. She tried to garner the gist of what had happened by the looks Maya provided, but the scene was all too confusing and much too layered to explain in gestures.

"Anna, Anna, Annabelle!" Reese mocked her by addressing her the way she used to in private. "I'd heard about this, but SEE-ing it is entirely different. You really have been welcomed into their perfect little world, haven't you?"

Anna narrowed her eyes, angry that she had spent years of her life defending someone this terrible.

"No need to answer, lovey…I already know. I'm well informed, remember? You have a new interest," she smiled at Brixton. "As everyone knows, I can't BAH-Lame you for wanting him. Kading is VERY WANT-able," she let her tongue hang out of her mouth for a single gross moment, before continuing, "…but I'm compelled to be brutally honest, since you and I have a not-all-ugly history together. Kading might be SOME-what into you, but he's not interested enough to BE with you. There's someone else. There always was…and he has this awfully good nature that won't allow him to betray his…heart," she took a speedy sip from the bottle since her mouth had suddenly grown dry. She took a second speedy sip and resumed, "I blame it on the philosophical junk he ingests, and that he ACT-ually BE-lieves in that whole ONE TRUE LOVE idiocy."

Brixton flinched. Among his four friends, he was the only one who knew where this train was headed. "Reese, don't do this," he let his voice soften. "You don't have to do this."

"I don't?" Reese looked at him, loving the suspense she had built and the emotions it had conjured within him. "I don't, do I? But, at the same time, I DO...I really want to...," her true feelings lay just beneath the surface.

"Think about what you're doing," Brixton looked in Reese's icy eyes.

She intentionally avoided his gaze.

"Just...this...once," he whispered, "think about it."

"I HAVE thought about it. I've done too much thinking on it, actually. And I'm tired of being the only one thinking about it. EV-ER-Y night. Why should I be the only one privy to the truth? Your friends here deserve to know. Why do you keep secrets from them? I'm tired of you treating me like I'm the problem, like I'm the one who doesn't fit in! Tell them why we could never work," she demanded at him angrily. "Tell them BRIX-TON!" she screeched, losing herself in her unearthed emotions for him.

Brixton no longer held onto hopes. He stood speechless waiting for Reese to blurt it out. She'd passed the point of no return and he knew pleading at this point would be fruitless. The moments passed too slowly in his mind. War was upon him, and he knew it. He stood tall and rallied the strength in his heart.

"Say it," Reese egged him on. "I want to hear you say it."

Brixton clenched his teeth.

Ethan's eyes reached the size of saucers.

"Come ON, KADING," she persisted with an overindulgent wink. "Do it for me."

"No," Brixton glared irately, "I wouldn't DARE take the glory away from you. You've earned it, after all. After. All. This. Time." He knew he sealed his fate with those four final words.

"Alright. I'll tell them," Reese stretched the muscles of her feet inside her sequined, pointy-toed stilettos. "You wouldn't be with ME, because you wanted HER!" she pointed a loaded index finger at Kila.

Baffled, Kila took a diagonal step forward and looked at Brixton's face to weigh the truth of Reese's statement.

Brixton looked at her assuringly, but she couldn't make heads or tails of it.

"You are full of lies," Kila spoke through her teeth.

"Oh Kila, for someone who was asked to skip a grade, you're awfully naïve. He's liked you for YEARS! Why else would he have turned down EVERY SINGLE person who has asked him out? It is a...rather decorated list. Or, maybe you didn't know about that. How CONVENIENT it was for you, not knowing the facts. As his former best friend, there SURE IS a lot you DON'T know about him."

Kila looked at Anna, then at Brixton, then back at Reese. *This can't possibly be true,* she traveled back to the memories in her mind just as **"Moments Passed" by Dermot Kennedy** negotiated with the volatile feelings in the air. *There was nothing questionable that happened between us. He never tried getting close, even when he could have. Near the end, I wanted to see him more than he wanted to see me. Then he eventually stopped seeing me altogether, most likely because he sensed MY feelings edging past the line. They were edging and he felt it. It was me not him. I remember it clearly. That confusion and that embarrassment.*

"No Brix, tell her," Kila touched Brixton's forearm. "You never thought of me like that, and we've barely seen each other in the last six months."

Brixton's prolonged silence caused a heavy veil to settle over the group.

Reese prayed he would retaliate, so she could tap into her reserves. But, when he looked at Kila the way he did, she could almost see the outlines of white flags in his eyes.

For once, Reese's outburst wasn't contrived. Like Maya and Ethan, Anna read the painful truth on Brixton's face; and, she couldn't bear for Reese to see her heart break in person. With strong, swift strides, Anna pushed the party behind her and escaped into the library to seek refuge among the old books. The shelves surrounding her held the most fantastic tragedies of all time, and if those characters could survive them, Anna planned to be as close to them as possible.

"I'm fine," Kila hushed the words to Maya, who was torn between staying and leaving. "Go check on Anna. She's more important."

Her choice having been made for her, Maya glanced at Ethan then dashed into the house.

With Anna and Maya out of sight, Kila eyed Brixton again. She eyed him the way she had wanted to since he had cut her out of his life, since she had learned what it was like to live without his companionship. Without his thoughts. Without his laughter. A dull, nearly six-month span, which had vexed each and every one of her playlists. *Brixton. It CAN'T be true. This doesn't add up. If it did we wouldn't be here right now. We'd be at Lazy Tortoise, having breakfast for dinner, arguing about song lyrics, and planning a drive up the coast.*

Brixton gazed back in return, regretful of his former decision to remain quiet. Feelings poured from his heart to his mouth, and, for the first time, he spoke to her without caring who would hear, "Kiki, I should have—"

"OH no!" Reese cut him off. "Hold on, Kading. You don't get it. There's no happy ending here. At least not for either of you," Reese basked in her ultimate power play. "Kila doesn't want YOU, she wants your best friend, and HE wants ME! Isn't it all so mismatched?" A sinister glimpse of pleasure swept across her airbrushed face.

Brixton closed his eyes. *Kiki DOES want Angus...* He let the spiked words penetrate his mind. *Did Reese just save me from embarrassing myself or was that a selfish act to avoid having to hear the truth from my own mouth?*

The crestfallen look on Brixton's face caused Kila to harden. She realized then that the music had never stopped playing. It had always been there. She had simply stopped listening.

Memories swam through her heart and she reflected on each. *Ethan's birthday, before the tree house, when we spoke in my room. Yesterday afternoon, by the pool, what Maya said. Last night, in the kitchen, his angelic voice.* Camp Fright, *in his lap, how he whispered to me. Tonight, the double hug, and plans to talk in the tree house. It can't be. It can't be like Reese is painting it. If it is, I've…I…really…m—*

The music stole the rest of Kila's thoughts away. Thoughts she had never dared to think before. Thoughts that had, up until now, always remained tidily tucked behind a door she thought she could never open.

"Reese. Hold up," Angus's calm words shocked everyone. He had slipped into the group, somehow remaining unnoticed until now. "Your story's comprised of some truths, I'll give you that. I think all of Cypress High knows that I wanted you."

Reese grinned until she realized he had spoken of his wanting her in the past tense.

Angus held onto his next thought until he knew she had made the connection. "But, what Cypress doesn't know is that I'm over wanting you. Finally over it. The aftertaste of your assumptions alone is enough to keep me away. I politely asked you to stop texting me this morning. If that wasn't direct enough, I didn't respond once to your bombardment of replies or answer any of your calls."

Reese's eyes flickered in a way Kila had never witnessed.

Angus DOES like me, Kila's endangered heart beat for him

despite her present feelings of confusion and nausea.

"It's true some of us may be mismatched, as you called it," Angus had more to say. "You're not the only one to have had a taste of heartache; but each of my friends here knows respect and love. Sadly, I've come to recognize, you know neither. And, from my perspective, coming here tonight with the ill-intentions and theatrics you brazenly bestowed upon us, I can no longer count you as a friend, either."

It was Reese's turn to hurt, and she felt it in the depths of her soul. Nearly certain she had held the winning hand, she had doubled down only to lose everything. Naked, even to her own fears, she wearily whispered her conditional request.

"Get rid of my pictures and poems, then, and I'll get rid of yours," she lifted her fingers to her eyes just in time to catch her tears.

WHAT? Kila's mind blew apart. *No, no, no—this can't be true. NOT this one*, Kila speculated, dreading the notion of a twice-broken heart by the same boy. Anything to prolong the pain. She looked at Angus uneasily for signs of confirmation or denial.

Brixton could nearly hear Kila's heart crack. His hands opened, wishing he could hold her to ease the pain.

"Consider it done. Totally over then," Angus replied to Reese. "Pictures and poetry gone." He looked at Kila, the pain on her face speaking volumes more than her words would have.

"And," Reese's voice wavered as tears dripped from her eyes, "never play...the song...again."

"I...won't," Angus's face softened just enough for Kila to catch the change, something Angus regretted instantly.

A song! Kila's stomach churned in disgust. *They had a SONG? What song did they have? God, I hope I never know what it is so I never have to hate it for the rest of my life. Ugh. He wrote her poems? Seriously? Then he obviously had feelings for her beyond the physical. What am I doing? What have I done? Foolish...that's what I am.*

And the pictures he sent her, at a minimum shirtless, at the maximum...uh—who knows? Gross, gross, GROSS! Once she had them, she could have shared them with anyone she wanted to—Josie, the whole school, the whole Internet, even...

Was he thinking about Reese when he kissed me? Is that why he kissed me in the dark, so he could pretend it was her? Was he kissing me or kissing her? Eww! I don't even want to think about it anymore. I'll never kiss anyone else ever again.

I'm a total amateur in life. Why did I trust him? Does he know how much I like him? I didn't say the specific words, but has he inferred them from the other words we exchanged? Can I make him think I simply went along with his kiss to be daring, and that our kissing means nothing to me now? I can pull that off. Right? I must be able to. No choice now, it's decided.

I'll only apply to faraway colleges. I won't go to state school, and I won't see him. I might even attend university outside the country. Canada? England? Both sound picturesque to me. I'll study, graduate with honors, open my boutique, and avoid physical contact with boys…that'll give me more time to paint and more angst to inspire my painting. Her disjointed yet powerful thoughts reverberated loudly against the walls of her mind, trying to teach her something.

Reese was spot-on about one thing: my naïvete! A night, which began with the perfection of kissing Angus, threatened to end in complete disillusionment. *Nice. I've wasted years of my life chasing a dream that's actually a nightmare,* Kila hardened at the thought. *Fine. I can accept my mistakes. But now, now I'll be as steel. No more of this.*

Everyone's eyes looked drained, and Kila refused to let Reese inflict greater damage. "Please leave my house," she spoke in an equally quiet and direct manner. "You have achieved what you came here to do. You can leave feeling accomplished. Exceptional work on the planning and follow-through."

Reese, caught in the avalanche of her own undoing, stood frozen in place.

"It's okay," Kila whispered slowly, "you're not the only one who's hurting, but you no longer have the option to stay."

Reese's slow nod took Kila by surprise.

Kila readied for a final outburst, but never received one.

"Will you…walk me…out…to…the front?" Reese barely pushed the words out.

"Yeah…course," Kila swallowed the lump in her throat. She placed a hand on Reese's back after seeing it tremble.

Reese tensed until she realized Kila was attempting to comfort her.

"We used to be friends, remember?" Kila whispered in her ear as they began walking together.

Reese nodded again, rubbing her wet eyes.

Kila prepared to engage more with Reese, when she felt the warmth of a hand on her shoulder. Seeing it was Angus's, she shrugged it off, coldly.

Angus reached for her again.

"Please don't...touch me," Kila whispered inflexibly to him. "I finally understand why you were so torn up in my room this morning...you two clearly shared more than you told me." While her eyes remained dry, her voice, which quivered, gave her feelings away, "...I can't BE...LIEVE you let me get... THAT close to you. The...whole time...tonight. How could you...do that...to me?"

Brixton shared a concerned glance with Ethan.

"Ki," Angus followed after her.

Without turning back, she continued escorting Reese through the yard.

"At least let me tell my side," Angus insisted. "I haven't spoken with her since we fell in the pool. That's when everything shifted. You saw me this morning. I was yours at that point. You must know that now, don't you?"

"Talking...isn't necessary," Kila gained control of her voice again. She eyed Reese's reaction to the conversation. "New details, new outcome. Consider that things have changed, that I won't be seeing you later, or next Saturday. Or ever again in that capacity."

No sinister signs crept across Reese's face. No room left for other emotions, it remained tied up in sadness.

Maybe she's human after all, Kila pondered. *Still up for debate after tonight's unfolding. I'm so foolish for believing what I wanted to. For letting my guard down...with HIM of all people.*

"This is what Reese wanted," Angus's heart bled as he pleaded to her. "I've never spent time with her alone, Ki—I thought I made that clear a little while ago," he hinted. "I don't want anything other than what we started today," his words revealed more to Ethan and Brixton than he would have preferred, but it didn't matter at this point. "I KNOW how I feel. What do you need me to do to prove it to you?"

Receiving no response, he turned to Reese, "Tell her it was superficial. We talked, but we didn't see each other. There was no affection. Reese. Come on. Why are you doing this to me, when you obviously still want Brixton anyway? Don't make me out to be twice your fool, when you know that's not the case. Tell her it was superficial. Don't let her think it was something it wasn't. If you were ever even just my friend you would do that for me now."

"Stubborn Love" by The Lumineers played in sweet sadness.

Reese lifted her tear-stained face to speak to Angus, when Kila spoke to her instead, "Listen. You don't have to say anything you don't want to. You don't have to give in to him...If only I had taken my own advice earlier," she huffed loudly.

The last comment cut Angus to the core, and Reese resolved to remain silent.

"Don't say that, Ki," Angus touched his palm to her shoulder, clutching the recent memory of their covert intimacy.

"Don't. Touch. Me," Kila looked him in the eyes, her impending tears struggling to hold the line behind her eyes. "You wrote her poetry. Writing is your secret passion. What you shared was more than skin deep, so don't pretend that it wasn't," Kila spoke through her teeth feeling the puncture in her heart. The pain had become so poignant she could feel it in her gums. *The poems were infinitely worse than the pictures. I've never even SEEN any of his poems,* Kila realized.

"Poems? Is that it?" Angus questioned, then vowed, "I'll write you a poem every day if you'll feel like you did earlier. If we could be like that again."

"It's not as easy as that. It never was, and it never will be," Kila swallowed another lump. "Just dissolve it, Angus. Forget it ever happened. Please."

"No," Angus inhaled, his dark eyes sparked with passion, "I can't! I could never forget. I will never forget how that felt."

Ethan pulled Angus back by his shirt when he saw him reach for Kila once more. "Angus, leave her be for a while. She's overwhelmed. You have to let this settle."

"E, you don't understand. I have to talk to her. I have to fix it…," Angus's chest ached almost as much as his mind.

"Actually, I think I do understand," Ethan made his position known. "She's not ready to talk to you right now. You can talk to her when she's ready and not a second before," his brotherly instincts had risen to full throttle.

Angus only then recognized the gravity of the situation. He placed his hands on Ethan's shoulders and nodded silently in submission. Next, he faced Brixton, who glared at him amidst his own agony. In gloomy contemplation, Angus walked back into the thick of the party feeling played, defeated, and empty. Insulated by the crowd, he escaped to his thoughts. *Brixton knew all about Reese. He may have even suspected she was planning something like this. He tried to warn me, but it was too late. I failed in grand fashion. Worse than before. At the most inopportune moment, she has rained down hell on our lives. I need to call Hunter. He'll know what to do.*

Ethan and Brixton stopped following Kila and Reese. The two talked about what Angus and Kila may have done earlier and fretted over just how bad it could have been. They agreed to stay in the front yard until Kila returned, and then to speak with her about it in as gentle a manner as they possessed. While they waited, Ethan paced the perimeter of the small lawn muttering to himself, and Brixton, with arms folded across his chest, proceeded to clench his jaw.

By the time Reese slid her car key into the ignition, streams of tears flowed down her otherwise flawless complexion.

"Reese," Kila swallowed another lump, leaning on the freshly waxed white Audi, "you're not letting me be mad at you. Isn't that what you wanted, for me to be furious? I want to be furious, and I SHOULD be furious, but I can't be furious when I'm this worried about you. I don't think you can drive like this. At least, not safely."

"I can. I'm fine," Reese insisted, gasping through her tears. "I'll be safe, I promise…not that that means anything anymore, but I need to get this out first. I…I have to tell you something."

Kila nodded, dreading the idea of more revelations.

"Okay," Reese looked in the rearview mirror to ready herself, "I did just want Brixton, but I knew he didn't like me…and then I started talking to Angus again, and I slowly realized what I hadn't seen before. It wasn't the way I felt for Kading, but it was…nice. He always called me…every single day. That's what I liked most about him…that he consistently cared. He made me laugh on good days and bad days. He excited me. I grew attached to the sound of his voice…so attached…he always checked in…my parents don't even do that…but, it doesn't matter…," Reese somberly looked at her lap.

"It does," Kila questioned the words coming out of her mouth as she heard each one. "Of course it matters. If you liked Angus so much, why wouldn't you see him in public? That's all he wanted—to take you somewhere, to be together, to shower you…with affection."

"I know," Reese's usually piercing light-brown eyes appeared glassy and washed out from all the wetness. "I wanted that, too. I really did. Even tonight…but, I CAN'T get over him. I

think I can until I see him. And then, he's EVERYTHING…,"
she sniffled, "everything in the whole world that I can't have."

"Brix?" Kila asked via whisper, shocked that Reese had
confided so deeply in her.

"Yeah…," Reese grabbed a T-shirt from the passenger seat to
dab the tears from her face and wipe the liquid running from
her nose. "Kila, I know you have no reason to believe me,
but Angus DEF-in-itely likes you. He might even LOVE you, I
heard it in his voice…."

Kila tilted her head in question.

"Yeah, the way he spoke to you," Reese explained, sniffling
again, "didn't you hear it? It's the same way spouses plead for
each other in the movies…."

Kila weighed Reese's current ability to distinguish reality from
fiction.

"…The real issue isn't Angus, though…it's Brixton. You
would have fallen in love with him in your own way had I
not forced him to stop hanging out with you," Reese wiped
the rest of her tears, feeling better for her reluctant honesty.
"I saw it happening whenever I ran into you guys, especially
on the weekends. How his smile belonged to you, how
he kept his station wagon spotless, how his eyes glistened
when he ordered your coffee, how you always seemed to be
whispering or laughing or both, and how even your strides
grew to match. Each time I saw you together it killed me,
and I didn't know how many lives I had left. I finally sent
him a note in class warning that I would tell you about his

real feelings if he didn't stop seeing you," she huffed. "I didn't think he'd actually do it, though," she looked up in annoyance. "He did and he was miserable…ugly miserable… and it only made him HATE me more," she shook her head, finally feeling a sense of regret.

Kila missed the majority of Reese's relevant confessions about Brixton. All she could think about was Angus. How he had minimized his relationship with Reese, and how she had been naïve enough to believe him. *I ALWAYS saw him texting. I should have known. The texts and those grins. I saw it so many times. I assumed it wasn't a relationship because it was an unconventional relationship. They shared words and pictures in place of kissing, possibly a more meaningful relationship than I've ever had or will have with him. Kissing can be shared by anyone. A good kisser isn't necessarily a good boyfriend.*

What song is it? I hope not one I like. If it is, I won't like it anymore, neither the song nor the artist. I hope it's not one of my favorite bands…I couldn't bear!

Kila chided herself for asking, but knew she had to, "What song is it? The song you mentioned? With Angus?"

The question allowed Reese to test her honesty again. She looked at Kila's hurt eyes, shaking her head "no" to relay she'd prefer not to say.

"Please tell me. I think, at this point, I'm more angry with myself than I am with you, and I…regret that we both changed so much," the truth in Kila's words touched her.

"We couldn't stay friends. How could we?" Reese looked at

the silver emblem on the steering wheel. "You were too smart for me, and the one person I liked my whole life fell in love with you. Friendship was impossible for me after that. Even if Brixton wasn't around, I still knew that your face was the face that he liked, your brain was the brain that he liked, and he liked you over me regardless of the godawful clothes you used to wear. Before Anna got to you, you looked like a cross between an old maid and a runaway nun."

Kila loathed that she laughed, but she couldn't help it. "How can you still make me laugh, even when I'd prefer to despise you?" she smiled through the pain. "Neither of us has what we want, so even though we're not friends, per se, we've found ourselves in somewhat of a parallel situation. I just want to know what song it is. Please, please tell me, because it will REALLY break my heart if I can't listen to music again. It's the one thing I have right now, and I can't bear to wonder every time I hear a song if it's THE song that was YOUR song with Angus. Please," she put a hand on the driver's door.

"That can't happen, Ki...I promise you," Reese responded slowly, praying she wouldn't have to speak further about it. "You've never heard it, and...you never will hear it."

The single nod and sudden tears that tumbled down Kila's cheeks relayed to Reese that more words weren't necessary. Kila understood and regretted having asked the question. Now knowing, she much rather would have had it the other way, always wondering which song and, possibly in the end, giving up music entirely until she was entirely over Angus Lyr.

At that point Reese did something uncharacteristic. She touched Kila's hand on the car door with her own. "I'm sorry for that," she looked in her light eyes. "I don't want to hurt you anymore. I mean it. I'm going to go."

Kila, lifting her fingers from underneath Reese's, whispered, "It's…not…your…fault." Those last words were excruciatingly difficult to push out, not because Kila didn't mean them, but because she did, and she wished she didn't. "Listen. I know we'll never be the same as we were, but I don't hate you. Not even for this. Make sure you get home alright. Do you need me to get Josie to drive you back?"

"No, Ki. I'm alright. I think," Reese forced a smile to reassure her. "Maybe we can meet up at the mall someday, midsummer, once this has all blown over?"

"Sure," Kila liked the idea, though she doubted it would ever happen. "Please drive safe…."

Reese nodded once, adjusting her side view mirror.

Though Kila knew Reese needed to leave, she felt strangely attached to her, like two people who had experienced the same tragedy, but from different angles. There was more she wanted to say, and those words made their way out just before Reese drove off, "You're more than you give yourself credit for. We both are. And, we shouldn't calculate our self-worth by adding the ones that want us and subtracting the ones that don't."

Reese's sad smile was more than Kila could have hoped for after the fallout, and Kila waved Reese off through her own tears. Dabbing her eyes with the backs of her hands, Kila took a step back onto the sidewalk that led to her house.

She could see her front lawn. She could sense the buzz of the party behind the house. But, she couldn't go back. Not now. Not even for the music. Her hardness had fallen away, leaving only pain and confusion and more pain. Throbbing pain.

He wrote her a song. An original. It was the first time those bitter words rang in between her ears and she allowed herself to grasp their meaning. *If he wrote it, the only way she could have heard it is if he sang it...so, he wrote her a song, then sang her the song he wrote for her...on the phone... multiple times.*

Her heart broke again and she didn't understand it. *I already felt it break. How can it keep breaking over and over again? I can't go back. I can't let him see me like this. I can't let anyone see me like this. I'm vulnerable.*

Ugh. I DETEST that word. I wish I could wipe it from the dictionary, and then from all of existence. No more vulnerability. Please. Especially for Angus Lyr. My one and only mission from here on out.

Pivoting on her feet, Kila faced the opposite direction and sprinted away. Running in platforms didn't faze her. They felt no different than her track sneakers. Right now, her only care was that the distance between herself and the party grow wide enough to accommodate her thoughts. And as she struggled to process everything all at once, she noticed an old olive-green Jaguar roll to a stop across the street, **"Train" by Brick + Mortar** blaring from its open windows.

DISCOGRAPHY: Music of the Chapters

Chapter 1:

Bishop Briggs, *The Way I Do*, Teleport Records under exclusive license to Island Records, a division of UMG Recordings, Inc., Track 3 on *Bishop Briggs*, 2017, Spotify.

Miike Snow, *Heart Is Full*, Jackalope Recordings Limited under exclusive license to Atlantic Recordings Corporation for the United States and WEA International Inc. for the world excluding the United States, Track 4 on *iii*, 2016, Spotify.

Moose Blood, *Knuckles (Acoustic)*, Hopeless Records, Inc., Track 2 on *Stay Beautiful*, 2016, Spotify.

The Cranberries, *Dreams*, The Island Def Jam Music Group, Track 1 on *20th Century Masters – The Millennium Collection: The Best Of The Cranberries*, 2005, Spotify.

Joss Stone, *Baby Baby Baby*, Virgin Records America, Inc., Track 8 on *The Best Of Joss Stone 2003-2009*, 2011, Spotify.

Chapter 2:

Dillon Francis, Kygo, and James Hersey, *Coming Over (feat. James Hersey)*, Columbia Records, a Division of Sony Music Entertainment, Track 5 on *This Mixtape is Fire.*, 2015, Spotify.

Franz Ferdinand, *Stand On the Horizon –Todd Terje Extended Mix*, Domino Recording Co. Ltd., Track 2 on *The North Sea*, 2013, Spotify.

The Neighbourhood, *Sweater Weather*, the [r]evolve group, Track 4 on *I'm Sorry...*, 2012, Spotify.

Bad Suns, *Cardiac Arrest*, Vagrant Records, Track 1 on *Cardiac Arrest –Single*, 2013, Spotify.

Chet Faker, *I'm Into You*, Downtown Records, Track 1 on *Thinking In Textures*, 2012, Spotify.

Chapter 3:

Eon Mc Etc., The Libra, *Love Right Now*, DeAndre Tinker, Track 5 on *Race Music*, 2016, Spotify.

Chapter 4:

Wolf Alice, *Bros*, RCA Records, a division of Sony Music Entertainment, Track 2 on *My Love Is Cool*, 2015, Spotify.

A Silent Film, *Lightning Strike*, Silent Songs, Track 2 on *A Silent Film*, 2015, Spotify.

Arctic Monkeys, *RU Mine?*, Domino Recording Co. Ltd., Track 2 on *AM*, 2013, Spotify.

Atlas Genius, *Electric*, Warner Bros. Records Inc., Track 1 on *When It Was Now (Deluxe Version)*, 2013, Spotify.

Journey, *Wheel in the Sky*, SONY BMG MUSIC ENTERTAIN-MENT, Track 6 on *Infinity*, 1978, 2006, Spotify.

Dispatch, *Water Stop*, Bomber Records, Track 3 on *Silent Steeples*, 2004, Spotify.

Dispatch, *Hey, Hey*, Bomber Music, LLC Manufactured and Marketed by Universal Music, a Division of UMG Recordings, Inc., Track 4 on *Silent Steeples [Remastered]*, 2004, Spotify.

Creedence Clearwater Revival, *Travelin' Band*, Fantasy, Inc., Track 10 on *Chronicle: 20 Greatest Hits*, 1976, 1995, Spotify.

Chapter 5:

Tegan and Sara, *Closer*, Warner Bros. Records Inc., Track 1 on *Heartthrob*, 2012, 2013, Spotify.

Kostka, *Motions*, Kostka, Track 1 on *Motions*, 2018, Spotify.

The xx, *I Dare You*, Young Turks Recordings, Track 9 on *I See You*, 2017, Spotify.

Chapter 6:

Copeland, *I Can Make You Feel Young Again*, Tooth & Nail Records, Track 3 on *Ixora*, 2014, Spotify.

The Cinema, *All The Lights*, marigolds+monsters recordings, Track 9 on *My Blood Is Full Of Airplanes*, 2011, Spotify.

The Strokes, *12:51*, BMG, Track 4 on *Room On Fire*, 2003, Spotify.

Chapter 7:

The 10x, Ben Schuller, *Skull and Bones*, The 10x, Track 1 on *Skull and Bones*, 2016, Spotify.

Broods, *Free*, Capitol Records, Track 1 on *Free*, 2016, Spotify.

Parade of Lights, *The Island*, Astralwerks, Track 3 on *Golden*, 2014, Spotify.

Darius, *Hot Hands*, Roche Musique, Track 2 on *Romance–EP*, 2014, Spotify.

The Naked And Famous, *Hearts Like Ours*, Somewhat Damaged under exclusive license to Polydor Ltd. (UK), Track 2 on *In Rolling Waves*, 2013, Spotify.

Chapter 8:

Fleetwood Mac, *Never Going Back Again–2004 Remastered Edition*, Warner Bros Records Inc. Marketed by Rhino Entertainment Company, a Warner Music Group Company, Track 3 (Disc 1) on *Rumours (Super Deluxe)*, 1977, 2013, Spotify.

We Are Scientists, *Make It Easy, Under The Sea*, Masterswan Recordings under exclusive license to Dine Alone Music Inc., Track 1 on *Make It Easy, Under The Sea*, 2015, Spotify.

Stevie Nicks, *Edge of Seventeen*, Reprise Records for the U.S. and WEA International Inc. for the world outside the U.S., Track 1 on *Crystal Visions…The Very Best Of Stevie Nicks (Standard Version)*, 2007, Spotify.

The Killers, *Shot At The Night*, The Island Def Jam Music Group, Track 14 on *Direct Hits*, 2013, Spotify.

Chapter 9:

Janet Jackson, *You Want This*, Black Doll Inc, Virgin Records Ltd., Track 4 on *Janet*, 1993, Spotify.

Sleigh Bells, *Young Legends*, Mom+Pop, Track 5 on *Bitter Rivals*, 2013, Spotify.

Chapter 10:

Bush, *Machinehead*, Round Hill Records–Zuma Rock Records, Track 7 on *Sixteen Stone* (Remastered), 1994, 2014, Spotify.

FAVELA, *Easy Yoke*, Favela, Track 6 on *Community*, 2018, Spotify.

Chapter 11:

Coasts, *A Rush Of Blood*, Warner Music UK Limited under exclusive license to Capitol Records, High Time under exclusive license to Capitol Records, Track 7 on *Coasts (Deluxe)*, 2015, 2016, Spotify.

Hozier, *Like Real People Do*, Rubyworks, under license to Columbia Records, a Division of Sony Music Entertainment, Track 10 on *Hozier*, 2013, 2014, Spotify.

Indian Run, *I Hope You Never Call*, Indian Run, Track 1 on *I Hope You Never Call*, 2018, Spotify.

Chapter 12:

Fink, *Hard Believer*, R'COUP'D, Track 1 on *Hard Believer*, 2014, Spotify.

Of Monsters and Men, *King And Lionheart*, SKRIMSL ehf under exclusive license to Universal Republic Records, A Division Of UMG Recordings, Inc., Track 2 on *My Head Is An Animal*, 2012, Spotify.

Chapter 13:

Ben Howard, *Only Love*, Ben Howard, Track 5 (Disc 1) on *Every Kingdom*, 2011, 2012, Spotify.

Ben Howard, *Old Pine*, Ben Howard, Track 1 (Disc 1) on *Every Kingdom*, 2011, 2012, Spotify.

James Bay, *If You Ever Want To Be In Love*, Republic Records, a division of UMG Recordings, Inc., Track 4 on *Chaos And The Calm*, 2014, Spotify.

Milky Chance, *Feathery–Slow Version*, Lichtdicht Records GmbH, Lichtdicht Records GmbH under exclusive license to Neon Records Pty Limited, Track 5 on *Sadnecessary*, 2014, Spotify.

Chapter 14:

Audioslave, *Like a Stone*, Sony Music Entertainment Inc. and Interscope Records, Track 5 on *Audioslave*, 2002, Spotify.

Florence + The Machine, *Shake It Out*, Universal Island Records, a division of Universal Music Operations Limited, Track 2 on *Ceremonials (Deluxe Edition)*, 2011, Spotify.

BANNERS, *Someone To You*, Island Records, a division of UMG Recordings, Inc., Track 1 on *Someone To You*, 2017, Spotify.

ELEL, *40 Watt*, Mom+Pop, Track 1 on *40 Watt*, 2014, Spotify.

Incubus, *Promises, Promises*, Sony Music Entertainment Inc., Track 2 on *If Not Now, When?*, 2011, Spotify.

Chapter 15:

Lydia, *Follow Me Down*, 8123, Track 10 on *Run Wild*, 2015, Spotify.

Big Data, *The Business of Emotion (feat. White Sea)*, Wilcassettes LLC under exclusive license to Warner Bros. Records Inc., Track 1 on *The Business of Emotion (feat. White Sea)*, 2014, Spotify.

alt-J, *Hunger Of The Pine*, Infectious Music Ltd., under exclusive license to Atlantic Recording Corporation for North America, a Warner Music Group Company, Track 8 on *This Is All Yours*, 2014, Spotify.

Little Daylight, *Overdose*, Capitol Records, LLC, Track 1 on *Overdose*, 2013, Spotify.

Banks, *Lovesick*, Harvest Records, Track 3 on *The Altar*, 2016, Spotify.

Chapter 16:

MGMT, *Electric Feel*, SONY BMG MUSIC ENTERTAINMENT, Track 4 on *Oracular Spectacular*, 2007, Spotify.

Bleachers, *Wake Me*, RCA Records, a division of Sony Music Entertainment, Track 5 on *Strange Desire*, 2014, Spotify.

Night Riots, *Oh My Heart*, Sumerian Records, Track 1 on *Howl*, 2014, 2015, Spotify.

The 1975, *Fallingforyou*, The 1975, Track 33 on *The 1975 (Deluxe Version)*, 2013, Spotify.

St. Lucia, *All Eyes on You*, Columbia Records, a Division of Sony Music Entertainment, Track 3 on *St. Lucia*, 2012, Spotify.

Chapter 17:

Disclosure, *Magnets (feat. Lorde)*, Island Records, a Division of Universal Music Operations Limited, Track 6 on *Caracal (Deluxe)*, 2015, Spotify.

CHVRCHES, *Get Out*, Glassnote Entetainment Group LLC, Track 1 on *Get Out*, 2018, Spotify.

Dermot Kennedy, *Moments Passed*, Riggins Recording Limited, Track 1 on *Moments Passed*, 2017, Spotify.

The Lumineers, *Stubborn Love*, Dualtone Music Group, Inc., Track 7 on *The Lumineers*, 2012, Spotify.

Brick + Mortar, *Train*, Merovee Records, Track 1 on *Dropped*, 2015, Spotify.

Ivy Cayden lives on the rugged, pinetree-lined Central Coast of California. Years ago, on her first visit to Henry Cowell Redwoods State Park, she fell in love with the tall trees in Felton and returns whenever she gets the chance. A vegan for over a decade, Ivy is passionate about supporting small businesses and all things indie—especially music. In addition to writing the CHORDUROYS AND TOO MANY BOYS™ series, she founded and manages the indie music blog My Multi-Track Mind, where she interviews rising musicians, covers new releases, and posts moody playlists.

Say "hi" to Ivy, find repeat-worthy songs, and learn about the next book release and more by connecting:

Instagram:
@ivycayden
@mymultitrackmind

Facebook:
@mymultitrackmind
@chorduroysandtoomanyboys

Spotify:
Ivy Cayden

www.chorduroys.com
www.mymultitrackmind.com

Made in the USA
Monee, IL
18 December 2022

22297253R00289